SISTERHOOD
BLOOD OF OUR BLOOD

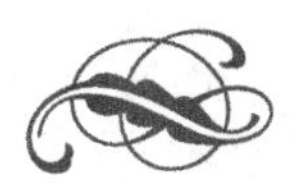

JAMES HENDERSHOT

Order this book online at www.trafford.com
or email orders@trafford.com

Most Trafford titles are also available at major online book retailers.

Printed in the United States of America.

ISBN: 978-1-4907-1480-6 (sc)
ISBN: 978-1-4907-1481-3 (e)

Trafford rev. 09/19/2013

 www.trafford.com

North America & international
toll-free: 1 888 232 4444 (USA & Canada)
fax: 812 355 4082

MY KINGDOM COME
MY WILL BE DONE
Lilith Series

Dedicated to my favorite RN, my wife Younghee, with thanks for financially providing for our family during my days of writing and to my sons, Josh & John and daughter, Nellie, newfound Mia and publishing consultant Love Blake.

TABLE OF CONTENTS

We are blood of our blood, and bone of our bone.
We give each our body that we all not be alone.
I give you my spirit until our life shall be done.
Transferred into flesh suits that every creature forever sees
Blood fashions every birth,
Crusading from one family to whole countries
The heart is the house of blood, whose rooms will never be full,
Whose red chambers are never silent?
As the ear of a shell covered in wool
Cultured for millennia like an exotic flower,
Heavenly clotting light into red,
We are bound, each to the other,
More tightly than we ever could have said
Blood is red soul crimson
Shaded in our mystery as we do now wed
Using our cherished love to keep us fed
Our mercy we now so freely shed
Eagerly penetrating to find every head
The inheritance of life
Before yielding to the dead

Chapter 01

REBIRTH

The crushing and mashing of bodies and spinning, up then bewitched by weird noises, I felt like stool being flushed down a toilet. What is time? There was a clock chasing me, and a peculiar eye watching me. Even the space now has a curious color, yet the color now is so much better than the red burning stinking fire consuming and frying spirits. Poor Bo . . . , whatever his name was, for his city is being pulverized, I think . . . . Currently I wonder, what is on the other side of that window? The door is tempting to open; however, as long as I do not hear that awful screaming, I will stay heeeerrrrrrrrrrrr, and something is pulling meeee. Oh, now everything is quiet, or is it? I can hear a baby crying. I can smell stinky blood. Who is that woman who is crying, and who are the other women are saying, "Push Prudence, push, just a bit more?" I wonder who Prudence is . . . and why does she have to push, or notwithstanding better. What is she pushing? Now I feel something in spite of more bizarre; I am becoming aware of my two hands and two feet; however, they are small and I cannot control them. My head is still in this warm water, and my feet are in the cold air. I can hear the group around Prudence giving her congratulations, saying to her, "It's a girl. You have a girl; someone inform Edward that he is the father of a young healthy girl." Where is the girl whom everyone is making such a fuss over? In addition, who is Edward? I can feel myself being held by a woman. I can hear her saying, "Oh you will be a beautiful girl as soon as we clean you. My friends please clean her and let her father see her." Then the women replied, "Yes it is important that our Edward sees his little daughter." I can now feel cold water on a rag scrubbing over my body. What and who is the old midwife? While laughing, said, "Do not cry little girl, this will make your skin tough and make it hard for demons to enter." Now it is starting to make sense. I must be this baby. I can see them cleaning up the bed that Prudence was lying on, as they help her to stand. Could Prudence be my mother, and Edward my father? Is such a thing even possible? Just less than one hour ago, I was given two more galaxies and a promise to marry a great god, and together we would have six galaxies, and at present, I am a baby in a small house somewhere and the time; I do not know. I at this moment in time remember the clock was turning them to the rear blazingly fast. Could I be to the rear in time? Now this person is telling me to smile for my grandpa John and grandma Elizabeth. John's hands feel so good wrapped around my head in this cold place. He then informs me, "I used to hold your daddy just like this." What the heck, I will smile. Come on, I hope my face does what it is supposed to do, as I truly have no control. Guess I was lucky that a smile came over my face when I wanted it to do. The one thing I am aware of now is that face move as I tell you. Oh, what a stupid body I am a prisoner trapped in this pain. Maybe something is wrong with me in this pain, considering that I have never heard my servants complain about pain in their infancy. Immediately, the woman they call Elizabeth is saying to me, "I am so lucky to be able to see you enter our universe as I gear up to depart." She has such warm, yet sad eyes. Her body looks so frail. She is leaving her journey into pain as I am beginning that weird whatever in pain. Someday, I shall create a body that does not get hungry, ill, and never has pain. I wonder if it is possible that she is staying alive, just to see me. That means this must be a good family. Then they yell, out "Edward, where have you been? It is time for you to take your new daughter." Then Edward replied, "I have been hitching up our carriage, and then we can bring this child to our church and get her christened." Now my grandpa John replied, "Yes, my son, that is so important, for the Lord gave her to us, hence we must offer her back." It has been a long time since I heard the servants talk about a lord, and that was far from my universe and so many ages ago. Oh my god; the lord . . . which lord? This cannot be from my galaxy, because I did not use lords, based upon my bad experience of being one. I wish my mouth would move when I tell it to do. This is absolutely awful. I am the only one who can hear my voice. I am a prisoner within this small flesh container. I am merely a mind inside a baby's body. How did all this happen? I wonder now about reincarnation, do we keep our cherished memories while we do not possess the ability to react. Oh well, they are wrapping me up. Then my grandma asks my father, "Why such a rush to baptize the child; we waited for five months for your baptism." I can now hear my father say, "I must have some special friends who will be with me for her christening this cold day in January." He promised them they would also see his child baptized. These grandparents will start their long journey across the ocean to the colonies tomorrow. They are now helping my mother into the carriage, as someone hands me to her. This is so strange, being held by arms so big and powerful for a woman. Then my father asks my grandpa, "Will my mother be joining us?" He replies with a sad crackling voice, "My son; your mother will not be with us much longer; she is too weak to go to our church. It was her dream to see your child, if she goes soon she will get this treasured memory with her." My father goes over and hugs my grandpa as they both have tears rolling down their cheeks. This is so sad; I really want to reach out and take away this misery from them. This is why my temples have angels on them and priests, so when a loved one gets ready to cross over to my side, they can enjoy it with them. What kind of situation would keep that a secret? It is as if whatever is on the other side here enjoys watching the living suffer. I know of only one situation like that, no, there is no way, it must be impossible. I helped destroy that atrocious place. Oh, it is so hard to think when bouncing in this carriage. My eyes now witness snow outside and this place is cold, much colder than the inside. Our convoy trots along, as if this is normal. I could use a commanding lightning bolt blasting into the wide-open universe currently, instead of freezing and being hungry in this tiny shell. Now our carriages are pulling into a barn, and the horses are given hay to eat. How such big strong animals survive on dried-out grass is still a mystery to me. They all form into a group of two men in the front and two in the back with rifles. I wonder why they would need rifles. I am beginning to feel apprehensive, as if there could be some danger around here. I was subsequently informed that the Catholics in this area liked to shoot at those who are not Catholic. I dealt with the Roman Catholics when doing my penance. What a concept, pick a god, say he is good, learn his commandment, "Thou shall not kill," then go kill others who revere him. The only thing that I do know is that the beast shall come from the Catholics. Now we are entering our church, which is a nice building, and thank god; it is warm. Therefore, there is a place, in this land, that is not cold. There seem to be many people here. My new family must have many friends. At this instant, the "parson" or whatever he is called, started to speak, "gabbb gabbb . . . We are united here on this great day, January 18, 1621 to celebrate the baptism of our newest member, the daughter of Edward Holyoke and Prudence Stockton Holyoke. "Have you picked a name for your daughter?" the cleric asked my parents. "We have; we shall call her "Ann Holyoke." He next motioned for my parents to bring me to him, and he stuck his hand in some holy water and after that starting, talking, and sprinkling the holy water over me. I figured this was it. Holy water and I never got along. That stuff, in my early ages, burned me. These parents are going to be embarrassed when the water burns me. I then heard him say, "baptize', father, son, and holy ghost . . ." Ouch, I do not get along with along with those three spirits. In fact, if they find me, I am in big trouble. Even so, oddly, for now the holy water is not burning me. Maybe I am someone or something else. I guess it could be possible. I hope that this is over at present. They currently started singing songs, from their Bibles, the book they call the Psalms. This was so strange, yet they all kept in tune and made it work. What is more eerie is I was there when King David wrote these psalms, as I both helped and beleaguered him. Then they all put down their bibles carefully and started to sing from their memory words somewhat like this,

"1. All hail the power of Jesus' Name; Let angels prostrate fall. Bring forth the royal diadem, and crown Him Lord of all.
2. Ye chosen seed of Israel's race, ye ransomed from the fall, Hail Him Who saves you by His grace, and crown Him Lord of all.
3. Sinners, whose love can ne'er forget the wormwood and the gall, Go throw yourselves at Jesus' feet, and crown Him Lord of all.
4. let every kindred, every tribe on this terrestrial ball to Him all majesty ascribe, And crown Him Lord of all."

Not a bad song, the way they sang it. The one word that stood out, and reinforced that I was in the dangerous territory, was 'Jesus.' I cannot imagine how something like this could have happened to me. I could uniquely hope that this was another Earth in the hundreds of other realities, or even in mine, far away from my galaxies, whose name I cannot remember at this time. My single question now is where I am, and of course do even so things happen in the other realities, or are they independent. I know that my reality is different from New Venus, yet I cannot be sure about the many other realities. That might help me guess on the dimension. My concern is if some are linked to the reality that held New Venus. I will listen to the conversations and next with some luck hear something. I subsequently hear a man talking to my father about the current business opportunities in Staffordshire, England. Where the 'heck' is that? Since I am a baby, I do not want to have a soiled mouth to go along with my filthy bottom. Then, as I am about ready to go to sleep, I hear a woman ask my mother, "Are you going to the Tamworth markets this weekend, after all we should get there early so that the hill people do not beat us who are from Tamworth from getting some good prices?" Ok, now this puzzle is slowly coming together. I was born on January 18, 1621 in

Tamworth, Warwickshire, England. I was christened one year before I was born and baptized today. I wonder how they knew I would be born on the same date, next year from my being christened. If I remember my biology, I did not even put an egg in my 'to be' mother at that time. Something must have told them that the being who was tasked to destroy this planet was going to be born. I never really paid much attention to England while roaming the old Earth, except for using their language as modified by between the wicked nations ever to exist on aged Earth, as my language given to my galaxies as our universal language. I hope I do not have to be crucified or anything comparable to that. I wish someone would replace the "diaper" she has wrapped around me. It is wet and smells bad. These bodies do not control their basic biological functions. Oh, this is so embarrassing. Too bad these little bodies do not have an effective means to reprocess the waste they produce. What even odd is how, while they are cleaning my mushing waste, they said, "Good girl!" I guess a bad girl is one who does not produce this recycled waste. I wonder how I can tell them I need cleaned, since the dingbats cannot smell it. I could try to cry, or will that be as everything else, and not heard. Ok, I will give it a shot. Waaaaaaaaaaa, hey their faces are moving towards me; it is working, and this is great, now I have a tool to fight back with waaaaaaaaaaaaaaa. This worked; they are cleaning my helpless body and removing the waste. I can never remember doing this before, all the flesh suits we wore did not consume matter nor produce waste. Today we are going back to our carriages when I see a man, and a woman with their necks bounded in a punishment device with everyone praying and screaming around them. All this screaming is giving me a headache. I hear my father speaking, "Looks like some of our boys found them some Catholics to torture." Then, utilizing some of the logic I have accumulated over the last millions of years, if you can find them, they can see you. I need to think of a way to speed these people up. Guess it is time to cry again, "Waaaaaaaaaa. Waaaaaa." "Oh, Edward, we need to get this baby home before she gets sick," yells my mother. Then the obedient response, the one I always enjoyed from my male partners, "Yes, Prudence, I'll go as fast as I can safely." Actually, I thought he was going to say 'yes dear' however, yes with her name following it also conveys the message. I must confess that Edward and Prudence do not appear to accept the typical Puritan marriage. Prudence had the security that failure to provide was a reason for an approved divorce, yet Edward's family was extremely rich, and Edward provided over-abundantly for them. Moreover, considering husbands and wives were forbidden to strike one another, there were no concerns about physical violence, although Prudence always joked how Edward would not even hurt a fly, not as a sign of weakness, but as a sign of tenderness. She still remembers their bundling, as they were put to bed conjointly and tarried all night with a bundling board between them. Edward joked about that there must be something special between Prudence's legs because her father bound them with each other in a bundling stocking that was tighter than two coats of paint. When he whispered this to Prudence, she started laughing and could not stop. Edward, whose face turned red, when he realized what he, had said humbly begging her for forgiveness. She then told him he would only be forgiven if he were to marry her. He quickly agreed, promising to make her a wonderful husband. Moreover, Prudence always told this story to everyone up until her death on September 1, 1665. That would indeed be a sad day for me when it comes. This is terrible, to know what they are going to pass away and be able to do nothing about it. There is nothing like an overload of misery, in this little helpless body. I wonder what they serve for food around here. As we enter our nice home, the servants great us at the door, as Edward asks, "What fine meal have you prepared for us, my friends." The servant subsequently said, "To celebrate our wonderful new gift today, "Pasty of venison, four capons roast, chicken pye; burred [buttered] capon, umble pye and tart." Prudence afterwards replied, "My, that is an excellent meal." The servant then replied, "Ma'am, we have to rebuild your strength." My parents then took me upstairs then went down to eat. Something is not right about this. I am the guest of honor, or newcomer, should not I be with my parents. These adults are going to need subjugated. I decided to see if I could grab some sleep now, however, I could not sleep because I am hungry. It is time to teach my parents, so here it goes, "Waaaaaaaaaaaa, Waaaaaaaaaaaaaaaa aaaaaaaaaa." Now my mother comes rushing in. She had not gone downstairs; she was in her room, removing the tons of things that made up a dress and had brushed her hair, pinning it up so that it would not get in her eyes. Someone already created a nice fire in this room. She came over, picked me up, then sat down on a soft loveseat by the fire, and put my face to her chest. I began to wonder, what is going on here? I do not believe my body is ready for sex, not even with a female, especially my mother. I locked my eyes on her as she smiled, holding my hand as my mouth was now centered on her breast. I do not know what to . . . . wow, my mouth is locked on her nipple, and I can feel myself sucking, what am I sucking . . . . wow, that is delicious, something is leaving my mother and going into my belly. This substance tastes good, is filling, and I can feel my body absorbing it. This is a rather unique idea, mothers prefilled with food. Guess that insures babies did not go hungry. I must be a lucky baby; because my mother has a lot of milk in those big jugs that carries her milk. I feel so special! I think I'm going to like this. It is amazing that my spirit has created trillions of female flesh suits, and they not at any time told me that babies lived off this, for I thought only animals drank from their mothers. In addition, during my intimate times with my special females, they at no time produced this food. Strange indeed, although this is a pleasant surprise that I cannot stop emphasizing, cause this stuff hits the spot so fantastically. Moreover, to top everything off, she dressed me in some special clothes. I have a wonderful mother, I sure am glad she hides my milk bottles when she goes in public, cause. I would hate it if I had to get rough on another baby for trying to get my milk from my mother. Now my stomach is filling up, however I do not want to let go of this nipple. What would I do if she stops making more milk for me? Even worse, what happens if she finds another baby? Oh, I am now starting to feel relaxed. It is time for me to sleep now. Goodnight, whatever dimension, or universe that has placed me in this small baby. I also quickly lose my memory, as events, people and details are going blurred. I have yet to see a familiar face. Wonder whether I will ever see my family again, or float through the sky as I once did. All I seem to be filled with is mommy's food and tons of questions. It is time to go to off into lullaby land now. Why it so dark now and everyone is was asleep, except for me? I am hungry and I need to have my waste removed, wow, all that waste from mommy's food. It is liquid going in and definitely not white going out. It is time to put my action plan back to work. "Waaaaaaaaaaaaaaaaaaa . . . . Waaaaaaaaaaaaaaa. Darn, takes more effort to wake these clowns up at night. Waaaaaaaa, oh wow, someone is lighting a candle. Oh, good, it is the one with the milk jugs . . . . I will be cleaned and fed in one trip. Come on mommy, talk to me . . . . You put your breast in someone's mouth and little by little talk, and sometimes sing. Her songs loosen every muscle around my bones and little by little ooze the pain out of me. . . . . "Well, my little Ann, you will soon be almost one day old. You had a very busy day yesterday. You made a good impression on everyone your first day." Now my time is off, since one minute I am just born and ensuing I am six months old. One second my grandparents are going to the colonies and now they are here. This is too much for one forced to reason within a baby's head, even though I am so many millions of years old, I know nothing. Well, she is talking nice, so I had better excite her with a smile. I need to keep this one on my face, because she is holding my milk and that stuff so gracefully hits the spot every time. Oh, no, no . . . . Something is blowing up inside of me. It is like a giant balloon wanting to blast me apart, wonder what rather curse this is., better cry, and get some help . . . Waaaa, . . . Then that warm one who has my milk speaks to me gently saying, "Now Ann, it is going to be ok . . ." Now she starts tapping my back repeatedly and suddenly, I can feel the air rushing out of 'burpppp' of me. Wow that felt amazing! This milk person knows what she is doing. It is as if she knows everything about me. I hope she stays around for a while. Well, guess I had better get back to sleep and let her get some sleep. I like this turning on and off, as long as when I am off, my mommy is close by. I feel so safe when she is around me. Oh wow, it is daytime again. How did I get here? What did I do before I came here? I can recall only a few voices here and there, yet they do not seem to fit together. The purely thing I know is that I am so alone. I am trapped inside this small body, which merely craves milk to make waste. It seems so strange, put it inside of me, and let it go outside of me. It would be so nice if I put it in, and it stayed in. Then I would have to be careful not to put too much in, only enough to fill me in as I grow. I find myself enjoying my time with the one who says she is my mother. She is always telling me so many excellent stories. Even though I do not understand them, she makes them feel so pleasurable for me. She gets most of them from the Bible, because she says this is very important. I can do more things now than I did before. Wow, this being a baby is not exuberant. I am nearly all grown-up today, mommy tells me this is my first birthday, and I will be one year old. It almost felt like an eternity. I can crawl fast now. Dad is teaching me how to take steps. I do not really think it is teaching. He stands me up, and then relinquishes his hold on me. I know he likes it when I try to stand. When I do, he cheers, and I do enjoy the cheers. They really make me joyful, because I am making the ones who work so hard caring for me to be merry. The longer I stand the louder he cheers. It makes mommy happy also. I try to stand as long as I can, yet my legs get wobbly, and down, I go. I can hear him say with pride, "My Ann is going to be walking soon." Moreover, my mother, smiling, caresses me with her hand. That does feel good, I must admit. Mommy tells me that my birthday is important because many babies die before they are one year old. She says there is a bad demon who kills them. I wonder who would want to kill Adam's babies. This must have been a bad demon. Maybe one who was served an injustice? I cannot think what that injustice could have been. I am glad I made it past the first year. Mommy says soon that I will be able to eat some big people food. She is going to give me some cake, whatever that is, tomorrow. She says many big people like it; however, a woman can only eat small amounts of it if they want to fit in the nice formal gowns for church and weddings.

I often wonder why she tells me so many things while I cannot talk back. She tells me that someday I will understand. It is nice to have someone talk to me so much. I just like watching her eyes and mouth. She tells me we are an aristocrat family, and that means we have lots of money and the friends who money buys. I do not know how to tell her about the strange dream I had last night. I saw this beautiful woman with long hair, a color different from mommy's, with soft clothes on. She was standing in the sky with dark to her top and blue clouds to her side and an ocean, like the water that some of daddy's ships stay in, by her side. She was standing too close to the edge. This is very scary indeed. Mommy told me not to stand on the edges like that. Every time I do, she runs over, picks me up, and says "no." I despise that word! Every time I am exploring or getting ready to do something fun, all the big people always say no, no, no. I wonder if they know how to say yes. This large person does not look sad, so why is she wanting to make a boo boo. I do not think that even adults can walk where there is no ground. She is pretty, not as gorgeous as my mommy, but prettier than many of her friends. This is a dream about nothing I have ever experienced, however I feel that I have been there before, hopefully not standing on a ledge like that. I will put this back in my mind and then someday when mommy teaches me how to talk to her, I will tell her. The only thing I want to think about now is the cake. Mommy says the people are coming to our big house to eat the cake and some pies and other sweets. She does not want to get me started on the other sweets. I am thinking that if milk made me this fat, what will happen when I start eating big people's foods. I might turn out to be as round as I am tall, like some of the old women from our church. I will worry about that later. For now, I will enjoy the cake, because mommy says I only get one birthday cake a year. That just does not seem fair, yet I know that my mommy would never cheat me out of anything that was for me. It is my birthday today, and everyone seems happy. They keep coming up to me, pinch my cheek and say, "Oh what a pretty little girl." They are not fooling me, because I know that if they do not, my daddy will yell at them. He is too kind to hit them. The man who invariably talks too much, because he unfailingly puts daddy to sleep, on Sundays at our church is waving for all the children to join around him. He yells over to my mommy, "Prudence; Ann is one-year-old this day, so it is time for her to join these story times." He started by telling us, "Today, I am going to tell you the story about David and Goliath." He started out as follows: "One day, David was delivering food to his brothers who were battling the Philistines. He was the youngest one, and his daddy would not let him fight. He heard a Philistine shouting and making fun of them. He was calling them injurious names and saying they were all scary cats. "Who is that big black-hearted man?" asked David. Since he was easily two times taller than little David, and all the Israeli soldiers were so afraid of him. His brothers told him about Goliath, the mighty warrior. No one could defeat him or would even attempt to fight him! Nevertheless, David was not afraid of the giant. He was angry that this awful man was saying terrible things with his lord, who had saved him so many times already in his young life. When King Saul heard of David's bravery, he called David before him. "Do not worry, I will go fight that giant," said David. "However, he is a warrior," said Saul. "You are just a boy." If he kills you, we must all surrender to him. Many would die if you do not win. "I killed a lion and a bear to protect my father's sheep," said David. "God will help me defeat this giant." Two times, when his father's sheep were in danger from large beasts, he called upon the Lord, and the lord gave him sovereignty to kill them. David always prayed to the Lord and had Faith Maria that the Lord would also deliver him from this giant. Saul gave David his armor and weapons. However, they were too big for David. Therefore, without any armor, David went to tackle the giant. He stopped by a stream to pick up seven stones and placed them in his bag. He believed that one stone would do the trick; however, Saul had told him that Goliath also had many brothers. Then David stood before Goliath. He stood brave and kept thanking the Lord for giving him a chance to liberate his people from this invading army. "Am I a fool than Israel comes at me with their babies?" bellowed Goliath. David looked up and said, "You come against me with, weapons, but I come against you by the name of the Lord Almighty. This is God's battle!" Then David put a stone in his sling and swung it around and around until the sling whistled. The stone whizzed through the air and whacked Goliath right in the forehead. Likewise, the giant fell to the ground with a mighty Earth-shaking thump! All the Israeli soldiers started to cheer, as the Philistines ran away so fast, they did not even pick up their tents. If a little boy from Israel could defeat a giant, then their soldiers could destroy cities. They wanted to go home and bring their families to the safety of the mountains. All Israel knew that Jehovah was alive in David. They would be safe with David. They now sang songs in the streets, "King Saul killed hundreds, and David killed thousands." David's father was currently sad, because his youngest son would live with him no more, now belonging to Israel. King Saul loved the way that David sang, so he brought him to the palace because his singing took away his headaches. This story tells us that no matter how large the problem is god will deliver you from it." That is not what that story tells us. It tells us that if I want my daddy to love me, I must kill lions and bears. Maybe I should start on some of the giants (compared to my current size) in this church today. I would, except one important thing is holding me back. The absence of seven stones is crippling me. I hope my daddy does not remember this story, so he will still love me. Maybe my birthday cake will give me the power as soon as I learn how to sling a slingshot. That stupid minister, he did not tell me what a slingshot looks like. How is a baby supposed to kill giants if they do not give him or her slingshots? Thus, I am in a situation that I cannot control. I really hope daddies forgive their children when placed in situations such as this. That was an interesting story. On the spiritual side, I am wondering why I never had any David's to help me with all the evil I fought on New Venus and in Ereshkigal. I remember that as lord of New Venus, we destroyed more demons than any other planet in their history. Even so, in that bedfast of evil, I created three heavenly angels and not only a Garden of Eden where Eve's seed was not cast out, they also had a land of batters saints destroy a demon whose wicked deeds surpassed most planet's complete history. The rebellion was led by two great saints from the immoral demon's womb. I also had goddesses from other realities to fight. With all this topsy-turvy, I still had to escape with my painful demise following close behind me. When I think of all this, I am comforted knowing that as a baby, I only have to worry about mommy's milk jugs. I still have so many unanswered questions, though. Mommy says that when I get bigger, I can hear stories like David every Sunday. I can see where that can be fun. For now, I simply want to stay warm until summer comes again. Mommy says she will let me play outside a lot this summer. Maybe I can find some good bugs to eat and cats to pull their tails. That is definitely something to look frontward. Exciting days are ahead, as soon as all these big people stop kissing me. Daddy keeps talking about a King James, I of England. I do not know why, but that name sounds familiar. Wonder who the other James was . . . Someday I will remember. For now, I am going to enjoy my splendid dad and super magnificent mom, and want to be free of my questionable past. Mommy says soon that I will not need the milk, which comes from her body. That is very sad, because I seriously like the way, she holds me when I drink her milk. I honestly like being their baby, and I am going to try to be a very good girl for them. As I have now grown tired mommy is putting me in my crib, that daddy brought me. I like it because I can hold on to the rails and play without getting a boo boo. Booboos do not feel good, and they make me cry; however, mommy's kisses make the boo boos feel better. I wonder what magic is in her kisses. Now, I am confused, as it is almost my birthday again, as my mother is telling me for this party, they have rented a large ballroom and invited all their business friends. Mommy says some of the people do not even go to our church. I wonder why people would not attend our church; they must be the bad people our preacher tells us will go to hell. My only question is, "what or where this hell is?" The way he talks about it, I do not want to know.

Mommy says that tomorrow I will be two years old. It just seems like, not that long ago I was celebrating my first birthday.

I can say a few words now like I love you daddy, and I love you mommy. I just have a strange vision in my mind, which told me my mommy, is going to die in the same year as me. My daddy will be sad in that year that has a 1 then 6 then 6 then 5. Now mostly when I find that vision, I scream and yell, sometimes for real and mommy comes in, holds me, and wipes away my tears. Mom just made me some food to eat. I think it is more fun to throw it on the floor; however, when I do that mommy yells at me. Mommy just dressed me very well. She bought me some nice boots that do not get wet or make my feet cold in the snow. She said so many little babies do not have shoes in England. We are so lucky to have a great daddy. He always lets mommy buy things for me. He bought some new larger horses for our carriage. He told me that since I was getting so big, we needed a bigger carriage and horses. I think that maybe he was teasing me. He said I was going to get a wonderful est present ever. I cannot wait to see what it is. Oh, look at the beautipul red house in the so w. Something in wong wit my wordies when I peak. In my head, they are ok. We are getting close to my big party, Oh, so many carriages. My daddy's business is going so well. It is nice to be rich, although daddy gives a lot to the poor. He gives them things at his workplace. He says he does not want them to come begging around our house. He is afraid they will get into the house and hurt mommy and me when he is not here. That is good because I do not want mommy and me to get hurt. Now we are standing in front of everyone, as all come up, lay down my gift {yeahhhhh} hug mommy, kiss me {yukee) and tell me happy birthday, and shake daddy's hand. One woman asked me, "Do you know what today is?" No, birdbrain, I was wondering why everyone was giving me birthday presents. So I said to her, "tooda isy me birthdaaa and mommy and me daddy rubs me berry muchhhy." She then kissed me and handed me a great present." She then hugged mommy and daddy. I said to mommy, "Who dat preddy bige gurl," and she told me, "She is Elizabeth of Denmark, Queen Anne's older sister. Our queen died two years before you were born. We named you after her. You have a queen's name, even though she was Catholic." Yes, I have the name of a dead queen. That is scary but at least they had good intentions in their wonderful hearts. Daddy is now telling everyone to join us and see my birthday presents. Subsequently my eyes saw the most beautiful thing in the whole world; it could move. Subsequently daddy told me, "You can hold your new English Cockapoo but be courteous. If you are mean he might bite you, and you will make him sad." I had to touch him (daddy said he), and I was so scared when I put my hand out to touch him. I hope he does not bite me, because I think, I am a good girl. When I touched him, he did not harm me. He moved his face to mine and started licking it. He must like the way I taste. Hope it does not make him hungry. Then daddy told me, "His name is Charles, who is one of King James's sons. You can call him Charley." I am so happy. I kissed mommy and daddy, and Charles licked their faces. Mommy said, "Now you have a friend who can stay with you and sleep with you and help against those bad dreams you have." Little I did know that the dreams were only starting.

CHAPTER 02

BLOOD SISTERS

Mommy told me that I need a friend to help me through the terrible twos, whatever that is. Charley is so nice. He loves to sleep under my blankets. When he hears a noise, he growls. However, he stays beside me. Moreover, that helps make me get unafraid. Sometimes he plays with my toes. That is fun because I tease him by moving my toes. Everywhere I go, he goes with me. Mommy will not let anyone else feed him, only me. She gets him some nice bones on the market and we give him a lot of meat. Mommy says we need to keep that a secret because so many families cannot afford meat. She told me that the reason we do not see many children is what daddy calls it the "financial revolution." She says that is making some people greedy and buying the kids from the poor people. They are bad people. In addition, they are making a lot of pollution that makes the air stink from butchering animals and stacking their garbage to burn. Mommy says someday many people will get sick. That is why we now live outside of town. The air is better here. I asked daddy, "Does yew maka rittle kidees wok in yur praycess?" He said, "Ann, I cannot be that cruel, my business buys things from other countries and sells them here and we buy things here and sell them in other countries. Your daddy loves kids and could not hurt them." Then I started to cry and said to him, "Onee rub me, I ams yur rittle gurl." He then hugged me said, "Of course, you are my little baby girl. Daddy then said to mommy, we must have somebody read many stories and talk to her. That will help her pronunciation, because I want to start sending her to some special schools next year. Then mommy smiled and gave him a kiss so I suppose it is safe for me. We shall soon see. Something about the word school is eerie, however I do not know why. I just have a feeling that children are not supposed to like school. I figured out why when mommy told me that children are not permitted to bring their pets to school with them. How unbelievably, against everything I can think of barbaric. Charley needs to learn the same things like me, so he can talk with me and help me with my homework. I do not really know what homework is; nevertheless, mommy told me it was good for me. It seems like my brain is filled up with so many memories of my mommy and daddy that all that yucky stuff that was in me, I am now relieved. It must not have been important since it is gone. Anyway, if it was without mommy and daddy, then I want it forever to leave my mind. My mind is for my mommy, daddy, our preacher who has the only church where the people are saved, and the wonderful people that work in our house. Someday I have to figure out what saved means, yet for now, I will pretend that I know. I do not want people to think I am a dumb one year old.

Mommy now asked daddy, "When is your painter going to draw a picture of our little Ann?" He then said, get her dressed, he will be here shortly. Yikes, when I have to get dressed, that means no playing, no feeding, and no having fun. Then my mommy got angry, "He is only going to draw her? How are you?" Then my daddy said to her, "Oh, no my dear, he draws real fast then goes back to his studios and paints them over some really exciting backgrounds." Then my mommy kissed my daddy and she said, "Thanks, Edward." Then the man came and made a fast drawing of me with his magic pencil, and then he drew Charles. When he drew Charles and showed me the picture, I gave him a kiss. Mommy and daddy clapped and laughed when I did that, and I laughed because I was so happy. When the man brought back the picture, mommy was so happy. He put Charles and me in the picture with water plashing behind me. She made daddy put it up in our living room, taking down the picture of them. She put that picture in their bedroom on the wall behind their bed. I saw daddy smiling, wonder why . . . ? Now my life was getting ready to change as daddy introduced me to Henrietta, the demon! That is what I call her. She had a white thing wrapped around her head and wore a black robe with a strange necklace around her neck. She was always reading the bible when mommy and daddy were looking. She would talk one-way to Charley and me and different when mommy and daddy were watching. The first thing she told me was that it was not a good thing to sleep with a light or lantern burning. Charley and I like it very much. Charley barks at her a lot. Then she told me, "Once there was a little girl who was afraid of the dark." I told her, "I notta fraid, Charley is." She continued, "Every night, she would leave her lanterns on when she went to sleep. After a while her mommy and daddy said she was a bad girl and needed to grow up for doing this and they got mad at her." I then asked her, "is me parots going to get bad ata me becuz of Charles?" She looked at me and said, "Maybe," then continued, "But the bad girl kept on sleeping with her lanterns on. So then, her mother and father would sneak into her room at night, hit her doggy, and blow out her lanterns." Then I said, "u isa tuppids, my mommy and daddy nebers hit Charley." She then slapped me and said, "Never hit an adult or I will tell your parents that you are too bad to teach. In this story, one day her parents got mad at her and left her alone in her big house with no servants for a whole week. She got very hungry and scared because she could hear many new noises and things walking on her floors." Now I was going to pay attention because I have heard things walking on our floors at night. Henrietta continued, "She would cry every night for her mommy and daddy to come back home and she would sleep in the dark with her doggy. Then one night when her parents were still away, someone snuck into her house and took her doggy. She found her doggy in the morning with his head cut off, but his body was missing. That night she could her doggy walking in her household as he kept running into the walls, because he lost his head." She then said it was time for me to go to bed. She then went over to light my lanterns and said, "I want your parents to leave so I can cut off your toes." I then yelled, "I want to live in the dark." She then blew out her match come over and hit me (not very hard) and Charley bit her (not very hard). Her hit was more like a reward for getting stronger. She then exited the room and closed my door. I heard her tell mommy, "I don't think she is going to start sleeping in the dark now." I heard my mommy say, "Really?" Then I went to sleep with my best friend ever, Charley. That night I experienced my first real bad dream. First, I saw what Henrietta really looked like. She is so very ugly and has strange eyes. I think she lives with that bad thing our reverend is always talking about in church, a place with a whole bunch of fire. There was fire in her hands and no bible. Then as I fell asleep, I saw a family moving into an old house beside ours that had been empty for many years. At first, everything was nice for them in their new house, just as it was for us when we moved into our new house. Their house was not as big as ours, that is because mommy keeps telling me, "We are aristocrats and you will be going to many nice schools so many important people will love you." I do not care how many people love me, just so they do. Then they started smelling some strange odor in their home. At first Victoria, their little girl's name, thought her mommy made a boo boo in their kitchen. They did not have servants to prepare their food. Mum tells me many people do not have servants to prepare their food. I asked her once, "Mama, hoo cooks der pood." Mommy then told me she did not know. Then one-day Victoria's parents told her that smell was the smell of flesh that had been burned. This made Victoria cry, and she was now so distressing. Then one day, her daddy came home and was very mad. He had found a story in the library newspapers about a bad man who had come to their house and killed all their cats and dogs and even their parrots. He then burned them. The sheriff came and found all their parts except for her doggy's head. It was now that I looked over and saw Henrietta with Charles in her hands. I started screaming very loud. I then began hitting my bed and then gave one of my dolls and kept on crying. By a miracle, my mommy came running in and said, "Ann, it is OK now, mommy is here." I then cried to her, "Where did Charley go?" She said, "Let us go find him." We walked around the house and downstairs to the kitchen. There he was, in the middle of the kitchen eating garbage he found from our garbage cans. The servants forgot to take them out that night. Mommy said, "We need to get back to bed, our servants will clean this in the morning." I gave her a big kiss and a hug. She then said, "See mommy can make everything so much better, now I need to let you get some beauty sleep so someday the boys will like you." Yucky, I hate every boy except for daddy and granddaddy. Maybe if I stay up all night, every night, then the boys will not pester me. If they pester me now, I will hit them and tell Charley to bite them. I grabbed a hold of my Charley as mommy put my blanket over us, kissed me, and patted Charley (he likes that very much) and said Goodnight. Mommy is right; she can make everything better. I hope someday that when I am a mommy my babies will like me, if so; I will have a whole bunch of them, if daddy says it is ok. I will buy the babies at a nice store, if daddy will give me the money. The next day was so wonderful, especially when mommy told me Henrietta was ill and would not come today. I asked mommy, "Can we pray whole bunches?" She said, "Yes (started running) catch me if you can." Charley and I started chasing her. She is so fast even with the big dress on. She says someday daddy will buy me a whole bunch of those dresses if I do not let any boys in them. I thought that was so stupid, why any girl would ever let a boy in them. That is only for girls. I told her, "I promises neber a boy see insidy, if he treyes, I will hit him hards." She looked at me and started laughing, saying "That is exactly what I told my mommy before I married your daddy." Daddy is different, because I am going to find a boy exactly like him, because I cannot marry my daddy, mommy, and the reverend told me. That must be a punishment for little good girls. I bet all the bad girls get to hook up with their daddies. The next night, saw me sleeping without my lanterns. This time I tied Charley to my hand.

Then when I went to sleep, the bad people came again. A man who fights in wars had taken leave to head home for a short vacation. His clothes were a different color than the red uniforms the men wear that guard daddy's ships — to pray to the holy images, and to bow down before his parents. Mommy said some countries, the kids bow to their parents, but not a whole bunch in England. Moreover, as he was going his way, at a time when the sun had long set, and all was dark around, he walked pass by a graveyard. Henrietta said that is where all my friends will sleep someday. Just then, he heard someone running after him, and crying, "Stop! Escape is fruitless!" He looked back and there was a man, with decayed flesh, who was supposed to be sleeping on the ground, running after him and gnashing his rotten teeth. The soldier jumped to one side and with all his powerfulness ran to get away from it, spotted a little church, and run straight into it. There was not a person in the sanctuary, yet stretched out on a table lay another forever-sleeping man, with candles burning in front of it. The soldier hid in a recession, and remained there not knowing whether he was alive or dead, but waiting to see what would happen. Then up ran the first sleeping person, the one that had chased the soldier, and hurried into the chapel. The one lying on the table jumped up, and shrieked to the first sleeping person. They now talked so fast that the soldier could not know which one spoke, "What hast thou come here for?" "I've chased a soldier in here, so I'm going to eat him." "Come now, brother! He has run into my house. I shall eat him myself." "No, I shall!" "No, I shall!" They set to labor fighting; the dust flew everywhere. They would have gone on fighting ever so much longer, only the roosters began to crow. Then both the corpses fell lifeless to the ground, and the soldier went on his way homeward in peace, saying, "Glory is to thee. O Lord! I am redeemed from the bad things!" I do not really know why this story scared me; I guess it is because the men who were supposed to be sleeping on the ground were running after the man who fights for his country. Mommy said that when they are put in the ground they would stay there for a long time. She says their families buy them pretty boxes to sleep in. I am so afraid when I think of dead people and of being dead. At least in the boxes the skinny worms will not be crawling through you. Mommy says they did not get any food or toys to play with. It sounds terrible to me. I think this story is like the David and Goliath story I discovered a long time ago when I was a little baby in that the Lord saved them. I think I am going to stay away from graveyards. Mommy says we are going to be buried in a graveyard with a whole bunch of good nice people. That means I can play nice with people forever. I still think I want to wait a long time for this. This evening I will be brave and not cry. Charley will protect me. It was time for me to go to sleep. I must go to sleep so Charley will go to sleep. He needed his rest. Morning will come and I can kiss mommy again. Mommy told me when we were eating breakfast; she always lets me sit on her lap, "Today, your storyteller will be here to teach you some new things." I thought to myself, yucky. Then the beast came to our house and took Charley and me upstairs with that bible in her hand. Then when we got in our room, she put me on her lap and said, "I am going to make you very strong, because you have a very important job to do someday." I hope that job is putting her in a trashcan. She told me, "Once a long time ago there was a nice man named Vlad the Implaler. He lived almost 200 years ago. He was an important man who kept the Muslims, they are the bad people who pretend to believe in our god, and we have been fighting them for many years we will fight them, out of the eastern part of the European Peninsula. I feel sorry for the Muslims because they do not go to our church, which is the only way to be saved. He was defeated a couple of times, yet stopped their advance the last time by impaling 20,000 people outside his capital of Târgoviște. She said he had found a way to impale them without killing them, so when the enemy saw them screaming and crying on the poles, they ran away." I then asked her, "Wat is impala?" She first said, "Someday a car, but for this story it is when they stick a pole in your butt and make it go out of your mouth." I said then, "Yu aar a ryer?" I then asked her, "What is a car?" She had a puzzled look on her face denying any knowledge of automobiles. She then told me that, "As people get older their mind sometimes plays tricks on them. That is why mommy and daddy will need you someday to take care of us." I told her, "I will take care of my mommy and daddy very good. She now told me, "I am sorry little Ann, this tale is true." She then told me that someday they will tell stories about men who drink women's blood so they do not die and call them vampires." I asked her, "Hoda u knows dis?" She told me, "I know many things my child, but we must keep it a secret, if you do not tell, I will not tell the reverend you are a bad girl, so that they do not burn you in front of everybody." We then shook hands and she gave me a kiss on my cheek. I was so surprised. At first, I thought she was going to take a big bite out of my face and make me an ugly baby. Perhaps she was not the best I thought. Maybe she was really making me strong. Therefore, I told her, "Tumsay I gonna kills dose bad men." She then surprised me by saying, "That you will do and you will be higher than anyone or thing in another entire universe." Then I said, "Not hiwer dan our god." She said, "I now will tell you a secret, but never tell anyone or they will kill you, but you will be so high that you will have to live in cities in the space above the clouds." Then I told her, "My daddy told me that the clouds were the pinnacle of the whole world." This woman is sometimes strange. She then went downstairs, then I was looking out the front door for her to pass, and then she came back into my room, with some cookies and milk. She asked me, "Why are you looking out your window?" I then told her, "t-u waves goody bye bye to yew." She then told me, "I made some real good cookies just for you, and do you want some?" I said to her, "Prease." She then told me, "You have to give me a kiss first." I think it is so amazing how so many big people will give a little girl like me so many things for just a kiss. I am glad I have something they are willing to do things for me. I then hurried over to her and saw a big plate with cookies and some brown milk. I gave her many kisses, because this was a whole bunch of cookies, then I asked her, "Whod putty dirts in da milke." She then told me, that she had melted some good chocolate, the stuff they make Christmas Candy with and put it in my milk. I took a drink and wow, it is delicious. Henrietta must know many good things for a big kid like me. She had many kinds of cookies on the plate, some I never had seen before. Mommy and Daddy like German cookies. She then told me, anytime you have any more bad dreams call my name and I will help you. I then wondered how she could go inside my head, then she scared me, by saying, "Ann I can go inside your head." I hugged her and she asked me if Charley and I would like to walk downstairs with her. I told her, "Yes." She stuck out her hand, we walked downstairs together, and she told my mommy that I was a very good girl today. Mommy smiled and gave me a big kiss. I got many kisses today, so I am starting very important now. Then when I dozed off, I watched a pretty forest, nice and green with a road under it. I went to step on the road and all of a sudden, the trees turned red. This frightened me, and I called out for Henrietta and there she was inside my head saying, "Do not fear Ann, I am with you and will protect you. Tonight you will learn about people who drink blood." I told her in my mind, "People who drink blood are bad," this is nice because in my mind, I do not talk baby talk. She told me, "Yes, Ann, however you need to know why it is bad." She further told me that the reason the trees turned red was due to the blood of innocent people. She then told me, relax and we will watch this together. This will be a big story. A soldier was allowed to go home on furlough (that is what we call their little vacations). Well, he walked and walked, and after a time he began to grow near to his home village. Not far off from that village lived a miller in his mill. In his younger years, the soldier had been very intimated by him; why should not he go and see his good friend that he missed so much? He went on. The miller received him demonstratively and at once brought out liquor; and the two began drinking, and babbling about their previous happy times, and what they were now doing. All this took place close to dusk, and the soldier stopped so long at the miller's place that it became very dark. When he proposed to originate in his village, his host exclaimed, "Spend the night here, trooper! It's really late now, and perhaps you might bump into something bad." I then stated, "The trooper needs to stay." Henrietta told me that only she could hear me. She returned to this story, "Why must I continue? "God is punishing us! A wicked witch has died among us, and at night, she rises from her grave, wanders through the village, and does such things as bring fear upon the very bravest! How could even you help being afraid of her?" I knew I was afraid; even so, I am just a little girl. Giving back to our story in which I wrongfully interrupted, "Not one piece! A soldier is a man who belongs to the crown, and 'crown property cannot be submerged in water nor burnt in fire.' Wow, I think maybe someday I might kiss a soldier and make him a whole bunch of babies like mommy made me. They would be good to have at night when scary things happen. He replied, "I will immediately go to my family, I'm very anxious to see my family and friends as soon as possible. Onward he went. His road went from the front of the cemetery. On one of the graves, he saw a large fire blazing. "What's that?" he thought to himself. "I had better have a look." When he drew close, he ensured that the witch's head was on fire, and she was burning boots in her hands. "Hail, sister!" calls out the soldier. The witch looked up and said, "What have you come here for?" The soldier said "Why, I wanted to understand what you're doing." The witch threw her work aside and invited the soldier to a wedding. "Come along, comrade," said she, "Let's enjoy ourselves. There is a wedding going on in the village. "Come along!" says the soldier. They came to where the wedding was; there they were given alcohol, and treated very kind and gracious. The witch drank and drank, enjoying drinks' parties where she could see them, and then became infuriated. She chased all the guests and relatives out of the house, threw the wedded pair into a slumber, took out two vials and a bradawl (a tool for piercing small holes), pierced the hands of the bride and groom with the bradawl, and began drawing off their pedigree. Having done this, she said to the soldier, "Now we must depart." Well, off they went. On the way the soldier said, "Tell me; why did you draw off their blood in those vials?" "Why, considering that the bride and bridegroom might die. Tomorrow morning no one will be able to wake them. I alone know how to bring them back to life." "How can you do that," asked the soldier? "The bride and bridegroom must have cuts made in their heels, and some of their own blood must then be poured back into those wounds. I have got the bridegroom's blood stowed away in my right-hand pocket, and the bride's on my left. "The soldier listened to this without letting a single word go past him. Then the witch began boasting again." Whatever I wish," says she, "That I can do!" "I think it is quite impossible to get over on you?" said the soldier. "Why impossible? If any one were to create a pile of poplar branches, a hundred piles of them, and were to burn me on that pile, then he would be able to defeat me. Only he would have to look out very careful when burning me; for snakes, worms, and different kinds of reptiles would slither out of my inside, and crows, magpies, and jackdaws would come flying up. All these must be caught and flung on the pile. If so much as a single maggot were to run away, then there would be no help for it; in that maggot, I should slip away! "The soldier listened to all this and did not forget it. He and the witch talked and talked, and at last, they arrived at the tomb. "Well, buddy," said the hag, "now I'll tear you to pieces. Otherwise you'd be telling all this." "What are you talking about? Don't you deceive yourself; I serve God and the Emperor." The witch gnashed her teeth, howled aloud, and jumped at the soldier, who withdrew his sword and started babbling about him with sweeping blows. They fought and struggled; the soldier was all but at the end of his strength. "Oh!" Thought he, "I'm a lost man, and all for nothing!" Suddenly the cocks began to crow. The witch fell lifeless to the ground. The soldier took the vials of blood out of the witch's pockets, and went on to the house of his own people. When he had got there, and had exchanged greetings with his relatives, they said, "Did you pick up any disturbance, soldier?" "No, I saw none." "There now, we have a terrible thing going on in our village. A witch has been haunting it! After talking for a while, they lay down to sleep. Next morning the soldier awoke, and began asking, "I am told you have got a wedding coming up somewhere here?" "There was a wedding in the mansion of a rich man," replied his relative, "but the bride and bridegroom have died this very night, from what, nobody knows." They went with him to the mansion. Thither he went without saying a word. When he arrived there, he found the entire family crying. "What are you moaning about?" he said. "Such and such is the state of things soldier," said they. "I can take your young people to life again. What will you give me if I do?" "Take what you like, even if it is half of what we have!" The soldier did as the witch had instructed him, and brought the young people back to life. Instead of crying there began to be happiness and rejoicing; the soldier was very well handled and well rewarded. Then, left, about face, off he marched to the sheriff, the people who protected them, and told him to send for the peasants together and to get ready a hundred lots of aspen wood. Well, they got hold of the wood into the graveyard, dragged the witch out of her tomb, placed her on the pot, and set it alight; the people all standing round in a circle with brooms, shovels, and fire-irons. The pile became wrapped in flames as the witch began to glow. Her corpse burst, and out of it crept snakes, insects, and all sorts of reptiles, and up came flying crows, magpies, and jackdaws. The peasants knocked them down and flung them into the fire, not leaving so much as a single maggot to creep away! Therefore, the witch was thoroughly consumed, and the soldier collected his ashes and scattered them to the winds. From that time onward, there was peace in the village. The soldier received the thanks of the whole community. He stayed at home some time, enjoying himself completely. Then he went back to the czar's service with money in his pocket. When he had done his time, he retired from the army, and began to live a very comfortable life. Henrietta then asked me, "Did that story scare you?" I told her (in my head), "Come on, I am just a little girl." She then told me, "But you are a very special strong little girl. This story taught you that all evil could be defeated, no matter how impossible that sounds. Someday you may have to fight some very evil people. Just be very hardy and do not be afraid, because you are a very special little girl. She then asked me if I wanted her to sleep with me for a while. I told her; "Yeps" Come on, what kid is going to turn down an offer of having a big person sleeping with them in the dark. She then told me, "Keep quiet. Only speak inside your mind, so that your mommy does not hear you." I answered back as I was bribing her with my powerful kissed, "Ok, my favorite Henrietta, good night and thanks for loving me. You are the bestest" I wonder how I could have been wrong about her; however, I never knew that someone could talk in your head and keep you safe at night. I then asked Henrietta if she would sleep in my head more, and she said yes, because she saw everything in my head and would keep me safe from it. I asked her if I could see in my head, and she said, "Just one peak, ok." She let me see it, and I asked her, "Is that inside me?" She told me it was a little blurry and stretched however, that was what kept my brain safe. I saw her in there also, and asked her, "How can you be in there?" She then said, "Queen Anne sent me from Denmark." I then told her, my mommy said Queen Anne was dead, how could she have sent you?" Henrietta then said, "The Queen is not dead, she only lives in a new spot where most people cannot understand her or talk to her." I asked her, "Where is that place and can I see it?" She told me I could not realize it at present, because I might accidentally tell someone and we could be burned as they performed the "Maid of Orleans" a few hundred years ago. I told her ok, since she does know many things and in can be in my dreams keeping me safe. Even Charley likes her whole bunch now. I burned my finger once trying to touch the white stuff that is under the wood in our fireplace and that was a big cheese. Consequently, I am going to keep quiet about this because I think burning while tied to a pole would not be fun. Anyway, today is going to be a great day, because daddy is going to bring a new doll home for me. He says I am the best doll in the whole world. I asked him, "Ams me a dull baba"? He then said, "Only to me, my little pumpkin." I do not know what a pumpkin is, mommy will teach me this someday, however when daddy says it, he is happy, then that makes me happy. I told Henrietta and she said that not all dolls were good, sometimes they let bad things get in them, so she would test the doll first, to make sure it was safe for me. She put me on her lap and we watched tonight's story together. We saw an old couple who had hired a new house cleaner to help in their house. (We have many nice people who help around our house.) The wife delivered a huge doll collection, and the house cleaner was told to dust them once a week. So once a week the house cleaner walked into the room where the dolls were stored and viewed them in disgust. She hated dolls. While she was dusting, she came across a particularly strange doll. It was a talking doll and it had a cord in the rear. The house cleaner was amazed and pulled the cord. The doll said, "Hello." The house cleaner pulled the cord again. "I love my mum," said the bird. The house cleaner put the doll back and continued cleaning. A few weeks later, while dusting off the dolls, the house cleaner accidently knocked a doll over. It shattered as soon as it hit the ground. The old woman heard the sound and went to inspect this noise. When she walked into the room and saw her shattered doll. A very sad expression came over her face. The house cleaner saw this quickly and said, "I am very sorry. I did not mean to break her. I will not do it again." The old woman looked down at her sadly, broken doll and told the house cleaner that she could only hold her job if she promised to be extra careful about the dolls. The house cleaner agreed. The next day, the old couple gave the house cleaner alone while they went out to do some routine tasks. The house cleaner was in such a bad mood that she failed to do her job. While she was sitting in the kitchen enjoying some of the couple's fancy chocolate, the house cleaner thought of a ferocious idea. She slowly walked into the room where the dolls were. She thought for a moment about how sad the old woman was about her broken doll. The house cleaner picked up a doll and said, "She must really love these dolls," and threw the doll on the floor. It shattered and the house cleaner smiled. She loved the feeling of breaking dolls. Something close to the crushing sound made her happy. She threw more and more dolls on the floor. She was still in her doll killing rage when the old couple came through the doorway. The old woman ran to her broken dolls. She looked up at the house cleaner with a threatening expression and asked, "What are you doing?" The husband, seeing his wife so upset, immediately told the house cleaner she was discharged. The house cleaner gathered her things and left in an even worse disposition than before. She was so angry that later that night she snuck back into the old couple's home. Knowing they would be sound asleep, she crept into the kitchen, found the biggest knife she could, and made her way to the bedroom. The next morning, the house cleaner returned to the house, acted like an innocent bystander, and told the police that she worked for the couple. She pretended to be the sorry victim that had lost good friends. She told police that the old couple was nice, loving caring people, and she had no idea why anyone would want to kill them. At that point, she slowly walked into the house, saying she wished to make sure no one had hurt the old woman's beloved collection. When she got to the talking doll, she lifted it up and pulled the cord. "Hello," it said. She pulled the cord again, and it said, "Why did you kill my momma?" The house cleaner looked horrified. "What did you just say?" "Why did you kill momma?" asked the doll. The house cleaner stared in shock. She kept pulling the cord. "Why did you kill my momma? She was a nice momma. I loved her very much. Why did you kill my momma?" The house cleaner stared at the doll. She could not believe this was happening. "You killed my momma!" The doll screamed. The house cleaner threw it to the ground and ran from the house. The next morning the house cleaner was found dead in her bed. In her arms was the talking doll. When investigators pulled the cord on the dolls back it just kept repeating, "She killed my momma. She killed my momma. She killed my momma . . ." "So, Ann, be careful around your dolls, because they do have eyes" Henrietta told me in a slow strong voice, "Make sure if one is around, you do not speak of any secrets or do anything that your mother and father may not like. Because your dolls may tell on you, as their job is also to help you be a good little girl." Then she told me a true story that happened in Denmark to her neighbor when she was a child. "This story is about a young Danish girl named Caroline. One day in 1599 in Hjorning, North Jutandic Island she was on the way to the market, when she stopped in front of an old cabin. Caroline was a girl who enjoyed the terrifying things and wanted to go into the cabin just to alleviate her curiosity. When Caroline got out of her carriage, she smelt a horrible smell that smelt kind of, similar to rotting flesh. Every step Caroline took her the smell became stronger and stronger. When she stood up to the cabin, it was taciturn. "Hello, hello is anyone in here?" Still, Caroline got no response. Caroline went around the cabin just to investigate. She stopped at a room that looked like it could have been a nursery one time. Caroline went into the room and then suddenly Boom! The door slammed shut behind her. Caroline ran over to the door and pounded on it as hard as she could, screaming "Let Me Out! Let Me Out!" She heard a laughing that sounded like a ten year old behind her. Caroline slowly turned around to see that there was a sick young woman with dark hair and a white ripped up clothes. She also noted that her mouth was sewn shut. Her name was Cathy. Caroline screamed at the top of her lungs and then kicked the door down. She went outside, got into her carriage, and took off. Caroline rode as far away, as fast as she could . . . . Then all of a sudden, the same girl that she witnessed in the room in the cabin appeared right in the middle of the road. Caroline pulled for her horses to break off and fell out onto the ground and fainted. Cathy took Caroline back into a strange spot in the cabin. It looked like a surgeon room. Cathy sewed Caroline's lips together just as Cathy has had hers sewn. Caroline went missing and when the sheriff found her, Caroline's lips were sewn and she died 'Because of too much blood loss. Three years later another young woman named Elizabeth went into that same cabin, and killed by Caroline by getting her lips sewn. So remember, never, I repeat never get into the cabin, or any place that you do not absolutely that you are safe, alone or the same thing could happen to you. So make sure you do not go into places that you cannot see or the bad people might take you. Dark and secret places can, and most times do, hide bad things." Then I asked her, "What about going to the kitchen at night, and sneak some good things for Charley?" She then said, "I would not, for all traps are baited and those who take the bait lose themselves." That was the conclusion of our story time today. It was better today, with seeing one and being told the other. Because I think I would be very scared seeing Catherine's lips getting sewed up." Then we went to sleep. In addition, while I was resting very nicely, Charley was trying to wake me. He would push his head against mine and whine quietly. When I awoke, he commenced licking my face. When I moved my hand, he jumped off the bed, ran to my door, and started scratching at it. I immediately knew what Charley wanted. Therefore, I got up and followed him down the steps and into our dark kitchen, loving Charley more than my previous warnings. We had a special little door that he could go in and out of when he had to do a number one or number a number two. Just then, I heard my mother calling for me. I went halfway of the stairs; however, I now heard my mother was calling me from the kitchen. I went to the kitchen, but now my mother was yelling from the cellar. Right away, I decided to find a spot to hide, so I went into one of the closets that our house cleaners kept their brooms. I tried to sneak in there very quietly when a hand reached out and grabbed me pulling me into what I prayed was safety. The other hand covered my mouth, I was now so scared. Why had Henrietta abandoned me? Why would a big woman leave a little girl in such a crisis? This monster was going to sew my month closed. Was this the witch, which killed the bride and groom? I have not even kissed a little boy yet, which I am in no hurry to do so. I honestly do not ever want to, except for my daddy and granddaddy Maybe it is one of those poor people daddy said might want to hurt us, because we are not starving. My heart was no longer beating; I think I might go to that place where the people cannot speak to us. Then all of a sudden, a soft voice whispered to me, "Ann, it is Ok, it is me?" I then said, "Mommy, why yew curing me from anywhere?" Then my mommy whispered to me, "I heard that also, so I went to the kitchen to find you. Then all of a sudden, something started scratching on the door. My mommy started kissing me very slow. I was now so scared I could feel some number two in my pants. Nevertheless, mommy's kisses felt like gifts from heaven now. This is a time that I am so glad we go to the only church where the members are saved. It has been so long since I did a number two in my pants. Nevertheless, I knew mommy could smell it; still she did not move or say anything. I hope she does not tell papa, because he might get mad at me. I hope these bad things do not kill my mom. She has been such a good mommy and should not have to die simply for saving her little girl. Then the door flew open and in came Charley. Mom and I both started laughing, and then she said, "Let me clean you boo boo." I told mommy I was so frightened I did not do it intentionally. She told me "I know Ann, I almost did it also." Then she started laughing and kissing me again. I really feel so good when she kisses me. I often think she knows everything about me, which makes me so happy to be loved so much. I now think I know what is happening, as it came to me why Henrietta did not come inside my head. We have to keep this a secret from mommy. She gave Charley some food and put both of us to bed with her wonderful kisses. Then Henrietta came sticking the top portion of her head out of the dark, with a white circle surrounding her. She did not have her uniform on. I could see her baby milk bottles. I said to (inside talk), "Henrietta, why did you forget your dress." She replied, "Ann, I was taking a bath, when I could feel something strange from the house beside you, so I wanted to warn you. I hope you are not upset by my body." I then told her, "You look so much better without that white thing over your head. Do you have babies for your milk bottles?" Henrietta then told me, "No Ann, you are my only little girl. All women have breasts, or baby milk bottles as you describe them, however they only make milk when the woman has an infant to feed from them." Then I told her, "But I do not have them." She then laughed and replied, "You will someday my little angel. I am going to get dressed and then take you to your neighbor's house. As she departed I then said to Charley, "Henrietta is a big girl and beautiful just like mommy. Mommies' milk jugs are better; however, it does not matter now since I eat big peoples food. How do her milk bottles know that I am not a baby anymore? I shall have to meditate on this one for a short while. Let's get some rest before she comes back and gets us." A short while later, she woke us up and took us up to one of my neighbor's houses. I have seen their children playing in their back yard. Sometimes they look like they are playing fun games, however mommy says that an aristocrat girl would not be seen outside behaving like that. I am beginning the think that aristocrat means no fun, and just looking and acting pretty. The house seemed normal to me. The kids always say hello to me. Mommy does not let me talk back to them. Nevertheless, I always wave at them behind my back. I can hear them say, "Thank you." First time mommy asked me, "Did you do something, to make them say thank you?" I turned around and saw them playing with some other kids. I then told mommy, "Look they have more friends, and may I meet with them?" Then mommy turned me back around and forced me to go in her friend's house. She never asked me that question again. Their daddy cannot walk, so he rides in a chair with wheels. It is nice and shiny. I sometimes think that it would be fun riding in a chair everywhere. Maybe I could have friends that would ride in their chairs and we could play games together. He never moves outside of his house or back yard; even so, I have witnessed him in their back yard. Those youngsters have their mommy, daddy, grand mommy, granddaddy, and another big person they call their uncle. At night, they always close all their curtains. I thought they saw someone looking in at them. Maybe one of them had seen me. I do not care, because Charley will protect me. Now, Henrietta took us in the house. We were invisible people, which Henrietta said was because of her magic. It did not scare me because Henrietta always held me and I always held Charley. He was always very quiet when we were being invisible people. Then I looked down at the floor and saw things that looked like empty people. Henrietta told me that those were flesh suits. In some way, this seemed normal to me. Then we looked in the kitchen and now that scared me! There were things sitting at the table and they were built from bones. I asked Henrietta what they were and she told me, "These are dead people working as spies to find out if anyone is being bad or different. Now that we know that, we will close our curtains at night and be very careful around them, Ok Ann?" I told her I would do as she asked. She then put me in my bed. I have a nice big bed with a pretty canopy on the upper side. Mom says it is a King bed, just like the kings. She used to sleep with me some, however now; she just gives me a kiss, tucks me in, and says good night. Now she sleeps almost all the time with papa. Henrietta now gave me a big kiss, tucked me back in and said, "Goodnight. If you need me, just call for me in your mind, so we do not wake up your mommy." It still joyfully amazes me how all the big people like to tuck a kid into bed. I let them do it because it makes them feel safe. This night is a lot different, since I found out the bone people. All of a sudden, I could feel something go into my bed. I could hear it taking big breaths. Now it is lying next to me. Maybe, Henrietta turned herself invisible and forgot to turn herself on for me. Anyhow, I am going to shut up so mommy and daddy do not hear me. Maybe Henrietta is testing me to see if I am getting to be a big girl. Now, the thing is breathing next to my ear and going down my neck. Now, it is getting up and shaking my bed by jumping up and down. Perhaps it is a kid or even my neighbor kids. Whatever, now I am calling Henrietta who comes in and starts fighting. I can hear it really breathing hard now. Then I can see her tying something up and dragging it off. Sadly they are both gone now. I can hear my mom saying, "Ann, stop playing on your bed." I used to do that a lot at night, however not much today since I am going to be a big girl. I now yelled back, "Sorry Mommy, Goodnight." Then she said Goodnight to me. I was afraid that she might come into my room and see the messy sheets. I hope that thing did not make my blankets dirty. That would make mommy very mad. She told me that my sheets cost her lots of money. It is the only one of its kind. She paid some woman a lot of money and it took her a long time to make them. Now Henrietta came back and asked me, "Are you ok, Anne?" "I am OK, what was that thing who was playing on my bed?" Henrietta told me, "It was the spirit of a kid who saw your bed and wanted to play. I took him back to his house and his dad is going to make sure he does not bother you anymore." I then asked Henrietta, "Will you tell me a story? She said sure, "However I have to take another bath, because that thing made me very dirty. Can I tell you the story while taking my bath? I then quickly answered, "Of course, my favorite friend." Then Henrietta starting talking strange again, by saying, "I am more than your friend; I am your protector and servant." I then asked her, "Don't mommy and daddy protect me?" She then said something that made a lot of sense to me, "Of course, however, I can protect you from inside also." I agreed and thanked her for her help. Now, some of her started to come out of the dark. I asked her where her other leg was, and she told me, "It is in a nice lake being cleaned. Are you ready for this long story?" I told her that I was. Then she withdrew her head, opened her mouth, and began singing with a chilling voice. I think this is going to be a good story. Mia is walking into her family living room and sees someone standing beside the family's open window. Mia notices it is Mr. Hendershot, someone to visit her aunt. Mia smiles at Mr. Hendershot. "My aunt will join us soon," says Mia. "Until then, you must try and endure me. May I take your coat and hat? "Mr. Hendershot is a frightened man. He timidly smiles back at Mia. "Thank you," he says. He gives her his coat and hat. Mr. Hendershot apprehensively looks around the living room. He looks at all the pictures on the walls and the sofa. He looks at the open window. He looks at the green lawn just clear of the open window. Mia closely watches Mr. Hendershot. "You just moved to the woodland?" she asks. "Yes," says Mr. Hendershot. He fiddles with his hands. His right eye twitches twice in succession. "I moved here to benefit from country life. Country life is relaxing and slow." "Do you know anyone in the country?" asks Mia. "No one," says Mr. Hendershot. "Your aunt, Mrs. Veszprém, is my first new friend." Mr. Hendershot takes a deep breath. His body trembles. "My sister, Váci, lived in the country four years ago. Váci met your aunt then. Váci says your aunt is very nice." "So you don't know anything about my aunt?" asks Mia. "I only know her name and address," says Mr. Hendershot. "Is she nice?" He asks with a swallow. "Oh, yes, very nice indeed," says Mia. "She is nice despite the misfortune." "Misfortune, what do you mean?" asks Mr. Hendershot. He twiddles with his hands, twitches his eye as his body shudders. "The misfortune happened about three years ago, since your sister was here," says Mia. Mia looks directly into Mr. Hendershot's eyes. "You may wonder why this window is open," she says. "I had noticed it," says Mr. Hendershot. "The view is very pretty." "Pretty and dreadful," says Mia. "Three years ago today, my aunt's husband, two brothers, and their favorite dog left through that window on a hunting trip. They never returned home. They had gone hunting on the dirt hills. When they crossed the rolling hills, they fell into a deep bog and were never seen again." Mr. Hendershot's eyes widen with anxiety. "On the anniversary of their deaths," says Mia, "My poor aunt leaves the window open. She believes that they will come back. Moreover, you know, Mr. Hendershot, on such a lovely day as this, I sometimes think they will. "Mia's aunt walks into the room." "Mr. Hendershot," she says, "I am sorry to keep you waiting. I hope my niece has made you comfortable." "Y-y-y-Es," says Mr. Hendershot, his eyes looking quickly from Mrs. Veszprém to Mia to the window. "I do hope you don't mind the open window," says Mrs. Veszprém. "My husband and brothers are hunting on the dirt hills. They should return soon. They always come back through this doorway. I do hate how they track mud onto my carpets. Those dirt hills are so muddy, you know." Mr. Hendershot listens with horror. He twitches with his hands. His body uncontrollably quakes. His eye twitches. Mia watches Mr. Hendershot. "I-I-I see," says Mr. Hendershot, nervous and wanting to change the subject. "I am delighted to see you. I will be in the area for a few months. I moved to the area for the benefit of my nervousness. My doctor says I absolutely must relax. Country life is relaxing and slow, don't you think?" Mrs. Veszprém turns from the open window. She looks at her guest. "Yes, it is, Mr. Hendershot," she answers. "And the hunting in the country is very good, too." Mrs. Veszprém turns back to the open window. "I wonder how the hunting is today?" she asks. The living room was completely silent. Mr. Hendershot restlessly tries to fill the silence. "My sister, Váci, met you about four years ago," he says. "Váci said the area would be very beneficial for my nerves." "Look! Here they are," says Mrs. Veszprém. "And they're back just in time for tea." The older woman walks towards the open window. She looks out across the green lawn. "Goodness! Look at all that mud. They will surely ruin all of my carpets today." Mr. Hendershot cannot believe his eyes and ears. What a catastrophic situation. This poor Mrs. Veszprém needs more help than he makes out. Mr. Hendershot turns to Mia to show his sympathy, but the child is staring out the window.

Mia's eyes are wide with horror. Mia sees the hunting party returning from the woods. Mr. Hendershot frets with his hands. His eye shudders. His entire body quivers with anticipation. He turned his head to look out the window. Far across the green lawn, a dog runs toward the drawing room. Following the dog is an older man with a shotgun resting on his shoulder and two young boys carrying sacks. Their boots are covered in mud. Mr. Hendershot screams, "AAARRRGGGHHH!" Mr. Hendershot grabs his coat and hat. Without turning back, he goes from the drawing room and out the open window. He runs across the lawn and disappears from sight. In his hasty departure, he nearly knocks over the returning Mr. Veszprém. Mr. Hendershot runs out of the house without turning back. "What got into that young man?" asks Mr. Veszprém. He treads on the clean carpet with his muddy boots. Mrs. Veszprém shakes her head and looks at the mud. "Such an odd, nervous fellow," Mrs. Veszprém tells Mr. Veszprém. "He fidgeted with his hands. His eye twitched. His body shivered and shook. He talked all about his nervous condition. Then he went away without saying good-bye. This is so very distressingly atypical." "He was probably terrified of the dog," says Mia. She bends to scratch the dog's head. "Makes sense, really," Mia continues. "He told me that he was very scared of dogs. Said Mia years ago, he was hiking in the mountains. While following a dark and narrow trail, he stumbled upon a pack of wild dogs. The dogs chased the poor chap for three days. Mr. Hendershot finally climbed up a tree and shrouded in the branches. Under him, the dogs walked back and forth, snarling and barking, for a whole week. "Mia sweetly smiles at her aunt and uncle. Mia likes to tell stories. The end." "Henrietta wasn't she happy that her uncle came back after so many years" I asked her. Henrietta told me, "Ann, Mia was making up the story, just like she invented the dog story about Mr. Hendershot." I told her, "I suppose that is lying." Henrietta then told me, "Be careful what people tell you, sometimes they want to hurt you or make you look stupid." I then said to Henrietta, "It is easy for me to look stupid, because I have never gone to school and discovered everything yet." Henrietta then replied, "Do not worry, I will teach you until you go to school." Then I started crying, and sobbingly said, "But I want you to be my teacher forever." Henrietta then answered swiftly, while giving me a kiss on my cheek, "Do not worry Ann, my boss has better plans for you. We will keep you safe." Then she said "Goodbye," then Charley and I went to sleep. When I awoke, mommy fed me, put a real nice dress on me, and then told me, "One of my childhood girlfriends is coming to see us today. She wants to see my pretty little girl." I just looked at mommy and said, "I love you," giving her a hug and a whole bunch of kisses. She got that big happy grin, and then told me, "You are everything in the world to me and your daddy." I asked mommy why and she told me, "Because we made you. We wanted to have somebody who was from me and your daddy." I then asked mommy, "which part of me is from my daddy," And mommy told me, "Your brains and muscles and strong legs and smile." I then replied, "Wow" Mommy said, "You are mouthing your words well now, just like your daddy did when he was little." I then told her, "I am so lucky to have a beautiful mommy and smart daddy." Then mom said, "I have to get my bath now, so why don't you come in and sit in the hot seat while I tell you a story my grandfather told me when I was a little girl." I said, "Yeah" and went to the room we all took our baths. We were lucky, because mommy said many people did not have such a room. Our servants would make the water hot and bring it upstairs to this room. They would refill it for us when the water began to get cold, however we had a little wood stove under it that would help keep it warm. Mom told me never to fiddle with that stove, and that is why she or one of our servants watches me all the time. Mommy has been walking a lot doing things on the floor lately that she calls exercises. After she takes a bath, she puts black paint around her eyes and eyebrows. I sometimes watch her do this. She said that she used to do that when she was in high school. She attended high school in Ireland. We are not permitted to do that right away, so I had to promise her to keep it a secret. She wants me to recognize all her secrets. I then asked mommy, "Why are your baby milk bottles still so big, I don't drink that milk now."

She told me, "You helped make them bigger honey, so now all the men talk nice to me and daddy is so happy now, just because of you. Thanks so much honey." I then said to her, "I do not like all boys, except for daddy, so I am glad that they do not talk to me." Mommy, then said, "Someday that will change. Are you ready for your story now?" I smiled, then sat down on the chair, not slouching and said, "Yes ma'am." She smiled then started, "It was the very coldest part of the year; it snowed, as the dark was rushing in, the evening on December 31st, 1620. In this, cold and darkness there went along the street a poor little girl, bareheaded, and with naked feet. Her mommy and daddy did not have any money. When she left home, she had slippers on; however, what was the good of that? They were very large slippers, which her mother had previously worn; so large were they; and the poor little thing lost them as she scraped away across the street, because of two carriages that rolled by very fast. One slipper was nowhere to be found; the other had been taken by a tramp, and off he ran with it; he would be saving it for a crib when some day he should have children. The poor people do not get nice beds like daddy got for you and me. Therefore, they try to find anything that can use. Thus, the little maiden walked on with her tiny freely exposed feet, which were quite red and blue from cold. Do you remember how the snow felt when you and were throwing snowballs at each other and you lost your glove. And mommy had to take you inside and warm your hands up fast and you got scared and thus started crying." I said, "Oh, mommy, snow on any part of a person is not good. She should have gone into a shop, school, sheriff office or our church and get saved." Mommy, then smiled at me, and took up the story again, "She carried some matches in an old apron, and she had a pile of them in her hand. Nobody had bought anything from her the whole day; no one had given her a single bit. She inched along trembling being hungry and cold, looking filled with sorrow, a very representation of sorrow, the poor little thing! The flakes of snow covered her long pale hair, which fell in beautiful curls around her neck; but of that, of course, she never once now thought. From all the windows, the candles were gleaming, and it smelt so deliciously of roast goose, for you know it was New Year's Eve; yes, of this, she thought. She sat down in front of two houses that formed a corner that cringed each other, of which one advanced more than the other did. She drew her little feet she nearer to her. Nonetheless, she got colder and colder. To go home she did not try, for she had not sold any matches and could not take a piece of money. Her father would certainly whip her, and at home it was also cold, for above her she had only the roof, through which the wind hooted, even though the largest cracks were temporary sealed with straw and rags." I called for mom, "Why would her daddy whip her for not selling the matches? I think he is a bad dad. When I get bigger will he not let me live with you unless I earn money?" Then mommy replied, No Ann, remember we have too much money already. If you made more money, our house would be filled up and we would have to sleep outside in the cold and maybe die. Please promise not to make us cold and die?" I then promised mommy I would not make any money and hurt us." As mommy smiled, she nodded her head and continued. "Her little hands were almost numbed with the wretched cold. Oh! One match might afford her a world of comfort, if she only dared take a single one out of the pile, draw it against the wall, and warm her fingers by it. She drew one out. "Oh, my god," how it blazed, how it burned! It was a warm, bright flame, like a lifesaving candle, as she held her hands over it. It was a wondrous light, which almost lit the whole sky. She hoped that it would render a light for the angels to go steady and then save her. It seemed really to the little girl as if she was sitting before a large iron stove, with gleaming brass feet and a brass ornament on top. The fire burned with such blessed authority; it warmed so wonderfully. The little girl had already stretched out her feet to warm them too; however, the small flame went out, the stove disappeared; she had only the leftovers of the burnt-out match in her hand. She rubbed another against the wall: it burned brightly, and where the light fell on the wall, there the wall became transparent like a veil, so that she could see into the room. On the table was spread a very white tablecloth; upon it was a splendid chinaware service, and the roast goose was steaming famously with its stuffing of apple and dried plums. Moreover, what was principal to behold was, the goose hopped down from the dish, reeled about on the floor with knife and fork in its breast, until it came up to the poor little girl; then it went out, then there was nothing but the thick, cold, damp wall left behind. She lit another match. At this time there, she was sitting under the most magnificent Christmas tree; it was still larger, and more decorated than the one, which she had seen through the glass door in the rich merchant's house. Thousands of lights were burning on the green branches, and happily, colored pictures, such as she had seen in the shop-windows, looked down upon her. The little girl stretched out her hands towards them when, the match went out. The lights of the Christmas tree rose higher and higher, she saw them now as stars in heaven; one fell down and formed a long trail of fire. "Someone has just died!" Said the little girl; for her old grandmother, the only person who had loved her, and who was now no more, had told her, that when a star falls, a soul ascends to God. She drew another match against the wall: it was again light, and in the gloom, there stood the old grandmother, so bright and radiant, so mild, and with such an expression of love. "Grandmother," cried the little one. Oh, take me with you! You go away when the match burns out; you vanish like the warm stove, like the delicious roast goose, and like the magnificent Christmas tree!" She rubbed the whole bundle of matches quickly against the wall, for she wanted to be quite sure of keeping her grandmother near her. The matches gave such a brilliant light that it was brighter than at midday, never before had the grandmother been so beautiful and so tall. She took the little maiden, on her arm, and both flew in brightness and in joy so high, so very high, and then above was neither cold, nor thirst, nor anxiety; they were with God. However, in the corner at the cold hour of dawn, sat the poor girl; with rosy cheeks and with a smiling mouth, leaning against the wall, frozen to death on the last evening of the old year. Stiff and stark sat the child there with her matches, of which one bundle had been burnt. "She wanted to warm herself," people said. No one had the slightest suspicion of what beautiful things she had seen; no one even dreamed of the majesty in which, with her grandmother she had entered on the joys of a new year." Then mommy said, "Why are you crying Ann." I told her that, "The poor little girl dying is so sad, yet I also remember when my grandmother passed away. She must not have loved me, because she did not take me with her. In addition, the little girl must have gone to our church if she was saved. Why did not anyone in our church help her?" Then my mother said as she was wiping off my tears and kissing me, "Oh, honey your grandma loved you a whole bunch. She told me she wanted you to stay with me because you were such a beautiful child and you are my child. Ok princess. I believe this story is real old thus our church people are new now and we should help any little girls who are hungry or cold, my little angel." I then still am crying saying. "Mommy, that is a sad story, "I am glad that daddy gives money to the poor people, so some of those kids can have shoes. I do not like it when little girls die, because that is fewer friends for me. Nowadays when I see snow I am going to think about that little girl." Then mom told me, "That is good, we must always remember that the poor get hungry and cold just like we do, the big difference is that they stay hungry and cold for a long time. Your daddy does help many of them; he told me he actually gives enough food to feed three hundred fifty of them. The rich people are so meticulous about the freshness and excellent taste that they waste a lot of food. Rather than giving this food away like all the other traders, he applies it to the poor people. He then gives them money to buy shoes and clothes. We should be proud of him." I told my mommy, "I am proud of my daddy, I think he is the greatest daddy ever in the history of daddies." She then smiled at me and said, "My friend will be here soon, so I had better get us dressed. You want to wipe my back and my lower legs, so mommy does not have to bend over." These made me so happy; mommy was going to let me do real work to help her. I jumped up, kissed her and said, "With all my love, ma'am" She then said, you are such a polite young lady." She had never called me a woman before. So now, I wiped her back and kissed it. I had to tell her, "Mommy your back is so beautiful, will mine look like that someday." She then told me, "Oh yes, Ann, because when you were in my belly, I put some magic in you to make you look just like me when you get big." "Oh, wow mommy, you have magic just like Henrietta," blundered out of my mouth. I caught it just in time to add, "'s stories?" Mommy's face now turned from serious to calm, as she said, "The big difference is that my magic is real and Henrietta's is only in stories." I had pulled my foot out of my mouth just in time. That was a very narrow escape. I do not know why whoever made little kids gave them little bodies with a big mouth. It is so hard to catch words as they fly out of your mouth. Something somewhere saved my most wonderful friend (Henrietta) and me on this one. I rather nervously finished wiping mommy's legs, and I think she noticed it by asking me "Is everything OK, Ann?" I told her, "Sorry mommy, I was just thinking of the little girl's feet." Mommy then gave me a kiss and asked me to help her get into her clothes. This was a big task; as two of our girl servants had also, to help her. The dress was heavy, so I asked mommy, "Why don't you have some of our boy servants' help, because they are so much stronger." One of the girl servants said, "Oh no, Anne, a lady cannot let a boy, that she is not married to, help her put on a dress." I then said, "But she already has all those white clothes on below it." Then mom said, "Sorry Ann that is the rules. If your daddy ever caught a boy, that you are not married to, helping you put on a dress, he would beat him and have the sheriff put him away in jail. Also, remember when I told you that daddy would buy you and me many dresses as long as we did not let any boys go inside of them." Then I told my mother, "If I ever catch a boy in my dress, I will tell daddy so he beats him and puts him in jail, because I hate boys, except to granddaddy, daddy, and our boy servants." The girl servants then painted mommy white, put a wig on her, and gave her white gloves. I said, "Mommy, why do big people paint themselves white and put wigs on" as I have also seen daddy do this? She then told me, "That is the style that ladies and gentlemen use when going in public or greeting long lost friends. I then asked, "Do I have to be a lady when I grow big like you?" One of our female servants started laughing, then stopped as fast when she saw mommy's angry look at her. Mommy said, "Only if you love your mom and daddy." I said, "Then they can paint all of me white forever." Mom gave me a big kiss. She could not hug me, because it was too hard for her in her dress. Then something strange flashed in my mind for about one tenth of a second, and I mean a real fast flash. I thought I had seen some people who were whiter than mommy is now, in a place I have never seen before. I wondered who these people were and from where. I would ask Henrietta about it later. Our butler knocked on my mother's door. He knew not to come in since two girl servants were in her room with the door locked and that meant one thing. No boys are allowed, of course. He told us through the door, "Ma'am, you have a lady friend to visit you." My mother then said, "William, bring her up please" and he answered, "Yes ma'am." Mommy always told me, to always call our servants by their first name and always say please. She stated they are here to help us; they are giving time out of their lives, so we must express our appreciation. In a few minutes, we heard a knock on our door. Then a few seconds later, the butler came and said to us through the door, Ma'am there is a Ms. Fejér here to see you. She claims you invited her." "That is right; tell her I will be with her in our family room real soon, and thanks William." Then William asked another strange question, "Are you sure, Ma'am?" Mommy simply replied in a normal voice, "That I am William." Then off went William. Mommy told us, "William is acting strange today, what you girls think?" We all three replied, "Yes, Ma'am", Yes Ma'am", Yes Mommy." Mommy had asked William to bring her friend upstairs, yet he did not, instead once again coming to our door to verify her simple request. Then we all walked down to our family room. I was so excited finally to see Mrs. Fejér. Mommy always talked about her and told me that until she had many great stories from her dad. Mommy told me that she had dated the man that Mrs. Fejér had married. Of course, that is in the humongous list of the secrets she had told me. That is what makes her a special mother. When I came out of her, she is putting herself in me. As she is with me, I cannot share everything with her, especially Henrietta. I feel guilty about that sometimes. We were almost to our family room and I was so excited, although if she was like mommy, all dressed up, and painted white, she would be boring. Nevertheless, she had been mommy's friend for a long time, so she might tell me some things about mommy that mommy forgot. That would be wonderful. Now we were walking into the family room and when mommy saw Mrs. Fejér, she was shocked and fell to the floor. The servants gave her some smelling salts and she awoke. Mommy looked at the woman in detail, and then said, "Who are you?" The woman, replied, "Rich girl, it is bubbly face." Then mommy got up next to her and looked at her again in detail. She then said "10, 001," and bubbly face replied, '10,002.' Mommy then looked at her chin, ears, and then opened up the top of her dress and looked at her baby milk jugs. She then stuck her hand down the top of bubbly face's shirt and moved it around a little and Mrs. Fejér replied, "Oh it is time for the storm." At this, mommy removed her hand, hugged Mrs. Fejér, and said, "Welcome to my home my best friend ever, Mrs. Fejér." She then looked at mommy with a tear rolling down her cheek and said, "It is not Mrs. Anymore, for my Mr. Died two years ago." Then mum said to her, "Why did not you tell me Fejér?" One of the servant women said to me, "Fejér is not her last name, but her given name." She shook her head yes, looking sad on the outside. I was happy on the inside, because Fejér looked like someone I could play. Fejér answered mommies question by saying, "Because Ranlyn put all that he had into three ships for international trade and Spanish pirates raided them and killed all but a few men, who as excellent swimmers swam out of sight, and then the pirates sunk all three ships. We lost everything we had. The bank came and took our house, and none of our friends would help us. Ranlyn was put into debtor's prison. We could not live with the thought that I would a fugitive on the streets as a beggar, thus he took his life." I asked one of the servants, "What is taking his life?" Likewise, they told me, "Killed himself, or committed suicide." I then asked, "Why is she a fugitive?" They told me, "Because the debtors took everything he owned and according to the law, he owned her, thus they owned her." I hate that law. That means daddy owns mommy, which is ok, as long as none of daddy's ship are taken by pirates. She had been hungry living on the streets like that little girl who perished with her grandmother. This is so very sad. Mommy started crying when she heard that Ranlyn had committed suicide." The servant girls came over and wiped her face, telling her everything would be ok. Our servants truly felt like they were a part of our family and they did love us, because we loved them. Fejér then replied, "Prudence, your servants truly give you outstanding service and look as if they care." Then both servant girls looked at Fejér and replied, "We do this because she is our mother in love as Ann is our sister in love. Then mommy looked at Fejér and said, "Why not you, and Ranlyn came to my house, I have told you so many times how we serve the poor, and we would have shared with our allies, as you very well know." Then Fejér answered by saying, "That I did tell Ranlyn, yet his shame and pride would not release him yet to me.im even to me. I came here today to beg for a lower job in your house." She then sank to her knees and began crying. This was so bad, that even mommy and I started crying. Mommy motioned for the two servant girls to help pull her up as they helped. Mommy hugged her, and I grabbed one of her legs and squeezed it. I do not know for sure why I did that, I just know that mommy really loved her so I should love her also. At this time, Fejér looked down at me and replied, "Prudence, your little girl truly has empathy." This scared me and I thus looked up at one of the servant girls who whispered, "That means you care for people like it was you." Fejér then replied, "And your servants appear to care about little Ann very much." Then the two girls replied, "Everyone in this house loves Ann and her puppy, Charles very much." That made me feel very good, then my mother replied, "You shall not have a lower job in my house. (Tears began rolling down Fejér's face as she began crying.) You shall possess the highest job in my house; for you shall cherish the thing, we love the most in this house. As I gave my heart to you so many years ago, I shall give my daughter to you." Fejér now started to grin. She immediately said, "Ann, behold your twin mother." With this Fejér again started crying as she cries so much. She then told me, "I always wanted a little girl;

however, Ranlyn would not let me have any babies until his business became successful. I remember when my mother told me that Prudence had a new baby, how happy I was for her and told my mother that Prudence was such a blessed woman." Wow, I did not know that your child meant so much to so many people, yet so many youngsters are dying from hunger every day in this country. I smiled at her and said, "I am the lucky one because my mama and daddy and the people in this house that help us so much all love me so much." Now all the big people in the room were smiling. Chalk one up for the kid. I got them all off balance now. Now would be a good time to get some candy, yet I want to know more about mommies real good friend. Then mommy said to our servants, "Please prepare some hot water for a good bath. Mommy then motioned for me to come after her. That always makes me happy. Mommy then told me, "Make sure your new 'other mommy' is clean and that she gets everything she needs, ok, my big girl?" I looked at her in shock then answered, "Yes, number one mommy ever." Then I followed her, four of our female servants, and Fejér into our bathing room. The female servants prepared the oils and lotions since mommy had told them to put out the best. They put out a wide range of towels and the servants started the stove under the tub. This would warm us and keep the water warm. The servants started removing Fejér's clothing. Mommy told them to throw the clothes away. I then called for mommy, "Is Fejér to be unclothed in our house?" Mommy shook her head no. As we looked at Fejér's appearing as unclothed, we were taken aback. She had bruises and many scratches. Mommy touched a few of the bruises and Fejér started twitching as in pain. Mommy, then told one of the girl servants to bring up our "boo boo box" which is what I called It, and now everyone in our house calls it that. She also asked her to send one of the boys to get our doctor. Now William knocked on the door, Fejér rapidly, wrapped herself in a towel, and the boys filled the tub with piping hot water, plus some water in my baby tub, which the girls had put beside the tub. The boys departed as mommy and the girls guided Fejér to my baby tub. They started scrubbing her feet and some dirtier parts of her skin. Her body did not look well, appearing as a bag of torment and abuse. She told mommy that some bad men had beaten her on the streets because the people would give her more food than they would. Therefore, they beat her and took it. Some men would pay the boys to beat her and rip off her clothes. Fejér said I learned real fast how evil men are and how they will do anything to violate a woman if they think there is a chance. How could something so little be worth so much to so many men? I had no idea what they were talking about, as I was looking around for something little that would be worth 'so much.' As we scrubbed off what could, which was not that much because some of the dirt was so deep inside her sores, and scrubbed her as hard as we could without making blood, then let her rest in the big tub. My baby tub was now pitch black from the first layer of dirt we got off Fejér. Now the girls used the soaps and oils further to clean her skin. We were making good progress and now had her face cleaned up, except for some black spots that mommy said the doctor would take out and put some medicines in it to prevent infection. Now our doctor was here, so mommy and the girls dried her, wrapped her in a towel, and took her to our changing room while the men cleaned the tubs and put new fresh hot water in our tub with some special oils to create a relaxing sensation. They also put a lot of wood in the tub's stove to boil the water because the doctor told them he would be awhile. The girls removed her towel and the doctor started working on her. He touched, sometimes pressed, and then said, "The good news is you have no broken bones. You do have a lot of bruises that will need some of my salve rubbed in them each day." I instantaneously yelled, "I will mommy, I will," as our doctor then gave me a kiss on my cheek and said to my mom, "I could not think of anyone any better for that job." Mommy and Fejér said together, "Nor can we." I then thought about the doctor kissing my face, because he was a boy; however, he is a boy that is allowed to see girls freely exposed, so that must be good and he did say good things about me, so I guess it is ok that he kissed my cheek. He gave mommy the salves and showed us how to use them. There were three types of salve. Then he gave us four types of oils and showed us where they went. This overload made me start to cry. Mommy then asked me, "Ann, why are you crying?" I then told her, "I do not think I can remember all that stuff." Mommy and Fejér started laughing together, just like real twin sisters, "We will help you honey." I then stopped crying and started fighting to get a smile to cover my face. I then discovered they both said the words together. The doctor then said to mommy, "You will need some pills and more shelves as you run out, just send one of your pretty girls to my place to get what you need." All the girls and mommy smiled back at him, giving the innocent girl laugh and blush. Mommy said, "Thanks" and then "Which of you girls want to see the doctor out and all four said, "I will . . ." That doctor had the girls under his spell, although I would have liked to walk him out; however, with my little legs, it might take a long time. Mommy, then said, "Ok, you all can walk him out. I will take Fejér to my bathing room. I decided to go with my mommy and my twin mommy. I will have to ask Henrietta what a twin mommy is because I never heard that before. Just as I was thinking about Henrietta, she popped in my head and said, "Ann, my time in my body with you shall soon end, however I will still be in your head for your dream and exciting stories at night. I then told her, "I love you so much Henrietta, I need to see your body in the daytime also so I can hug and kiss you." I thought putting that kid hug and kid kiss out there would bring her back in my life during the days. Henrietta then told me, "It is not my will. Those who I serve that truly love you feel it is time for you to have two mommies in the day." I yelled in my head and said, "Henrietta, I do not have two mommies." She then told me, "You have your mommy, plus now my master has given you a twin mommy. My master wants you to love all the time. However, I still get to be in your head anytime, day or night, when you want me. It is just that my master will not let me put on a skin suit and cross over to you in the day." I then said to Henrietta, "Tell your master he is making me sad, because I want mommy, Fejér, and you. I want all three of you loving me all the time." Henrietta then said to me, "I will, now go help your twin mommy." I remembered my new question and asked her, "What is a twin mommy." Henrietta said, "In the kingdom of love she is the same as your mommy and can also be a sister." I thought to myself, wow that is amazing. I am really a lucky kid. I do not know what I want more another mommy, or a real sister. Now I rushed in to help Fejér, because she really needs my help. I have to work hard to save her so I can have two mommies and a sister. I think two mommies will be better than one mommy will. We all scrubbed her hair and brushed it out. Mom helped me put the oils and salves on her violated skin. Mommy said we would make it pure again. Fejér does not have baby milk bottles as big as mommy or Henrietta; however, they are bigger than mine that is if I ever get some. I hope I get along someday, because I do not want to look like a boy. That would be too terrible! I would have to stay inside my house all the time. We tried hard to clean Fejér toes; even the dirt was too deep so we would have to let the salves draw it out of her hide. She does have wonderful eyes and when I checked them out, I slowly reached over and kissed her face saying, "Thanks for being my twin mom. I want you to live with us forever. You can share my room. Please." She then said, "Ann, I have dreamed so long to see Prudence's little angel. In my dreams you have wonderful big wings and fly real high in the sky." Then it hit me, she was talking to me in my head. I thus said back to her in my head, "You can talk to me in my head?" She said, "Yes, just like Henrietta." I asked, "You know Henrietta." She told me, "We were sent by the same master." I then said, "Who is your master." She once again replied, "You are." Then I replied, "I am just a little kid, how can I be your master?" She answered me by saying, "Someday you will understand. If you want me to stay in your room with you, you have to ask your other mom. I really would love to sleep beside you and Charley at night to keep you safe." I then asked her, "How did you know about Charley?" She then told me, "Everyone knows about the most famous dog in the universe, right?" I then realized that she was right and answered, "Right, Wow, you are just like my other mommy in that you know everything in the world." I then gave her a big hug and many kisses. She continued, "We had better talk so your mommy can hear us, ok." I then said to Fejér, "If you will be my twin mommy, I will love you and do everything you tell me except for one thing." She asked, "What is the one thing?" I told her that is to let the boys go underneath my dresses." Fejér answered, "I will never tell you to do that, and I will make you a promise that neither of us will ever let the boys do under our dress, because I hate boys." I told her, "I hate boys also; I think we have many things in common. Then my mommy said to us, "With all my heart and all the love I have had for you for my entire life. My daughter shall be your daughter. In addition, you shall live with me for the remainder of your life. I will now show you to your new room." She took her to the room between hers and mine. It was a big room and had many of my toys in there. When mommy opened the door and picked up my toys, she remembered this was my playroom. She then looked at me and said, "Where do you want me to put your toys." I then stated, "Wherever my other mommy's room is." Fejér then said, "Oh, Prudence, I want the toys to stay here, so Ann can teach me how to play them." I then said to mommy, "Mommy, please have our boy servants take down the door between our rooms." Then mom said, "Ann, Fejér loves you may be more than mommy and daddy, yet just like your parent's, and big girls like you do not sleep with their mommies and daddy. She needs her privacy." I then said to mommy, "I know all her privates, as I must clean all of her each day. Her privates are like mine, just larger. Please, mommy I am still a little girl with a whole lot of love inside of me." Then Fejér said, "Prudence, I have dreamed of being loved by a little angel so I beg that you not separate us. I want your child to be the happiest little girl ever to exist. My life is gone, hence I am dead, so I pray you let me live inside of her." Mommy was outnumbered two to one. She thus said, "Well, at least until you get healed. Let me remind you that your life is never over as long as I am alive." Mommy, then gave both of us a kiss on our cheeks and said, "Are you sure?" We both nodded yes. Mommy then laughed saying, "I guess I am dealing with some crooks." What made my room so good for playing in was that the canopy bed that was tucked into a corner. Our servants liked to have meetings in there; however, there are still some vacant rooms on the third floor, where many of our servants stay. Some servants are married and want to live in their own homes. Some servants have kids, yet the kids are not allowed to play with me. All the big people are ok with that and mommy says it is a social law. I do not want to go to jail by breaking a social law. That would make me a criminal and might make daddy not love me anymore. Mommy had the girls help her take off the dress. She had been cleaning Fejér with only her inner under clothes, or whatever, they call them. I always get confused. She had the girls get off that white paint, as she told Fejér; I truly hate this paint, wig, and those dresses. They both chuckled. My beautiful mommy had the girls clean her, and she was not with us in the powder room that had bright quilts and fresh flowers, and plenty of mirrors. The girls were looking for two casual dresses for in the house. Fejér looked at mommy and said, "You still look so wonderful," as mommy replied, "and so do you Fejér, and we will soon get you fixed up and we can play again if you still want me." Fejér answered, "I have always wanted you." I then said to Fejér, "My mommy has big baby milk bottles in case someday I get really hungry." They both chuckled as mommy answered back, "The one thing I am so proud of is that I did breast feed our baby for as long as she was on milk." Than Fejér complimented her by saying, "You did good Prudence, for many rich women do not give the time and patience for that." The mom told her, "Our mommies fed us that way, so I thought it important to carry on that important tradition." I then called for mommy, "Why do you and Fejér have hair down there and I do not." Then Fejér replied, "Our little Ann is going to be a scientist, because she is very observant." Mommy then taught me by saying, "Ann, you are still a little girl, so when you get bigger you will have it just like Fejér, as for me, daddy does like it, and then I trim mine to make him happy." I then asked mommy, "When I get my hair, should I also trim mine to make daddy happy." Then both my mommies said very loud while laughing, "No," then mommy added, "Daddy's are not allowed to see that hair, however daddy will give you to your future husband, and he will tell you how to dress your hair down there." I then asked mommy if my husband would be a boy." Mommy told me, "If you want babies?" I told mommy that Fejér and I hated boys and thus, I would buy my babies from the baby store. I know there are baby stores, because our minister at church told me to be careful or someone might take me and put me in a baby store." I thought this was so strange, for why would daddy not get to see it; he was the one that made me. However, mommy knows everything so I said, "ok." I then had to confess to them, "I am very lucky to have such beautiful mommies, and Henrietta that loves me so much and teach me all these strange rules so that when I grow up I will know everything. I see many children with fat mean mommies." Actually fat is ok, the big disadvantage being that they cannot wear the fancy ball dresses as mommy had on today. Mommy says all the girls hate them but the boys love them. She now was helping Fejér put some make up on her face, helping her to conceal the remains of past facial beatings. Mommy helped her wrap her hair in the back of her head. She looks so wonderful and lovely. Mommy said the better that Fejér looked when mommy ask Edward if Fejér could live with us, the easier it would be to get a yes. They both laughed and said something I did not understand, nevertheless it was about boys so I do not want to know. Fejér said, "Get one head on a boy excited and the other head will follow." They both laughed heartily. I may not know much about boys, however I see them walking on the street sometimes and I know they only have one head like daddy and William. Am I really that much smarter than they are? Someday, I will have to teach mommy, notwithstanding I will pretend to not know for now so she will not get afraid of me being so smart. Then Henrietta knocked on the door and asked to come in. I cried, "Yes, hurry." My mommies looked surprised, for in walked Henrietta. She seemed surprised to see both of them appearing as created by the Gods, very nude and she laughingly replied, "Should I strip down and join you." Mommy, then replied, "No need for you to undress, because as soon as my girls get back with our dresses we shall join you. You can wait for us in our meeting room on this floor. Henrietta then kissed me and excused herself. The girls did return and my mommies got dressed, then my mommy said to Fejér, "Please take Ann into your room." She then asked me, "Ann, you help Fejér get settled in, see what she wants, and tell William to get it for." William knew that if I said mommy said it, I was telling the truth. Therefore, we went into her room, and we talked with our heads. I said to her, make a list, and I will add to it, because you will get the best. I added things such as pain powders, special candies, and perfumes; make up, some alcohol, books, and lanterns. I handed the list to William and he sent someone out to buy them. I told him to make sure a girl was with whoever he sent, and he shook his head yes. For some strange reason he does not like Fejér, however since she is my third mother and can talk in my head, he had better be nice or I will tell my real mommy. Mommy went into our meeting room to talk with Henrietta. They started with the normal small talk and then Henrietta said to her, "Ma'am, you know my love for Ann is great, however my sister in law is seriously ill now, and I must help my brother tend to his children until she regains her health. I will of course stop by and say hi to Ann what few times I make it to town and will write many letters. I pray that you would give her the letters." My mother looked at her in shock and said, "Oh my God, yes of course. You are such a big portion of her life and a total break could break her heart, which so much belongs to you. I can never imagine our life without you, and the great things you have done." Henrietta then said; "I will stop by and spend a few nights with her if you would grant me permission." My mother asked her a question, "How far is your sister in law from here?" Henrietta answered, "About three hours in a carriage." Then my mother said to her, "We will prepare a special room here and save it for you. You send me a letter and tell me when you want our carriage to pick you up and we will bring you here and celebrate each time with a nice large dinner." Henrietta then hugged my mother and asked her if she could take little Ann out around the neighborhood and explain this to her. My mother quickly agreed. Henrietta then went inside my old playroom and after entering the door, she closed it. She went straight up to Fejér and wrapped her arms round her and they shared a great kiss. I guess two mommies know how to give good kisses, so they will be able to kiss their babies and husbands. Then Henrietta said the Fejér, "Take good care of our master." I will have to teach the both of them someday that bigger people are supposed to be the master and the kids are supposed to do what they say. The adults in this house are confused. However, this is a bigger problem to handle than is the boss. I guess if they are stupid enough to think that boys have two heads, you just about could expect anything from them. Fejér promised Henrietta, "I shall treat Ann as if she fell from my womb." Actually, I was glad to see them kiss so lovingly, so now I absolutely trusted Fejér, for if Henrietta and my mommy loved her, then I would have to love her twice as much. Henrietta now dressed me and we went to the park at the other end of our street. There were kids playing and I just watched them. At least Henrietta lets me watch them, and not rush me off as mommy always did. Then Henrietta said, "Your mommy said I could come and spend some nights and sleep with you. Would you like that?" I, while crying, said to her, "With all my heart, I wish you could sleep with me every night in the real world." Henrietta then told me, "We could hear your mother thinking and she was getting suspicious of me, planning to spy on me. They were afraid that she might see me. We learned that her friend Fejér had died with her husband, and no one knew about it so we got a new Fejér just to love and care for you." I asked her, "When you say 'we' who do you mean?" She then gave me another one of her silly answers by saying, "Your servants, and armies." Someday I will have to explain that little girls do not have armies. I believe my future is going to be very busy teaching all my knuckleheads that I love so much. They all are so happy that I enunciate my words so easily. Henrietta can stop time when she is in my head by taking us back in time and returning us just a few minutes after our departure. When we are back in time, we practice all the language repeatedly. This way, even though I am in the physical structure of a two year old, I was really much older by spending all that time in the past with her. At any rate, she wanted to tell me a story about her mother's grandmother. She began by saying, "My great-grandmother lived alone in the mountains in her cabin. Her husband had died, thus she was there all alone. She only had one friend, and that was her loving dog, as you have Charley who loves you so much. They both loved each other very much and the dog loved her and pleased her. Every night as she was going to bed, the dog would lick her hand to let her know that he was there to guard her. One night, she had gone to sleep and the dog had licked her hand as he had performed regularly every night since her husband passed away. However, this night was not the same. She had awakened in the middle of the night because she heard her dog whimpering. She wanted to calm him and let her know she was there for him, so she stuck her hand out by the bed, and she felt the dog gently lick her hand like permanently. She thought he was just cold so she went back to sleep. Her dog's whimpering woke her up a second time in the same night so she stuck her hand out, the dog lapped it up and she went back to sleep. This happened a third time, and she stuck her hand out and the dog stopped whimpering, came, and licked her hand. She stayed awake a few moments later and the dog had stopped whimpering. She went back to sleep right afterwards. In the morning, she woke up and stuck her hand out by the bed, but nothing licked her paw. She believed that the dog had already woken up and was simply in the front room. She rolled over, got out of bed, and heard Drip . . . Drip . . . Drip . . . Drip, so she walked into the kitchen and turned the handles on the sink faucet, but it was not dripping. She continued into her bathroom to take a shower. As she walked in, the drips got louder! She turned and looked above the bathtub and Screamed! There, hanging from the light by his tail, was her loving friend, with his blood dripping into the bathtub. She screamed and began to cry. Wiping her eyes and sobbing, she turned around and looked at the mirror. In the mirror, she saw the dog hanging. Moreover, written on the mirror with a finger, in her dog's blood with drips, and streaks hanging down from each letter, were the words . . . Humans Can Lick Too!" I asked her, "What is this story about?" Henrietta said, "It is based on the bible when a prophet from a long time ago named Daniel interpreted the king's dream of blood on a wall. It is nowadays believed that when you see a message written in blood is a warning about your future. She most likely would be attacked by a bear or mountain lion. She would lick her wounds and die." I was still confused so I asked her again, "What are you teaching me in this my favorite teacher?" Henrietta told me, "Give attention to warnings. If you get this warning, get it interpreted, and avoid your deadly future situation. If you get the correct adjustment, you will be able to hold out. If my great-grandmother would have concluded that something killed her dog and brought it into her home, it could cause the same thing to her. She should have left that spot at once. Do you now understand?" I then asked her, "If I were to be in peril, would you warn me?" Henrietta got up and then fell to her knees giving me a tight hug and saying, "With all night, and all my soul my master," as she was kissing me with tears coming out of her eyes. I could feel her love for me. She has given me so much in my new life, and her support and loyalty has advanced me in my old age. I then said to her, "Never leave me Henrietta, because nothing can replace the spot I have given you in my heart." Henrietta then reinforced her previous promise, "I shall visit you every night and every time you are in danger, plus I shall put on my body suit and spend the night with you a couple of times each year, until you outgrow me." My search for the truth continued as I asked her, "Do you have that bone body like my neighbors had when they get out of their body suits." She then scolded me by saying, "Oh, no Ann, I have my spirit in my flesh suit. My bones turned to dust very long ago. We must go, I hear Fejér calling for you." I then asked her if I could say goodbye to the other kids here. I want them to know that I like them. She handed me her approval as long as mommy never finds out. I went over and said goodbye to some girls standing by the fence. They smiled as asked, "Can you stay and play with us?" I was getting ready to answer them when their big sisters came over and pulled them away from me. They were yelling at them saying, "That is one of those rich girls, she will get you in big trouble." They looked back at me in horror thinking I would betray them. I waved goodbye to them and blew some kisses. The big girls waved back at me and as they forced my friends escape with them and ran back to me. They then asked me if I was going to betray them and I answered, 'Never, I just want you to know I want to be your friend. My mommies do not allow me to talk with you." They asked, "How many mommies do you have." I told them I have three mommies and they looked at me with shock. They told me that one mommy was hard to sneak away from; therefore three would be hard. I told them, "That is true, that is why I came with my third mommy today. She goes away tonight for a little while, so this is one of my goodbye gifts. She is standing over there." I pointed to her and waived for her to come over. The girls got scared as she was walking towards us. Their sisters rushed up behind them to take them out to safety. Henrietta now rushed towards us, hollering at the two sisters, "Stop, please do not take Ann's friends away from her." The sisters were frozen in fear. As they froze, their trusting little sisters went back to me. This time we hugged each other. Their sisters fell down to the ground screaming. Henrietta slowly walked over to them. The sisters stood up on their knees and started begging Henrietta, "Please don't take our little sisters away to kill them since they did not recognize what they were doing. Please, please let us have them back." Henrietta got down on her knees, and gave them both a hug and said to them, "Your sisters are in no danger, would you like to be with them also?" They shook their heads yes, as Henrietta gave them both a big hug. They helped Henrietta up and the three young women folk came over to us as my friends were presenting themselves. The first girl told me her name was Ruth, from the bible and the second girl said her name was Mary, from the bible. I then told them they were lucky to have names from the bible, I only had a name of a queen who was now dead. She was friends with my parents and her family said it was ok. The two elder sisters were there right away. They asked, "Your family knew the queen?" I then told them, "Yes, and my mommy hates when they go to the castle to see the king, because she has to put on a big heavy ball dress and paint her face white and put on a wig. The King likes blond haired women, so all the women were blond wigs." The four of them told me how lucky I was. I told them, "However today is a sad day for me, because Henrietta, my best friend in the whole world (she now lowered her face and gave me a kiss on the cheek and I kissed her on the lips) is going away today and I will only have my two other mommies to play with." Ruth then said, "Henrietta must be a great mom because she let you kiss her on her lips." Henrietta then said, "I have loved Ann every day since I met her." Then Mary said to me, "I will be your forever friend." Ruth, Joy and Faith (the big sisters) then they, promised to be my forever friends. I hugged each one, and then I asked, "Why when I hug you very nice girls, I feel mostly bones? Henrietta started feeling underneath their shirts and Joy said, "Ann, we have very little money so many days we do not eat. Sometimes Faith Maria gets lucky with the boys. They pay her five cents per boy when she lifts up her shirt. Sometimes there are ten boys in the group. They also pay her twenty-five cents each boy if she lets them touch under her shirt. They do not want to see under my shirt, however they pay me five cents each boy if I pull down my pants and twenty-five cents apiece if I let them put their hands deep down my knickers. We have to keep it a secret from our parents, because if they knew they would be very angry. We like doing it because we get to eat and take some food home for our parents and the boys always say how beautiful we are and when they have their hands under our clothes they say real nice things to us." I looked at them and said, "I could not do that, because I hate boys and do not want them to say nice things to me." Faith Maria now came over, and put her hands on my shoulder, and kissed the tip of my head and began singing, "I hate all the boys also, Ann, yet I have to make sure my sisters do not starve to death like our neighborhood kids have." I looked at my new friends and said, "I promise I will find you some food beginning today." Then Henrietta pulled out some cookies she had in her pockets and also gave them fifteen dollars." Faith Maria then said to her, "That is almost all the money in the whole world. Now we are rich, we will be able to eat for two weeks with this money. Thank you so much Ms. Henrietta. We will love you forever." Next Mary told me, "Oh Ann, we know how to be hungry, we do not want you to be hungry and suffer to feed us." I then told my friends, "We always have surplus food. I can have my servants give you some." I then asked Henrietta, "Do you think my new mommy will let me give my friends food?" Henrietta then said to us, "If they are your friends, I will show them where my friend lives, and let them eat all the food they want." I then asked Henrietta, "Where will you get the food?" Henrietta told me boldly, "I will beg it from your new mommy," I then jumped up to get into her arms and started kissing her cheeks crying, "I love you so much, my best friend ever." At this Henrietta motioned for our four new friends to join us as we all screamed and everyone kept saying we love Henrietta and Ann, our new best friends ever." I could feel the passion pouring out of their skinny, dirty, and bony bodies. All the suffering they have through done not matter now for we all were sharing our hearts and souls. Nothing in the whole world mattered now. They thought I was lucky to wear nice clothes and I thought they were lucky to wear clothes that they could play with. We each thought the other side was so much better, yet all we wanted now was to be best friends and let that caste system crap stay away from us. There was no thinking that I was better than they were. They promised not to blame me for all the bad things that the rich people did to them. Nowadays, with Henrietta, there were six hearts trying to fill the other members in our new special club with a surfeit of love. Then Mary said she had a real good idea. Her family lived close to this part, on the other side of the railroad tracks. She told us she would be back in one minute. Mommy had been so wrong, because she said all the people on the other side of the railroad tracks were evil and bad, and would kill me if they got a hold of me. I told my new friends what mommy had told me and added, "She was so wrong." Then Faith got down on her knees (she was the biggest kid here) and looked me in my eyes and said, "Ann, my love, we love you so much, but never ever go across those tracks because there are bad people there, and they would hurt you. Not everyone knows how wonderful you are, they just know you are from a rich family, and because of that if they can kill you, they will." I asked Faith, "If they came over here and tried to hurt me, would you help them or me." Then all three of them told me, "We will protect you, and if they kill us we will die for you." I then told

Ruth, "I do not want you to die for me, I want you to live with me and be my best friends." Then Faith Maria said, "Never cross to this side of that sidewalk, over here unless you see us and we tell you to come over; promise me my new little bundle of love?" She is a big girl, the biggest kid here, so she can call me little. I shook my head yes. It just hit me that Faith Maria is fourteen years old, so even though she did not have big baby milk bottles like mommy, her milk bottles were the biggest ones in our club. I bet they are beautiful, since the boys pay so much money to watch them. I then made my oath to Faith, "I promise." Then Henrietta told me, "You are so lucky to have such great friends." Just then, we could see Mary running back to us. She can run very fast, I think maybe as fast as a horse, well maybe. I then told my friends, "Mary can run real fast." They told me that everyone had to run fast to stay alive. I then remembered how lucky I was not to have to live in this kind of danger. Mary then showed me some shorts and a ragged tee shirt and some torn up soft play shoes. Mary said, "Ann, put these on and you can play with us." I told Ann, "I cannot put them on out here; some bad people might see me." Then Henrietta and the girls formed a tight circle around me and started taking my clothes off. When five girls undress you, the clothes go off fast. Henrietta put my tee shirt on while Joy and Faith lifted me, Ruth and Mary pulled up my play shirt. They then put my shoes on. Then Ruth and Mary said to me, "You look the same as us when you are naked, except you do not have bruises and sores like us." Joy then said, "Maybe you are really a human being." I then told them, "Show Henrietta your sores tonight and I will get some medicine from the doctor to fix them." They then told me, we did not know that they could be repaired, because everyone has them. Then Henrietta said to them, "We will get them fixed, so you will look just like Ann when you are naked, showing your fat bellies." Mary then said, "We do not have fat bellies. Then Henrietta said, "You will after we fatten you up with some good food." They all then cheered as Faith Maria said, "Maybe the boys will pay me more." They taught me so many fun games. We played hide and go seek. We would all hide and one of us would attempt to get us. That is what makes the game so much fun. Skinny kids can almost hide in the wide open. They were hard to find. That is what makes it so fun for me. Then we play ring around the posy. That was just so much fun. Plus I could keep up with them in this game. We then went to play a game called tag when Henrietta came up to me and motioned the other girls to get us together. She said my mom was on her way. We had to change me fast and so fast they could. They really did not want to get me in trouble. Henrietta then wiped off my hands and face. Then she told the girls where to meet her, and how to go to her house to wait for her. I then asked Henrietta as she was walking with me up the sidewalk, "Do you suppose I can tell my new mommy about my new friends." Henrietta then looked at me and said, "Just tell her that if she keeps it a secret you will give her a big kiss." I then looked at Henrietta and said, "Wow, your kisses have magic also." She looked at me and said, "Only when they are to get you something," As we were talking, we were not paying attention, then we heard, "Hello Anny." I looked up and it was mommy. I knew I had better give her some sugar for letting Henrietta play with me. So I reached up and let her lift me up and gave her a big kiss and said, "I love you mommy." Then my mother smelled me and said, "Why were you sweeting?" Henrietta said in my mind, "We will tell her we were playing hide and go seek." We both told her at the same time. Mommy then said to Henrietta, "Would you like some tea before you leave today?" Then Henrietta looked up at the sky and said, "Oh, I am so sorry Ma'am, Ann and I have had so much fun, I lost track of time, I must hurry to catch the stagecoach to my brothers." I then said to her in our mind talk, "Why don't you stay with your friend who lives nearby?" She then answered back, "That is what I am going to do, I am just telling you mommy I am going for away so she will let your other mommy sleep with you." I then replied, "Henrietta, how did you become so smart. She fired back, "From you my master, from you." I did not want to teach her that the real master is supposed to be her, and not me. I wanted to save these last few minutes for kisses and hugs. She then knelt down and I hugged her, and gave her a kiss and said, "Please promise me to come back soon my best friend forever and ever." Henrietta then looked back at and said, "That is a promise that I shall keep." Then mommy said to me, "We must hurry and get you home and get you a bath." I then asked her, "Can Fejér give me a bath, and I want to teach her how, now so she will know." My mom told me that was a good idea. I really wanted Fejér just in case I had some boo boos from the exuberance of playing the best games in the whole world. She then told me, "You might have to give her some sugar." I told mommy, "Don't worry mommy, I know how to give you guys all the sugar in the whole world" She started laughing and said, "I guess you are a little professional at that." I then called for mommy, "Is that a good thing." Mommy rushed over to me and said, while she was hugging me, "Oh Ann, it is a very good thing, because if I did not have your sugar I would die." I then told my mommy, "Here is a whole bunch of sugar for letting me play with Henrietta today." I then started kissing her a whole bunch of times. When I finished, she stood up, carrying her heart and said, "Wow, I have enough sugar to make it to dinner tonight." We then laughed as I took my sweaty body up to Fejér's room. I was so afraid that she would get angry over my new friends, if she found out. What if she betrayed me and told mommy? What if daddy took the police over there and put them in jail? This was going to be the biggest risk I had ever taken. Why does life have to be so stressful for a little pretty girl? Then I heard Henrietta say to me, "Be brave my little hero." That is something that truly amazes me. Have all adults forgotten what it was like when they were little?" Adults know how to be courageous, because they have had a good deal of time to rehearse. Kids have not had a lot of practice in being brave, and we have small nerves that cannot convey all the pressure like adults with big nerves can. Go ahead and tell a kid, be my hero, you are really saying for that kid to do something that you are too afraid to act. You are saying for that kid to stick their heads in a meat grinder. Thanks a lot people! Then just sit back, and look innocent and say, give me some sugar. Why is it taking my little body so long to climb up these giant steps and down that long hallway to the doorway? When I finally arrived there, I could hear my heart pounding louder than my hand on Fejér's door. She stated in her tricky soft voice, "Come on in." She was going to get to grind this little girl's precious little head. I walked in and tripped over a rug on her floor. She rushed over and picked me up. I was so afraid that she was going to throw me on the floor. Then it hit me, I had not asked her my criminal "bad kid" request. I then kissed her and she told me it would be all right and I would feel better soon. I knew I was not going to feel better soon, because after I asked her, she would pick me up and throw my poor little kid's body across the room. I was now looking around the room to see which wall could hide a kid's blood the better. That would be the wall, which would shatter my head. I just do not care. I would rather die saving my best forever friends than live and watch them starve to death. Sometime a little girl must grow up and accept responsibilities for those who depend upon them. I then asked Fejér if she would help me take a bath, by saying, "I was hoping my new mommy would take a bath with me." That got her off the hook. She said, "Yes, my daughter, it would be my pleasure." Darn, when they say daughter, you are in for a challenge. She then pulled our servant's cord and as one of the girls came in, I said to her, "Maria, would you please have the boys get us some hot water. I am going to bathe with my other mommy." Maria looked shocked, said, "Yes Ma'am," and rushed out of the room. I asked Fejér, "Why did she look so strange, she always loved me before?" Then Fejér answered by saying, "Ann, she still loves you, it is just that she did not tell them about me yet. For you to give me a title as mommy in just one day is a lot for them to understand. That is the greatest title for your mommy in this house and for you to say your other mommy; it makes me look like I am trying to steal you from your wonderful mommy. Your mom and I will explain it to them soon." Then William came in and told us that our water was ready. He asked to speak to Fejér and I yelled, "I do not want people talking about me to my mommy unless I can hear it also, right mommy?" Then both Fejér and mommy who came rushing in said "Yes, of course Ann." I saw mommy behind William when I was talking to William. Mommy then said, "William please meet with me in our meeting room. Fejér, please bath with your daughter." William's face turned red as he followed my mother into the meeting room. Now Fejér and I were in the bathing room. She had undressed me, and given me an emergency towel in case someone came in. She made me so proud when she said I could undress her. I was pulling down her skirt when mommy walked in. I immediately wrapped my towel to cover my legs and said, "Mommy, Fejér is letting me undress her so I can see where her boo boos are." My mother winked at Fejér as she gave her a kiss and whispered in Fejér ears, "Children are so enthused by the most routine opportunities." My mother quickly agreed with her. To my great joy, I could hear what she was saying. She was protecting me and I liked that. Mommy, then stuck her head back in the door and said, "Ann, you will be glad to know that all our servants are being told now that you have two mommies." Fejér began to weep and I ran over, with nothing on and gave my mommy a big hug. Mom hugged me tight and said, "You were dressed like this when you came out of my womb. Oh, dear, what are those bruises on your leg?" I told her, "I am sorry, I was a bad girl and fell down outside and in Fejér's room." Mommy touched each of the bruises, gave them a kiss, and said, "Oh, dear, do not be grim, kids always come. That is why mommies always check them." I then asked her, "So you don't hate me because I am ugly now?" Mommy kept on kissing my cheek repeatedly, "Saying, I will never ever hate you, and you are still very beautiful and always will be beautiful now." She had a big grin on her face as she went over and kissed Fejér and tickled her belly very fast. Fejér then laughed saying, "Just like the old days when we took baths together." Mommy said, "Yes, indeed my forever ever best friend." She then left the room much happier than when she came in. Fejér then explained to me, that mommy was worried that I did not love her anymore. She feared that I was trying to stay away from her. When she saw the bruises then she realized why I was hiding from her. I then gave Fejér a big kiss, as I knew I had a bunch of sugar to get out in the open in order to smooth things out when I dropped the big bomb about my new forever friends. I then asked her if we had her salves and oils in here. She pointed to where they were and

I rushed over to them. I started on her face, which is already becoming so beautiful. I told her, "I hope someday I have yellow bright hair like yours and a beautiful face." She then took hold of my hand, and put it on her belly and said, "Since you are my daughter, you came from in here, so you will look like me and your mommy." I looked at her and said, "Wow. Can I change how I look?" She nodded yes and said, "With love from the heart all things are possible." I then started putting the salves on her soars. I asked her before each one to make sure it was the correct one. I wanted to make sure I knew how to do it for my best friends forever. I had to bring this out in the open, so I asked her, "My wonderful mommy, may I sneak in my new best friends forever and will you help me hide them?" Fejér nodded yes, and to my surprise asked me, "Where can I find them." I then told her, "They were the four poor boney girls that I had hiding across the street. Do you hate poor girls?" She told me, "Oh you should know that I love poor girls, because I am also a poor girl. I will sneak out now with the servants and get them in here. I will be back as fast as I can." She threw on a thin dress, wearing nothing under it, rushing out the door. Henrietta was hiding with the girls keeping them safe in case someone called the sheriff. Soon, Fejér came in softly with my four best friends. I asked her how she found them so fast. She told me, "Henrietta was hiding with them and told me where I could find them. I then ordered them to take off their clothes and handed them to one of the servant girls who helped Fejér sneak them in our home. The wonderful servant girl said she would wash them with the servant's clothes and sneak them back in tomorrow. We then had them move into the big tub, one at a time as Fejér and I washed them and coated them with salves, oils, and lotions. I was so happy today as I was putting these on my new best friends forever and ever. I saw some new red marks on Faith's baby milk bottles and reached up to see if they hurt. As I touched them, I asked her if it hurt. She said no, it was the new dress and how they scratch on the body. I then told her, your baby milk bottles feel different from my mommies. Yours are harder and smaller. My Mommies are bigger and softer. I told them to look at Fejér's to see what I was saying. Faith Maria then explained, "That is because when you were a child, you did not drink the milk from my baby bottles. I then blushed and said, "I am sorry, I forgot, will you forgive me, they are still so very beautiful. Mine is still so small. Is it true that some boys give you money for lifting up your shirt so they can see? Do I have to pay you for ensuring your big very pretty baby milk bottles?" Fejér then said, "You are a little girl that grew in here in your mommy's womb, (pulling my hand back to her belly) and then you get to look at mine for free. Sorry, it is true that boys and later enjoying your body paid you money to see in your shirt and skirt and to put their hands inside them. How did you know about that?" I looked at her and started crying. She stated, "My precious Ann, I wished you loved me enough to trust me.to trust me. Look at me; I am here with you together taking a bath. I trust you with all I have, which is only my body and freedom today. You know you can trust me. I brought in your friends and if I got caught will be beaten till I die and maybe your parents also." She gave me a big hug, and started kissing both of my checks and then began rubbing down my neck and spine. That did feel good as all my stress started going somewhere away from me. It was time to leap over the cliff. I then had my four friends hide in my bed after we all cleaned the bathing room extra good. Then I had Fejér sleep in the other room. Now I walked down the steps alone to find my mother. Charley joined me. Now is a time I really need to have Charley at my side. I then found mommy and sat on her lap, just in case she was going to kill me, she could choke me, which would be much better than being kicked and hit until I died. Mommy was sipping on some wine and relaxing. Once get got me on her lap she put down her book and started massaging me, and kissing me all over my head and face. I wondered if she was testing my body to see if it would taste good after she killed me. I then told mommy that I had the most important question in my life to ask her. She asked me what I had to tell her. I then confessed, "Today I made four new best friends forever. They are poor and the biggest girl had to lift up her shirt and let the boys play with her little milk bottles. The next biggest girl does not have any baby milk bottles, so the boys pay her to pull up her skirt and more money to put their hands down her skirt. They do that so their little sisters and they will not starve and die. Am I bad for loving them?" Mommy was now wiping the tears from her eyes. I asked mommy, "Have I been so bad that you hate me now? Are you going to choke me to death or throw me on the floor and beat me to death, and then feed me to Charley?" She immediately grabbed me. I thought, oh no, I am too young to be drowned in a tub. I wonder if my daddy will have to buy a little casket for me. She then wrapped both arms around my little body that had no heartbeat and started kissing me. Yahoo, I have been around long enough to know that when adult women kiss you, you are off the hook. Just in time because I was almost ready to do my last number one and number two. You will be alive until your daddy comes home. She then whispered into my ear, "They all told me about how wonderful and full of love you are, and I never really believed it until now. I am so proud of you and so glad you trusted me. Please, start breathing again. (Then, just like magic, my heart started breathing again. I do not think I could have stayed alive much longer unless it started to beat again.) If they are your friends, they are my friends and if you play with them, I will play with them. Moreover, we both will give them a whole bunch of good food. We can have the girls find out where they live and take some food to them. You can never go to their house because bad men will get you. They like to eat little girls for dinner. Ann, never ever tell your mommy. You can tell Henrietta if you want. (I decided to let Henrietta tell her just in case she was setting me up and wanting to take down my accomplices. Henrietta never taught me how to say that word better yet, I was guessing hard) Can I tell you a secret?" I kissed her on her cheek and said, "Yes." At this time, Fejér came walking down the steps. Mommy called her to come see her in the waiting room we were in, as mommy likes to drink some wine before daddy comes home. Now mommy asked me where my little friends were. She said that we needed to get them cleaned, fed, routine medical care and hid before daddy got home. I told her I had them hid in a secret place in case the neighbors or the police were snooping around in our neighborhood. I am trying hard to keep them a secret. I wanted to make sure I did not lie to my mommy so I designed my words carefully, because I was trying to keep them secret, that is why I had them hidden in my bed. Mommy now called Fejér in to ask her if she needed anything. I was scared to death that she was going to punish Fejér and had only been setting me up. I need to either decide mommy will not hurt me and loves me, or not trust her. I am going to go with she loves me. There is something mystical about the relationship between a little girl and her mommy. Fejér now told mommy, "I was just going to get some milk to drink before going to sleep and get Ann some. I could not find her upstairs." Mommy then asked Fejér if she would do, which will probably be the biggest favor in the world for her. Fejér then answered, "My forever best friend, I am a fugitive in which you can send one of your servants to the police and have me imprisoned. You own my heart as well as Ann has quickly melted my heart with so much sugar. I will do anything you ask, except play with boys, because Ann and I hate boys." I then looked at mommy and said, "Yes, I, or I guess we hate boys." Mommy then fired back, "That is good for now. Fejér, Ann has found some poor children she wants to keep as best friends. Will you go outside, find them, feed, give routine medical care and hide them from my husband, and please get the allegiance from my servants?" Fejér fell to the floor on her knees and said, "My best friend ever, you can trust me to do this as fast as I can." She now looked at me and said, "Ann will you whisper in my ears where you hid them?" I went over and whispered in her ear, "You are the best mommy ever and I am going to give you a whole bunch of sugar. Just pretend you are going outside and sneak a couple of the girls upstairs to wait with my friends." Fejér looked at me and said, "Ok Ann." She then looked at mommy and said, "Ann looked so scared I thought she would do better to whisper to me." Mommy, then told her to please get it done as fast as possible. Then out went Fejér into the dark and she came back in through the back door. Just then, someone knocked on our front door. I was scared that someone had seen my friends and had brought the sheriff.

Then William came in and told mommy that daddy had sent a messenger to tell her he would be working late tonight and would be home around nine PM. Mommy told me, "Little girl, I think you have some angels watching over you." I do not know about that for sure, however Fejér and Henrietta keep telling me that. Angel or not, we have a good fighting chance now. Fejér intercepted the message from William, so she now readjusted her time schedule to make this more believable for mommy. About one hour later, she came back downstairs and told mommy the girls were tucked away in my bed. Mommy then thanked Fejér for saving us in this situation. Mommy did not know that she was the one that was saving Fejér. Mommy, then looked at me and asked, "Ann, may I see your new best friends forever?" I now asked mommy, "Mommy, you do know that they are poor girls and do not look as good as me, however they are my forever best friends?" Mommy then kissed me on my cheek and told me, "Ann, my best friend has forever been also a poor girl. So we have something in common, do not we?" She smiled and gave Fejér a nice kiss, once again thanking her for doing such a dangerous thing. Fejér was so relieved, which she told me in our mind talk. She also told me that I was performing like a veteran in this operation. Therefore, up the stairs we went to my room. I had to pretend as if I did not know where they were, so we let Fejér lead the way. She led us into my room and told mommy they were in my bed under the sheets. Mommy went over and pulled down the blankets and there before her were four sets of scared eyes. She smiled at them and introduced herself. She told them she was their mommy now, and wanted to check them over to make sure they were ok. She asked them to get out of my bed and to stand in a row. Once they were in the row, she asked them to remove their clothing, where were some of my old dresses. She looked at one of our house cleaners and told her to search for some pajamas for these wonderful little girls. When she said that, Faith Maria started to relax, the Joy and then my two almost the same age friends, Ruth and Mary. I asked mommy if I could help her and she readily agreed. Thus, we started with Faith Maria and mommy checked her whole body. She then squeezed one of Faith's baby milk bottles. When I saw this, I told mommy she had to pay Faith Maria some money for the boys had to pay to play with her baby milk bottles. Fejér then told me, "Ann, the number one mommy in the house can touch everyone anywhere she wants because she is the one that makes sure everyone is healthy." I then asked Fejér, "When is someone going to teach me how to make sure we are healthy in case someday I am the mommy of my house." Fejér then said, "Ann, in order to be a mommy of a house, you must get married to a boy." I then said, "Yucky, I will never do that, therefore I guess I do not need to know how to check them." Fejér then asked, "Mommy is not it true that best friends forever can check each other's private parts for health reasons?" Mommy then went over, unbuttoned Fejér's shirt, and squeezed her milk bottles. She had a strange serious look on her face and then said, "Ouch." She looked at Fejér and one of our house girls and said, "I want the doctor to check this today, ok?" Fejér looked rather startled and one of our house girls went rushing outside for our doctor. I asked mommy, "What is wrong with my number two mommy?" Mommy then told me, "Ann, when you get your milk bottles you need to have someone squeeze them, and feel for the little lumps inside of them. Sometimes these lumps are ok and sometimes they are not. Only a doctor knows for sure." I then asked mommy, "What if they are not ok?" Then mommy said, "Fejér could die." I then started crying and said, "I have not healed her boo boos yet, and she is going to die." Mommy then told me, "She is not going to die, because I think it is just a regular boo boo in there. You can squeeze them to see what a boo boo feels like. This is something very important that all girls need to know how to check. Then Mary and Joy begged, "Can we help?" In addition, Fejér said, "Absolutely, because someday Ann could be busy and you two would have to save my life." There was some awkwardness at first with the three little girls trying to squeeze Fejér's breasts as best as their little hands could do. They had such serious looks on their faces as their trembling fingers searched hard. The Ann shouted, "I found the one mommy found." I had really found it and now I said, "Mommy number two, I think it is just a boo boo and you will be ok, I hope." Fejér winked at mommy and then said, "Mommy, I think our little girl may be a doctor someday." Mommy, then said, "That would be wonderful." Then, unexpectedly, Mary shouted, "I found another one." Mommy rushed over and verified it, giving Mary a kiss on the top of her head. Mommy then said to Fejér, she would need to have that checked out by the doctor also. Then Ruth asked, "What if the doctor is a boy? Can he squeeze number two mommy's milk bottles, and does he have to give her five cents?" Mommy then reached over, patted Ruth on the head, and said, "Daughter, the doctor can check everywhere just like a mommy can, and we have to pay him money for him to squeeze them." Then Mary said, "I am glad the boys in our neighborhood did not know we should pay them to squeeze our milk bottles. We would have starved to death a long time ago." Then Joy said to Mary, "Mary resolve not to be silly, only doctors get paid to touch, and that is because they can try to fix you." Fejér quickly agreed as mommy told the girls to line up again. I asked Faith Maria if I could squeeze her milk bottles to double check them and get some practice being a doctor. Faith Maria knelt down where I could squeeze them thoroughly and said, "You can be my doctor anytime you want to, Doctor Ann." I then said to Faith, "I have to wait until I finish Doctor's school. I think it might even be more than one day." Mommy then told all of us, "Yes, girls it takes ten years of college." I then collapsed to the ground. Fejér then asked me, "What is wrong Ann?" I told her that with ten years of college, I would be an old woman at fifteen years old before I became a doctor." Fejér then told me, "Your number one mommy and I will try to figure out some shortcuts for you, ok." Then Joy asked me, "Doctor Ann, do you want to make sure I am ok?" She knelt down to the floor beside Faith Maria as I said, "Absolutely, I want to make sure none of my best friend sisters do not die." I checked her, and told both of them it was ok. I then asked mommy if she needed to check. She told me that daddy always checked them and that was one of daddy's jobs. I looked at Fejér and Faith Maria and they both shook their heads in agreement. Then I said, "I am glad that daddy is helping to keep our number one mommy alive." It was so natural to make my new best friends a part of this family. It just felt like they belonged to her so naturally. Then mommy told me, "Our prison bait is all healthy, now get them ready to eat dinner. Fejér will have them staged and I will soften up your daddy for our big bomb, ok all my children?" She went down since it was now getting close to daddy's time to come home and she wanted our cooks to prepare a good dinner for him, as she also had them bring up a good bottle of wine. Meanwhile Fejér sat us all down to share some of our stories. She then told us, "When my husband died and I had no one to help me, I would let the boys and men see me freely exposed and touch me everywhere they wanted for money. That is why I have some bruises on my girl parts. It was either let my pride die or my body starve." I then told her, "Do not worry mommy, we will take care of you. I hate every boy in the whole world except daddy." I now started checking her baby milk bottles again noticed some dark under her skin. She had painted them with makeup, however in the tub; our water washed some of them off. I then washed the paint off and started kissing her boo boos saying, "Please get healed." She once again she started crying saying, "You are too innocent to carry these burdens Ann. That is the first time you called me mommy." I then told her, "Two days ago, I only had one best friend forever and I was bored most of the time. Today I have six best friends forever and love them all so much. I am the luckiest person in the whole world. To lose them would take away any desire for me to live." Fejér then told me, "You are truly as wise as the millenniums you have ruled." I asked her, "What is a mini emblem?" She then said, "Oh, it is just a little picture." I smiled then said, "I guess I do rule a whole bunch of little pictures in our house. No one else wants them. They all want the big ones." We both laughed and relaxed in the warm water as we let the oils sink into our skin. My four sisters had the big tub as Fejér and I snuggled up in my tub. Fejér told me that a woman's skin has to be soft to be a woman. I told her yucky. She gave me another kiss while we both laughed. We had been in there for almost an hour when mommy came up and knocked on our door, saying, "When are my six best friends ever going to finish and help me eat our dinner?" We then invited her to come in. Fejér apologized, saying, "I am so sorry, Ann and I were telling each other stories." I then said, "Mommy, it was my fault. She was explaining to me that you really do not hate me." Just then, Fejér flashed in my mind, "Wow, you are a genius; I think we are not going to get in trouble now." Mommy looked over at Fejér, and thanked her while kissing me on my cheek saying, "Mommies have to love forever and ever." She helped us all get dressed and we three walked down stairs together laughing and being stupid. Our servants could feel our happiness and love. The next day three of the girl servants snuck into my room and started kissing me. I was starting to think that these big people are taking this kissing a little overboard. They then whispered to me, "Please be quite so your mommies don't come in here. They said, we know Faith and she told me that you are now best friends forever with her, Joy, Ruth and Mary and that Henrietta gave them some real good food to eat yesterday, plus extra for her parents so she did not have to be freely exposed for the boys yesterday. I stretched out my arms as all five fit them in my arms; how they did that I can never figure out, and I said to them, they are my greatest best friends forever and ever. I love them so much and would love to have them live with me; however, Fejér and Henrietta said I could not ask daddy. Will you promise to keep it our secret? Fejér is going to let me play with them as soon as she finds a safe place for us." Everyone has promised to keep it a secret, to help take food to them and to find us a good secret place to play. We wanted to ask daddy last night, however after mommy felt him out, she said he was not ready yet. I now told my sisters that I truly loved them and they told me that I was truly an angel come down from the heavens above Earth. I asked them, "What is Earth?" They, while kissing me, (my face is going to be all gone if everyone does not stop kissing it) "It is the world we live in." Something all of a sudden was pounding in my side. I just could not believe that the place I live is called Earth. The word Earth gives me the feeling of a bad place, as the word boys make me feel bad. Earth must be a place where so many people starve and die, it does not feel like a good place for me. Maybe when I grow up I can punish all the bad people, especially the boys who make girls be freely exposed for money. It would be better if the girls were able to pay boys to be freely exposed, although they would starve if they were waiting for me to pay them to be freely exposed. I will only pay them if they jump into the water and do not come back up. When I think about the sores on Faith and Joy, which I have not seen yet, and the sores on Fejér that I have seen made from boys it makes me angry. It would be nice if I could throw them into one of our fireplaces and watch them burn away. Nevertheless, that is just crazy thinking, so I had better start thinking of the happy things like all the new friends I have. As Charley and I walked into our kitchen for our breakfast, all the servants got up and clapped for me. As they were, doing that William came in and started to yell. He said, "Get back to work while you still have a job." I then said, "I want them to play with me." He said "No." I started crying and then started yelling, "Mommies" as I was running up the steps. Both of my mommies came running out of their rooms rushing towards me saying, "We are coming Ann. What is wrong?" I then said, "I want some girls to play with and William said no very meanly." Mommy yelled, "William" and he came running towards her. Mommy said, "Did you say that Ann could not play with the girls?" He answered, "Yes, I did ma'am, not with my staff." Mommy said to him, "I have told you before that we will not play the caste game when alone in the house with my daughter, have not I? Moreover, as long as the girls do their fair share of the work, they can play with Ann. I also told you that any delay or failure to do something I want based upon playing with Ann is excused. What is your problem?" He then said, "I beg your pardon, Ma'am." She said to him, "I beg your immediate resignation and I want you out of this house in less than one hour. Summon all the male help now." William then motioned for one of the girls to do the summing while he went to his room and started packing. All the males came rushing into my mommy, saying, "What is your command, Ma'am?" She then told them, "Help William pack. I want him out of this city immediately, thus two of you will drive him to the sheriff's office and give them this letter from me. They will make sure he never returns." Everyone knew that when a rich womankind gave the sheriff a letter about a male servant his life was soon to end. Mother, fearing that the boys may try to sneak out of town, gave another letter to one of the girls to take by horseback to the sheriff. That would only take about five minutes and thus the sheriff would return before William departed. The sheriff returned before William departed and my mother summoned the letter from the two escorts who had already destroyed it. She was angry and had the sheriff take all three. They promised her that these men would never enter this county again. They were now dead men walking. The courts were for rich people when they argued; the jails were for poor people when they argued. My 'mothers' would now escort me to the kitchen. Fejér was talking in my mind saying, "You did a good thing Ann, for William would have told your dad about your new friends and they would have been beaten to death." The boys would have told the sheriff and with the reward moved to another part of England while your parents would have been punished severely. I then said to Fejér in her mind, "Thanks for helping me and keeping our secret. Henrietta has already told some of the female servants and they all loved me now." Fejér asked, "Henrietta knows, why you not told me that she knows?" I told her, "Because big people have to tell big people so we little people do not get anyone in trouble." Fejér squeezed my hand softly and said in my head, "Somehow, that makes sense" as she smiled at me. Then my first mommy said to me, "I am sorry you had to see that Ann. Are you feeling better now?" I then told her, "That bad man made my sisters cry." My mother then said, "William and the boys did not see them did they?" I told her, "We did not show him, unless he spied on us." Mommy then wrote another note and gave it to one of the girls to give to the sheriff. She told them not to worry about the letter, because all the girls in this house were safe. I then told mommy, "I guess I will have to make them happy, right." I rebutted, "I love you and right. Mommy, I hate all boys except for daddy. I do not want any more boys in this house." Mommy, then said, "Ann, we need some help protect us when daddy is not here, plus to carry the heavy things and do the hard work so your sisters will not suffer from great pain trying it." I then told me mommy, "You are right, I was not even thinking about that. You are the smartest mommy in the whole world." Mommy, then told the girls to all meet us in the family room, and to bring food and comfortable pillows to sit so all would be relaxed. We now have six young girls working in the house. Mommy does not want any old girls because she wants to keep the house energetic and happy for her daughter and daughters now. We all sat down on our furniture or nice cushions as mommy told the girls, "Put those nice cushions over there for Ann's sisters." It was so easy to feel so much love and happiness in our house now, since that bad man was gone forever. Mommy then said to her girls, "I want to thank you for being Ann's sisters and my daughters. She and I love you all so very much. We would gladly die to keep you. When I heard Ann cries on the steps today, I thought, 'What if she was to die.' I have been so concerned about making her a woman, that I forgot she is my little girl. My mommy would not let me play when I was a child and I hated her for that. All of us are going to put play clothes on and play in the backyard today. We are going to find some friends for her to play with. I did not care, just so they will love her. I beg that you will help me with this. However, the first things after we sing some songs, and eat our food, we all are going outside and play. Fejér then told me in my head, "Do not tell her that you have played with these girls before until she talks to your daddy to be safe, OK." I nodded my head yes. I knew she was right, because I have heard daddy yell at her before. Some daddies hit their wives. We are lucky; my daddy has not hit his girls, to date. He said God gave him two beautiful girls to love not to lash. It scares me when I think about how much power boys have. I hate that so much. Maybe someday women will have more power. As we were laughing and eating, as all us girls love to eat, a terrible thing happened. It started to rain very heavily. It was now pitch black outside. I started crying and said, "My only day to play with my mommies and sisters and now it is raining." Mommy said to me, "Why are you crying? We can still play outside, right girls."

Everyone cheered and yelled, "Yes ma'am." Mommy, then said, "After we finish with our inside party we will all put our old clothes on and play outside and get really dirty. We know that boys do not like dirty girls, so we will be making any that spy on us mad, would not we. Girls, here is my key, open the chocolate drawer over there, and bring out some of that chocolate." I was so shocked, because mommy never even let me eat that chocolate. The servant girls treated it as if they were eating gold. Our bond was stronger than most families and we were the only family that had this bond with our help and now my sisters. All our smiles chased the dark away from outside. The girls found us some play clothes, and got some old children's clothes that had been left by our previous help for us girls. Everyone helped us get dressed. My mommies started to change their clothes in front of all us girls (female help). Mommy looked at them and said, "Hurry, don't be shy." I think if a boy had walked in now, he would have thought he was in heaven, because our clothes were flying everywhere. This was something that none of us ever heard of, especially in a rigid caste system as in England, for the poor servant women to see a rich woman, above all, their masters naked. I think they were all afraid that the poor people would find out that they were human also. Then my mother commanded one of the servant girls to hit her in the arm hard. The girl did then fell to the floor crying as mommy showed everyone the bruise and said, "See girls, I am human also and stand here naked and bruised before you to try and prove this." She then reached down and pulled our girl servant up that hit her and gave her a big kiss. Now that was clearly a violation of every law in England, for to kiss a servant was implying that they were also worthy of love and feelings. Women were forbidden to show any affection to anyone except their family and other aristocrats. Men could have sex with servant girls as long as it was only for pleasure and no love was involved. Mommy told my daughters and Fejér not to worry for our daddy was a very pure righteous man. When the girls looked at my mother, they saw that she was really trying so hard to make a strong, well bonded, and family here plus of course, as social creatures we all wanted to be part of a family. She was a real human being, and not just someone who was trying to take everything from them. The sad thing is that in our country, the rich are the masters, appointed by God to punish the poor. That was not the law in this house. We all had hot blood in our veins and our hot blood was from love and not greed or lust. I then yelled out, "This is not fair." Mommy then asked why, and I said, "Everyone has big baby milk bottles except for me, Ruth and Mary." Then mommy looked around and said, "They all do have really nice baby milk bottles do not they." Then one of the girls said to me, "Ann, someday you will be big like us and have big beautiful baby milk bottles just like your mommy, yet we will all be old and our baby milk bottles will be almost empty." Now instead of being filled with envy, I now felt sorry for them. Mommy, then said, "Leah, I could not have said that any better. Thank you so much for being so smart." I then ran over to her and said, "Do not worry; you can live with me, because I will only live with the girls and will try to find doctors for you all to fix your broken milk bottles." They all laughed and said, "Time will tell." Now this was the happiest time in my life so far, even happier than yesterday and it was just starting. Mommy asked the girls if they knew any rain games and they said, "We can have a rain race or play rain tripping." Mommy asked, "What is rain tripping?" The girls then told her, "We will divide into two teams and whoever trips all the players on the other side wins. Sorry Ann, this game would be dangerous for you, so you can play 'dig a hole to bury the monster and you can cheer for your mommies." I then told the girls, "That sounds like the greatest game that was ever invented." The girls then asked mommy, "Will you put us in prison or have us beaten to death if we trip you." Mommy looked at them and said, "Only if you do not trip me." She then kissed each one of them. I was so happy when I saw that, because for once my face was not being slobbered on by a big person. Then they divided into two teams, after the girls gave me a nice little shovel to dig my hole. I started to dig the hole when Fejér knocked me into the mud. Oh, the mud felt so good, for once, the dirt was a part of me, and I had the most wonderful wet dirt all over me. I just lay on the wet soft ground laughing so hard. I said to Fejér in her head, "Thanks so much for that." She replied, "Anything for my only daughter." My mother went over to Fejér and gave her a big hug. She then said to Fejér, "I wish I could do that. Will you teach me?" Fejér then said, "It will be so easy to whip you." My mother then said to me, "I will be a handful for you. Did you forget how many brothers I had?" Fejér then said, "Only the ones I did not sleep with." My mother fell to the ground laughing so hard. Her virgin ears had never heard someone talk like that. For anyone to say that, even if upper class like her, and be reported upper class would go to jail, and lower class would be buried. How could Fejér trust her so much? The only reason must be from deep love and trust, the exact kind of woman she needed to be in the bathing room with her daughter. Fejér's bad luck was our good luck. She rolled in the mud and threw mud balls at me, who came over to her, plastered in mud, and rubbed mud on my mommy's face. Her mother hugged her, as both laughed so hard. Fejér and the girls could see the freedom of a Lady as she turned into a human. Then mommy went over to Fejér and sealed their bond by saying, "My brothers told me you were easy." For mommy to say that could put her in prison, however mommy did not care. This was a dream come true for her and she was going to enjoy it for the most. This was like expensive chocolate for her and she was going to enjoy every little bite. Fejér simply looked at my mother and said, "That is because they knew I liked three at a time and they could not keep up with me." Mommy then said to her, "I was able to keep up with you?" Fejér then replied, "That is because your grapes make the softest smoothest wine I ever tasted." They then hugged and kissed each other on the lips. We all looked so surprised but pretended like everything was normal. The girls had never seen girls kiss girls on the lips. They only heard of witches kissing each other and that would mean being burned at the stake like Henrietta had told me. We had to protect my mommies, because to lose two mommies, would be so unfair. I made the girls promise never to tell anyone and they gave me a special oath that went like this, "cross my heart and hope to die, stick a needle in my eye." I looked at them and asked them,

"Does that mean yes, and they told me, "It does for neither could we now live without your mommies." Then the rain tripping game started. The girls lined up my mommies against each other. They trusted my mommies, yet still had the fear that if anyone else saw them touching my mommies they would be beaten to death. No one wanted that, so my mommies pretended it was simply the way the cards fell. They lined up in front of each other and the game began. My mommy's arms locked on to each other and they pushed and pulled. One would be gaining the edge until the other one revived and shifted back and forth until I decided to break this tie. I walked over to them, completely unnoticed, and gave them a push. Down they fell into the mud created by the rain races the girls had ran. My push was enough to tip them, as they both were so exhausted. As they fell, I just stood there and laughed. They both were initially shocked until they realized I had done this. Then they laughed and splashed mud on each other. The girls were all down, and now were wrestling each other. My whole back yard was nothing except mud faces and brown baby milk bottles. Then the entire back yard froze, as standing in our back door, with his nice dinner robe on, was my daddy. My mommies and the girls did not know what to do, so I decided to help them. I walked up to my daddy and said, "Daddy will you have fun with me?" We were all shocked when he threw down his dinner jacket and now standing in his swimming pants grabbed me, ran across the yard, and slid to the ground with me in his arms. He was instantaneously covered with mud as we both laughed so hard. He then got up, picked up my mommy, and did the same thing. They both just laughed and laughed, and then started kissing. I never had seen them kiss like that. They then held hands and then went up to the door where my daddy had a couple of buckets of water. He washed some of the mud off my mommy and she washed some off him. He then said to all us girls, "My ladies enjoy your games as long as you wish. I will fill all our tubs and heat some buckets for you at the door. Have fun. We will be using your tubs." He and my mommy went inside and took a fast bath. They then went to their room that was above where we were playing. They forgot the girls always opened the windows. All of a sudden, I heard my mother screaming and my father moaning. I started to cry as I told my other mommy and the girls, "My daddy is killing my mommy." They all started laughing. I kept on crying and said to them, "How can you all laugh? My mommy is getting killed." Then Fejér said to me, "Ann, your mommy is not getting killed but is having a great time. She is making your daddy the happiest man in this whole country now." Then they all started laughing again. I looked at the girls, and said, "Is this true?" They all agreed with me. I knew they all would not lie to a poor girl, like me, so I was relieved. Now I got curious and asked them, "How can mommy make my daddy the happiest man in England from their sleeping room?" Fejér now informed me, "That is a secret that only married women know. Let's go get cleaned up before someone gets sick." Therefore, Fejér and I helped wash the girl's heavy mud off and their feet, then we all went to the servant's bathroom. They had many tubs in there, so we all could help each other. The first thing they did was scrubbed me. I had one person per foot, and arms, one on my belly, the other on my back and Fejér on my head. They all treated dirt on my body as their enemy and they were going to win this battle. Finally, Fejér wrapped me in a big towel and sat me on a chair beside her. She then removed her clothes and jumped into the tub I used to bathe. The six girls just stood there waiting. My four new sisters were already scrubbing away as fast as they could. Our six girls were supervising them. Fejér then asked them, "What are you looking for? Jump in while the water is still warm." They looked at each other and then said, "What about Ann?" Fejér then said, "Do not worry, if it doesn't swing, she can see it. Hurry, our friends." One started, and then soon they all joined and put their muddy clothes in a pile. Fejér then told them to put all the clothes together. This was in violation of every social caste law in England. Servants could never see their masters freely exposed, they could never put their clothes with their master's clothes, and when their masters were bathing, they could never sit down and above all, they could not be nude together, especially with three little girls watching. I went over to each one, without my towel and gave each one a kiss and told each one how beautiful they were, "Each one, with tears rolling down their face replied, "I love also, Ann, our sister." Wow, we are really becoming a family here, and I am the only kid to boss all these big people. That is going to be a big job; I hope they help me out by being good. Fejér and I helped clean the washing room and everyone began to dress in that room, while Fejér and I wrapped big towels (almost blankets) around ourselves and walked up to our rooms. She dressed me first, and then I helped her. I had to put the salves, lotions and oils on her like our doctor had told us to do. I then put the oils on my new sisters. Then it just hit me, "Why did not daddy ask about them?" Then Fejér told me in mind talk, "He probably thought they belonged to the girl servants, since the kids were always kept hidden. Then we went to mommy and daddy's room and I knocked. They asked, "Who is there?" I then replied, "Ann." They then told me, "Come in." I then asked them, "May Fejér approach also?" Mommy said, "Of course." As Fejér opened the door, I went running into their room, bounced onto their bed, and then ran up to get in between them. It just hit me; this was the first time since I was a baby that I had been in there. I now lay there in between them as each one puts an arm around me. Fejér sat down in one of their chairs. I then told my parents, "I love you both so much." My daddy then said, "We love you also Ann, and now we are going to start playing more with you and just being stupid, Ok?" I told them, "Wow that is going to be better than anything in the whole world." Daddy then told me we were going to have a big family meeting with all the girls and a family picnic in the family room. Henrietta had never taught me picnic; however, the way daddy said it, it must be good. Daddy then said, "Who is that beautiful woman sitting in the chair and where is Henrietta. Wow, it just hit me that daddy did not know about Fejér. Mommy then asked him, "Honey, do not you remember my best friend forever?" Daddy then looked again and said, "Now that you mention it, I never had seen her before except in a formal setting. Where is your husband Fejér?" Mommy then told him how her husband lost his ships due to pirates, and had been put in prison thus committing suicide. She further told him how Fejér was a fugitive and that if she were caught they would kill her. Daddy said, "I could never live with knowing I was part of getting such a beautiful woman killed. We will hide her here. There are enough extra rooms to stay hidden in this house, or better yet, we swear everyone to secrecy and let her make friends with our servants, if she wants to do so. I know it is a step down to socialize with servants, however we do, so you may also do if you wish." Fejér now started crying for joy, saying to my daddy, "You have saved my life and your servants are such wonderful girls I would love to serve with them if you will let me do so." Daddy then further asked, "Were all those other girls your daughters?" Fejér then said, "Yes and no." Then mommy said, "They are Fejér and my daughters and Ann's best friends ever sisters." Daddy looked at me and said, "Ann is that true." I started shaking and crying saying, "I love them so much daddy and want to keep them forever please." Then daddy said to me, "Why are you shaking honey, if you want to keep them, I will do the papers and adapt them." Mommy, then said, "Honey, you do not have to adapt them, Fejér bought all four of them for fifteen dollars." Daddy looked at Fejér and asked, "How can you buy all four for only fifteen dollars. They must be starving poor children." Then I said, "I promise to feed them a whole bunch, and put some flesh back on their bones. They may even have my food and I will eat the leftovers from our servants, please daddy." Daddy then said, "Ok honey, but you know if we get caught we all could go to jail, so you must promise to keep them hid. I will have my company build the walls around our back yard higher and have our basement remodeled." Mommy and I started kissing daddy a whole bunch, then I asked daddy, "Can Fejér kiss you also?" Fejér now sat quietly as her face turned red. Daddy calmly said, "If mommy says it is ok." Then mommy said, "Well, since she is my best friend ever, get over here and show him how I taught you." Without thinking, she bounced on mommy and gave my daddy a whole bunch of kisses over his face while tickling my mommy. She then asked my mommy, "Do you always laugh when your best friend is kissing your husband?" Mommy fired back, "Only when is someone inexperienced like you." Fejér then fired back, "Move over, I can make him moan much louder than you did today. It is time he saw how a real woman pleases." Mommy and daddy now looked embarrassed realizing that all the women and kids in this house heard them while they were having sexual intercourse. Fejér then said, "Ann, give them their sugar and let's go down and tell your sisters about the picnic." I then gave each one their sugar, since parents need to have sugar from their baby girl, and off we went downstairs to tell my sisters the great news. Before we went down, I stuck my ear up against the door to hear if they said anything new. I could hear my daddy tell my mommy, "It is good that she is sisters with the girls. I think that will give her a better life and have more people protecting her." Mommy agreed. At least I now knew that daddy was in agreement with me being friends with all of our girls. I want us all to take big bathes together so I can make sure everyone has a medicine on their boo boos. I want to take care of all the people who care for me so much. With them all around me, and all of us playing in the tubs, I feel so safe, by knowing that no one else is allowed in to see us. Therefore, off we went to our kitchen to tell the girls the good news. I told them, "Mommy and daddy said all of us are going to have a picnic in the family room." The girls then starting cooking baked beans, potato salads, chopping crunchy vegetables, frying some chicken, and rolling some noodles in addition to making some pies, a cake, and making some good grape juice from some grapes daddy got from France. This looked like it was going to be fun. The girls then asked me if I wanted to help so both of us, (Fejér and I) said "Yes." We jumped in and started to work. Daddy went to his smoking room where he smokes those fat brown things. I used to think those were dried out poop, then mommy lets me see inside a used one and I saw they were something else. She told me the leaves were grown in the good part of the colony ships brought them back to England. I thought, wow that is a long way to chase after some leaves just to burn and make the room cloudy and smelly. Mommy said we are the lucky ones because we do not have to choke on them all the time. Sometimes even daddy gets sick from the smoke; however, he says it is a man thing from men so he must do it to look strong for the other men. That is why I like our girl club, because even though Mary, Ruth, and I are very little girls or runts who have nothing, the big girls still love for us and treat us special. Girls are so nice to each other when in private. Mommy says they can get cutthroat and malicious when they are competing for the same boy. That can be war. Women may not look at a man's cigar chest, nor enter a room when a man or the men are smoking. This is forbidden in the barbaric prison for women called England, according to Fejér. We always stay away from the men in this house when they are smoking because we love daddy and want to make him look strong in front of his friends. Mommy says that is a way to show love for our daddy. I am glad we cannot enter, because the smoke makes me sick. I wonder how a person could breathe that in and enjoy it. Mommy then came in the kitchen and saw all the fun we had and asked if she could help. The girls said, "If it be they will, Ma'am." They always talk to mommy and daddy like our minister talks about God. Fejér started a song and we all started singing. It was like slave people being freed and singing their freedom song. We then got some cushions and started taking all this wonderful food in the family room. Mommy saw the only boy servant we had. His skin was a different color then ours. Mommy told me he was from British India. I always liked the way he said our words. They sounded so neat. Mommy told me, "It was his accent." He was always nice to me, so I liked him. He, our minister, and my grandpa were the only other boys, besides daddy, that I liked. Mommy asked him, "India, do you want to join us for a picnic in our family room?" He said, "No ma'am, I must guard our front yard and windows to make sure no one is spying on us." Mommy, then told him, "That is very wise, India. We thank you for making this sacrifice for our protection. I will have the girls make you something good to eat." He gave us a courtesy bow and excused himself. Mommy always told me that the thing she liked about India was that he did not follow William and his friend. He did as William said, however when he finished with his duties he went to his room and stayed there until time to work again. He was quiet by nature and mommy said those kind of people can keep secrets. He also seemed to be content with what he had. Thus, she did not worry about him stealing things. He was extremely loyal, which daddy liked, because he had said, "I feel so much better for you girls with India around the house when I am gone." William had always obeyed daddy without question; however, mommy was always complaining to daddy about him. That put William on daddy's keep an eye on list. He was actually happy when mommy told him she had William taken by the Sheriff's office for arguing with Ann. Anyway, now is the time to talk about all this food. Mommy let me sit on the cushions with the girls, as she and Fejér sat with daddy in between them. Everyone was laughing and talking as the food slowly started to vanish. Then daddy asked everyone if he could have his or her attention. He said this to us, "I want to thank all you girls, especially Prudence (now all the girls started laughing) for a wonderful time today. I apologize for leaving our window open; nevertheless, I have no shame with you wonderful people sharing this experience with us. Then all of Fejér and us girls started clapping, as mommy's face looked so embarrassed. I asked Fejér why mommy was embarrassed and Fejér told me it was a big girl thing and that mommy was being treated well by her other female things. She was not used to talking about this in mixed company. Mommy had been recently concerned that her Ann needed some friends to play with during the day. She had planned to ask you girls to find some little girls she can buy. In England, the rich could buy children from the poor; however, when they paid off the debt, and had reached the age of twenty-one they would be set free. This made me happy. Daddy continues with, "We are going to be a new family here from now on. I will build high walls in our back yard and have our basement and attic remodeled so we will have an abundant source of safe places to play. It is very important that no one tell anyone who is not here about this. One person could have the Sheriff here investigating and most of us here would pay a terrible price. I never realized how many beautiful women lived here until I saw you all playing in the mud, brown skin, big laughs, and bubbling eyes. I had to have that fun also, and I did. Thus, once again, I thank you for helping to set me free in this house, for I must put those chains back on when I go outside. That is not my law but England's law. We must find two new men to work with us here in this house, to help reduce any hardships or burdens that some of the hard labor could be laid upon you. I really would prefer to hire a couple of your brothers, thus protect our family environment. The pay is good and labor is manageable, with no more William to hassle you. I also want to hire one of your sisters to provide extra care for Ann and her new friends. I was going to hire someone to care for you Fejér however I have been informed that this job is already being performed by Ann." I ran over and kissed Fejér as we both hugged. She then added, "Yes sir, for only Ann can take care of me." We both smiled at daddy as he continued, "Prudence has asked me if we could select one evening during the week to have a picnic in our family room. I think that Wednesday would be the best choice, with only one girl being off. She can of course have a special picnic at lunch on Thursday with Ann and her friends. We know what we must do to enjoy and enrich this new experience, thus let us begin. We want to have Ann's friends settled in, in time for her big three year old birthday party next month." After we finished eating, all of us took the remaining food and plates to the kitchen. Even daddy joined us. After that, mommy and daddy vanished again and we finished all the work in the kitchen. It was so much fun helping in the kitchen, instead of eating, then going to my room and be bored with Charley. Charley really loved the picnic. He was able to beg food from everyone. He was so excited. This had been a wonderful day in this house, with two picnics in the family room, and playing in the mud plus daddy accepting the four friends I bought. I think the reason the church approves of the buying of children is that it gives some money to the parents and creates a legal obligation for the owner to educate and provide for them. Any serious punishment had to be executed by the crown for indentured help. That made me happy, because I would want my friends to be educated and given food. Then all the girls and Fejér encircled me. They then asked me if they could be friends with my new little girls also. I told them yes, "Faith, Joy, Mary, and Ruth,"

The master-servant rules only apply to the government, and the rich people live. In the poor people's area, where the rich are forbidden to go, there are no laws. I wonder how my sisters had survived so long under those terrible rules. The crown does not want to waste any money protecting them. I knew the girls, as even Faith Maria and Henrietta had stressed, they were saying this to protect me, so I gave them each some little girl sugar and begged them to hurry. My father gave the girls many gold coins; he was actually giving them almost double, what the current rate was. He wanted this deal finished as soon as possible. The girls then told him, "Master, we will find the best of our brothers to serve in this paradise. With this much money, you will own them for many decades." That initially sounds so harsh; nevertheless, if that is the only way to keep us helpless little angels protected then so be it. I have the power to love them or punish them, as my parents always leave this to me. Of course, I love them with all my heart. I have drilled in my heart that if I ever and to own another human I will treat them as if they are part of my body. I am buying them to have some friends to love, thus I will use my power to love them. The girls were gone for about one hour then came back to our house with my new friends new play clothes and dresses. I want to dress my girls where they will look like beauty queens. I will love playing 'dress up' with my Fejér and sisters. I love scrubbing their boo boos and making them happy. I heard our servant girls tell mommy that, "Big Ann works so hard taking care of her sisters and mommies." Mommy told them that she was very proud of me. Now I want to fix them all again.

The girls returned and gave daddy most of the coins back, saying they got a big discount by getting them from their families. Daddy told them to keep the extra money and save it in case their families ran into more hard times, which was all England had to offer. Daddy then looked at the brother's thin bodies and then said, "Take your brothers, clean them up and have them show some of their strength to mommy or Fejér and Ann to approve the deal." One of the girls came and got me and as I entered the kitchen.

"They are always playing in the park when mommy and I walk past. The girls told us they were their brothers. I could hear them calling each other's name and see them always playing." Daddy then said, "Oh that makes sense. I used to listen to the poor kids playing when I walked with my mother a long time ago. Ann, do you want them to be your protectors against the bad men that may attack us? Your life could rest in the balance. " I said, "Oh yes, I will introduce Charley to them, and show them where they are to sleep. Charley will teach them how to fight." Daddy said, "Very good Ann, I can see that you are going to be responsible with your new family members, so enjoy." Joy asked me, "Are we your family members?" I told them, "That is the only way the King will let you live with us is if we make you our livestock, so by law we own you, so you have to let me feed you cakes and pies and give you a nice bed to sleep with me at night." Then Mary said, "How late can we stay here today?" I then told Mary, "Oh Mary, you now live here in this big house." Then Ruth said, "Really?" Faith Maria then puts her arms around them and says, "What Ann says is the truth. You will no longer have to be hungry." Then Mary asked, "Is it true that kids who live in rich people's home cannot play?" Now, Fejér replied, "I will tell you a secret that you can tell no one, in this house kids are allowed to play." Mary then cheered. I think this is how the big people keep their kids on their side, by telling them the things about the other side, which the kids will not like. It did not matter now; the girls had baked some bread and pastries and were serving them now. My friends were grabbing big chunks and eating as fast as they could. The girls were now serving our remaining picnic food. My friends were now starting to slow down as they ate and ate. Ruth said afterwards, "This is the first time I have ever had my belly filled with 'only rich people' food." I looked at my friends, and told them, "You will never go hungry as long as you live with us. We eat three times a day and have snacks in between our meals. Even my girls eat so much that they have to exercise in our basement to stay pretty for the boys" Then Mary said, "I never knew that people could eat more than one time a day. How can exercise make the girls look better for boys?" I told them,

"I do not know, however if the boys like it, I hate it." Fejér then, changing the conversation before going to the basement to exercise, said to me, "They have been so hungry for so long, it will take some time before we can recharge and rebuild their bodies. We will have to have them eat a lot of healthy foods and later give them more sweets." Now Joy asked, "Ann, who is she?" I told them, "She is one of my two remaining mommies and she will sleep with us at nights also." Then Ruth said, "Everyone I know only has one or no mommy. How can you have two mommies and how can you grow inside two mommies?" Then Joy said to Ruth, "Ruth, are you stupid, have not you ever heard of twins? If one woman can have two babies, then one baby can have two mommies. Why do you think we have two of these?" She now pointed at Faith, pulled up her shirt and touched both of her nipples. Ruth then said to me, "I am sorry Ann, I was not thinking. It will be so nice to have a grown up sleeping with us to help love and protect us." I gave her a kiss and said, "Do not worry; our mommies will love you also." Ruth and Mary now said, "Thanks Ann." Mary then asked, "Will we get to live with our mommy and daddy some?" Then Faith Maria told them, "Sorry sisters, mommy, and daddy have moved far away to the new world." Many of the poor people, when they got some money, would move to the New World. It is hard to think of parents going so far away; months across the long ocean, forgetting their children, yet the current caste system made this a way of life. I hated a system where parents had to give up or lose everything they had just to stay alive a little longer. The new world lured them with hope and hope is a hard thing to destroy. As Mary and Ruth cried, Joy and Faith Maria tried to soothe them. Faith Maria was personally worried because she was quickly approaching the age that her mother delivered her. She did not want to fall into this trap, to be locked in a small house with little food and watch the one she married scrape for every bit to feed them. She knew there was something else in the future, and now she had a chance to live that dream. To be loved, by us, and to be able to eat three times a day was more than she ever thought was possible. Sure, she had heard of that, yet had never seen it, so how could that be true? Part of this mystery is the need to keep situations where humans love each other in their love a giant secret as the crown would destroy this instantly if discovered. Fejér now motioned for all of us to go to the family den. This was the room where daddy would spend a lot of time. It had so many books on the wall and a large desk that daddy always sits at plus many chairs for when the churchmen come to visit him. I never went in here much because books are not fun to play with and every time I put them on the floor to make a play fort, someone gets mad at me. They always told me that these books needed to stay on the wall to look pretty and make daddy look smart. We all sat in the chairs while Fejér sat behind the desk. She told us that each day we would get to learn a new scary story and that some of the girls would be teaching us letters and words so that we would be able to read. I thought how bloody crazy could she be. Why would we want to sit down and look at those boring pieces of paper when we could be outside playing in the mud? I really have to teach the facts of life to these big people someday. For now, I would go along with it, since Henrietta had taught me so much; it was only fair that Fejér be rewarded by teaching my friends. She then turned down the lanterns, and started speaking in an eerie somewhat creepy voice and went straight into the story. Something dreadful happened to a ten-year-old girl who had braids. The little girl had been wearing her braids in a ponytail for the longest time, and seemingly the braids were old, at least two to three months old, and the mother never took them down to wash them or let them air out. Nevertheless, the girl had been complaining to her mother about having a headache for about two weeks, but her mother just ignored it, supposing that she had hit her head against the wall or something. One morning the child complained again to her mother about having a headache while getting ready for school. Again, the mother ignored it. When the child got to school, she told her teacher that her head was hurting. The teacher assumed that the braids were too tight in the child's hair and attempted to let the ponytail down. When she removed the hairpiece and let the braids loose, there was a spider in the girl's hair. The spider had laid eggs in the child's hair and the spiders were eating her scalp. She was rushed to the hospital, where she later died. The crown had messengers tell everyone about it. They told all, "Parents, do not leave braids or any kind of hair extensions in children's (or your own) hair for no more than two to three weeks!" Fejér now asked what this story really taught us." Mary answered, "That there are spiders in Joy's hair." Faith then replied, "That we should comb our hair at least every two to three weeks." I then told them, "Oh, no, here we are allowed to wash and comb our hair every day. Plus we can use some neat stuff to help wash it and we can put some neat stuff on it afterwards to make it look pretty." Fejér then asked me, "Why don't you and I go to the kids washing room (They put some more tubs in mine, plus Fejér's tub, because I had to take care of her also.), And teach them now?" I did not know about the new tubs so when we saw them, we all were so happy. They were folding their clothes so perfectly, as we undressed so I told them, "Oh no my best friends forever, we put them in this box (I opened the lid and dropped my clothes in there) and the girls will get them, clean them and put them back in our bedroom." Ruth then said, "You guys wash your clothes? We always stood out in the rain to clean our clothes. This is so tidy." Just then, I looked over at Faith and saw her small baby milk bottles. I then said, "Oh, Faith, I promise to give you a nickel when we go back to my room because I just saw your baby milk bottles!" She then looked at me and asked, "Do you think they are pretty?" I told her, "Everything about all four of my friends is beautiful." Faith Maria then said, "Then you get to see and touch them for free?" I said wow and ran over to exercise by new freedom. As I looked at all four of them, I could see many black spots and bruises. Fejér then joined me in the inspection and pointed for me to get her salves and oils from our doctor, and we both got to work. We told the girls to relax in their tubs as the girls brought more hot water in and started the big fire stove, using it to warm us more water and keep the cold out of our room. They all looked so amazing, thus, Fejér and the girls gave them big kisses on the cheeks. I promised them that I would love and care for every part of them. We slowly started to work on the big black spots. We knew, as on Fejér, it would take a couple of weeks to get all that junk out of them. We also had some pills from our doctor that would help get all that bad stuff out of them. Fejér had told me before that sometimes people get worms in them. We had to warn her so those things would not move around in them and especially around their hearts because I wanted everything from their hearts. We would do the same thing to my new friends. It makes me so sad that so many people suffer like this. Some of those bugs can kill. The girls brought in some candy for them to eat while they were being cleaned. We scrubbed them, put oil all over them, cleaned their heads putting a special soap on them that would help kill the lice like all the poor people had. Then we put some good stuff in their hair and salves all over their bodies. We brushed and brushed their hair. Some of the girls helped cut the ends of their hair to get rid of the double ends, oh sorry, the split ends, which made it a lot easier to brush. Then Fejér told me some scary news. She sat all of us down and said, "Sisters, you know you have lived outside in poor conditions for too many years, thus just like everyone else out there in the cold hungry dark, they have lice and other bad things living in their hair eating at their heads. The good news is that our doctor can give us some wonderful medicine and heal your heads so one day you will be bad bug free. We will have to trim your hair down to almost look like a boy." I then cried out, "Can I get my hair cut short also, so it will not bother me when I am playing in the mud?" Then Mary and Ruth each yelled out, "me too . . . me too." Fejér looked at me and said, "Ann, both your mommies will have to ask you're your daddy about you getting your hair cut off. However, for you and your sisters, it is your decision." I then asked Faith, "What should I do, because I want you all to have two good things we can give you?" Faith Maria then said to her sisters, "We need to do this before one of us dies like the spider girl." They all said yes and I looked at Fejér and nodded my head yes. Fejér then told me, "Your mommies will ask daddy when he is in a good mood, which lucky for us is often." When daddy does come home in a bad mood we all hide so he can relax or fix the problem that is making him mad." Mommy always tells me how lucky we are to have such a wonderful daddy, because so many daddies go to their homes and beat their family severely. Moreover, according to the crown the daddy owns his family and may even kill them if he wants to. I hate that crown, even though I am named after our dead queen.

Faith now looked at Fejér who was also cleaning, with my help and said, "Fejér, your body is so beautiful." Fejér looked at them and said, "Ann and I will make your bodies beautiful also." We worked so hard and they did turn out to be, "Ladies that had boys fighting over them, once their hair grow back out." After we finished and put on our new clothes Fejér said to me, "Why are we not showing them in our room now?" I said that was a great idea, and when we all got dressed in our pajamas we went down the hall. Actually, this hall was in our chamber, which had doors that exited into the hallway. That way we did not have to worry about boys spying on us. Mommy number one said that daddy wanted to make sure his women kept their honor. The girls had purchased new night clothing for all us "little angels" as they called us. We paused while we all helped clean up the bathroom. Fejér looked at them and said, "That is a good idea." We joined in and had our washing room looking good. The girls begged us not to do this, but we told them that we had to prove to them that they were part of us. They helped us, and kissed us repeatedly. There was so much love explodes in this room. No one was better than any other was. I made sure to work extra hard, since technically, I was the enemy. Fejér had started singing and we all joined her. It was so much fun. We were molded into one family. We discovered that someone had removed the temporary wall between my room and Fejér's. We now had a very large room with two fireplaces and five beds. My friends' beds were queen size and the one Fejér's and I shared was King size. My new friends did not care, as they asked when they looked at their beds, "How only one person could have a giant bed like these?" They never had beds before and only slept on the floor inside during the cold winter months. The rest of the year, they all slept outside. I thought, "How lucky, to be able to sleep outside, and look up at the stars and see the trees as the birds slept in them. They even told me about sticks that could move. If they bite you, death would gain you. I thought, oh, how dangerous. Fejér then told me, "Never touch the snakes." I thought how it is possible for these moving sticks could bite me. She then told me, "Someday, you will know." I now thought, wow, someday someone will be telling me a whole bunch of something. I am not going to worry about that now, I will worry about it someday. Fejér then told us about the ultimate bond we could create as we were walking into our room. She said we could become one as blood sisters and that she would teach us and be our sister. We all agreed and she began the process. She then said we each had to give the oath, and that one had to be the leader. Everyone elected me. She began as we all followed, "I do with all my heart promise to serve and worship Ann for all her days and to defend all in this group with my life it need be." She then poked a hole in my finger, and rubbed the blood on her finger and stuck her finger in her mouth swallowing my blood. She then said, "With your blood we are one now, my loving and kind master." Each of the girls did the same thing and when Mary had finished Fejér said, "We . . . are all now one inside Li . . . uh. Ann. May our service make you get on your throne." Faith then said inside my head, "Where is Ann's throne. Fejér then said, "Someday you shall enjoy the greatness of her throne." Then Ruth said, "Wow, I can hear you guys talking in my head." Fejér said, "This is because we are now one, forever, until our deaths when we will go to Ann's throne." I then asked Fejér. "I am only a little girl, how can I have a throne?" Fejér then said, "Someday you will see. The important thing is that we must all keep this a secret, for if one of us tells the secret about Ann, that person will be eaten by dragons every day for eternity." Fejér bowed to me, and then all the girls joined. Fejér then said, "This is our secret club's customs, which we know great days shall come." I then told Fejér that I did not like playing this game. She told me, "Sorry that is the rule. We could only use you as the master because our blood is filled with bad things, however now your blood in us will make us clean and free from many bad things." Then all my sisters gave me a big hug, thanking me." I then said, "I do not understand." All of them looked at me and said, "Someday, you will." Little did I know that they would become so much of me, that the old little girl was gone and now had a body with five new people living in it. To my great surprise, Henrietta appeared in front of us. Faith rushed in front of me and cried out to Fejér, "Who is this spirit." Then I told her, "It is Ok, she is my other best friend." She then appeared in flesh and took her hair to wipe my feet. I asked her, "What are you doing Henrietta?" My new blood sisters were on their knees, scared silly. She said, I am begging you Ann, to let me worship you also and have your magic blood in me, please . . . ." I looked at her and said, "Henrietta, if you want my blood, you can have all of it, for in each drop is my love for you." Fejér then poked my finger and Henrietta started sucking on my finger. Then finally she stood up and starting kissing my head and all my sisters, promising them her protection and love. Then she wrapped her arms around Fejér and they kissed each other's face then their lips. Faith Maria now said, "Wow, I never saw two women kiss on the lips and yet today, I have seen it twice." Then Fejér replied, "Is this not your blood kissing your sisters?" Faith Maria then said, "Yes it is, may I also join you." Then Henrietta said, "Let us all join, with Ann in our arms and reward her for the divine blood that runs in her veins." I do not know what divine means, yet I will wait and ask someday, since that is what they will tell me to do anyway. For now, we just all enjoyed being one. Henrietta then told us all in our minds, "Today we are truly blessed." Then Joy said, "Wow, she can talk in our heads also." We all had that additional feeling of peace knowing that we would never be alone. I then asked Henrietta if she would tell us a good scary story. She then said, I should tell you the story about my cousin, and his wife who lived in Nógrád. "My cousin and his wife lived in Nógrád with this huge Doberman in a little house off Szikszói Road. One night they went out for dinner and some drinking in the bars. By the time they got home, it was so late and my cousin was more than a slightly drunk. They went in the door. They were greeted by their dog that was choking to death in the washing room. Her cousin just fainted, but his wife asked a neighbor to get the veterinarian, who was an old family friend of hers, and got her to agree to meet her at the surgery. The wife takes the carriage, and dropped off the dog, but decided that she had better go home and get her husband in bed. She goes home and finally slaps her husband trying to wake him; however, he is still drunk. It takes her almost half an hour to get him up the stairs, and then the neighbor knocks on the door. She was enticed to ignore it; however, she decides that it must be imperative or they would not be visiting this late at night. As soon as she gets close to the door, she hears the veterinarian's voice screaming out, "Thank God I got to you in time! Leave this house, at this instant! No time to explain!" Then the veterinarian runs away to tell the sheriff. Because she is such an old family comrade, the wife trusts her, and so she starts getting the husband down the stairs and out of the house. By the time she has made it all the way out, the sheriff is outside. They rush up the front stairs past the couple and into the house, but my cousin's wife still does not have an inkling what is going on. The veterinarian returns and says, "Did they get him? Did they get him?" The wife asks, "Did they get who?" starting to get mad. "Well, I found out what the dog was gagging on – it was a human finger." Just then, the sheriff drags out a dirty, stubbly man who is bleeding copiously from one hand. "Hey Sheriff," one of them screams. "We found him in the bedroom." Therefore, make sure you lock the bedroom door when you leave it. Fejér and Henrietta really wanted to make sure that Prudence could not go in there and snoop while we were gone. Then Henrietta stood in the middle of us and said, "Goodbye, my sisters," as she disappeared. Joy asked, "Is she a magic woman." Fejér then answered, "We are all magic women now. So we must not tell or they will burn us like witches." Then Ruth asked, "Are we witches?" Then Fejér answered, "No, we are servants of Ann. England will not know the difference. One mistake and we could be in a lot of trouble. We can save ourselves, excluding our girls, India, and our parents. Do you girls crave me to tell you another story before we dress for dinner?" They all said yes, and then we have to dress for dinner?" Then Fejér said, "We want to look real pretty for our father, since he is our master of the house." She started by saying Baranya's friend, a girl in her teens, was babysitting for a family in Nógrád. The family was prosperous and has a very large house, although smaller than ours. Anyways, the parents are going out for a late dinner. The father tells the babysitter that once the children are in bed, she should go into this specific room, and read their books, because he does not want her meandering around the house. The parents take off and soon she puts the kids into bed and goes to the room to read. She tries to read, but she is troubled by a clown statue in the corner of the room. She tries to ignore it for as long as possible, but it starts freaking her out so much, that she cannot handle it. This clown statue was really creeping her out. Thus, she very fast and so scared got the kids, and went next door. The neighbor then sent one of his servants to get the sheriff. The sheriff arrives just as the parents are returning home. The father asks her, "So, really, what's going on?" The babysitter tells him, "The clown statue was really creeping me out." He answers, "We do not have a clown statue." He then further explains that the children have been complaining about a clown watching them as they sleep. He and his wife had just ignored it, believing that they were only having nightmares. The deputies arrive and capture the "clown," who turns out to be a midget, a midget clown! I guess he was some homeless person dressed as a clown, who somehow got into the house and had been living there for several weeks. He would come into the kids' rooms at nights and watch them while they slept. As the house was so large, he was able to avoid discovery, surviving off their food, etc. He had been in the reading room right before the babysitter came in there. He also loved to read books When she entered he did not have enough time to hide, so he just froze in place and pretended to be a statue." We all then started to scrunch together, because we knew our house had so many rooms. Fejér then said, "We are lucky that in our house we keep the doors to the rooms locked. So each time you walk past a room make sure it is locked, if it is not locked call for one of the girls to come and they will lock it. If we do not make sure they are locked instead of getting a clown that pretends to be a statue, we may get a clown that is a killer who, like the dog, wants to eat little girl's fingers. I do not want to scare you, that is why we teach you these easy ways to keep us all safe inside this wonderful house where everyone wants to make sure our sisters are safe and can be happy so we can love them a whole bunch. We shall now get dressed, go downstairs, and eat dinner. I will tell you what to do in your minds, like which silverware to use and how to drink from a glass and remember, always eat slowly with your mouth closed. No burps or farts and by all means no laughing unless I say to do so, ok my big sisters. I will tell when to laugh when daddy tells us something. If daddy likes something we like it, if he hates something we hate it, and if he says something is true we agree and disagree when he disagrees." I then added, "If Fejér does not speak, I always look at mommy and do what she does. Since my daddy is such a kind and strong man, mommy says we need to make him feel very important, since that kind of stuff is what makes men for big and strong." Then Ruth adds, "Why are men so strange?" Fejér then laughs and says, "Ruth, all the women in the world asks that question and as of yet, none have found the answer." Fejér then added, "This world gets stranger every day I live in it." We all agreed. We all rushed over to her and hugged her. Soon we were all dressed, hair professionally put up, putting on our nice long dresses and make up on and our new fancy dinner shoes. Ruth told us, "We have never looked this good before." Fejér then told us in our minds, "You all look like beautiful angels in Ann's army. Fear not, for now that Ann's blood is in you, you shall have these luxuries for eternity. We belong to Ann." We looked at each other and started hugging and kissing each other easily not to harm our makeup. Then down we descended to our big family dining room and waited in the hall for mommy and daddy to come. When mommy saw all of us, she immediately started to cry saying, "Oh, my god, I never saw so many beautiful angels like this coming down from heaven." My father dropped to his knees and gave each of us a hug and big kiss saying, "I never thought you girls could look so wonderful. I think we may soon be able to go out and eat in a big restaurant." Faith, who looked gorgeous said, "Sir, we have never eaten in a restaurant before." Then Fejér added, " Sir, I will insure you that there will be no need to worry. Everyone who sees them shall acclaim, "What beautiful angels they are." My father then looked at Fejér who was the epitome of a glamorous woman of the courts, "That I believe with all my heart, my fair ladies." Fejér told us to stand back in a line against the wall, smallest to tallest with her in the rear. My father looked so amazed at how we all did this so smoothly and exactly. He then said to my mommy, "Prudence, do so how well they execute our social protocols with such precision?" My mother, reaching over to kiss and hug Fejér then said, "Fejér, you are an amazing friend who can do amazing things. We are so lucky to have you as a forever member of our home and family." This made us feel so good, for we all so very much loved our Fejér and wanted her to be with us every minute of every day until we have no more days. Fejér then bowed and said, "Ma'am, I bring into our heart so much joy that we have pleased you." We all knew she was teaching us, so even we started bowing before my parents before we spoke. They were especially surprised when I did so. They always hugged me and told me how much they loved me. I knew that by practicing this all the time, it would be casual and normal for us when we were entertaining guests. My parents now went into our big dining room and sat down, one on each end. This table had twenty seats and where we sat made a difference. Fejér told us exactly what to do. We were first would go in front of my father, bow, then turn around and kiss his hand that would be extended. We would then go to the other end and do the same for my mother. As we were walking down to our mother, we were to casually look at the table and see if our name was behind any plate. Fejér had a good idea where we would sit, so if we went past our plate, she would tell us to glance back quickly, and then proceed to my mother. Ruth went first, then Mary then me, followed by Joy, Faith, and Fejér. The girls started to bring out our appetizers. When they brought out the second, Mary said, "Wow, I thought the first plate was our food." Then I told them, "We will be getting a lot of food so just enjoy. I will start talking when we are allowed." We all had such big smiles, as my parents could tell that they had indeed found the perfect new children in our family. Daddy started the talking by saying, "I found a new church for us to go to. It is in a town about one hour from here, yet in another church demonization. We will be able all to go to church together. I asked daddy if the people in that church would be saved also and he told me yes, they would also be saved. One of our girls, who had brought her brother to work here, will be one couple with Mary as their child. The widow Fejér shall have Ruth as her child. Prudence and I will have Ann, Joy, and Faith Maria as our children. We all agreed and thought this would be so fun. Daddy said the girls would help us get some nice new formal church appropriate gowns. My sisters said they could not wait to see them. As the meal was reaching its end and desert was now being served, my friends were talking a hundred miles a minute in our heads. They said each bite was like heaven. Then the girls served us our evening wine. That was the good thing about aristocrats is that the children get to drink the same wine, smaller amounts at dinners. Fejér told the girls to slowly wiggle the wine in their glasses, then sniff it, afterwards blow in it slowly to smell the wine's odor, and then slowly sip it. When the girls sipped it, they started screaming in our heads, "Oh my, this tastes so strange." Fejér told them that it would help reduce the pain in their bodies and make them feel good. Soon they had started feeling good as daddy led us all to the family room, where he drank some alcohol and we girls drank some more "girly wine." We all talked about our day, and the things we had done. Mommy said, "I hardly saw you girls today, you must have been so busy learning things." We all stood up at Fejér command, bowed, and said, "Ma'am, indeed we did." Daddy then said, "I do believe this is the only house in England that has so many beautiful young high class ladies." We all said thank you, after mommy thanked him first, we went down our line little toward big. We had so much great fun talking and then daddy told us some funny stories. He also told us stories that made him look stupid, like the time when I was in the Navy on a ship playing and he accidentally knocked the first mate into the ocean. He then jumped as fast as he could into the water and saved the first mate, which to his shame could not swim. For his punishment, he was put into the ship's prison for thirty days and only given bread and water. He would have received a much larger punishment; however, in exchange for not telling the crew that the First Mate could not swim, he only got the thirty days. The First Mate pretended that the fall knocked him unconscious. We all, including mommy who never knew this, just laughed and laughed along with daddy who would start laughing harder. It was so nice to hear all this laughing and we all could feel that something very special was here. This was a family with one heart and soul and you could see the love that we all had for each other and mommy and daddy were a big part of it. We could go high class and we could wallow in the mud, it did not matter as long as we were together. Mommy then asked why all the girl's rooms were still untouched. I then said to mommy, "Oh mommy my best friends forever are going to sleep with Fejér and I." Then daddy said, "Yes Dear, I did hire a company to remodel their rooms, in order to insure more security for Ann, with only two males (as the girls were requiting available brothers), and India, on our staff." Mommy, then said, "Great thinking Sir." She always spoke like that to him when she felt he had done very well. Mommy, then said, "Tomorrow, I will teach you Naughts and Crosses/Draughts (tic tac toe) and Knickers (marbles)." That really got us excited as we went up to our room. It would be so fun to learn some games we could play in the house, most likely the kitchen, since that is where all the cake and pies are kept. Joy said we could all play All Hid (hide and seek) again in this house in addition to Hopfrog (leapfrog), Lummelen (keep away). We now took our tired bodies up to my room. On the way up Ruth said, "Wow, this new life is good, all you do is put on clean clothes and eat, plus keep a lot of secrets." I took her hand as we continued into my room. Fejér the then showed each girl their nice new beds, yet they kept following me. Fejér then asked, "Why are you not in your beds." They then replied, "We want to sleep with Ann because we love her." Fejér then bowed and asked me, "Can your blood sleep with you" As we all jumped in my bed, I have to sleep on Fejér with my back to her body and her arms wrapped around me and my head securely anchored on her chest as my pillows. Ruth and Mary slept on each side of me with Faith and Joy next to them. We all were snuggled tight as Fejér told the girls, "Our new friends, you have so many things to learn so you can be cast as an aristocrat. Henrietta will be teaching you with Ann. Do not worry about time, she will be taking you back in time and bring you back here in just about twenty seconds our time. Each night you will get about two weeks of training. Enjoy and good night, my blood sisters and Charley who worked his way into our bed sleeping at our feet.

CHAPTER 03

SISTERHOOD

Henrietta worked endlessly on training my servants or blood sisters as we continued to bond. Henrietta and Fejér then one told us that, "We were going to take real mind vacations in other parts of this planet and maybe even this solar system. In addition, to protect our identity we would give 'temp suits or new bodies for that trip only' which would look and speak like different girls most times almost the same age." We all thought that would be so fun and exciting. As we awoke in the morning, my sisters were all so excited about the many things they learned the night before. As I watched them throughout the upbringing form into social elites yet at the same time, we would toss the clothes and play in the mud. Fejér continued to tell us stories to help mold us and protect us. They then told a secret story about one of Henrietta's ancestors. Henrietta's great-great grandmother had been ill for quite some time, and finally passed away after lying in a coma for several days. Her great-great grandfather was devastated tremendously, as she was his one true love and they had been married over fifty years. They were married so long it seemed as if they knew each other's innermost thoughts, as we in our sisterhood are working so hard to obtain. After the doctor pronounced her dead, her great-great grandfather insisted that she was not. They had literally to wrench him away from his wife's body so they could be ready for her burial. Now, back in those days they had backyard burial plots and did not drain the body of its fluids. They simply prepared a proper coffin and put the body in its coffin to its permanent resting place. Throughout this process, my great-great grandfather protested so fiercely that he had to be put under and to bed. His wife was buried and that was that. That night he woke to a horrific vision of his wife uncontrollably trying to scratch her way out of the coffin. He ran to the doctor immediately and begged to have his wife's body exhumed. The doctor refused, but my great-great grandfather had this nightmare every night for a week, each time frantically begging to have his wife removed from the grave. Finally, the doctor gave in and, together with local authorities, exhumed the body. The coffin was pried open, and to everyone's horror and amazement, my great-great grandmother's nails were bent back and there were bloody scratch-marks on the inside of the coffin. The doctor had made a mistake. If you feel strongly about something you should stand against others for it." Mary then said, "What kind of coffins will we get when we die?" Fejér then looked at her and said, "My sister, do you not know that those with Ann's blood in them never die." I then asked her if I would die. Fejér told me, "Oh Ann, do you know that it is the blood in you that will save us?" I then said, "Ok, thanks." We all then put our daytime clothes on, and all but, I put on their salves and oils. We did this in the morning so the extractions at night would be more fruitful. ? As we were leaving our room, my mommy was at the door and asked if she could enter. Fejér quickly agreed and stepped aside. Mommy asked, "Why are all the beds made except for Ann's." I then answered, "Mommy, they are all my best friends forever and they all wanted to protect me." Mommy, then looked at them and said, "I thank all of you for helping protect Fejér and my daughter." All five of us girls then gave her a bow and said "Thanks." When daddy is not with her, we can be a lot more informal. Mommy likes that, for it tells her that we are beginning to trust her more. Mommy was also dressed very casual. We knew we had to include her in our daily activities so she would not feel rejected. Therefore, we would just talk and play around her, speaking of all things except our secrets and of course take turns bothering her. She was nice about hugging my new sisters, a term that soon I would not be able to use. Daddy told us that since he knew the brother of the King of Denmark. They were now in a thirty-year war helping the Protestants and thus understood the rigid line the new groups had formed. Now that one of our female servants had recruited her twin brother and youngest brother, who were twenty years old, to join our family we were now stable in our house. Mommy wanted to buy some female servants to help Fejér with all the children, however we all insisted on having only Fejér, in which she also joined our plea. Daddy liked that because it saved him money. Daddy had sent one of his ships to Denmark for trading and a messenger to the King's brother to get some false family documents for one of our female servants and one of the new brothers and the four new girls. Fejér did not need new papers since she was still registered. England did not register poor people since so many of them died at young ages, and many of those who did not, were bought by trade companies, government agencies, and private companies who needed disposable labor. Their lives were so little value, being considered less than the family pets. Little they did know the love that was hidden in them as we had learned from our four new bundles of love and happiness. The king's brother was not a stout reformist yet a Sunday church member, and then the rest of his time he helped other believers that needed the help of a rather handsome donation. He usually dealt with matters where the receiver had a lot more to lose than did he. That kept the world's wheels greased, as he would say. In the meantime, he continued to praise them on their elegance repeating so many times, "England shall desire the company of such royal class ladies." Of course, the king's brother would find a loose part in their family tree and fill it in to create another group of long lost relatives. Our titles for our new servants would go like this, the servant brother and servant girl would be titled Viscount/ Viscountess Håkon of Norway, while my four girls would all be Countess Ruth, Mary, Joy, and Faith Maria, all of Denmark. Daddy said that since they had Christian names it would be ok, as long as we spelled it like the king's brother spelled it. Faith Maria then asked, "Will I be a real Countess. My father then said, "Countess Faith Maria of Denmark, a title verified and registered by the King of Denmark. Fortunately, all documents produced by the King's brother were rubber stamped by the King's ministers. It was a common practice in our day to invite those of titles from other kingdoms to live with the extremely high aristocrats of England. Then I asked daddy, "With all these new titles, will we still go to the new church you promised?" The powerful, "you promised" tool gives the kid power of the parent, for they have no defense against it. Daddy then said, "Oh course Ann, for they can have honor everywhere, save here." Joy then said to Daddy, "Such a wise thing you have created. Ann was correct when she told us; you are the smartest daddy in the whole world." My daddy looked at her and replied, "Thanks for the compliment Joy; however, the honor is not mine but the Bible's." I then told my servants, "When you go to church, they will teach you many great stories like the time a small boy killed a big mean giant." Mary is looking at me and says, "Is that really a story we will learn in church?" Fejér replied, "That and many more." My daddy liked seeing that enthusiasm in them for church, since the church controlled so much of our lives. A few weeks later, daddy had the papers. He got them registered by the crown, which gave him a paper to show to public places when wanting the titles announced as they entered. We then prepared for our first restaurant visit, which upon seeing our papers prepared Danish food with menus. Daddy was shocked, yet Fejér told him not to fear, for she knew Danish. Henrietta did an emergency class in the past to give them time to practice pronunciation, and to order from the menu. They did not have to worry much about talking to others in the restaurant since they were countesses, and as such would not talk with lowly aristocrats, except for a yes or no. To be safe, Henrietta drilled them very solidly on Danish during her nighttime classes back in time. We practiced with them during the day. Fejér would tell them in their mind how to respond and what to do, such as allowing certain people to kiss their hand. Henrietta trained them hard for about ninety days and then flashed them back exactly when they had left, thus did not even miss a step. Owners of the restaurant seated the countesses as Fejér told them how to respond and to alert these 'servants' on the seating order, which for this event all the girls would look at the youngest, the Danes did youngest to oldest while the English did oldest to youngest, except in our home. The 'servants" would pull the chair out. The child would sit in it and then two servants would pick them up and scoot them in, being careful not to drop them. To drop them meant a public beating. When we all were seated, my parents, Fejér, and I had no titles so we sat at the table next to them. Fejér then told the restaurant managers that she had been commanded by the King of Denmark to watch these girls. She had also worn Danish gowns like the countesses. The managers immediately announced to the girls that Fejér was going to join them. They each, from youngest to oldest nodded their approved and then stared at each other, because a countess would not eat or drink with servants around the table. Fejér then seated herself and motioned for the managers to leave. Everyone had their eyes on the girls as Henrietta had her eyes on them. Daddy had added another touch to tonight's public show. One of the servant girls had also dropped of papers on Viscount/Viscountess Håkon of Norway. Upon the young couple's arrival, completely dressed as Danes with a horse and buggy, and being announced all stood except the girls. Another test passed by the socialites. The door announcer then informed them that a table was filled with four Countesses. They immediately went to that table and bowed asking in Danish if they could rise. Ruth gave them permission. They both kissed the girl's extended hand and then proceeded to their table, on the other end of the restaurant being seated with their escort Henrietta of Denmark. Test number three had been passed. These four young women were for real and were most likely of sufficient title to date the children of the monarchy of all Europe when of age. The possibility of being a future Queen of England could not be ruled out. Henrietta handled all the talking with the staff for the new couple and told them how to eat, and, in the correct order which to use our silverware. Young couples of title always let their chaperone do all the talking. They had also practiced the protocol at our home. There was a complete different protocol enforced at their table. Most knew that many of the rigid titleholders in Denmark would not let a young boy and girl (even married) be in public without a chaperone. The chaperone primary duties were to help the female, ensuring that was not placed in any compromising position, since young boys were thought not to be responsible enough to protect a young woman's virtue and honor. They ate slowly, since to leave before the countesses would be a serious protocol violation. When the countesses were finished, Ruth simply raised her hand and lowered it. The staff immediately came, pulled their chairs out slowly, and then helped them stand up. As Ruth the first to stand, stood up all in the restaurant stood up and remained silent. Then the countesses departed. My parents and I followed them to our carriage as some socialite idiots tried to give us the look as if we were their servants. Daddy told me that they are always looking for a way to downgrade others. That is why we are prisoners outside, confirming to foolish rituals to verify we are civilized. As we returned home, the house was once again buzzing, as everyone wanted to tell the girls about the evening's events. One of the girls commented, "My, we were popular tonight." We had to gently take our evening gowns off, and hand them to the girls, who would take them to a special place to clean tomorrow. They had to drop of my parents and mine at one place, the countesses at another and the viscount/viscountess at another. Social protocols are making me nauseated. Hallelujah, it is time for some kid's amusement. Mommy begged Henrietta to stay for a few days, which since she had sent the carriage to bring her from her 'brothers' she felt obligated. Mommy and daddy excused themselves for the evening as they were 'bloody well tired' as daddy put it. That was not the case for us kids. We were wound up and ready to play and make noises. Thus, Henrietta asked one of the boys if they would fire up the basements stoves. She no longer hid her beauty, thus they rushed downstairs to obey her command. She told us, "I think they were hoping it would be so warm that I would take off my shirt."

Mary quickly asked, "Would you make them pay five cents to see you?" Henrietta said, "Mary, I would make them pay much more than that." I then said, "I have seen her without her shirt on and I would absolutely pay much more." She then told me, "For you Ann, it is always free for you to see, since you created me." Mary then asked me, "Did you create us?" I then told her, "I do not remember, however Henrietta is so much smarter than I am. Returning to Henrietta, I then said, "Wow, I am going to be able to save a lot of money taking baths with you guys." We all laughed. The wonders, joys, and mysteries, of childhood logic produce a variety of surprises. We all huddled around in our slips, since our outer garments we being saved for the cleaners, one of the corners stoves provided enough warmth as Henrietta told us she would tell us a story about a baby killer that lived long ago. We all crunched up in a small bundle with Fejér protecting our backs. When I would think about these tight huddles later, I would marvel about how five girls could occupy such a small amount of space, yet always marveled how Joy, Faith Maria and Fejér, would always hover over us, as if they were hiding gold from thieves. She began by saying, "In the ages before a living man settled on this planet, came a spirit from a planet called Lamenta and later on Earth named Lilith." As she said this name, my heart started beating harder. Fejér and the sisters could all feel it. Fejér then motioned for the girls to let her hold me. She rubbed my back and arms, kissing me all over, yet that name felt like it was stirring a hidden spot inside me. I soon started to feel better as she now said to me, "Fear not Ann, for we will all, always protect you." This really made me feel so much better. Fejér and Henrietta winked at each other as if to say, "Something good just happened." They dare not talk in their heads since we all could hear them. Henrietta then continued, "She searched for men who were sleeping alone, then seduced them and sucked their blood." I then said, "I hope it made them die because I hate almost all of the boys." Henrietta then continued, "That it did Ann; she was also a great danger to any boy under the age of eight, or any girl less than twenty days old. To protect them, parents were advised to draw a charcoal circle on the wall of the room, and write inside of it "Adam and Eve, barring Lilith." On the door they were supposed to write three names "Sanvi, Sansanvi, Semangelaf"." Faith Maria then said, "I remember seeing our parents do that for Ruth and Mary." I then said, "I am so glad they did" and gave Ruth and Mary each a smooch. Henrietta also gave them a kiss and continued, "According to the myth, these three names belonged to the three angels whom God sent down to get Lilith back into Eden with Adam, and who eventually struck the deal mentioned above with her." I then said, "Our minister at church told us that Eve lived with Adam in their garden." Fejér then added, "Ann, this is a secret time before Eve moved there. Everyone, do not mention this in church or we could be in big trouble." Later that night, inside my dreams I could see a woman who had a head of fire. Fejér quickly told me to be quiet as she turned off my mind reading. Then at morning time, she turned it on again. I asked her why she did that. She told me it was because Lilith was looking for babies to kill in this town. I told her I was over twenty days old. Fejér then told me, she also looks for kids who can hear others talking in their heads and for me not to worry, for anytime she was near we would all mask ourselves. I then asked her why she would want to kill me. Fejér said, "She does want to kill you, yet could by accident and thus kill herself." I started to ask and then stopped saying, "I know, someday." She gave me another kiss, which I always liked her kisses. We now decided to take our tired little bodies upstairs and go to the washroom, what was where we were making such a great headway on the black spots on my friends. They were almost gone as their skin was now so soft just like mine. Faith Maria was now maturing both physically and mentally, as she now appeared to have a need to be appreciated for her beauty, which we all detected and would make extra efforts to appease. She would always undress first and lay on her bed waiting for us. She had to do things that we all, except for a little on Joy, did not have and that was fast growing baby milk bottles and plenty of hair where mommy kept trimmed nice for daddy. Little girls know almost everything about their mommies. We would all rush over and ask Joy if we could play with that hair, since none of us could understand why we would have hair there and why as we did not have hair there yet. We wondered if we were disabled or defective, by Faith Maria explained to us with our favorite words, "Someday." She enjoyed the attention and would let us all play, and sometimes even Fejér would play with her, as she would also allow Faith Maria pet hers, I think more out of curiosity about what to expect as her body continued to mature. She still had some scars and sores on her body, however we did not care, and neither did her, since she no longer had to pull down her pants for money from the boys. Faith Maria was a great sister to have as we could see what would be happening to our bodies in the future and not go through the pain as she matured, only to discover that the boys knew what was happening and they wanted it. Too bad Lilah, or whoever Henrietta taught us about, did not get those boys. She told us all her story as also did Fejér. We were so glad to know that, however not as glad as Joy was since it was starting on her. She had a few black hairs growing down there and Fejér and Faith Maria would play with Joy's bragging her up so she would not feel all alone in the middle. We all now had special friends that we liked to scrub extra good. Faith Maria enjoyed Fejér, as she was really a lot of skin for me to work on. I enjoyed Joy because I wanted to be a part of her blooming so I would be stronger, and Ruth and Mary enjoyed each other, not wanting to rush out of their being the babies. They were truly soul sisters, having survived terrifying beginnings, yet young enough to pull through without any permanent damage. Faith Maria would be able to pull through since she had invested herself into saving her sisters and now that they were doing so good, she was able to rebuild herself. Of course, Fejér and Henrietta worked endlessly to rebuild her both as a woman and to my surprise a mistress. As I walked into one of our playrooms, I saw Faith Maria kissing Fejér on the lips and Henrietta conquering her privates. I asked them if I could watch. They paused for a second, and then started back again. I then asked Henrietta, "What does that taste like down there, and Fejér then said, "Go ahead Ann, taste it. Henrietta positioned my face and said, go ahead and lick slow so you do not hurt Fejér." As I started licking, some old skills I had buried somewhere started to return, and I licked as passionately as someone, my physical age could, and then all of a sudden Fejér started to moan softly and her body got stiff as a board and she started releasing her special wine in my face. Henrietta then said, "Hurry Ann, help me drink this up. This is the good stuff." It had tasted better than this wine, however to me this wine tasted good also. I then asked if I could drink Faith Maria also, and she said sure, "rolled over on her back and opened her wine bottle as my lips softly buried itself around her wine bottle. Henrietta rolled over as Fejér started enjoying her. This was so much fun. Soon Faith Maria started releasing her 'wine juices.' They tasted good, I guess since they were fresher since she was younger. We now squeezed each other's breast, that is what Henrietta said we have to call them when with other girls, although since Faith Maria had me and my breasts were still inside me, she massaged them with one hand and my small bottle with the other. It felt so good and wonderful. All I could think about now was teaching Joy, Ruth, and Mary. This was a new freedom for me, for now I could enjoy my life without boys, and could only dream of a day when this would be considered normal. Even at my young age, I could feel the anti-social chains pulling against this "evil" as our minister called it. Oh, please someone; get rid of all those bad boys. Fejér said that tonight I would get to teach each one starting with Joy, while Faith Maria and she would do a demo for Mary and Ruth. I told them that I was so glad they were a part of my life. They then told me I was the hero today, for I made two of them release their wine. I asked, "Is it a good thing to make the one you are enjoying to release their wine?" and they all three said, "That is the reward both ways, Ann. The bottle opener gets to drink some of the best wine made by a woman and the woman gets the joy of a heavenly experience. Make sure you keep this a secret." I asked Faith Maria if she ever saw this before, and she said yes, "One time a rich man took her to his house and paid her thirty pounds to enjoy his wife. After I got the money and thought about it, I decided that it was also fun." I then replied, "It seems like rich people get a lot of things with their money, do I have to pay you?" Faith Maria said,

"Remember Ann, you made me enjoy this heavenly experience, so I should pay you?" I told her, "Do not worry, because I love you so much I will serve you whenever you want me to. I am glad our bodies were created especially to enjoy this. It is as if they were made for this purpose." She then replied, "What if I want you to enjoy me a lot?" I then said, "Then I shall enjoy you a lot, because I like playing with the nice hair you women have down there." They all laughed and said, "Let's go and get the gang and go to the basement and tell another story, since Ann has made our day very happy." Fejér began the story, "Two dorm mates in college were in the same Math class. The teacher had just reminded them about the midterm the next day when one dorm mate, I will call her Julie was asked to this big party by the most handsome boy in the college. The other dorm mate, Meg, had no interest in going and, being an assiduous student, she took notes on what the midterm was. Over the entire period of flirting with her date, Julie was utterly unprepared for her test, while Meg was completely prepared for a major study date with her books. At the end of the day, Julie spent hours getting ready for the party while Meg started studying. Julie tried to get Meg go, but she was insistent that she would study and pass the test. The girls were rather close and Julie did not like leaving Meg alone to be bored while she was out having fun. Julie finally gave up, using the excuse that she would cram in homeroom the next day. Julie went to the party and had the time of her life with her date. She headed back to the dorm around two a.m. and decided not to wake Meg. She went to bed nervous about the midterm and decided she would wake up early to ask Meg for help. She woke up and went to wake Meg. Meg was lying on her stomach apparently sound asleep. Julie rolled Meg over to reveal Meg's terrified face. Julie, concerned, turned on the desk lamp. Meg's study stuff was still open and had blood all over it. Meg had been murdered. Julie, in horror, fell to the floor and looked up to see, written on the wall in Meg's blood, "Aren't you glad you didn't turn on the light?" I then asked, "Why would she be glad that her roommate had not turned on the light?" Fejér then replied, "Oh no Ann, if she would have turned on the light, she would have seen her roommate still alive. The thing we must remember is that by being in a sisterhood, we must always make sure each other is ok. Then Faith Maria Maria wanted to tell a story she heard some girls tell on one of the corners one night. As I heard her start to talk, my heart was pounding new heated blood that wanted her to spray my face again with some wine. Wow, this is a great feeling that I hope we all will have as we take our sisterhood to the cherished level tonight. We all now got excited, because now one of us was going to tell a story, since Faith Maria was stuck in the middle of kid and adult. She followed the same line as Fejér did, and her story went as follows, "In his life, George was a good-looking guy who liked the girls. Once he had dated all the available girls in the area, he started seeing a girl in the next town, not knowing she was married. Eventually her husband discovered what was going on and promised revenge on the two of them. He told his wife he was going out of town for the weekend, and then hid in the woods behind their house. As he had predicted, that evening George showed up to take the wife out. The husband followed them to the nearby Blueberry Hill. Things were getting pretty hot and heavy and when all of a sudden, the carriage door was jerked open and George came face to face with one very huge, very angry looking man carrying a hunting knife. "Oh no!" screamed the girl who had started all the trouble in the first place. "It is my husband!" "That is right, you cheating wicked man!" yelled her husband. "And I am about to teach you a lesson you will never forget!" He pulled her off George, rammed the knife into her, and tossed her aside. Then he turned back to George, grinning eccentrically. "Do not hurt me!" George begged. "I swear to God I did not know she was married!" Nevertheless, the wronged husband would not listen. He dragged George out of the carriage and skinned him alive with the hunting knife. Then he went to town and turned himself in to the sheriff. When the sheriff arrived at the crime scene, they found the woman, who was astoundingly still alive. However, George was nowhere to be found. They say he is still hanging around Blueberry Hill, waiting to catch a couple and "teach" them the same lesson his girlfriend's husband taught him. He is described as a bloody skeleton in 1300's clothes, carrying the knife he himself was. All the teenagers around here grow up hearing "Don't go to Blueberry Hill if you don't want to be Skinned George's next victim!" Mary immediately asked, "What is Blueberry Hill." Fejér then told her, "It is a place where boys and girls go to kiss." Joy then took the words out of our mouths by saying, "Yukkieeee." Faith Maria then said, "Tonight Fejér, Ann, and I will teach you something better to kiss than yucky boys." Then Joy complains, "How come Ann knows and we do not know." I then told her, "I learned just today and I promised to teach you tonight when we sleep." Then Ruth said, "Oh boy, another night class." Then Fejér said, "Training you will enjoy for the rest of your life." Then Joy asked, "Why did the husband get angry about George for kissing his wife?" Then Faith Maria said, "Because once you get married to a man, you must kiss him when he says to and be his slave plus you can never kiss another man or you can be punished, sometimes by being tied in the middle of town and beaten to die." Then Ruth said almost crying, "I think to be married to a man is very dangerous." Then I told her, "Sometimes you can get lucky like my mommy and meet my daddy." Now Mary said, "Ann, your daddy is already married to your mommy." Then I said, "Oh that is right." Faith Maria said, "Tonight we will teach you how to get love without being married to a man." Since it is always dangerous to be married to a man, a woman can never have happiness. Then Fejér said, let me tell you all another story before we go eat our lunch and play in the basement. I then asked one of our girl servants, "Where is my mommy?" They told me that she had gone to the market with a couple of the other girls to get some special food for you young hungry angels. Fejér now began her story. "A newlywed husband and wife (a man and woman who just were married) went to London for their honeymoon (the special first night when the woman must let her husband do anything he wants or be hated by her mother, father, and friends and the marriage cancelled), and signed into a room at an inn. When they got to their room, they both noticed a bad odor (they could smell something bad). The husband called down to the front desk and asked to speak to the manager. He explained that the room smelled very bad and they would like another suite. The manager apologized and told the man that they were all booked because of a convention (all the rooms were reserved for a business meeting.) He offered to send them to a restaurant of their choice for lunch compliments of the hotel (free) and said he was going to send a house cleaner up to their room to clean and to try and get rid of the odor. After a nice lunch, the couple went back to their room. When they walked in, they could both still smell the same odor. Again, the husband called the front desk and told the manager that the room still smelled bad. The manager told the man that they would try to find a suite at another hotel. He asked every inn in the area, but every inn was sold out because of the convention. The manager told the couple that they could not find them a room anywhere, but they would try to clean the room again. The couple wanted to see the sights and do a little game of cards anyway, so they said they would give those two hours to clean and then they would be back. When the couple had left, the manager and all of housekeeping went to the room to try to find what was making the room smell so bad. They searched the entire room and found nothing, so the house cleaners changed the sheets, changed the towels, took down the curtains and put new ones up, cleaned the carpet and cleaned the suite again using the strongest cleaning products they had. The couple came back two hours later to find the room still had a bad odor. The husband was so angry at this point, he decided to find whatever this smell was himself. Therefore, he started tearing the entire suite apart himself. As he pulled the top mattress off the box spring he found a dead body of a woman." Ruth started by asking, "Why do so many men like to kill women?" Faith Maria then said, "Because they are smaller than men, so by beating and hurting them it makes them feel stronger." She knew this from being beaten a few times by crazy men. I was now getting very angry and said, "Someday I will punish the bad men." Fejér then said, "Indeed you will, my great master." I then looked at her and said, "Will you promise me you will try to savor, the location I really love?" Fejér said, "I shall try so hard to bring you any joy for me you desire, my master."

Fejér then said, "Let me tell you another story about bad men."
Ruth asked, "How many stories are there about bad men?" Fejér
then said, "Thousands my dear, thousands. Here is a story my
wonderful mother told to my friends and me when I was about
seven years old. You can imagine I was scared to death . . . A
woman and her husband were on their way home from somewhere
one night, and suddenly his horse died. It was about one in the
morning and they were completely alone in the middle of the
nowhere. The husband stepped out of the carriage, saying
comfortingly to his girlfriend, "Do not worry, I'll be right back. I
am just going to go search for some help or buy a horse. Lock the
doors, though." She locked the doors and sat restlessly, waiting for
her husband to come back. Suddenly, she sees a shadow fall across
her lap. She looks up to see . . . not her husband, but a strange,
crazed looking man. He is swinging something in his right hand.
He sticks his face close to the window and slowly pulls up his right
hand. In it is her husband's amputated head, twisted horribly in
pain and shock. She shuts her eyes in horror and tries to make the
image go away. When she opens her eyes, the man still being there
was grinning crazily. He slowly lifts his left hand, and he is
holding her husband's marriage ring. He then beats and breaks the
window of the carriage and pulls out the woman by her hair,
scratching and cutting her face. When he got her out, she fell to the
ground crying from all the cuts on her face. Her clothes were
ripped. He pulled her hair into the woods and then tied her hands
around a tree. He then put a rag in her mouth so if she would
scream no one would hear her. He then opened wide her legs and
tied them to other trees. Now he cut off all her clothes. She now
knew what was going to happen. He then did what she thought he
was going to do and raped her. When he had received all the
pleasure he wanted, he put a rope around her neck and tied her
hands behind her back. He then raped her again, that is when a
man puts his 'down there' into your 'down there.' It hurt her each
time, and afterwards he beat her each time. His friends paid him
money so they could violate her also. She was horrified the next
day when she saw them bringing her husband's body in. They cut

him up into pieces and cooked him in front of her and all sat down and ate him. She was now horrified and did not know what to do. That night, she found a small branch on the tree broke it and slowly was able to cut the rope. She immediately went for this evil man's butcher knife, which he kept in his outside shed. As she got one in her hand, a dog jumped on her. She immediately thrust the knife in the dog and then cut his throat, so he could not whine. She then saw a bow with some arrows. She grabbed them, then ran up the nearby hill, and made her a small camp where she could see everyone who went past her. In the morning, she found a stream and cleaned the old blood from her skin. As the stream ran down hill, she could see some dogs following the stream away from her. She thought she was safe until she looked over and saw a man following his dog straight to her. She calmly placed her arrow into her bow and when he was about five feet below her, she shot him straight in his head. She then grabbed her knife and once again stabbed a dog as he was about to bite her. She now knew this place would not be safe, so she started thinking about which way to go. These hillbillies were everywhere. She heard a noise behind her and in fear ran as fast as she could further up the hill. She paused to look back and saw that it was a rabbit. She hid in the brush to catch her breath. She now knew that the men with the dogs would catch her unless she had a miracle. However, no miracle was coming. She was also very hungry and knew she had to eat something to keep her alive. She looked around and saw an apple tree. She searched through them and started eating as fast as she could. She could feel the sugar from the apple flowing through her body. She grabbed a few more of them and started running again. As she was running, she slipped on a branch and could feel her leg in pain. She could only hope now. She wanted to get the leg in a stream so the water would help with the swelling and infection. She saw a stream a little ways up the hill, hopped over to it, and rested her leg in the cold fresh water. Her heart was now pumping harder as the cool wind and cold water was dropping her body temperature. She now thought about how her life had changed. Last night she was riding with her husband in a nice carriage on their way home from enjoying a good evening. She was pure for her husband, with only him ever doing the marriage thing with her. She loved him and he loved her. Now she had been raped by about ten ugly beasts. She had watched these sick things eat her husband. It was only a matter of time before they caught her. She looked at her knife and thought about killing herself, yet she did not have the courage. She could only hope that some civilized people would be on a hunting trip and find her. As night started to fall, she felt very weak from the constant pain. Then in a flash, three of the beasts ascended to her. Immediately they picked her up and started tying her. She was too weak to fight them. They then put her on a large tree trunk with a dog also tied to it. She could not move and if she tried, the pain from her injured leg made it impossible. Very early the next morning, they all came to get her. They laid her on the ground and each raped her. They knew her leg injury was going to disable her for a while. They had planned to work her hard in their small rocky gardens; however, that no longer proved to be viable. The men complained that the sheep and horses were better than she was for sex. They then tied her up to a tree and decided to beat her to death with their special whip that they used to tenderize animal flesh. Each lash cuts with many small razors attached to it. She soon died and they feed her to their dogs. They had made one big mistake. In their rush to capture her, they forgot about the carriage, and soon some people who were traveling back to the same hometown, they had slept in a hotel, saw the carriage and the bloody doors. They quickly rushed to their hometown, and told the sheriff, who alerted the crown that someone was living in his private hunting grounds. The crown sent 1,000 soldiers who killed all the hillbillies. All were amazed that they had lived there so long without being detected. Now everyone fears going into forests, for you never know who is living there." I told Fever that this story was very scary and asked her why so many people were so cruel to a woman. There is something very wrong about this." Fejér then told me that men have traditionally violated women only to satisfy their desires. The hunger becomes so great in them that taking and destroying is the only option. A bit of good news for you, the aristocrats seldom violate each other, and the men have freely violated their servants and disposing that threat." I then told her, "I am so lucky to have a daddy that does not do that, because I love all our female servants." Fejér then added, "We all love them too, as we all love each other in our sisterhood for we have made the blood oath. Let us look at our basement now. I then asked Fejér, "Who made the men like this?" She answered, "The same one who forbids us to drink each other's wine." I did not understand this so I just pretended that I understood it.

"Ann's daddy has remolded the basement for us," broadcasted Fejér. We all walked down into the basement. It now had a nice large play area with baby cribs and dolls and things to roll the babies in. It also had a nice table that we could eat. We walked down the long hallway with rooms on each side. I guess it had twenty-four more rooms, and it had many washrooms. Guess he thought that if we played in the mud, they wanted us clean before going upstairs. We had rooms packed with play clothes and toys. It was like a play version of our house upstairs. One part of the basement was blocked off. This is where we kept our burning wood. We played for a while having a lot of fun. Fejér played with us, as also did Faith. Laughter flooded through the basement as the lanterns gave us all the light we needed. We also had a nice library of fun children's books. There was one large room with little tables and all kinds of books, papers, a big chalkboard, maps, and other creative posters about parts of the body and the stars, with a desk in the front. The door to the room next to it was locked. I asked Fejér what was going on in these rooms and she told me, "Your daddy wants you girls to get some education called home school; it will be before you actually go to college." I then was curious about if we would all go together, especially with Joy and Faith Maria is so much bigger than we three younger ones. Fejér said that would be something that I should talk to my daddy about. I told her we could worry about that later. For now, it was time to have some fun. Fejér said we could go into one of the smaller rooms and lock the doors. They had a nice flat white strong sheet with a fence around it that we were told was a wrestling mat. Thus we said, "Sure, why not." We divided into the big group and my group. Fejér and Faith Maria removed their dresses and said to the rest of us, "What are you waiting for?" However, we all did not know what kind of game we were going to play, so we went along with it. It was nice for me, because when I saw them standing beside each other I could remember them flooding my soul with wine. It was as Fejér said, 'wine from heaven." Down went Fejér and Faith Maria immediately went down and started enjoying as Fejér now had her heart opened as far as they could go. The remaining four of us crowded around them, looked at this awesome event that was in progress. Faith Maria had absolute control and was pleasing Fejér. At this time, Fejér told Joy to come and rest with her. She wrapped her arms around her. Within minutes, Joy's rock hard trembling body melted and she then took both of her hands and started playing with Fejér's nice large milk jugs as Faith Maria moved her hand up opened Joy's wine bottle shaking it. Joy totally loved this. Then Faith Maria looked at me and said, "Ann, show Ruth and Mary what you learned today. Ruth and Mary lay down and let Ann make you real happy." We wasted no time. I told Ruth she could watch what I was going to Mary, and then I would share our wine with her next. Mary's body was rock hard out of total fear, of what was happening and not wanting to be the odd ball, because Faith Maria and Joy were doing it to Fejér, so it must be ok. I am slowly starting to open her wine bottle as Fejér told me; I searched each part and wriggled my bottle opener throughout her wine container. Her body, like Joy's, started to melt. She started to moan, and crying out, "I love you Ann, take all of me." Sadly since we were both four now, there was not that much to take, however what she had I took. When I finished, she just lay there smiling with a glow on her face as she took hold my hand and starting moving it around. That was fun yet I looked over at Ruth watching beside us and trembling. I got up and slowly escorted her body to the mat. Then I motioned for Mary to rub her hands massaging Ruth's rock hard body. She was now the only newbie and oddball. All of her sisters had enjoyed this, what looked to be, wonderful experience and was alive and so happy. She could see our spirits pulsate with a new power, a brick wall that had been broken down. Nevertheless, what would happen to her if she did not like this? Her young life would be ruined, she would be without sisters, have no friends, no home and no food. Her body started to melt as she grabbed hold of Mary and started kissing her as tears of joy exploded. This was a first for Mary also, who had seen Joy and Fejér kissing and Faith Maria and Joy kissing as if the capture each ones souls. If her two older sisters liked it, then it must be something good. They wrapped their arms around each other and kissed frantically. A kiss to us had a special meaning, as we all so much wanted to join with each other and form one body. We knew we were made somewhat the same, with a few exceptions, so what one enjoyed most likely would be enjoyed by the others. This was our special way of showing how deeply we wanted the others to enjoy themselves, and it created the deep satisfaction that we had created that joy. This was a joy, which could not be faked, or if so, we did not want to know how. I could taste her love releasing what they could as she swayed her body back and forth under my face. She was so limber that it actually took her about five minutes to regain control of her body. What a wonderful surrender and unification. I now asked them if they thought they could do it to me. They formed a wonderful team each working together to sip and they even liked to imbibe while kissing different parts of my unification entry. This felt wonderful, powerful, and explosive. My sacred parts were now theirs to enjoy and I enjoyed surrendering myself to them. This was what at that time we felt, the greatest act of proving we valued our club more than our current lives only to later discover that the actual surrender of your life was greater. However, Henrietta or one of the big girls told us we would never die. When I explained this to one of our girls (servants) she told me that there never was a person who died who believed they would someday die. We had now established a freedom among us, a freedom to be bonded forever with our bodies also united with our hearts and souls. We not only could talk in each other's minds we could share our sacred gifts making this public for our bond. After our wonderful experience, the three big girls let us sip on them. They had no more 'heaven's wine' to share; however, they did have bottles to mold with our sippers. It was now getting close for our dinning hour, so we had to get all dressed up for a nice formal evening. Fejér now stressed to us the importance of always locking our doors, for everything on the other side of that door would try to destroy us if they discovered our special warm secret. Some of daddy's friends wanted to meet the elite countesses at our house. They would be semi-formal, yet socially casually reserved. They would be allowed to smile some, to show their great comfort in being served by our family. Fejér now gave us another surprise as we helped dress each other. That was impressive to me, as girls usually are in a rush to clothe themselves first, we did not care about ourselves but about the most important thing in our lives, our other sisters. Fejér showed us a secret hallway that went straight to our room and came out behind one of our bookshelves. We would have never known this. She owed us which books to push on, and luckily, for me, they were on the lower shelves. She then showed us how to close the door behind us. She did the same at the door to our room. We all really thought this was so neat. We could go to the basement a private way. It was as our massive play area was in our room. We all started to put our gowns on with one temporary delay. Fejér and the big girls lay on my bed with their bottles opened and Fejér invited us three little lovers to their bottles, and spun them easily. That was fun, yet we could only do it for a few minutes. When we finished I stuck my finger into my mouth to get any 'heavenly wine' off my finger and into my system. Ruth and Mary saw me do this and quickly did it themselves, as we all did when eating some sweets. As we all finished, we quickly bathed a new way. Everyone cleaned and put lotion on someone else. Our new rule was that we could not touch our own bodies. This was another method for bonding of our sisterhood, womanhood, and maybe even motherhood, if we could figure a way to make babies without being owned by a man. The four countesses put on their lovely gowns, which were of a royal Persian style and not English style. Countesses were allowed to wear exotic elegant gowns from royalties throughout the known world, since they made up a part of the inner circle for the wives of other kings. Most kings would ordain them as Princesses before they married a Prince from another nation. The kings believed the countesses' strong family bonds would help secure favors in the future relations between the nations. The Danes were well known to work with the formal Vikings and trade for things that most of Europe did not know, and if the Danes had it, my daddy could and would trade for it. He made sure that all his countesses, for he had adapted them, in promise as sisters to me, would look delightfully. The seating ritual was different now that we had guests here to dine with the four countesses. Over the past almost two years, the countesses had become rather popular in our part of England. Father told us, he did not want the countesses to become too popular, least King James 1 attempt to marry them. Although he was single, all women avoided him not trusting his sanity to hold. Faith Maria looked so supreme with her necklace and jewel trimmed purse that even our new male servants fainted when they first saw her. Was this the same being that was pushing dolls around with her little sisters and jumping on the wrestling mat in the basement? How could this be? They themselves chatted with their sisters and the other girls in the kitchen, asking them if this was real. They laughed at them and said, "Brothers, you have not seen anything yet." Joy, Mary, and Ruth all had the same gown fitted for their various bodies. This time we all stood against the wall with our guests at the end closest to the kitchen or farthest from the hallway entrance, our countesses would enter. We of course were the hosts of the countesses and would be the first to greet. They each descended our wide stairway one at a time with Faith Maria at the end. They each stopped in front of us as we each bowed to them, one at a time, and kissed their extended hands. As I kissed their hands, I could also taste their 'heavenly wine' they had shared with me. It was easy for all to see that the countesses favored me, which brought great pride to my father when they told him, "Your Ann will have a great reputation among the royals of Europe." As that story spread through England, my reputation grew. We finished our bowing as they entered and immediately sat at their assigned seats of privilege. My daddy had told them where to sit in advance, so it would look like a normal event in our home. One of our male guests fainted when he kissed Faith Maria Maria's hand. Daddy told me that was the first time that our little muddy girl was going to be an elite countess. The evening went smoothly, as the guests extended every form of courtesy to these famous countesses, their home nation never yet published, as it is the custom for the kings' courts to conceal that information. The guests asked normal questions that England was curious about. The countesses answered the questions completely in accordance with the tale so far and within complete pre-royal constraints, with Henrietta telling them what to say. The evening finished as we all retired for the day. We had a new spirit as we all snuggled into our favorite positions in this one large blob of seven females (Henrietta joined us). Looking at us, you would not know so many were in our group. Our bodies molded into one container of a single heart and spirit of a rock hard sisterhood. Henrietta had heard of our new adventures today and wanted to show the countesses and me her wonderful skills during our long nightly class in her time protected zone. Her skills were like a pure exotic lotion as it tangles each part of our 'well shared wine bottles.' She also let us enjoy her wonderful well aged and cured wine bottle with wine we could not get enough as the five of us worked her over all at once. She overflowed Faith Maria and me with her 'unbelievable wine'. I could not believe that so much of this precious liquid could be shared. She actually placed Faith Maria into another realm as she could only become vertiginous in Henrietta's arms crying about how much she loved Henrietta. Henrietta loved all of us and worked so patiently and diligently to improve us. We were much better trained than any prince was or princess was, to such perfection that a guest would faint as his lips touched Faith Maria Maria's hand. During the remainder of our class, Faith Maria Maria could not let her go as she explored all of Henrietta and asked a strange question none of us had ever conceived. She wanted to know if she could marry Henrietta and be her slave for the remainder of her life. She figured that if marriage made a woman the slave to a man, then would this not make her a slave to Henrietta. Henrietta told her that the world would not allow this and would execute her painfully. Faith Maria then asked if she could have Henrietta's name as part of her name. This flattered Henrietta to the point that she cried, saying that no one had ever loved her so much. I then asked, "Why do we not change her name to Henrietta Maria?" All of us agreed as Henrietta asked Faith Maria one more time if she knew what she was doing. She told her she knew this was something that she wanted and begged Henrietta never to stop bringing her to her nighttime free zone. Henrietta said, "Rest assured you who now have my name shall be a cumbersome part of me that I shall never struggle to be free from." We always saw those holding hands, kissing or siting on each other's lap all the times we were in Henrietta's nighttime world. Fejér later told me that this was something very strange that she only heard the witches did, thus if Faith Maria was discovered, she would be burned at a stake as was Joan of France. I had another strange feeling that this custom was something that I approved of, yet since I was still a little girl I had better keep my mouth shut. Henrietta was also able to recharge our wine reserves, which added another great touch to our nighttime training and explorations. Henrietta now wanted so much to return to our home. Henrietta now asked me if I would ask my daddy for 'Henrietta Maria.' The argument would be how Henrietta was a strong influence on Faith Maria and how I missed Henrietta. I would of course run this by my mother with such a good little girl's plea. If mommy knew that inside I was rolling some of Faith Maria Maria's 'heavenly wine', she would be surprised and devastated. It probably would be better to keep her from getting surprised. Henrietta's nighttime world now included Fejér who would always beg to tag along with us. She always pleaded for us to forgive her for wanting to be with us always, in which we always thanked her for sharing our love. The next morning I came into mommy's room as she was still sleeping, after daddy had left to manage his enterprises, and jumped in bed beside her. It is amazing how a child can always join their mother in bed without a response from her, as if she knows even in her sleep who has invaded her bed. I think they pretend not to know so they can sneak some more sleep. As she saw me, she reached out, pulled me into her arms, and started kissing me, and telling me how much she wanted to serve me. She then asked me if I was ok. I think it must have been close to the time she wanted to wake up. I told her I was and that this was because I missed her so much lately. I did not want to overdo it, since she now was becoming a larger part of the social circle in England, the aristocrat that shared her house with four countesses, as the rumors flourished were from different countries and showed the international prestige that they commanded. She told me that my mother had to do this to protect my friends. I gave her a big kiss and told her thanks and that I understood. I then told her I missed Henrietta. She asked if Fejér was not taking care of us. I then told her that, "Every ounce of blood in Fejér was dedicated to us, and that was not the problem, it was the emptiness that I had filled with the memories of Henrietta." My mother told me, "Ann, I have made every attempt to get Henrietta back, however she must care for her brother and his family, which is blood and I could never demand that she return. She knows that every time she wants to visit, I send a carriage and bring her here." I told my mother, "I understand. What if I added Henrietta's name to one of my friends, since I own them?" She then asked me, "Which one do you want to rename and I told her, "Faith Maria to Henrietta Maria, since she is thirteen and to one that is closest to Henrietta's age." My mother then replied, "Ann that is a brilliant idea, since royalty commonly change their names when becoming of age. I will tell your daddy to approve it." I then gave her a kiss and pretended to go back to sleep. She woke me about thirty minutes later, as the girls were coming in to dress her. Afterwards, we all enjoyed our daily activities, saving our wine drinking for our other world and reducing our chances of being caught, especially since the servant brothers were taking every opportunity to be close to us. I told Faith Maria that my mother had approved my request for her name change and she told me, "I will give you some of my special wine this afternoon." I thanked her very much. Our tasty afternoon soon passed, as we got ready for our family room picnic tonight. This was a special day as we saw through our records. Ruth, Mary, and I could already read perfectly thanks to the so many years of excellent teaching by Henrietta on her special road. We now would read stories in our world now, because we were tired of the real stories that the big girls would tell us because they were so scary and filled with killing, which we were terrified of now. In books, we could check out the pictures first, and then if they looked safe, we would take the chance. You always had to be careful because adults always liked to put tricks in the stories.

Our family picnic nights in the family room had always been special to us, as 'our' parents completely relaxed and we have to share each other's lives. Of course, we kept our special secrets. I completely shared my parents with my sisters. Mommy and daddy were reserved about this initially; however, I would yell at them making them call my parents mommy and daddy. Initially, it was like a special title, notwithstanding it later became as if it were real, which I wanted so much for it to be genuine. My need for them to have parents was just too prodigious. My parents detected this and enjoyed it. Daddy had some news for us tonight. The king's brother in Denmark reported that some "reformers" were investigating all his previous work submitted to his brother's court. He did, however have many corrupt friends in France and thus had arranged, for a fee of course, to have the countesses nation be France. These friends of his were able to get the older girls documented as attending prestigious schools, registered in churches and 'fictitious parents' with records placed through ten of the king's courts, covering all aspects of life, to include being registered as attending many special events in the king's palace. These papers were so amazing; father could only shake his head in unbelief. The paperwork they gave dad to register them in England was comprehensive. He would go to London to register them. It was easy to justify the change, since it was common practice to register them from other nations for security and warfare reasons.

We were all so excited, yet little did we know that London was the best place to register Henrietta Maria. This simple act lost Henrietta Maria from us, for one greater than us would snatch her from our hands, and leave our small sisterhood with one less member during the daytime. However, before we lost her from our house, we were lucky enough to celebrate her 14th birthday, and celebrate we did as this angel left all at her party with memories of beauty to last them a lifetime. Daddy once again had her dressed like the best countess in all of Europe. That night over twenty men fainted when she allowed them to kiss her hand. Many painters were making fast drawings so they could go back to their studios and paint from their memory. Most painters did not want anything in the background to take away from the French countess Henrietta Maria. She allowed all who went through her line to kiss her hands and for the females who bowed, she let them kiss her hand, which told them she had respect for the women of England. This rocketed her fame and support through all the female rumor networks. There was one man, poorly dressed who snuck in the line. The other noblemen ignored him and allowed him to stand in line, knowing this great countess would not permit him to kiss her hand. Contrary to their belief, she stuck out her hand. Before this man kissed it, he asked, "Are you sure that one as low as I could kiss the hand of one so mighty?" She answered him with grace and dignity, "Are not we all low?" He kissed her hand just in time for the hotel managers to start hitting him and grabbed him to throw out of the ballroom. Henrietta Maria demanded that they stop, saying, "Do not hurt him, for so many like him allow such greatest as me to have our great honors. Give this man some of the food from my plate that he may tell all I shared with him." Every person in that ballroom stood in shock and amazement. Many then understood that the truly great ones also honored all people. Thus, they would be loved by all people, which gave them the loyalty they needed to save their nation during great times of tribulations. She then asked him, what is your name?" He told her, "Many call me Charles" and immediately with her food in his hands walked out the front door. We could hear many saying, "How dare he disgraces the King's name. Once the ceremonial seating's was finished, my daddy said to her, "Henrietta Maria, I am so proud of you and your courage to stand up for all poor people without fear. I can now say that you someday will have a greatness that so few will ever attain." Mommy spoke to her also with tears in her eyes, "My great countess, you have filled my inner soul with great pride. I can only dream of the greatness you showed us tonight. I could never be that brave, to show the mercy on the ones our family has come to love so much. You are the queen of my heart." If she only knew, what she had spoken in this world. Yet, we all did not know that our Henrietta Maria was going to be pulled away from us, and escape the jaws of death by a mere hair.

CHAPTER O4

DISCOVERING OUR NEW QUEEN

Our parents were not the only ones who were proud of Henrietta Maria. Henrietta also praised her, as also did Fejér who had the honor to experience this. Fejér asked her, "Henrietta Maria, why did you do that?" She said that her sisters had filled her up with so much love, and that if it were not for Ann, she would have been much lower than that high man, according to birthrights was. I cannot ever be able to pay Ann back for her warm heart in loving the ugly poor, so how could I not love the ugly poor, although I wish his name was not so close to the name of our treasure house Charley." At that time, Charley jumped into her lap and licked her face. She then continued, "Is this not love from a little heart, then should not we who have big hearts also not love more, because Charley is not afraid to love those who are different. Now I jumped into her lap and started kissing her face, promising to love her for eternity. She gave me such a wonderful hug. It was so strange, because now that she was fourteen and deeply in love with Henrietta, she seemed to have changed, yet she had not discarded any part of her inner self. If she had you in her heart, you grew with her. Joy, Mary, and Ruth have also matured so fast, with Henrietta's love pulling them higher. Yet they never forgot they were real sisters and had struggled hard for their chance in life and chance that I was dedicated to ensuring they got. Now, a special time I enjoyed was our singing songs in the family piano room in which one of the girls would play for us, while the other servants would dance with the 'brothers.' We have started feeling ourselves attracted to some brothers who served us with their true hearts and of course one of their sisters watching. They now, could feel the special spirit and harmony in our homes, and had never seen a house where the master and his wife would not only associate with them but occasionally would help them with their duties. They now willingly shared the burden of our confidence and security. Our songs would roll, as we would give the entire house, including mommy and daddy, a show each week. Henrietta taught us the songs and added special parts to them that would have my parents standing up and clapping. How very special and exciting family times. The boys, while on their routine duties, one day came into the house with a woman screaming and trying to bite and kick them. We sisters were downstairs playing, except for some strange reason Henrietta had called Fejér and Henrietta Maria up to our bedroom. The remainder of us stayed in our bright gray basement and took care of our babies, giving them their daily bathes, and stroll around the basement in their nice outside clothes. We also pretended they could talk and would create their conversations. We actually learned a lot about ourselves by doing this. With all the screaming and noise from the kitchen, we decided to break the rules of the house, which were that we must stay behind locked doors, and went up into the pantry and watched this crisis unfold. They finally tied the woman's feet and arms securing her to a wall beam. Then we walked into the room, Ruth and Mary ordained in bright spotless white, and to the servant's scolding watched the rest of the events unfold. The servants begged us never to take such a chance again, for if we were to get hurt it would crush their hearts and destroy their lives. This woman, who we called the crazy woman, started screaming, "I have watched you people and seen the social laws you have violated. I shall see you all burned by fire, and you shall suffer like my husband William did suffer." The girls told her William had to die for being disloyal and harmful to Ann. Crazy Woman argued that, "William served you as no other served you and you discarded him to get someone younger and people who would dishonor England and hide your terrible secrets. You are all truly witches, especially the way you women kiss each other." This is when we knew that if we left her alive in our lives would be in danger. Then Henrietta told me, in my mind, demand that the sheriff be summoned, in which I did. A couple of the girls went and got the sheriff. In the meantime, Henrietta Maria was dressed extremely formal and waiting in our receiving room with its bright white walls, which helps in promoting an image of honesty, for the sheriff to report to her.

The sheriff and about thirty deputies came rushing to our house on horseback. They could take no chance of an incident in our house with its four famous countesses. The boys had gagged crazy woman's mouth, so no one could her words. The remaining girls escorted the sheriff to our receiving room. Two guarded the doorway while two entered, bowed, and when given the command to rise, reported to the countess, "Oh great and honorable Countess Henrietta Maria, the sheriff has arrived by your command." The countess then said, "Have the sheriff escorted in." The sheriff, now trembling, entered the room, and bowed and when given the command to rise, reported to the countess, "Oh great and honorable Countess Henrietta Maria of France, how may I humbly serve you?" The countess then stuck out her hand, as the sheriff rushed on his knees to kiss it. The countess now spoke to the sheriff saying, "You shall find a woman tied in the kitchen. My servants found her hiding in my room with a knife. She confessed to us that her goal was for me to lose my life. I then commanded that she never again speak. Must I call upon the King of France for justice or may I call upon you?" The sheriff, still on his knees answered, "On behalf of King Charles 1, I beg that you permit us to take the life of this terrible beast." The countess then replied, "I wish to see her as her life departs so I can call upon St. Peter to forbid her entry." The sheriff then said, "Your wish shall be our command." The deputies tied her to a beating pole on one of their wagons that just arrived and they started beating her with their razor beating whips. She surrendered her life in a few minutes. They lowered her body, cut off her head, and showed it to our countess, who now wore a red scarf to show her heat of revenge. When she saw the head, she put her hand on it and yelled, "St. Peter, forbid this entry." Seven deputies fainted upon hearing this. The power in her voice, as Henrietta had coached for a long time to perfection, radiated in her command, as if she were truly talking to St. Peter. This also hinted that she was Catholic, as Catholic's were now being discriminated against in England. Henrietta had her do this to reinforce her role as a French countess with no fear, for no one would dare discriminate against a countess, especially one who is now fourteen, which is a ripe age for many young princes to become interested in escorting her. The deputies then put the remains of her slashed body and head in a cheap bag to be buried with garbage. Many feared touching her in case when St. Peter dropped her to below, she would drag them. The countess then waved her hand across her body that meant it was time for this event to end. She rushed inside, had the girls lift her out the gown and in her body garments rushed downstairs to play with her sisters. The girls had rushed to cover the eyes of the boys. Henrietta Maria told them not worry about it; all who lived or worked in this house was part of her family, which she loved, and belonged to her heart. The girls and their two brothers were awed at how a great one of so mighty words newfound power could instantly turn into a child playing with her sisters, half freely exposed with no worries. It just kept reinforcing the greatness of living in this house, as they too received special honors among the other servants whom they were acquaintances because of their honor of serving countesses. A countess represented the absolute purity of the human race. If they were walking outside and it began to rain, men would rush to the ground in front of them so they could walk on their backs and have no dirt touch them. Few knew that these countesses loved to wallow in the mud. The servants in this house knew greatness was here, and greatness was there, however it was in the one they least predicted yet was the foundation that the others launched. Each wanted the other to do better and worked hard to advance the others. Henrietta Maria usually had her sisters with her or at the least Joy who would be the next one to reach age fourteen. I was able to live their lives with them, and we wanted to make sure we did not lose what we had. We only knew of one way to keep what we had and that was to share and love our servants. We continued our tradition of helping them at least one hour per day. Our servants had trouble with this, claiming that their greatest reward in life was that of being able to serve us. We would look at them and say, "Tell us how we can serve you now." This humbling gave us a greater sense of worth knowing that we were repaying them for so much love they always gave us. We were all locked so tight. Yet that bond of oneness was going to take its first big hit.

Daddy came home late one night with a couple of men and rushed into his downstairs den. We could hear them screaming and arguing. Then daddy sent one of the girls to get mommy. He spoke with mommy for a few minutes and then mommy took one of the girls with her upstairs and sent another girl into daddy. Then that girl came out with tears in her eyes and asked where Henrietta Maria was. She then found her and escorted her to my daddy. As she returned to the kitchen, where we were all now in shock, as all five of us huddled into our small ball and froze in total suspense. When the girl came into the kitchen and started to cry, we begged her to tell us why. She said she could not tell us because Ann's daddy has not given her permission. Then daddy opened the door and called for a girl to come to him. The girl who cried did not respond, so another girl proceeded. As she left the kitchen, we could see the sweat rolling from her tender body. She immediately entered my father's den and then she and Henrietta Maria rushed upstairs. We could hear Henrietta Maria crying. At this time, Fejér arose. I could see her face turn red. This precious container of 'heavenly wine' now looked mean like the crazy woman who was previously here. She rushed into my father's room and we could hear her screaming. Suddenly her screaming stopped and she rushed back to tell us not to worry. Then Fejér rushed upstairs to my mother's room first and then with my mother went into our room, bringing the girls with them. As they entered the room, Henrietta Maria was on her bed crying. That gorgeous face of the countess that men would faint to see her, was now a pitiful red swollen face with paths of stains from the tears that rolled from her face and her now wet hair from the stress consistent with a major event in one's life. Mommy asked her why she was crying. Henrietta Maria told her, "Daddy says he must take me to France and that my sisters cannot go with me." Fejér then said, "My dear precious gift from the heavens, this is not a bad thing." Then mommy added, "Your beauty has reached the King of France who wants to enjoy your beauty for a meeting in Chamford Castle." She then said, "My beauty is my curse, for inside I now feel ugliness and emptiness." Then Fejér asked her, "If I were to go with you, would you like that." She then said, "I would love that so much, yet can I take you away from Ann and my sisters?" Then mommy said, "Why do we not explain to them that you will be coming back to England and let them decide?" Henrietta Maria then asked Fejér, "Would that be fair?" Fejér told her, "If it be their will, then it would be our duty." Henrietta Maria then said, "Your comfort with me shall be the anchor to hold my ship through this terrifying experience. Fejér then added, "My sister, there are things worse than having a nation marvel at your beauty." Then Henrietta Maria replied, "Yet, I am from the poor, an ugly slum slut." Then my mother told her, "Now Maria, do not believe that for those who love you the most care not what you were but are thankful that you allow us to live inside your pure, clean, immensely rich heart." Henrietta Maria then added, "That is what makes our temporary separation hurt so much, for how can I leave those who love me so?" Fejér then said, "Because we who love you so want you to be recognized for what we know you are entitled, for we would hate ourselves if we selflessly took that gift from you." Henrietta Maria then loudly said, "Fejér, why can I never reject your great wisdom?" Fejér then said, "Because only men can reject me without effort." With this statement, we all three laughed as the heavy burdens seamed to break down somewhat. Mommy then told one of the girls to have Henrietta Maria's sisters assemble into the family room. She then went with Henrietta Maria and Fejér to speak with her husband. She instructed them to hold hands and hug a lot in front of them and lay their heads on each other's shoulders when such opportunities arose. They then entered the room. The men immediately stopped talking and prepared to give their undivided attention. They knew that this had to be given priority since mommy was the woman of the house and men would never deny her that right. She then asked my father that if Ann and the sisters approved the request for Fejér to accompany Henrietta Maria to France would he approve. She was careful to leave the other two men out of the decision making process since she had no control over them. Daddy then asked Fejér and Henrietta Maria if this was acceptable for them. They both told him it was their will, if the sisters approved it. Then daddy sat back, scratched his head, and finally said, "Let's ask the sisters." With this recommendation, Fejér hugged Henrietta Maria as tears flowed from both eyes. This was enough to melt the three men as they looked at each other fighting not to cry themselves. For few men could not feel the pain of a lady crying. Daddy then said, "You both shall come back to England or I shall ask Charles I to send troops in to free you." The three women now excused themselves and proceeded to the family room where four girls now sat frozen being tortured by the suspense. Mommy sat in the middle of three nice chairs that the girls had positioned. Before she began, she asked Fejér to call for all the servants to join us. They were all assembled in the kitchen and upon learning about their invitation rushed into the family room sitting behind the sisters, in the event the unknown news would require their immediate support. Mommy began by saying, "Young ladies, Henrietta Maria has been offered an unbelievable opportunity for a young countess as herself. She has been invited to Chamford Castle in France as a guest to one the king's social events and to remain for a short period with meetings that daddy will also be attending to insure she returns to England." Fejér then added, "This is an opportunity created by the people of England's love for your sister. Our people have bragged to the King of France about the beauty of one of his countesses. She will not go unless you girls approve and you allow Fejér to escort her." I looked at Fejér, mommy and the countess and could feel that this was a great thing for her. I thus ran to her and put my hands up, which notified her that I wanted to be picked up and held by her. The instant that I could wrap my arms around her I started kissing her and telling her that I loved her. I then told my countess, "I know that you would give your life for each of us, thus we should give you the life you are entitled. Promise to keep me in your heart." Our countess started kissing me, and as tears rolled down her face, she told us, "My sisters are my life and I could never forget my sister, for I shall always love you all." At this time, all my other sisters rushed to our oldest countess, and started kissing her. She had to drop to her knees so we all could reach her. I of course shared my position with my sisters. Then mommy asked us, "What say the sisters of Henrietta Maria?" I told my mommy, "We want our countess to receive this honor that we give her every day of our lives. We plead that Fejér be with her, thus ensuring her safety. If something were to happen to her without Fejér beside her we could never forgive ourselves." Then mommy said, "I know it is hard to share your loved ones with people you do not know. I am proud of the love you sisters have for each other, based upon giving and reframing from being selfish. Now, will you sisters take our countess to her room, help her pack and make her beautiful for the people of England." We escorted her to our room and we all worked hard along with Fejér to make sure England did not forget the countesses return of King Louis XIII. Mommy reported to daddy that the girls had approved the departure of both. Daddy and the two other people released a loud cheer. The power they gave us little sisters was astronomical. They gave this power because they wanted to insure we had a happy childhood and maintained the sanctity of our individualism and synchronization, a gift they had to surrender during the beginning years of their lives. The men continued to talk, in front of mommy, as if she was not present. This gave mommy some added peace of mind, as daddy would stop every few minutes and asked her for input on a part of the subject they were discussing. Then in a short time, one of the girls knocked on the door. Mommy answered it, and the girl whispered in her ear. Mommy, then peaked out into the hallway and with a stammering voice announced, "Gentlemen, the Countess Henrietta Maria." She then entered the room and all gave her the ceremonial bow. She said to them, "You may rise." Henrietta had taught her all the proper protocols and how to refuse to respond unless they were rendered. She was not involved in the separation discussions, since they would still share their nighttime world. I could see an added peace of mind come over daddy. He had been distressed when the man who got him the countess's papers reported that the courts of King Louis XIII had discovered their cover up and reported that the King wanted to discuss this with them. Their time was now starting to run out, thus daddy motioned for his carriage to be brought to the front door and for his guest's wagon to be brought forward. He would escort the countess and the other two men would be their guards. We all said our goodbyes and I told my daddy, "Make sure you return to your girls." He assured me that we could not get rid of him that easily. The girls helped our countess into the carriage, which had its insides dressed to the nines. Daddy saved this carriage for escorting the countesses. We all surrendered our kisses and said our goodbyes taking care not to disturb the countess's make up. They then start proceeded to the dock when 300 soldiers came rushing up. Their leader said to daddy, "The King has ordered the countess be escorted to the royal dock." Mommy and daddy were now stunned. This game was for real now. The neighbors on both sides of our street were all in their front yards looking at what they thought would be a great historical event. The poor people on the other side ran to hide. For them the King's soldiers meant pain and punishment. Our convoy then proceeded straight to and through the middle of London to the nearby port. In London, both sides of the streets were crowded with people. Our carriage had a removable top roof thus, the countess asked daddy to open the roof. She then stood on her seat, popped the top part of her body through the roof, and gave a royal wave to the crowds. London was now a city packed with the thunder of the people's cheers. Now many of the King's knights escorted this countess. My father and the brother to the King of Denmark were astonished. How did this craving develop? My dad then thought to himself, "Oh my God, these people have no Queen; they are looking for some national image to fulfill that role. With the King's soldiers and knight escorting them, only fueled the fire. With Henrietta Maria gives them a royal wave, their hunger increased, as they could find no way to fill that emptiness in them. She was their image of beauty, purity, love, honor, justice, chastity, and hope for new children born into not only her elite circle but also even the people belonging to the poor and sick circles. To have such beauty and dignity escorted by their King's Knights and Soldiers of the King of France, borrowing what was his according to court documents, was a once in a lifetime event. Many fell to the ground, in front of the tents they had lived in to get a good position, crying out, "We love you mighty countess." Nations are strange when selecting an icon. There are no rules. They truly felt that she cared for them, for why else she would expose herself trusting them, an act seldom seen in a royal carriage guarded by so many. That can only be from her Faith Maria and understanding of them, and unquestionable evidence that she was a leader, willing to stand face to face with what many considered dangerous. No human could be all that the people thought she was, yet for that discretion, she could easily be forgiven, for no human had ever walked that great. She was the closest thing they ever had seen in the image. I do believe that if someone told them she was really a dirty poor slut, they would forgive her, yet that Cinderella was buried deep in history, for now it was the "Countess Henrietta Maria. She was never a slut to me; she did what she had to in order that her sisters could survive, and by doing that she gave me three additional gifts of love, for which that alone created a debt that I may never be able to repay. This in my mind proves everything the people were saying to be true. Daddy did not know exactly how they were going to France, thus he had one of his ships also waiting. He was now glad he took the precaution, for if they were to wait at the port for any amount of time, all of London would be here honoring their 'national icon.' As they arrived at the port, 300 French soldiers were in a formation in which allowed us to drive safely to the ship. It was one of the King of France's ships. As we proceeded towards the massive gray ship, the soldiers retreated behind us. This was a show title. This proved to all that the lady in this carriage was protected by kings, yet also loved by all who served the kings. They quickly rushed the countess into the ship and within one hour were on their way to France. England also provided two ships as escort and protection until the English waters met the French waters, where two more ships that are French, provided protection all the way to the Le Havre port. There the countess and her three escorts were placed into a carriage and escorted by 300 of the King's soldiers to Paris and then to Chamford Castle. Three hundred seemed to be the magic number for her protection. Then Daddy started to wonder, for a queen only received 200 escorts. Any number 200 and above were reserved for royalty. Henrietta Maria was only a fourteen-year-old countess. It was nighttime when we reached Paris and the Countess received another wonderful surprise. Crowds had formed along the route with so many candles burning. The countess had her carriage stop when surrounded by this crowd. She had daddy and the people to put on top of the carriage. She stood up, raising her arm. The crowds came to an immediate still, not a noise could be heard among the crowds. She then yelled out, "Vous êtes des gens merveilleux." She told them that they were wonderful. Henrietta had taught her fluent French. She spoke these words with power. The crowds started cheering so loud that all in Paris could hear them. She had won this nation in just a few words and her willingness to expose herself to them unprotected. Even the soldiers were now cheering, for if anyone dare hurt this gift from the heavens they would not live to the next minute. The crowds would destroy them. The crowds now yelled back, "Vous êtes notre cadeau du ciel" which means, "You are our gift from the heavens." The French had taken possession of their countess. She belonged and was a part of them and their identity. Daddy and his friends carefully returned her to the ground, insuring she had no discomfort and that they touched her in only authorized places. These places were handled by Fejér. She whispered in the countesses ear, "We have to do this more often." The countess started laughing. She has not only held her dignity but added fun and laughter into her role. She also shocked the crowds when she gave each of her male 'servants' a kiss and Fejér a hug. This told the crowd that these servants were loved and trusted by her. She also showed them that those who served her had her respect. This heavenly saintly quality actually added to make her immortal. She then had them seat her as a shotgun beside the carriage driver. The soldier who was sitting there now marched in front of the convoy. Fejér seated her back to back with the countess, to add the expected additional protection. The countess continued to give the crowds her royal wave. Once a person had the assignment to escort the now "most famous countess in history," they would not relieve themselves, but would search for another way to serve and still be a part of history. The countess was within such a short time, actually less than thirty minutes in Paris was locked into the lives of these Parisians for the remainder of their lives. As they started to depart Paris, the countess and Fejér returned to the carriage and the soldier returned to his shotgun position. As they left Paris, it became apparent that the crowds had not ceased. Through the countryside, the rural population found itself forming on both sides of the road. Fejér told Maria that she would give the royal wave on her side and the countess could give her royal wave on the opposite side. It was easy for all to know where she was, even though her carriage was hard to see with so many people standing along the roads. All were careful not to touch the road, as he could alert the soldiers. The soldiers were relieved by the king's orders once they left Paris, however begged the countess to continue providing security. They told her, "Nous ne pouvons pas prendre un pari sur sa vie", which means, "We cannot take a gamble on her life." The countess gave her approval. The King's ministers were surprised to learn that the soldiers had volunteered to escort her. This told them that combined with non-stop cheering and lit candles for a far as one could see or hear the countess now belonged to France and to in any way defame her could start a revolution and even the possibility of war with England. The carriage entered the castle gates and stopped to unload the countess. She gracefully got out of the carriage and followed the castle escorts into the castle as her gang followed behind them. They all went to their chambers as the King has requested an early morning audience. They did sleep and in the morning were served breakfast. Then the Kings guards came to bring them to the king's judgment hall. As they wait to enter, they were still confused as to exactly why the King picked out these four to appear before him. Falsification of countess papers when no profit or commercial gain had deprived one unjustly was a matter handled by smaller courts. If they were defrauding the English no one cared, for it simply reduced the king's need to do it. They had never used the king's name so he should not be involved. Then a group brought in a guillotine. This now sends a Shockwave among the group as Henrietta Maria started to cry. Fejér now trembling held the countess. Daddy now told the group that his game was his fault and begged them to forgive him. He then looked at the Danish king's brother and said, I guess your head will be heading back to Denmark. The two men just looked at each other and started to cry. Henrietta Maria then told the group it was her fault, she said I had been nothing but a poor slut and the feeling of pure fame felt so good. It was so nice to take away their pain and give them hope. Fejér then told her, "My child, your heart is so pure the lord will let no bad thing come to you. Just pray for the rest of us.' Our countess now cried out, "Oh no, you and my father are my blood, I will beg for your pardon. I will give anything to me to those beasts." Fejér then said, "My child, you may not have to give everything, just enough to excite the buds." At this, she caused my daddy and his two friends to blush as she stuck both hands into the top of the countess's dress and lifted her breasts up. Then she placed some handkerchiefs under her breasts to lift them up. She now stood back and said, "My friends, does it now look mouthwatering?" Daddy said, "It makes me sad to be her father, for now I cannot compete for her fruits." Then our countess started to smile, reached over to my daddy, wrapped her arms around him, and gave him a kiss. She then told him, "Yet unlike those who may have the fruit, you own the tree." Fejér thought to herself, "How does she come up with the perfect solution each time." Daddy then said, "And since I own this tree, I shall make sure no one else cuts it down." She then kissed his cheek again and said, "That is why this tree shall always belong to you." Daddy then thought to himself, "I am so lucky to have so many wonderful daughters. This experience within itself was worth death, for death would only be a small payment on such a big gain. Moreover, to think it was little Ann who got the ball rolling. Bringing home those starving balls of walking mud and having the honor of seeing them grow so magnificent was a once in a lifetime experience." Then the doors opened as guards with swords came out and told us to go report to the king. They all then entered all dropped to their knees before the King and bowed. The King now said, "The one that is the countess, stand before me." Henrietta now rose and stood before the king. King Louis XIII then looked at her and said, "You look like one who is honest and pure. Tell me, are you a countess." She answered, "Many say I am; what say you?" The King then looked puzzled then stood up and said, "I shall ask you one more time, "Are you a countess?" She then said, "What do you want me to be?" He looked at her angrily and said, "I want your head in that guillotine." Henrietta Maria then broke out in tears saying, "How can you be so evil?" The King then asked, "How could I put a head so beautiful and young into a guillotine, I probably do better to behead those who force you to do evil things." The countess then stood tall, wiped away her tears and said, "To kill them is to kill me, for if you kill them, I will kill myself before your people." The King then said, "I shall ask you the third time, "Are you a countess?" She then said, "For you I am nothing but a toy to cause pain and to give you joy at my suffering, I might be better to be a dog." At this time his mother, Marie de' Medici entered from behind the King and began to yell, "Louis, how dare you torture this child?" King Louis XIII said to his mother, "She will not tell me if she is a countess." Marie then screamed at him, "Do you not know that no countess will talk about such things to a man, not even a king. That is the same as asking her to stand freely exposed in front of you. When she confesses this to a priest, as she must, that priest will immediately appeal to the pope that you are disgracing the aristocratic ladies." I shall beg her forgiveness. She then fell before our countess and beg forgiveness. She then said, "He threatened to behead me and my friends. God should punish him for that." Marie then said, "I shall confess to all the courts that you are my daughter. If he touches any in your group, I will personally deliver to you his head. I hereby today declare that when you presented yourself as a countess you were deceiving the people of Europe. You have been living a lie." Then did a hush fall upon all in the court. Henrietta could now see that the king's mother must be able to uncover all secrets. Her dome was now at hand. The King looked at me and laughed, "Liar, liar, your pants will be on fire. The countess looked over to Marie and said, "That which you must do to me, do quickly." Marie said, "Ok, let us begin. Call in all the ministers now. Furthermore, get this cursed guillotine out of here. Put in in Louis's chamber for our talk later today while the others kiss Henrietta's feet." Henrietta actually was thinking now she would be killed and the murder made to look like a mistake, to save them from a riot, and the people to kiss her feet as a sign of respect. Henrietta stood strong, her head hung down, and solid as a rock. Marie now said, "My daughter, why do you look so sad?" Henrietta Maria, "For I know my death and the death of those I love is at hand." Marie then yelled, "Child, why would I kill a Princess. You have been hiding as a countess when you were really a Princess. No one should die for that reason. I am going to declare you the daughter of Henry IV and myself and beg France to forgive us in hiding you. Henry's wish was that you be kept pure. However your pureness has become so famous that must now confess the truth." She then looked at Louis and said, "You and I are going to have a long talk," The King then spoke angrily, "Very well, however I demand that they will report to my chambers tomorrow morning. You may attend if you want. You must bring your own breakfast." Marie then said, "You who are the Princess's servants, rush her to my chambers and put her into one of my new gowns and paint her face as you in England do." The guards now escorted all of them to Marie's quarters. Inside the quarters, they all hugged and kissed the new Princess. Fejér then said, "How did you have the courage to tear the kingdom apart and be within a second away from losing your head as a countess to now being a true Princess." My daddy then added, "I heard it, I saw it, yet I cannot believe it, yet you not only saved our lives, you conquered France. If I start hugging you, do I have to stop?" Our new Princess looked at him and said, "Fear not that I will make you stop, for I plan never to let my master go." Fejér then said, "There you go again, you have just conquered France and care not, for all you want to do is be Edward's daughter." The princess then replied, "Is there anything greater than being an Ann's sister and having the same father that she has." They all just marveled at the depth and innocence of her mind. When she got something greater new, she always wanted to go back to where she was before. Born with nothing, beaten, starved, raped by so many, yet forever a servant of Ann and her pure love. She then added, "I know not how I can ever be greater than Ann." Fejér marveled at the truth of this statement, yet knew that Ann would swear she could never be greater than Henrietta Maria, or her special Faith Maria. We all rushed as we cleaned her and redressed her. She had no shame among those whom she loved. The men were shy and being conservative. She yelled at them, "If I can stand before a King and try to trade my life for yours, then why would I hide myself from you and not let you help me? I need your help now, stop being silly, I know my breasts are small but please forgive me for that and help me." All three men said, "Henrietta Maria, your breasts may only be fourteen yet they have in-between the large heart on Earth today." She then said, "Thanks guys, I hope you enjoy my freedom." Then one of the men who did the papers to make her a countess said, "Angel, your freedom has made my heart a prisoner." She then bent over and gave him a kiss. Soon they were done scrubbing and oiling her, massaging, and spreading lotions and perfumes on her. Fejér now was wrapping the female undergarments on her as daddy was putting the jewelry on her and the other two men were bringing her dress beside her.

Fejér then started working on her hair as daddy was putting her makeup on and the people were putting her dress on and then brushed the dust from her shoes. Like a team who had done this every day of their lives. They had her in her sunshine dress shoulders exposed, hair darkened and combed straight. Her power was shining through, clear elegance, and confidence. If you are powering you, do not have to overdo it. She now, with her servants stood behind the King's throne as Marie stood in front of the people. She began by saying, "The one who calls herself a countess and has come from England is not a countess." The crowd then started yelling, "She is true. She is true. We want Henrietta Maria . . ." Then Marie raised her hand and as all became quiet, she continued and said, "I too have failed to reveal the truth to you as commanded by your Henry IV of France. I gave birth to a baby girl. He decided to hide and protect her from the burdens of royalty. We kept it a secret from you and her. She however uses divinity and love to pull the people to her. I now declare on behalf of me and my former husband, King Henry IV of France that Henrietta Maria is my daughter and Princes." Then King Louis XIII came on the stage and said, "I do declare that my sister is of royal heritage and shall be now known as Princess Henrietta Maria. The crowd now broke into a loud roar as they all started singing. The Chamford Castle was now the center of celebration and Marie called all the garrisons to concentrate on the private royal chambers. It was now time for her to put on a special white and the gray toned dress when golden trim. The nation knew this dress had been worn by queens and elite royal functions for many centuries. As she reappeared with this epic dress of many legends with her mini crown, as a token for her being denied her royal heritage, yet King Louis XIII had a worried look on his face. His mother told him, "Do not worry; your sister is younger than you." The King told her that was not my worry, yet to think about the age I wish she were older than I was, then she could have these burdens. Then Maria said, "Do you understand why your father did this?" Louis then said, "Why did he not do it for me?" Maria said, "You were a boy, and your father wanted France to have a King and not a

Queen." Louis then said, "At least someone wanted me." Marie then said, "We .... I always wanted you." Louis then confessed, "If you would not have been here and off on one of your women stupid trips, I could have shamefully executed my own blood. How could you have done that to me?" Marie then responded, "How could I know that she would return from England and within a minute inside Paris win the love of our nation? I still wonder why she came here anyway." Louis then said, "I called her here to scare her and get her to do a great dead for our nation." Marie then shockingly asked, "What deed?" Louis then said, "Allow me to give her hand in marriage to a man from England." Marie then asked, "Which man of England would be worthy to take the hand of my daughter?" Louis XIII then argued, "At that time she was not your daughter, but a countess with papers that were not legal." Marie then asked again, "Which man of England would be worthy to take the hand of my daughter?" Louis then replied, "The King." Marie then said, "Of course, how could he deny her great beauty?" Then Louis said, "If I were to approve this, you would support it?" Marie then said, "What woman who has been the wife of a King would want anything less for her daughter?" Louis then were relieved and told Marie, "That was the intent of my meeting with her in the morning." Marie added, "I will ask her to attend and once you ask her, I will appear at your side." They both then heard a new load roar outside, as their highest minister was now introducing the new Princess and giving the proof. The minister then shocked all who were there when he began to talk, "I have today opened King Henry IV of France's sealed letter he had in his final tomb. This was specified in a letter he had in our official archives, which ordered to open if one come attesting a royal titled. He said that when that day came, to open his tomb and get the letter. We gave this letter to the church and our bishop gave us that divine right. They also requested that if she speaks to the people, she wears the holy outer garment, and that he is allowed to sit behind her show the people this was supported by the church. In the letter, he tells of how he had to give up a great gift from God, a child who resembled Marie. He said that the test was the birthmarks in her left eye, two special marks at three thirty P.M. and four P.M. from the pupil. This is the proof that she is in my blood and I pray that France will love her and give her the finest of royal rights. We only intended to hide her for the first decade of her life, and then to allow her to visit and regain some honors in privacy. Yet sadly, with the dangers in England, her appointed parents died of an illness and the baby was placed in an orphanage. We lost track of her after that, except that a couple of little means adopted her and one young girl. We sent spies all through England searching, since we could not notify the king, lest he execute her." The minister then said, "You people have suffered the loss of our Princess, who as we now know is one of great love for the people. I can only hope she will forgive her crown and people and agree to shake the hands of her people so they may verify the truth of her eye, a mark that cannot be created by any man. Princess Henrietta Maria, sister of King Louis XIII will you forgive crown and shake the hands of your people as a sign of forgiveness and speak unto them." The Princess now spoke, "My people and my crown, yesterday I felt the spirit of my father take hold of my body and I challenged my brother with such power that he commanded my head be cut off, only to be saved by my mother. I can hold to ill will towards my parents, for I have lived a truly wonderful life and grafted into a family straight from our heavens to love and care for me. Though they have no royal blood in their veins I will at any time until my death gives my life in their defense. For they have given me so much, made me aware of the ordinary people and allowed to love them. (At this, she had to pause as the crowds roared in excitement.) How can I hate or forget the wonderful love I have received. I once told a man, 'It is only through so many of you that one of me can be. If you can all love me, then I can love all of you. As your Princess, I shall hate all who hate you and only love those who love you." The crowds continued to roar as the Princess now stood before them giving a divinely appointed royal wave. Fejér, my daddy and both his friends joined in Fejér's chambers and watched to the crowds as they roared in hysteria over their new Princes. The roads from Paris were packed as so many came to see their new Princess. Fejér said, "A people will never give up their right to have their princess." Daddy added, "I have looked into Faith's eyes a thousand times and wondered what those two marks meant. I knew they had to mean something because they were so special. How could I have ever known that Ann, instead of bringing in a stray animal, she brings in a Princess of France?" Then the King of Denmark's brother said, "Nor how could I know that the papers you requested were of our royal duties. My brother shall have great honor when hearing what I did. For I will tell him, 'Something from above made me do it." The trip here was so long and the stress we all had did not bring out the best in us. I shall give back to you all money you paid me to do this royal duty. I shall do many great things you ask me in the future, as long as you are not disguising Princess from such great powers. The reward in the end justifies it, yet the flirting with death while doing it diminishes its attraction." Daddy then said, "I understand my friends, yet her great honor means we lose her bubbly little body wallowing and the floor with her sisters. That is a great loss for my family." Tears now rolled down his face, as Fejér now spoke, "We now know why she had such great noble wisdom, for it followed in her blood, and the royal spirits her. She is now one of the greatest royal family members not only in France but also in all of history. Her people loved her before she had her title. Millions would die for her as they now speak of her endlessly creating a legend that no human could ever live up to." They now want to see her on the stage as she was shaking people's hands. So many soldiers were lined behind the people shaking her hand. They were not there for her protection; they were there to catch the people as they fainted. So many were fainting; as they looked into her left eye, and then were overloaded when they received her heavenly handshake. She actually shook hands for three days with only small sleep periods each day. She said strongly to those who were caring for her, "If these people want to serve me, how can I not shake their hands and touch those who love me so." Unknowingly, all things she said were reported as the nation tried to learn as much as they could about their newfound treasure. Finally, she was able to stop shaking hands, later it was discovered that many from Germany and the Netherlands had made the journey to shake her hand. She was the hottest thing going in Europe, yet her fire was just getting ready to burn. She finally returned to her room, first stopping in to see Fejér, where she walked right in, without saying one word, dropped her dress, and clothing and immediately plopped on her bed and went straight to sleep. Fejér, not knowing she was in her room when returning from a dinning engagement, invited daddy and his two friends and a female reporter. As they all entered the room, there was an immediate hush, and then the female reporter replied, "The princess truly belongs to her loved ones. To shine in in front of so many and then return to your room and trust you with her body is the sign of her great bonding with those she loves. Fejér, do you have an extra blanket to put over her great beauty?" Fejér then put a blanket over her saying, "Our little yard ape is now a Princess." The reporter then asked, "Does she still play?" Fejér then answered, 'She has four sisters, three still very young that she loves with her entire soul. She plays with them, doing all the foolish things they ask, then when they stop playing she guards, protects and provides for them anyway she can, which in our home is simply asking one of the house cleaners. Yet she still makes sure they eat the proper foods, and controls the deserts and any other food that when in excess could make them sick. I try to help as much as I can, yet her ear is tuned to the hearts of her sisters." The reporter then asks, "How long are you staying in France?" Fejér said, "We came here by order of the King. We shall make audience with the King and do as he commands." The reporter then asked, "Can I use this information in a story about tonight?" Fejér said, "As long as you tell the truth, I will ask her to put her trust in you, for to say anything bad about her would be like cursing our God." The reporter then answered in great sincerity, "It will be so good that some may wonder if it is possible, which I can only answer yes. She can trust me as I search to discover the trust that she shares with her family. She has no shame among those who serve her, and will in an instant humble herself before them, not in her glamorous gowns, but in the clothing God gave her." This reporter left soon thereafter wanting to put together and share with her nation the greatness of "The humble one" a nickname that flooded France and fueled their love for their monarchy. Fejér and her companions each pulled up a chair and sat around the Princess looking at her. She had in such few years packed, a lifetime of memories for the family. Daddy said, "If she does not return with us, the sisters will be angry." Fejér replied, "Let them be angry if they cannot love enough to let her have the honor that is now, by her birthright duty to keep." After a few glasses of wine, the men departed to their chambers. Now Fejér put on a nightgown and lay down in her bed beside the Princes. Then about three A.M., soldiers came knocking on her door. Fejér got up to answer her door, having no idea why this time at night she would be disturbed. When she opened the door, she saw many soldiers and asked, "What service from me do you require?" At that time, she noticed some of the soldiers were crying. She then thought that maybe sometime terrible had happened. One soldier became brave enough to talk, and said, "Marie went to check the Princess in order to insure that all is well however, the Princess was gone. We have checked so many places and she still cannot be found. Will you help us?" Fejér replied with a big sigh of relief, "I will do better than help you, I will show you where my daughter is. Follow me." She took them back to her room and showed them the Princess. Fejér said, "The child is so exhausted and needs much attention and love to restore her depleted strength. She knows I will care for you with all my heart and my love that flows lives in her blood. I know everything about this child. Tell Marie that she will be made completely again, that she gave too much of herself in order to love the people of France. The soldiers put their hand under her nose to feel her breaths, and when they did, a great smile of happiness came over them, as they rushed to leave the room and waited for Fejér to come out. Fejér said, "Why did you rush to leave her room?" They answered, "Ma'am, she is a Princess and no man can be in her sleeping room while she is sleeping. We just had to for our nation, verify she was still alive. We shall report to Marie that her daughter or your daughter is being provided the best care possible and we thank God you are here to care for her. I do hope if you will permit soldiers to guard your doors, as they are also guarding the Princess chamber doors. With your permission we will depart." Fejér then said, "You may protect your Princess as you so desire." The Princess woke up two days later. Fejér had food waiting for her to eat. She slowly fed her and washed her with a tub of water she had placed in the room. All she had to do was say, "I need for the Princess", and in a few minutes she had it. When the Princess awoke, she was terrified. She reported to Fejér that Henrietta had appeared and told her she was angry. Fejér looked distressed when she heard this. She gave the Princess a total massage, rubbed oil, lotion, and perfume generously throughout her entire body. The Princes asked her to lie beside and hug her. She told Fejér that 'Too much was happening too fast. I miss so much the love I have for my sisters and Henrietta. She allowed me to share her name, yet now hates me. How long will it before my sister's turn against me?" Fejér to her, "Your sisters have the same blood as all you have; the blood of Ann. I shall search for the misunderstanding that Henrietta has. Once we get you back to a regular sleep pattern where you will be conscious, we will visit Henrietta and share our 'heavenly juices." The Princess told Fejér, "I have depended on so much in my short life and in all things you have surpassed my expectations. I also have always enjoyed your juices, wanting them still even after being in a relationship with Henrietta. Is that wrong?" Fejér then answered by saying, "Only if you deny your true heart then it would be wrong. We will talk to Henrietta about this, my lovely child." We must get you ready for a very important meeting today with your brother. "He has waited all the days you were sleeping, even coming into pet your head. I feel he truly wants to be your brother and has a hunger to put you into his life. Have you had any brothers before?" The Princess surrendered to a pale sad face and answered, "We had two brothers that our parents refused to sell. They always provided for them, telling us that as females, we were a burden and sons are an asset." Fejér then wrapped her back in her arms and started kissing her cheeks telling her, "That is so sad, yet now you have a brother given back to you." The Princess gave more detail to her earlier testimony, "I, for some unknown had no fear of my brother. Afterwards, I asked myself why I would be so stubborn to a man, who had a guillotine beside him ready for our heads. Something pushed me on. Poor person was blasted by his mother after she looked into my left eye. When she saw my so very rare birthmark, a mark that my previous father said made me defective and was the reason he tossed in my sisters in our sale, she instantly knew I was her daughter. She told me that only so very few people knew it, since they kept her so private. She can vaguely remember many different cold places, yet still cannot remember the King or Marie. She was now powerfully dressed to meet the king. She had her own style of clothing, almost half a millennium in advance. Her big thing was more with less. She refused to wear all the 'unnecessary extras.' She wanted a plain cloth with some variations, an economical, but powerful look. She enjoys sharing her female features. She was trying to show she was human, like the rest of the people. The glamour satisfied that creepy elite, the simplicity satisfied the humble poor. She never wanted to give up her origins of being humble poor. This put her defenseless self and sisters into the hands of a small child who led them all to love and absolute sharing. She told Fejér, "I can never give up you and my sisters, nor ever repay my huge debt for your love and bonding." Fejér told her, "Pursue your dream and those who truly love you will remain by your side. We shall now jump back into our mind time and have a sisters meeting after we find Henrietta." In the next instance, they were in the nighttime world calling for Henrietta. Something appeared in front of them with a terrifying beast beneath it. Fejér cried out, who are you, "I am the one called Baktalórántháza, whom you called Henrietta." The Princess asked, "What happened to you my love?" Baktalórántháza replied, "Call me not your love for I am hate only, and shall never have loved." Fejér then asked, "Why did you appear as Henrietta?" Baktalórántháza then replied, "I was sent by the queen of evil to destroy your sisters. Yet some unknown force protected them, even while in my nighttime world. My master wanted to know the source of this protection, which I could not find. I can only think it has something to do with your love. My master has tried to no avail to find the solution, yet this is the only thing she has met that will not reveal itself. My friend here is going to get your confessions today, for if you do not confess, your sisters shall suffer a torturous death." We were now all standing around the beast. The sisters started crying, and then I wanted answers. I first said, "It is not nice to have such bad creatures among us. Instantly, the beast vanished and Baktalórántháza fell to the ground where we all jumped on top of her, as Fejér started to tear off her wings. Baktalórántháza then was defenseless and begged to know, "By which power was the child able to destroy a protection beast of Lilith." Fejér then said, "The child is protected by a god in another realm who supports neither good nor evil in this realm. Another realm is trying to destroy her. She means no harm to Lilith. Tell your master to look deep in her heart as she will find this child hidden and secured deep within her." Baktalórántháza stood frozen for a few minutes, and then began to talk, "My master has found what you say to be true. She questions, 'how are you able to hide so deep inside her?' She also wants to know why she should trust you." Fejér then said, "Trust or no trust is not an option now, the child has done no evil that was not in self-defense to you. When the child is returned to her dimension in a few of your Earth years, all your questions shall be answered. Attempting to destroy the child is futile, and will only result in the termination of her and many of her daughters." Baktalórántháza then asked, "How do you know about the daughters?" Fejér then replied, "The gods of my dimension know all things even your future and shall protect the child and her sisters." Baktalórántháza stood froze again, then returned to normal and replied, "You can promise not to attack us?" Fejér then replied, "Have your master tell me, or you to me, those she wants to protect." Her master sent straight to Fejér the names and images as Fejér sent them through billions of small atoms back to her dimension. She received back a response, "Tell the one you call mother, she and her daughters shall have no violence from us, as long as this child is protected." Fejér shared the reception with

Baktalórántháza who transmitted it to the queen of evil, who replied, "That which you have requested shall be. I will also help protect the one inside of me." Baktalórántháza now looked over at the Princess and said, "If I could love, you would be the one. May you have a great life?" The Princess dropped to her knees begging Henrietta to return. Yet Baktalórántháza vanished and with her, all hope of a continued union with Henrietta. All the time that Baktalórántháza had spent with the sisters, she could never find out the identity of the growing child. The child's gods had provided a protection and concealment that none could penetrate, not even with her in their nighttime worlds. Our small group no longer had a nighttime trainer. The child's home dimension had prepared a new 'night time nanny' and she appeared in front of our group. The dimension did not want to take any chances with another from Earth, since the first one's identity was not discovered. Then appeared before them one whose name was Máriakéménd. She was frozen in the doorway and studying the children. The Princess remarked that she had some very special fabrics. Ann then asked her, "Are you here to be our teacher? You look like our servant India." Máriakéménd then answered, "The gods wanted me to give you a fresh look and did pattern my skin after the one called India to reduce your resistance. I want to be an cherished part of your league, and beg now for your love." She now removed her robe and sat down with her legs crossed in a mysterious way the sisters had never seen before. Ruth cried out, "Wow, do you see how she is sitting, that looks fun and yet painful." Joy then said, "I am looking at her thinking how good she can be with us." Máriakéménd now said to the group, "Touch me and do as you my masters, me and my body is here to serve you in all things. Then all of us, to include Fejér wrapped around have now laid her down, and enjoyed surrender of her soul is it blended into ours becoming now 'heavenly wine." She was perfect for us, warm, kind, big small, completely subservient. I asked, "Who gave us this dark angel?" Fejér answered her, "A very good friend." I then asked, "Can we keep her?" Fejér told the girls who were eagerly staring at her waiting for a response from Fejér, "If you promise to work for her in your studies as you did Henrietta and to love her, you may keep her." Everyone promised as the Princess said to her, "Sorry my great teacher, I have been lonely and under a lot of stress lately and need some more of that 'heavenly wine,'" as she positioned herself and performed the necessary arrangements to receive this wine. Her creators had designed her with a continual supply of this wine, hoping that would ease our loss of Henrietta and maintain our hard work for Fejér. The Princess enjoyed the way Máriakéménd's body was so flexible and smooth as she was able to express her emotions warmly and lovingly. The sisters watched in awe as they started to massage the princess in order to help her escape from her pains. They then rubbed some nice oils and lotions on her. When she had received another filling of the new heavenly wine provider, she rolled over and started to play with her starved sisters. They had a lot of catching up to do, and they made every effort to catch up. Then I asked her, "What is taking you so long before you return." The Princess said, "Ann, things are changing every day now. Your daddy and we are going to visit the King when I return and find out what he wants. Things have changed for me, thus I do not know when the King will release me." Joy asked with an angry voice, "Is he making you his prisoner?" Fejér then answered, "Oh, no my sisters, Henrietta Maria, who will be Maria for us from now on, has discovered her authentic identity. She has a special mark on her body that was given by the spirits so that those who loved her could find her. Her real mother discovered her. She is truly the sister of the King, for the woman who discovered she, is the mother of the King." Then Ruth said, "Where is the mark, for we all know every mark on her?" Fejér then said, "The two small extra lights in her left eye." Then I said, "That is no mark, it is her extra beauty." Then Fejér said, "We should let her have some time with her real birth families. We can still keep her here in our night time world, however to take her away from those who gave her life is wrong." The Mary said, "Then why did her parents give her to us?" Then Fejér answered saying, "They did not, she was stolen and sold many times and too young to know it. Our question is, 'Do we love her enough to put her back where she belongs and still have her with us in our night world where your sisters can spend an enormous amount of time with someone we were so lucky to have met, even by accident." Joy, then, who would now be our leader said, "We want to do what is right and just, for to do anything else could not have its basis in love." We all now started crying and agreed." Maria gave us all kisses as Fejér now remarked, "Joy, how did you get such great wisdom now? I think you will be a perfect leader for our group." We all laughed and started kissing her. She had been the child in the middle, tagging after her older 'sister' who was tagging after the big girls, and too big really to be appreciated by the little girls who at times ignored her. She would now have a positive position and we could see was eager to follow in her older 'sister's footsteps, for what would be, just a few hours during the day and their sleeping hours after their nightly visit to the night worlds." Máriakémténd was now trying to regain her strength after feeding all the sisters. She had a peaceful look over her face as she just sat there making herself available for the next thirsty sister. Fejér then said, "We are so lucky to have Máriakémténd here with us. I think she is going to add a lot of excitement and new things to our nighttime world. Now, my sisters, you may stay here and Máriakémténd will take you back home. We all agreed and accepted we would have a new host. I was now going to be more reserved. How we could have been so wrong about Henrietta is scary to say the least. She was after me, or something in me, I do not know, the only thing I know for sure it that it is not the time for me to know. Whoever is calling my shots appears to be working hard, because no one could even deny that Máriakémténd was truly a dark angel. Our new Princess had taken Fejér with her to go back to where daddy was. I think Fejér was now along to help make sure daddy made it back home for mommy and her daughters. I never thought that Maria was or would be a Princess. That helps to explain to me why she was so good at being a countess. We would now wait for their news, which I hope we get tomorrow night in our nighttime world. Fejér and the Princess arrive back into their chambers at the exact time they departed. The Princess quickly put on her new gray low cut in the front gown and was working on her hair when the rest of the gang came knocking at her door, standing in between an among a ton of guards. Fejér told the Princess in their secret mind talk to invite them in. Hence, the Princess yelled out in a warm voice, "Guards, allow my friends to enter." The guards asked Fejér since they had seen her so many times before and knew that the Princess loved them all, "How did she know it was you?" Fever simply answered, "By the way my knock penetrates her heart." They opened the door quickly and shook their heads. The only they knew for sure was Princess had identified them with the door closed and only through a door knock. Maybe what she said was true. The Princess's private escorts rushed in and finished the Princess, saying we need to get to the King. The Princess then asked, "Do you think he would cut off the head of his sister and those who protect her? Since I am his sister, he would expect me to exercise my female right to be always late . . . ." None could argue with that so they progressed at their pleasure with one-half of the Kings Guards following her. The other half remained to insure all the chambers belonging to her and her escorts were guarded since no one knew which one she would end up. The guards actually enjoyed this special feature of her personality as it made them feel that she was more of a people's person and not a royal self-righteous jerk like the rest of them. They believed that by her sleeping in the other rooms with her friends represented how she put friendship above status, being centered around her friends and not self-centered. Besides, these soldiers were feeding these stories first to their families who then spread it everywhere. When the group arrived, the Princess refused to knock and request entry. She told the guard, he is my brother first, then your king. Furthermore, I will see my brother. The guards stepped aside as she walked in. The King looked up and shook his head saying, "And now my guards obey you, will you please join me my sister?" The guards then retreated, as the King yelled out, "Tell the gang that protects her to enter also." The Princess asked her brother, "How did you know they were with me?" The King then told her, "They are always with you, so why should this time be different? Anyways, I summoned for them also." The Princess then asked, "Your court looks different now, why is that?" The King replied, "For now I am entertaining my sister, who has the same amount of my father and mother in her as I do. Why should one so special doesn't receive special attention, for the throne I set upon belonged to the King that is the father of both of us, and we did both enter this world from the same womb. You are as much of me as I am of you. Come sit beside me my sister and invite your protectors, which I too have a great debt for the fine job they have been doing. Let us make a circle out of these chairs. My father began the conversation, "Oh great and honorable King, we petition you to tell us why you called us to England." The King then said, "We shall not do all that honorable King protocols in this meeting, since I know beyond every doubt that my sister, like my mother, would rather be thrown into a dungeon than give me that honor. He then pulled out a letter and gave it to his sister saying, please look at the date before you read it. After she read it, her face became a charmed blush as she handed the letter to 'our' daddy. After my daddy reads it he said, "Congratulations my fair Princess" and handed the letter to Fejér. After she read it, she handed the letter to my daddy's partners, and turned to the Princess while looking at the King and said, "You mean we must break in another King. I still exhausted from this one." At this, the King and his ministers standing by the wall broke out a large laugh and applauded. The King looked at Fejér and replied, "With such a great soldier like you at her side, I do believe she will have a fighting chance against the King of England" as the court, to include daddy broke out in a big laughter. The King then looked at Maria and asked, "My sister, how do you feel about the killing and persecution of Catholics in England?" His sister replied, "I oppose all persecution and killing of innocent people. I will fight hard for the poor people to have a better life." The King replied, "Truly I have a special warm sister. I wish so much that you would spend a few weeks with me so I can show all which is yours." Looking at the king, Maria replied, "Is it not all yours, and could I not a threat?" The King stood and said, "I swear before my ministers that I shall exercise my divine right and return to you that which is yours without any form of retaliation." The Princess stood up, walked over to her brother, and kissed him on his head and said, "I am so sorry for saying such a cold thing to such a warm brother and they did hug as tears flowed from both their eyes." As the princess sat down, the King asked his guards, while wiping the tears from his eyes, "Do you not protect your King anymore?" They looked at the King and answered, "Since we would rather die than hurt our Princess." The King looked at them and said, "I too would rather die than hurt my sister." Now with all sitting down, the Princess asked the King, "What do you want me to do? The King now answered, "I know not, when you were an unknown countess I wanted you to do it, yet now you are my sister, and I have a longing to get to know the rest of my family, truly I do not know. I know two things, the people of France love you and the people of England love you. Now that you are forever of my blood, I could think of no other person who, while in England would serve all people with love and justice. I will both rejoice and cry at which ever answer you give." The Princess then looked at my daddy and ran to him crying dropping to her knees and laying her head on his shoulders, and saying, "What say my master that I shall do?" My daddy motioned for Fejér to join them. The King yelled saying, "My sister has no masters." My sister looked at him, still on her knees before my daddy and with Fejér massaging her back and screamed back, "I decide who my masters are and these two, I shall worship for eternity." The King then replied, "You are my sister and shall serve whom you wish." Then the King said, "Please take my sister back to my guest chambers and tend to her as if she were the most important thing in the world." Fejér looked at the King and said, "She is the most important thing in the world to us, for we too worship her." The King now stood and lowered his head saying, "Let me be included in those who worship her." Fejér said, "As well her brother would be her primary protector with her father died." The King looked at Fejér and replied, "I am willing to protect her with all that I have, to include my life and the lives of my armies." Upon hearing that his soldiers in the room gave out a large, cheer. The King looked at his soldiers then back to Fejér saying, "I believe my armies would do so, even without my command. My sister truly owns France, yet deserves to be a queen and not a princess." That was the comment that through Maria's escorts for their final lap and gave fuel to their arguments over what the Princess should do. They escorted the king's sister back to his guest chambers and Fejér started massaging her as my father started singing some songs he used to sing to her. This combination brought energy back to the one they loved so much. She once again asked, "What say my masters that I should do?" My daddy said, "For starters, "Please do not call us your masters in front of the king, Ok my little girl." She kissed our daddy on his cheek and said, "I love you so much, you were the best daddy I ever had, the one that loved me the most." My daddy told her, "It was so easy to love you and your sisters." She then replied, "I hate calling my father Henry." My daddy said, "As long as you live in France, you can have no father but the King's father." She then looked at Fejér and asked, "Why are you so quiet?" Fejér then said, "We have decided on our recommendation." The Princess looked at my father and said, "Tell me daddy, what you would tell Ann to do?" My daddy looked at her and said, "I would tell you both the same, and will carry the same when you leave me. I have suffered as all England has suffered. We suffer for many reasons, one of which for having no queen since the death of Anne. I have searched my heart and mind and cannot find anyone who would be a better Queen of England than you would. The English people loved you as a countess as so did the French people. As a Queen of England, you could do things that would make life better for your sisters and the lives of the poor people, which you know is not good or justified. The decision must be yours. I know that I could never under no circumstances ever give any of you up as babies to another family and especially cannot forgive a King who does it, be he your father or not." Maria looked at daddy, wrapped her arms around his head, and gave the yank that meant she wanted to be cradled like a baby. My father and Fejér then started rocking her and singing to her as she sunk into deep deliberation. She then once again opened her eyes and asked, "What say you my Fejér."

Fejér replied, "Why is a princess in a distant land when you can go back to England as the Betrothed Queen? You will be loved by both nations; France for doing the duty expected of a Princess, which is to marry a King, no matter how far or distant. By accepting this offer, you will be close to us and in a country that also loves you and close enough to me, that if you need my love, I can quickly come to you." Is that all you both have to say, Then my daddy, with tears in his eyes said, "What daddy would want for his little girl to be close to him and living in a nice home. Your castles, which are many, would qualify as good homes, and having armies to protect you qualifies as a security. There are so many ways to live worse than being a queen." Fejér then answered, "You should always pick what is best for you and your friends." The Princess then stood up and said, "I have decided, please come with me." She then returned to the court and told the ministers to bring forth her King. They all eagerly ran to the resting area of the King to tell him. She then asked Fejér, "How many ministers does it take to bring me my brother?" The soldiers all started laughing with her. Few would ever make jokes about the minister. Their princess was witty and daring. The King came forward and asked them to sit. He started by saying, "I hope you do not mind, I excused your two shivering friends." The Princess looked at daddy who shook his head up and down and then she looked to her brother and said, "A . very kind and warm deed my brother, we do thank you." As they sat down, the King asked, "My sister have you searched your heart and found peace." The Princess now looked at her brother and said, "Yes, I have decided to do my duty to you and to France and accept this offer. I hope it brings great joy to our family, as they will now have two royal heads on it." The King then said, "If this is true . . . Your" (he then looked at my daddy and asked, "What say you?" My father said, "Fejér and I agree with your sister. That it is her life and her duty." The King looked at daddy and said, "My sister is wise in the people whom she serves." The Princess now gave her brother a big smile. The King looked at her and said, "See sister, I can be trained as I am sure Charles will soon discover that no King is a match to you." Please, join me and bring our friends with you at my table for dinner, while I tell my minister to say in my letter back to Charles. After I am done, the minister will take both letters back to the bishop who will have the church in England to present it to the king. The church will notify me when to send you and 'our masters' back to England in my royal fleet." Maria then asked the king, "My brother, may I go back and put on another gown for our dinner?" The King said, "As long as you bring back that little bundle of joy (looking at Fejér)" Maria then said, "I would not leave home without her." Then they departed back to their chambers, with Fejér giving the King a little extra wiggle, much to the King's delight. Such are the games of boys and girls. The Princess put on another one of her daring gowns and they did proceed to the royal dinner, when they discovered another guest was among them. Their mother had decided to join them. When she saw his daughter she said, "How could one as beautiful as you come from my womb? I am glad that your gown covers some of your body although the more I would hope. I do not want all to see what Charles must marry to see." Maria then said, "Mother, I will save just a little special for only Charles." Marie then said, "Thank God. I have asked your brother's permission to join my children for dinner, a gift yet have I received. In addition, I want to make sure the response to Charles is strong enough to make his heartburn. We have decided to let you keep Charles proposal. It does belong to you." The Princess said, "Thank you mother, and mother, do you want to set beside me in case my top should fall down and all see my breasts." Marie then said, "My God my daughter, will you please be good." The King then started laughing, "My sister has done in a few minutes what I have failed to do in my lifetime and that is to embarrass our mother." He then motioned for the wine to be served first and said to his sister and mother, "I shall begin the letter and you may suggest changes as you will." He motioned for the scribes to assemble and began as follows: "My dear friend, Charles I, I have received your proposal for marriage to the countess Henrietta Maria, yet must gloriously report that her credentials are not valid. She is not nor ever was a countess in France. I will report to you her true title and position. She is my sister, who was in hiding as per Henry IV's deeds. Her true title is Princess Henrietta Maria, daughter of Henry IV of France. The decision to accept your proposal was given to this wonderful King tamer. Within a few weeks, she conquered France, and was by all her people loved, as your people had reported. I had feared she would not accept the proposal believed Kings, such as me, were too easy to handle. However, to my surprise, she searched her heart, and out of love for both my people and your people decided to marry you so that so many may live in peace. If you want the most daring, strongest willed and by far the most beautiful bride in Europe, you may have my sister. May our God bless you?" Then mother requested that another line be added to the protection of the Catholics in England that went as follows: Upon your promise to protect the Catholics in England you may have her hand in marriage." The Princess, my daddy and Fejér then all agreed. Then the Princess grabbed ahold of her mother and said, "This excitement is making my top fall apart, mommy, save me." Her mother immediately fainted. The King stood up and started laughing so hard that he had to grab his side because the pain was so great. The chief minister looked at the Princess and said, "My God, you have killed your mother and put a curse on your brother." Maria looked at him and said, "Shut up and sit down." She asked Fejér to tend to the King and motioned for a guard to bring her some water. She washed her mother's face bringing her back to conscience. As the King's pain went away and he was restored, his mother regained her senses and they both looked at the Princess who was now giving her normal "I am a little innocent angel look." Her mother then, along with the King, started laughing telling her, "We have not had a joy such as that in our lives." The King then said, "Makes me wonder how we ever lived without you Henrietta Maria." The King and his mother told her so many wonderful stories about the things that had happened in their lives. The King then asked his sister, "My sister, in order not to bring shame upon our family by future generations, may I have your permission to rewrite our history as if you had lived your royal life since childhood?" Maria looked at Fejér and my daddy who both shook their heads yes and she quickly responded with a handshake yes. Her mother then responded, "My daughter, by having servants you love and trust to advise you, and then depending and accepting their recommendations, you will seldom be in error, for three heads are better than one, except in a guillotine." The Princess laughed and said, "They shall be in my heart for eternity." The King looked at the two of them, then his sister and said, "You are truly blessed to have two so loyal.

For anyone who looks in their eyes and does not see you or in your eyes and does not see them is truly blind." At this, my daddy and Fejér each kissed the Princess on a cheek. Marie applauded adding, "I shall rest in much more peacefully at night knowing you are with my daughter." The Princess then retired with her escorts back to their chambers where she asked Fejér to join her for the night. They both walked between all the soldiers who were guarding her hallway to her door. Then one asked, "Has anything new happened today our fair Princess?" Fejér then looked at them and said, "Do not call her a Princess, for she is the Betrothed Queen Henrietta Maria of England." All the soldiers started cheering as word went like wildfire all the way back to Paris and throughout all of France. The ministers then rushed to prepare to official notify the courts, as the church had already notified all the churches. Anything that had Maria associated with it was the food that the people lived on. One Priest said, "History may never have another such great miracle in a young girl entering France from England with false accreditations as a countess, and within days is discovered to be our Princess and in is now returning to England as their betrothed Queen. Even the greatest storywriters could not dream up something as this, for they would be told their fiction was too far beyond reason to be believed. Only our God could make something like this happen." The nation was now being called Marianites because all were standing around the castle each night with their candles singing songs they had written about her. She would of course every few hours appear in her night robe and give them her royal wave. No one dared complain about her appearing in public with only her night robe wrapped around her, for all knew she was sleeping and thus coming from her bed to wave at the people who loved her, and whom she loved. They knew she loved them. As the night gave way to the dawn and daylight, the nation received the news. Marie, Maria, King Louis XIII stood with the bishops as the chief minister addressed the nation. "Today, the crown has great news to share with you. Our royal Princess Henrietta Maria has accepted, of her own true will and sadly supported by her brother and mother the proposal for Queen of Charles I of England. We can think of no greater honor for the Princess we have grown to love. She has accepted because of her great love for both her people of France and her people of England, being so much loved by both nations. She can do no greater royal duty for her nation than this, as so many people may now be able to raise their families in peace. May I introduce to you the Betrothed Henrietta Maria of England?" The crowds now cheered hysterically. Maria now stood before her people and raised her hand to signify she wanted to share her mind with them. "My people, as your Princess I can do no more than my brother, for I truly believe he would strive hard to grant my every wish. I have seen you stand during the long cold nights with your candles to show your love for me. It is now time I showed you my love and do my duty as prescribed by my father, Henry IV of France. In my heart, I have some battles. I cannot support the killing of other people who worship the same God in the name of our God. As I go to England and stop the killing of Catholics, I ask that you stop the killing of Huguenots. Do not slay any man who says 'Jesus is Lord' in the name of Jesus, for no man would kill himself. Fight to save your church by, working harder for your church. Feed the hungry and clothe the freely exposed, as those who discovered me hungry and freely exposed did clothe me and feed me. Give strength for the weak, as those who found me week did protect me until I myself had strength. My great wish has always been to find those who clothed me, and feed me and cared for me in my beginning years to thank them. All that they did they did for love. Thus, all that you do please do for love. For without their love, you would have not Princess before you now. Love the many poor, for it is so easy to love the few rich. You will have far more friends and opportunities to show that you are a true lover of Christ. These are the true battles of the righteous. Love all people, even those who do not love you, for it is easy to hate those who hate you and hard to love those who hate you. If you walk in love, no one can take from you the rewards the Lord has saved for you. You know I love all of you, so please love all of you as I do. Those who do this are the ones who truly love me and are the ones that will keep my love among you all the days of your lives. Love the Lord and his creations as I do. I must now prepare to serve you as the Queen of your enemy. I shall walk through the valley of death fearing no evil. God bless my children." The Betrothed Queen went back into her chambers. A minister approached the King and whispered in his ear, "The church is reporting the Charles I has accepted your terms and wished to marry his queen in June of 1625. As we talk, he has sent 500 soldiers dressed in white. They are now debarking in the Le Havre port." The King now stood before the people waving his mother off. Marie had seen the minister talking-to the King and wanted to know what the news was. The King stood before his people as the crowds did cheer for him also and spoke as follows, "I thank the queen's servants for extending me such a wonderful applause. (There now was more applause and laughter throughout the crowd as this was the first time the King had joked with his people) My sister asked me what to do about this proposal. She knew that it would break Charles's heart if she rejected it, or break my heart if she accepted it. Either way, one angel would make a King cry. What is more, cry I have and shall, not for sadness that she goes but for the sadness of not having my sister grow up. I thank our God that I did get to discover her before my death. Her love for her people is greater than her love for herself. I know that she will do well in England, for she is a King tamer, as she quickly tamed me. Again, the crowd laughed and cheered. Charles has a surprise waiting for him. He will be tamed by my sister. Once more, the crowd laughed and cheered. The church tells me he has accepted our Princess harsh terms and is sending an Army of 1,000 soldiers dressed in white to take her back to England in his royal fleet. We shall also have 1,000 soldiers ride with the English to our shorelines at Le Havre. God Save the Queen! Marie now stood before the people. The people were now feeling so much closer with their monarchy and feeling the painful decisions that they had to make for them. She began by saying, "Today, I stand before my people, not in the dishonor as before for hiding your Princess, but in the fear of her shame being exposed in future generations. I can only beg that your love for her will force you to help me rewrite history as if she had grown up with Henry and me. To shame us is not the issue, as I too shall soon join Henry, but it will shame our children as they rule two of the greatest Empires today. The question is, 'Do you want our Queen to be loved by future generations or her to be shamed by them?" As she departed the stage, the Princess came riding out in a white female pawn's riding dress on one of the king's finest horses and waving at the crowd. The people marveled at how the most powerful woman in the world today could also be strong enough to dress as she pleased, as one of them while riding one of the king's greatest prized horses. Maybe she was not only a King tamer, but also a world tamer. The sun now shined on the special oils she put in her hair to make it shine and amplify her beauty. It was so easy to see her big bright eyes that reflected the souls of the people who loved her so much. One man asked, "Are those the eyes that will launch thousands of soldiers today?" She rode among the people allowing all to touch her legs. She knew her people rightfully and justifiably wanted to touch the source of their new love and hope. She did not care if this broke royal law, as she felt throwing their Princess to the wolves was also not royal law. They had been cheated from her, and as many as could be going to leave today having touched their Princess, who returned to them just in time to do her royal duty to them and give them hope for a peaceful world to raise their families. Now Fejér, my daddy and a royal castle escort appeared before the crowd. Fejér broke the rules and wore leather pants with the church's approval for her safety among the crowds. They mingled in the crowd as their escort stayed on the other side of the fence. All knew them as the one who the Princes loves, thus wanted to touch them also. Later in the day, some 1,000 soldiers began to form and asked for the Princess and her escorts to form at the front. Daddy's two other friends wanted to stay in France and work on some new business ventures. Daddy told me they were looking for some thieves to rob blind. The people began forming on both sides of the road, from her to Paris and to Le Havre. The English was astonished and commented, "I do believe my lad, they bloody well love our Queen also. When they arrived in front of the castle, they were even more surprised. There before them was a pawn on one of the king's white horses. Their commander rode up and asked my Daddy, "Dear sir, may you show me where our Betrothed Queen may be?" "Daddy then said to him, "My dear lad, you have just made a big error, I recommend you ask the one who leads this 1, 000 man Army of the King." The commander looked forward and saw her in front of him and immediately got off his horse and bowed before begging for forgiveness. She told him, rise my friend, lest my brother worries about my safety. You have done no wrong, for it is my power that allows me to dress as this. Her brother and mother were watching from one of the towers. The King said to his mother, "My God Marie, it has taken her a whole minute to defeat a great English Army. She must be losing her touch. They both then hugged, which was the first warm jester they had since the days of his mother being the regent. The Princes said now for both commanders to report to her. To both Commanders, "I wish to show France and England to be now part of a bigger family, thus I want you to ride beside each other and the soldiers ride two French and two English per row, so that we do not hurt any of my servants who honor me on both sides of the roads." They both saluted her, called for their staff to reorganize the armies, as the French went down one side and the English went down the other side. Then the ride to Paris began with solid cheering and the queen leaning forward with both hands extended so any who wanted to touch her could. She then sat up and motioned daddy Fejér to ride with her. She had my daddy ride in the middle with Fejér and her riding on the outside, shaking the people's hands. The commanders were terrified, especially with so much of the world's power in one person who was to be protected by 2,000 soldiers. They pleaded for her to be more secure. She refused saying, "They stand here because they love me. I must trust them if they are to put their futures in my hand." They ride into Paris in the evening. The Princess was scheduled to sleep in a royal hotel. She refused saying it was not fair to the soldiers or the people along the roads. She then pulled out a nice dress and asked the commanders for some soldiers to give her cover while she changed. The commanders motioned them up and they circled her. She then told them, "Why do you turn your backs on me? You cannot seem to help hold my clothes as they are removed or hand me my garments to put on. Are you afraid of a female's body?" They turned around and said, "Only the most powerful body in the world." She removed her pawn outfit and handed it to one soldier as another soldier's hand her a fluffy slip. She then said to them, "This body belongs to the people and are you not the people. I feel that maybe you think my breasts are ugly." The four of them said, "Oh princess, they are the perfect work of a great God. How can you be so brave to stand topless among thousands of people?" She said to them, "By putting myself in your hands." The soldiers helped to get her dress on and quickly went to go back to their formation when she ordered them back. She told them, with her fake woman scorned look, "How can you enjoy by breasts and leave me without even a kiss and hug. Each soldier kissed and hugged her as the crowds roared. When the soldiers retold this story, they all claimed she had white wrapping around her body. They told how her love and trust of the people was like others breathing. They did not want either King to know the beauty they had seen or they would lose their heads. The Army then paused for about one hour as the Princess, Fejér, shook hands and the citizens gave food to the soldiers from both Armies. The English soldiers commented, "Never have any citizens fed us better." My daddy collected the food for 'his girls' so they would not suffer from hunger. The armies rode slowly through the crowded roaring city of Paris. The English soldiers now commented, "England is getting the greatest loved queen in history. She must be like unto a god." They thus proceeded now towards Le Havre. This has been the largest peacetime army ever to escort a member of a royal family. As the crowd could see the soldiers riding together, talking, laughing, and shaking, the people's hands a feeling of peace were now in the air.

Chapter 05

The Road to Le Havre

T he road now to Le Havre was now so crowded that the local garrisons had to go before the Princess' 2,000 soldier escort. This now elevated so much the princess and her escorts were now physically suffering from the noise. The princess then asked the soldiers about taking a back road for a few hours then switch back to the main road for a dash to the port. If they did nothing or kept on the same course the two hundred kilometers to the port could have dire consequences. Thus, they jumped off the main road and flashed through to fields heading west so they could line up on another road that branched about one hundred kilometers away from the port with two roads that would take them in straight into the port and Charles I's large fleet waiting for her. The Armies shifted as did the massive crowds. It was now that Fejér's fears were being realized. The crowds were angry at the switch. Then some poor young kid threw a rock hitting the Princess in her head. My daddy grabbed her fast, taking her from the horse she was riding. In an instant, the soldiers surrounded her. The remaining soldiers were now in a fight with the crowds who all started to throw stones now. The soldiers now drew their swords and any person they saw who threw a stone was executed. A local garrison was watching in horror from a nearby hillside and immediately started sounding their trumpets to alert other units to mobilize. They obtained a very heavily protected carriage with eight mighty horses, with a doctor inside, and rushed it to the Princes. They also used a special drumming code they had to alert the king. She was still one hundred kilometers from the port. Bodies were starting to pile up, as the soldiers were not fighting hard for each advancing small gains. The garrison force of 575 soldiers joined the fight. They concentrated on getting the injured to a nearby hospital. Even this started requiring musket shots, killing the attackers. The French soldiers were also trying to protect the English soldiers who had no warrior protection garments. The crowd had so quickly turned into a mob. The doctor worked quickly to save Faith, for she had a fractured skull. Since he was a young lad, the Princess had bent over to shake his hand and made herself a perfect target. The news going through the crowds was that she bent down and stabbed the boy in the head and that the commander had to hit her in order to prevent more death. The English and French in Le Havre were told that all the crowds had turned violent and were killing all in sight. They combined forces as the French gave their English co-parts heavy armor to wear. They also brought armored wagons filled with little people who could reload Muskets so they could maximize their kill ratio. They had mustered together another 1,000 soldiers and were now confiscating horses from the nearby town. There plans were to beat a path to the Princess so she could make a fast run for the port. Word had now reached both Kings as tremendous armies were being formed. The English was now preparing for a land invasion to the western side of Le Havre where they projected would be the least suspected and crowded avenue. The King had messengers sent to all his armies to "Save the Princess." He then led a 20,000 soldier, heavily armored Army straight to Le Havre, bypassing Paris. He brought many wagons to be packed with people who were to die on his new love, the guillotine. The King rode in front of this giant Army; as would Charles also lead his army. The next few hours' war raged. There was only one hope to reduce the bloodshed. The church had discovered the miscommunications and were going house to house to tell the true story and recruiting more people to spread the true story. In the meantime, the warriors protecting the Princess guided her into an old castle that was perfectly secure on two sides. They would easily be able to protect the front. They could only hope that they would be saved in a short period, as there were only limited amounts of rations available. Fighting continued to be fierce on both the two front sides, as the Princess remained unconscious. Additional doctors were smuggled in with additional medical supplies. Her recovery room was very large now pretty much packed with doctors and nurses. The Princess was still popular among the professional people. My daddy gave the true account about the childish deadly attack upon his daughter. All knew that the deceased King was her father, and that she was raised in unknown foster homes and that the princess considered my daddy her daddy. Now an entire day had passed and she had not regained conscience. My daddy then asked, "How could a rock thrown by a young boy so close do such damage?" The doctors told him that she had turned her head in defense and unknowingly exposed a more vulnerable part of her side skull. The church was now spreading that the Huguenots had planted a surprise assassination on the Princess and had spread the rumors so Catholics would die attacking their Princess. The Church then started having people walk in the holy robes crying in the streets, "How foolish slaves of the Huguenots, you have tried to kill the only one to ever love you." As both Kings armies marched to the abandoned castle, none would stand in front of such a mighty force. They played their drums and trumpets as the landsides rumbled as they rushed to save "The Queen" as both armies screamed out. Both armies had a cavalry and land marching force. The cavalry reported back to the Kings that "Chosen one" was unconscious and now in a deep sleep. Both cavalries now rushed their Kings to the castle. Their roads to the castle were empty, as all the rioters had fled to their homes, for to defy a King was death for you, your family, and even your village. Those punished in these riots would be executed without mercy. King Louis XIII ordered extra wagons to collect as many rioters as possible, and now when a citizen was questioned, and provided no names, they would be imprisoned in the wagon. All investigations were conducted by a local government or church official, who would receive the confessions. The King had a special surprise for these rioters. It is not wise or healthy to hurt a King's sister. Many times wives were hurt with the King only giving a token condolence, yet sisters had his blood in her and that was war. King Louis XIII's Cavalry got him and another herd of medicine men to his sister within a few hours. The King ordered that Cannons start firing throughout France to show his anger. He then sarcastically added, "And please do not attack the English who are to join me." Upon first seeing his sister, the King yelled in anger, "Prepare my sister in royal apparel, for if she is to give her life in France then all shall see the beauty we have given back to the heavens." He then called for Fejér who was just outside the door and asked, "Well you please stay beside my sister and use your love to bring her back. I shall give you another maiden to serve both your needs." It was then that Fejér, after viewing her sister, realized that the other sisters would soon need to be notified. Fejér answered the King with tears in her eyes, "As my lord commands." The King then replied, "With you my Fejér, it shall never be a command." He then kissed her on her tear-filled check and then started crying. Fejér then motioned for the new maiden to join her as they consoled the king, who continued to talk with his tears now rolling like rivers, "She is blood of my blood and the only that I have ever truly loved. He then motioned to sit in a regular chair that was in the room. That sent the signal out to all how much the King loved his sister, that he too was now willing to be humble. Soon, the Princess was completely cleaned and dressed in a beautiful gold trimmed nightgown with a gold headband that his mother had thrown into his war bag. When the King saw it he reminisced, "This is my mother's favorite, for she told me it was what she wore the night my father gave her his seed putting me into her womb." Then the sound of thunder came before towards the castle. As Louis XIII looked out, he saw a massive English army approaching, and yelled out, "Open the gates, so that they too may give honors to my sister." All rioters were now long gone, fleeing for mountains or caves or under churches. Everyone knew the blood was getting ready to flow. Then Charles I with his soldiers rode into the castle as the soldiers secured it behind them. The English started sharing their supplies with all other soldiers, thus a sense of calm had taken over the stressed castle. They reported that the countryside was now open, with no rioters in sight. The King escorted his future brother in law into the Princess's room. Charles I then looked upon her and replied, "I cannot believe this, her beauty is greater than when I first saw her." King Louis XIII told his guest, "There lies before you the only being that I have ever loved." Then Charles hugged him saying, "Fear not my brother, for I shall always love you sister also." Charles then commented, "Those maidens seem to serve their Princess with their hearts." Louis answered, pointing at Fejér, "She is her soul sister. You would be wise and secure by keeping her at my sister's side." Then did they both sit in chairs beside her as their armies outside made friends. The Princess spirit of love took over the castle. Then Louis asked Charles to join him in his tower. Then the King motioned, as the soldiers brought forth a riot who was begging for mercy. The King yelled out, "And did not my sister's spirit beg for mercy?" Then did the blade drop as the soldier held up his head. He handed it to another soldier who threw it into the wagon holding the other confessors. The body was tossed out over the long wall behind the castle. Charles remarked, "That is more efficient than the axes we use, why did not I know about this." Louis replied, "We are still adjusting it. I have been toying with it in my court to gain confessions, with great success until I met my sister, who was then your countess. I am so disappointed that you did not detect the family resemblance when you first saw her." Charles remarked, "Do not blame me; blame the King of Denmark for giving me false papers. At least her mother identified her. How did she identify her again?" Louis responded, "Only my father and Marie knew of the divine marks in her left eye, and when she saw it she knew the heavens had returned her to her home. I offered her up to half of our kingdom as I feel her birthright since she is blood of my blood and I hers. She denied the offer, wanting instead to stand for almost three days straight and shake these rotten scumbag's hands. No other saint deserved this." Charles asked, "What are your ministers telling you were the reasons for this?" Louis answered, "Jealous Huguenots over her pledge to protect the Catholics in England." Charles then looked at his host and said, "Her promise is now getting easier to keep my brother." They then went over beside the Princess when Fejér jumped up in front of Charles as to protect the Princess. Charles remarked, "My child, do you not know who is your King?" She looked at Louis who motioned approval and stepped back saying, "I now shall die before anyone whom I have ever seen before touches the Princess." Charles then laughed and remarked to Louis, "I agree my brother is would be wise to keep her at her sister's side, for I shall have no worries about her chastity?" Louis looked at her and said, "How could you question the chastity of my sister?" Charles then replied, "If I did, would I be here at her side?" Louis replied, "Sorry, the burden of this horrifying even is creating another me." They then shook hands. All Europe was now on hold as so many other nations gave their honors. The King of Spain, the Netherlands, Denmark, and the ruler of the Germans came to the castle, as did the Pope. Fejér laughed in her mind when she saw the Pope, for little did he know, she was not Catholic, nevertheless her secret was safe. The other kings had brought their best doctors as so many provided treatments. Then a doctor from the Dutch came out with great joy saying the Princess should awake in a few weeks at the longest. He said, "The point of impact had held strong enough to prevent entry to the inside of her head and was now showing signs of healing." The room filled with great cheers, as seldom in history had so many kings joined in peace. Many times during this wait, kings would excuse themselves, go into a nearby room, and discuss any differences they had. No one dared to yell or scream, thus the conversations tended to be more constructive as both sides were willing to compromise. More compromises and deals were worked out in these few days than in centuries before. When these kings returned to their nations, telling their people about the deals made and how they would prevent stupid additional wars and save so many lives that many wondered if the Princess was really a human being or an archangel. Sadly, though the nations found new things to fight. As the Kings started to depart back to their nations, additional supplies kept pouring in, so their Armies would be able to eat on their long journeys back. Louis had ordered the wagons with the rioters against his sister be taken back to Paris, yet first the biggest man in each wagon would be beheaded and his head thrown back into his wagon. The hopeless now could do nothing except wait for their punishment. So many wondered how such evil had filled their minds with anger and hate over the one that truly was their hope. Louis knew that if his sister discovered these people's plight so would forgive them. The less she knew about royal justice the better things would be. Then one morning one week later and still within the window of the Dutch doctor who had been commanded to stay on her side she awoke. Many stories were told about this what appeared to be a "miraculous event when Louis walked in to see his sister and was once again begging for the Lord's mercy to bring his sister back, when a bright light shined into the room, which had no windows. The light also appeared in the Pope's room, as he would not leave until the Princes was restored causing him to rush into the room. When the soldiers saw the Pope running for her room all became frozen and quiet, except for praying. She awoke and asked her brother, "My brother, blood of my blood, why do you stand over me?" Louis explained, "You tried to kiss a rock from a young boy and instead was struck in the head with a stone. My sister, you escaped death, yet this doctor saved you and now by order of his King is never to depart from you." She then started laughing saying, "I should stick to kissing my brother if you agree." The pope and Charles now came rushing in as the King was hugging his sister kissing her check saying, "Praise is to the almighty God." The Pope and Charles now came rushing in and seeing her beautiful eyes began, hugging and cheering giving glory to anything that came to their minds.

Fejér knew the true reason for Faith's recovery but kept her silence. The sisters had been pestering her every night for word about Faith Maria. They hated to use the "Henrietta" in her name.

Finally, Máriakémɛ́nd intervened and came to Fejér and investigated the situation. When she saw the tragedy, she began to call out into the heavens for mercy. She then volunteered to return to the sisters and tell them. Fejér argued that she should go with her and tell them, so that they would not blame this on Máriakémɛ́nd. They both went back and summoned the sisters. Fejér began by saying, "I am very happy to see my little bottles of the heavenly wine, yet tonight I have some bad news for you. Faith Maria had been assaulted by a little boy and has been fighting for her life." I immediately yelled, "Has someone punished that bad little boy?" Fejér said, "He died at your daddy's hand and your daddy saved her during the following raids until many strong armies came to save her. Many good people, to include many kings, doctors, the Pope, and so many others are working hard for her to wake up." I then said, "My daddy said he would bring her home thus she must come home for I love her so much and want her to be with me for eternity." Little Ann knew that her words had so much power and that she would have all her sisters with her for eternity. Fejér then knew of one thing that would surely save Faith and she asked Ann, "Would you give her some more of your blood to save her?" I answered quickly, "I will give her all my blood?" Fejér said, "A few drops will do." Fejér then said to Máriakémɛ́nd, "Prepare the sisters to meet their Faith." They then appeared before their sister, and tears began to fall as Ruth, Mary and Joy all begged Ann to make her well again. Then Ann stuck up her finger to Fejér and she stuck a small needle into her finger. Then Ann as if by instinct opened Faith's mouth, stuck her finger it wriggling in on her tongue, and said, "Blood of my blood and the love of my heart, awake to me so that I may enjoy your heavenly wine." Then did the flash appear, as Fejér said to the sisters, "Sorry, I must go now, Máriakémɛ́nd will take you back after you see Faith Maria restored," and then Fejér departed to be with my daddy. I now wondered, "Where did this power come from?" I truly did not know however I did not care, because before me was Faith Maria and she was waking up. We all rejoice and then wrapped around Máriakémɛ́nd asking, "Will you give us some of your wine to celebrate?" She then said, "Come with me my children and let me take away your thirst." We really enjoyed her warmth and compassion. She was a grownup who treated us like adults and would be a kid if we wanted her to do so. We now would flood her with good deeds, because she had the good things she opening and with love would share with us. I liked the way she so resembled India. I now accidently discovered a new gift. I went to go back into Fejér's mind; however, I accidently went into my daddy's mind. I could feel a barrier between his mind and my mind, thus could not hear his thoughts. I guess that is a good thing, yet I could see his recent memories. I then copied them into myself and got out of there fast. I now could see what my daddy had seen since he left. I was glad that he was a perfect aristocrat and true to my mommy. He was truly dedicated to protecting and serving faith, which I would never be able to repay him. He had risked his life to protect my Faith as thus kept every promise he made to me. My sisters and I rejoiced when we watched this unfold before us. We all rejoiced that we had such a wonderful daddy. I think even Charles, who now joined us in our night world was excited, for he had many wonderful times with Faith. King Louis allowed the Pope and Charles see his sister awake, and then forced them to leave, saying to Charles, "I shall have her prepared for your first meeting." Charles said, "How can she ever look better than she does now?" Louis answered, "I agree with you, however women think differently, and if she were to discover I allowed you to see her before the girls prepped her, she would release her wrath on me. She has trained me as she will train you." Charles proceeded to leave the room with the Pope saying, "Our Pope, can you think of anyone who would be better to train me than her?" The Pope answered, "I can think of no other and I do fully ordain your marriage. She will give you many good children. Enjoy this gift from the heavens." The Princess was once again resting, rebuilding her strength. When she woke up, Fejér and her maiden prepared her to meet the fiancé. Charles had also dressed in one of his best suits to meet her officially for the first time. Fejér had dressed her in a beautiful white gown on top of clean gray sheets and incense burning in the room. Charles then gently knocked on the door as Fejér called for him to enter saying, "Your royal highness, behold your Betrothed." As he walked in, he knelt by her side as she took her hand to touch his face and replied, "We have met before." He replied, "We have my Betrothed." Then it hit Faith like a lightning bolt, "You were the beggar at the dinner ball?" He looked at her and said, "You gave me food when I was hungry and words of kindness in an ocean of hatred." It was at this time, Fejér replied, "Faith, you are right? I never put the connection together." Charles asked, "Who is Faith?" Fejér answered, "She is the sister of our sisters and is only called Faith Maria by those who live in her heart." Charles then replied, "Then soon, I hope to call her Faith Maria also." Fejér is so quick effortlessly to handle every situation. Faith Maria now said, "Without Fejér and my sisters, I would not want a life." Charles then told his Betrothed, "As soon as that Dutch doctor, who owns you now, gives me permission, I shall take you back to your new home in England, with your permission of course." Faith Maria answered, "I had so hoped to have been there by now." Charles replied, "As so have many others; the important thing is that you are still on this side of the border of life." She then said, "I was dreaming of a little girl in one of my childhood stories that with a match could see into the other side. At times in the last few weeks, I could see into the other side, and as I started to feel, the match would go out. I trembled each time the match would light and rejoiced each time in went out. Do you think that is strange Charles?" Charles replied, "Oh by no means my Queen. I shall always pray that your match never lights again; and shall also pray that you share with me all stories in your mind and all feelings in your heart." The Princess then said, "I would kiss you, yet if my brother with his stupid head cutter were to see you, he would behead you." Charles laughed and said, "I do believe that is true my love. I still wonder why you gave me food and warm words." The Princess replied, "Because you were hungry and your heart was all alone. No person should be hungry and without kind words." Charles then replied, "What you say is so true, and I can think of now greater woman to carry my seed in her womb."

Charles then left the room and saw Louis in the hallway saying to him, "No greater woman exists in the world today. Did you know she gave me food when I was hungry and warm words when all other cursed me?" Louis replied, "That I did not know, yet I do know that few live in France now that she has not. I beg that you tell me the story. However, I can tell she has tamed you. I was disappointed that it took her a whole three minutes. She must be losing her touch." Charles then answered, "No my brother, your sister had me at the very first minute. The time with her after being merely me giving thanks and the first minute was me on my knees begging." Then they did laugh as Charles told him his story. Louis asked afterward, "Am I to believe in front of all those horrible self-centered aristocrats, my sister gave you her food and warm words in front of them? How can one be that strong, for even as I have so many times longed to cut off their heads, I swallowed my words, wishing I had that strength?" Charles then added, "That night, I ordered my ministry to find her papers which reported that she was a countess in your empire and begged you for her hand, knowing that no greater hand had ever been made." Louis then told Charles, "I shall send my soldiers back to Paris to prepare for my arrival and my special punishment for those who dare assault royalty." Charles told him, "Do not to return alone, for other killers will be waiting. It is your choice, return with one of your garrisons or one of mine. I cannot stand to see your sister suffer anymore." Louis agreed, "Thanks, my brother for your wise words. I shall keep two of my cavalry so that Paris will hear the thunder of my entry." Faith now returned to the night world to see her sisters and to thank Ann for her fresh blood. Upon their reunion, they all did shout with joy and honor. She was afraid to return to the memories of Henrietta, a name now that she would be cursed with until her death. The sisters told her about the great love and warmth of their new nanny. They said Máriakéménd, "Was created specifically for them. She treats us all like big girls and, she will jump into the mud and play with us. She really wants us all to take a trip to a very fun place. She has a big girlfriend that wants to meet, love, and protect us. Máriakéménd wants some time with you before you become our queen. And her wine is so good." Faith Maria then said, "Let us go." We all got new body suits since this was in the real world and some of our body suits had a lot of hair, down there that we all liked to play with. We have to swim in a nice pond, play a hiding game with all the rocks and we have to eat some fish cooked on a campfire. They also had some rubber boats that we could go into the deepest part of the pond and see how far down we could swim. Máriakéménd for some reason made herself the smallest. We asked her, "Máriakéménd, why are you so small?" She said, "You all get to small all the time, this is my turn to have all the fun of being the smallest." We did not care, for except for Julie, Máriakéménd's friend we were all almost the same size. We were so happy to discover that Julie also had the refillable heavenly wine bottles, so one of us was drinking her wine nonstop. We felt bad that she did not get to play all the fun games, however Máriakéménd told us, "Julie can come here to play every day. She can only serve you today." I asked, "Is she going to visit us again?" Máriakéménd said, "She is going to start teaching you some things that a teacher your daddy will be bringing home will teach you." Then I asked, "Why then must she also teach us?" Fejér then replied, "Because we want you girls to be great like Faith." The sisters then remembered why they were here and that was to have some time with Faith. Anyway, once Faith Maria had ended with Julie she joined us, as Fejér has to join Julie. I told Faith, "I was able to get some memories from my daddy about your trip in France. If I can sit on your lap, while you watch them with us?" Faith Maria then asked, "Are you the only sister that wants me to hold her?" Instantaneously, all four of us were on her lap. Faith Maria then hugged all of us to tight and said, "You girls are the most important thing to me, and it is so sad that I cannot spend the daytime hours with you." I told her, "We understand, you have to get married and make babies like my mommy did." We then started watching the great deeds our daddy had done for Faith. She replied, "I now stand in fear about how close we came to death if not saved in time by my mother." Later she added, "He saved my life, he was willing to die to keep me alive. Ann, your daddy is the greatest." I looked at her and said,

"Blood of my Blood, my father is our father. Why do you not want him as your father?" Faith Maria then said, "Oh, Ann I so much want him to be our father, I just did not want to make you angry." I told her, "How can a sister make me angry?" We all laughed and started poking and tickling each other. These big girl suits did not take the kid out of us. We were just all so glad to see what a truly wonderful daddy we had. Faith Maria said, "When I return I am going to give me a big hug and kiss and tell him he is the greatest daddy in the whole world and I care not who is watching, because like all of you, I am his daughter threw Ann." I was so proud, because it made me feel so good to know that my sisters also loved OUR daddy. It was now time to play more games and have some more fun. We now all jumped in the pond with a pointed stick to see if anyone could get some fish. We got eight of them in thirty minutes, which insured a good tasty fish fry for dinner. We then went with Máriakéménd to gather some special roots and leaves. She knew a lot about living off the land. She told us that as a child, her family was poor and hungry all the time. Her sisters taught her how to gather roots and leaves and that is what kept them alive. Faith Maria then told her that she and her sisters were once from a poor family. She now told us something new, her father would get drunk and bring in nasty women, giving them the food in the house, and if there were not enough for his lover, he would beat their mother. Fejér then hugged her as Máriakéménd added that her father did not drink; however, he loved to beat my mother and my sisters. He always complained that women were no good. One day when he was beating my mother, I stabbed him in the back with a knife. We turned and started to beat me. My mother and sisters then stabbed him many more times. I watch his eyes, as he died telling him, "You are the devil, and we hate you." We had only one thing of value and it was not of value in our home village, so we packed our few clothes and walked to the big city. Then all seven of us, to include our mother, started selling ourselves. We made a lot of money fast and were able to buy a nice home to take our patrons. We were warned by many others that we had to hire a big man to protect us. My mother immediately hired one and we allowed him to live with us. He was our lifesaver many times, as occasionally we would get an evil greedy patron who decided he wanted to beat us and thus not pay us for our services. Big Jake, as we called him, would come get me and capture the bad man and break their necks and put them in a bag and when we were finished with all our work, Big Jake would have us locked into the door and he would go throw the body into a river. He always let me watch him do it, because he said I was his angel. I always watched in order to justify in my mind that bad men would die for being bad. Yet bad men kept being bad and Big Jake kept breaking their necks until one day, a man had a poison dart and shot it in his neck as he was trying to grab the man's neck. Big Jake died instantly. I screamed as all my sisters and mother came rushing in with knives. We stabbed the man repeatedly until he bleeds no more. Mommy then said, 'We have much money, we shall move to a smaller and safer town.' We packed up all our things, sold the house and moved to a small town far away. Mother bought a nice little farm for us and some cattle, chickens and pigs. We planted a garden and worked hard, yet had a good life. We all agreed not to invite men, for we knew the only thing they wanted and that they would lie, cheat, steal or kill to get it. Mother bought some muskets from the British, and some swords, spears and some crossbows. We made many arrows. Sad to say, that in this beautiful land, evil men would give way to their lusts and come after what they thought were helpless women. When they made their raid, we immediately went into war mode and started killing them. We had signs painted, 'no men allowed.' Those who could not read met their deaths. We had a zero trust rule. We could survive no other way. She said we would pic some vegetables, fruits, and sit along the river cleaning them. We would also wash our clothes and our bodies in the clean fresh cool water. Things were going well, until one day our mother got sick. We did not know how to save her and were too afraid to take her to the nearby town, yet still we asked her if we could take her. She refused and never recovered. We then decided to divide our savings and five of us left. I returned to visit a few years later to see them both tied to stakes where they were burned. I then found my crossbow, filled a bag with our hidden arrows, and went up to a cave that overlooked the town below. I made three trips to get all the arrows. The cave had black magic stones that would burn for a long time. We also had found a few side tunnels that had a black liquid that would soak into straw and burn strong. I gathered straw and wrapped it tight over hundreds of arrows. I let them soak in the oil and started a small fire with the black stones to fuel it. I then ignited the heads of the arrows and shot them into the straw roofs of the homes below. Within about thirty shots, I had the town ablaze. I have now watched for people to escape down the road. I was able to kill another 100 people. Bodies were now stacked on top of each other. I was afraid to kill people who were going out the other road for fear they would be able to determine where the two points intersected and discover my location. I was however able to shoot some arrows straight up and let the wind and gravity disguise their origination, however my successful kill rate was low, just enough to create terror in their attempted escapes. I now had every building on fire so I removed the black stones from my little fire and put them in the cave. I had shot some fire arrows in some dry grass on both hillsides of the village to fill the air with smoke. My job was done, I put on the extra bag of valuables I collected from our home and headed out another secret exit we had discovered long ago. I was able to find a small farm nearby, bought a horse from them, and rode away. I left standing tall and strong. With only one serious burn mark from a bad man long ago, I decided it was time to find a new world and thus rode and rode until I ended up in what you call your holy land and they learned English and was preparing to go to England when Fejér discovered me. She took me many places and then when she trusted me, she told me about you girls who were all sisters and she told me once again I could have sisters to love. That is why I want to be loved by you all so that my sisters who are died can now live with you girls." Faith then gave her a solid hug and asked for some more of her wine. She consented and when finished Faith Maria told her, "We must have you join Ann by blood." Faith Maria now called Fejér and the sisters to see her mind and shared with them the story of

Máriakéménd. When they finished watching it, I stood up and said
to Fejér while extending my finger, "Take from the blood you need
so that Máriakéménd may now be forever a part of us, blood of our
blood. Then Fejér stuck the needle in Ann's finger and said, "Let us
all drink again so we all may be the blood of Ann's blood and Ann
shall be in all of us." Likewise, they all did drink and we now had a
new oath of sisterhood for eternity for if someday my dreams were
to come true I would have six more sisters forever with me. We all
did sing a new song that would now be our oath,

> We are blood of our blood, and bone of our bone.
> We give each our body that we all might not be alone.
> I give you my spirit until our life shall be done.
> Translated into human fuel that
> every creature forever sees
> Blood remembers every birth, battle from one family
> to whole countries
> The heart is the house of blood, whose
> rooms will never be full;
> Whose red chambers are never silent as
> the ear of a shell covered in wool?
> Cultured for millennia like an exotic flower,
> heavenly clotting light into red,
> We are bound, each to the other, more
> tightly than we ever could have said
> Blood is red soul crimson shaded in our mystery
> as we do now wed

We now felt a deeper peace come over us. Fejér had yet to tell
us her story, yet we knew that would someday come. We knew that
we have all crossed over into a bond that would take a lot of work
and travel many roads. Our work with the Queen to be would be
our first test. We would not be around her, except for a few visits to
the royal castle. We all know it is the daytime hours that appear to
define our reality, since that is where our physical being exists, the
part that gets ill, hungry and expresses our emotions. The pains

and horrors seen in the daytime world do not exist in the nighttime world. All we can do is wipe away our tears and hope, we can someday be like Máriakéménd, and live in the nighttime world. Then an interesting question came into my mind. Why does Máriakéménd live only in the nighttime world? I asked Faith who did not know, and then I asked Fejér who told me, "For she has crossed over into only the nighttime world. She no longer has a daytime world." I asked why and she told me, "She lost her life at the hands of a bad man." I then asked, "How did she get into our nighttime world?" Fejér then asked me, "Do you not know my child? It was the love from one very close to you." I asked, "Who is this one closest to me?" Then Fejér said, "Someday . . ." Oh, I hate that word, yet I know Fejér's inside heart and if she were allowed to tell me, she would. I can only hope that someday comes fast. As far as now goes, I wish my daddy would hurry and return to my daytime world. I know mommy is starting to miss him a lot. She does not have our nighttime world so she knows nothing about what my daddy is doing. In fact, she had been taking me at night and putting me in her bed. I now go straight to her bed. She smiles and pulls me up into 'our' bed and hugs me. She asks me if I want her to tell me a story. I now hate stories, because just like real life, they are most times about bad men. I tell her every night, "You are so lucky to have married the best man ever." She tells me, "What about our Faith, she will be our queen?" I tell her, "The King is not as good as my daddy." She always kisses me and says, "I agree Ann; however, we must keep that a secret." We then laugh as asleep we fall and reunite with Máriakéménd. Faith Maria now said shockingly, "Oh blood of my blood, I must go back to Ann's daddy." She knew when she said she was returning to our daddy, I would support her departure and in a sense, she was being very truthful. Our daddy's life was in her hands as well as Fejér's. They were lucky to have their lives' in her hands, because they were hands filled with love for them. Faith's life had only one value and that was in saving her sisterhood and the parents thereof. They were as we all are 'blood of our blood." Faith Maria awoke with the aroma of fresh flowers. The room was filled with them. She had makeup on her face and another wonderful gown on. Where were these gowns coming from? Her faithful maiden was at her side. The maiden was not allowed to talk to the betrothed Queen; however, as all knew this royal highness wrote her own rules. The maiden refused to talk, and Faith called her to her side, wrapped her arms around her, and kissed her cheek. I shall kiss you until you talk to me, and if Charles walks in I shall tell him I want to marry you instead. The poor maiden's head and face had rivers of sweat rolling down. She forced as hard as she could with her head bowed, "Oh please my Queen, let not the kings take my head." Then Faith Maria released her and started wiping her head dry saying, "No one who talks to me with my permission shall lose their head. You talk to me by my command; you must not obey the commands of your Queen?" She now is on her knees said, "I shall obey all the commands and wishes from my great Queen." Faith Maria now worried that in order to talk to anyone; she would have to go through this process. She would speak to the King about this. A crew of doctors now appeared and started their examination. They asked my virgin to remove my gowns. She then looked at me, and I shook my head yes. They laid me on a nice very large silky soft light blue blanket as l lay there with a soft smile smelling the sweet odor of the incenses burning in the room and bouncing off some parts of my body. My maid inquired, "How can you be at so much peace with all these men seeing you?" I answered, "My fair maiden, for I have what they have not. I lust not for them. They lust for me. Eyes cannot not hurt me, however sticks and stones can. I am their Queen, if they wish to shame me, so be it, for I can have their heads. They are making sure that danger does not beset me before my throne seats me." The maiden said, "My queen is so wise and so strong. My days shall be great if you take me to serve you." Faith then said, "Absolutely, if you want to serve me then I shall also serve you and if you love me I shall love you. What is the name of my new maiden for my life?" She answered, "I am called Heidi." "Why do they call you that," questioned Faith. Heidi replied, "I lived in the mountains of Germany when raiders captured me and killed my family. They then sold me to some traders. One of King Louis's ministers saw me and bought me for the King's service, which is an honorable rewarded service." Faith Maria then said to Heidi, "I can give you freedom so you may return home." Heidi then said, "My Queen, go back to what? Even if I still had my family, I am now in love with you and want to serve only you until the day that I die. I hope you will get my papers changed to make me yours." Faith Maria looked at one of the Doctors and said, "Tell my brother to make this so, for I want to have and keep Heidi for my life." Faith Maria then asked Heidi to hold her hand and whispered in her ear, "I feel a little lonely with all these men staring at my breasts and vaginal hair. Do you think that makes me weak?" Heidi then whispered back into her ear, "That means you are a real woman of great honor. I am surprised that the queen mother is not here now to protect you. May I kiss the cheek of my master?" Faith Maria shook her head yes, and Heidi kissed her cheek. The doctors now had seen the absolute proof, Heidi was now the Queen's, and no other could ever have her. Any who did not obey her would be in trouble. Heidi was now the intimate personal damsel, for the queen. She would be permitted to sleep with the queen when she was not sleeping with the king. The doctors asked the queen why her entire body was tanned. Faith Maria said, "In my brother's house there are many sun rooms." The doctors agreed and quickly shifted the subject, for this freely exposed female was not only a betrothed Queen to a foreign nation, she was also their King's sister, and had the same blood in her that the King had. Faith Maria now asked, "I got hit in the head, why must I be freely exposed in front of you for so long?" The Doctor replied, "Your brother said to check every ounce of you if we wanted to keep our heads." Faith Maria then said, "My idiot brother and his head cutting. Take all the time you wish and tell me how I can serve you and thus help keep your lives. The doctors then laughed, and said, "Truly you are a great royal highness." Faith Maria then said, "Do not all women look as I look?" The a few doctors replied, "None could ever hope to look as good as you look. You bring great honor to your family. Our reports will read, "Her body is of absolute royalty, complete and perfect worthy to be called the Royal Highness Queen." Faith Maria then winked at them, "It is so rare that I can be freely exposed among such honored men." They then told her their work was done and helped Heidi put back on her clothes. As the doctors departed, then Marie came in followed by Fejér then daddy. Faith Maria asked Marie, "Why were you not in here to protect me?" She then answered, "Your brother would allow no one to answer. He forgot about your maiden there." Faith answered, "I was in no danger, except to have old bald men staring at what may have been a long time for them to see." Marie then said, "My child, they see it regularly, for when I first received this examination, I now insist being checked once each month." Faith Maria then hugged her mother as they both began to laugh. Faith's mother told her, "I shall write many letters to you; my daughter for you shall know all things in my mind. A daughter has that right." They hugged tight, as Louis walked in saying, "Hey, wait for me, I am a part of this family am I not?" Faith Maria and Marie opened their arms and let him join their family hug. Faith Maria then remarked, "Oh, men these days." Marie, quickly answered, "When can we go my daughter." The King then replied, "Ladies, if I wanted to hold those who hate me, would I not go to my dungeon." They both then looked at him and started yelling and slapping him. Marie yelled, "You will never be loved more than the female blood of your blood." Faith Maria then said, "That, my brother you should know to be true." The King looked at both of them and said, "I know even to the depths of my heart this to be true." Then Charles entered and asked, "What must a bridegroom do to see his bride?" Marie looked at him and said, "You shall be taking the foundation of our family with you. If you ever do her harm, I shall call upon my Henry IV to petition your father, James VI to place a curse upon you. Do you understand?" Charles answered, "Yes mother." Marie then said to her children; let us make room for my newest child." They created an opening between Marie and Louis and welcomed him into the circle with Louis laughing." Louis looking at Charles said, "You did not think we would let you touch our flower in bloom until the Pope says, "I pronounce you King and Queen, did you?" Charles laughed and said, "Fault me not for trying my brother" as he winked at Faith Maria who now gave the sky innocent girl giggle. My daddy, Fejér and Heidi sat on the chairs in the corner and whispered to each other. Fejér then said to Heidi, "Faith Maria tells me that you are to be honor chamber maid of honor. Does that make you happy?" Heidi asked, "When did she tell you this, for I watched her leave the room and go straight into her mother's arms. Fejér simply replied, "I read it in her eyes, a skill that you too shall someday have." Heidi then said, "I so much want that skill for my life shall be hers to do as she wills." Fejér replied, "Her will is to only love." Heidi said, "I do know that." Fejér then said, "I know you shall be great for her and her sisters." Heidi then said, "I knew not that she had sisters." Fejér said, "That is our secret. She will invite them to the castle. They are the blood of her blood." Daddy then said, "The King is ready for us to begin our march. Our Queen and us, to include you Heidi, shall ride in her carriage." Heidi then started counting us and said, "We are too many for a royal carriage." I shall ride behind." Fejér then said, "Heidi, I do not think you understand, "We shall all ride in her carriage." Heidi then said, "Of course, I shall ride at her feet." Daddy then laughed, "She will ride at your feet before you ride at her feet. You have a lot to learn about this special creation from the heavens." Heidi then said, "And a lifetime to learn it" with a big peaceful smile." Then they all started laughing as the Queen came over to join them, "My loves, what is so funny, will you tell . . . , Hey brother, wait for a minute." She ran to the King and said, "My brother, (pointing at Heidi) she is to be my 'chamber maiden of honor'." The King looked at her and said, "Oh my sister, I will get you many so much better, why would you want that ugly thing?" The Queen looked at him and said, "When she first came in to care for me, she never left my side, giving every ounce of her energy only for me. That kind of loyalty I must have with me when my husband wants me not." The King started laughing, "You are so strange, it would not matter if a bird were locked into a room with you alone, you would find some way to love it also. That which you ask for you shall have, for I am now glad I did not put a one legged maid in your room." He then motioned for his minister to bring Heidi before him. He then raised his hand as all in the hallways and room stopped talking and said, "Today I appoint . . . Looking at her, when my daddy said to him Heidi, Heidi to be the lifetime chamber maiden of honor for my sister. You shall be by her side all the hours she is in her chambers, and only you may sleep beside her when she sleeps not with her husband. You shall know her better than herself and answer to God only while caring for her. This is your command, today your life ends, as you now shall breathe the same air and eat the same food, as does she. Only death can free you from this divine ordination. Rise now and wipe her feet with your hair." The King knew not what he had just said, yet soon realized the error of his ways. As Heidi went to bow before Faith, the Queen rush to bow first and commanded her with a loud voice, "Air that I breathe give unto me your feet." She motioned for her to extend her leg placing both feet in her hands. Faith Maria then, with tears in her eyes of great joy, wiped the tears from her face with her hair and then started wiping Heidi's feet. Heidi was in such shock she fainted, as did a few in the room. My daddy and Fejér quickly started nursing her, as Faith Maria kissed her cheeks. All knew that the creature that just fainted was the Queens and only answered to the Queen. The King now shook his head, laughing said, "Only my sister would wipe the feet with her tears and hair of her bound servant." I had better surrender her to Charles before she wipes the feet of all in France, or knowing her all of Europe." He and his mother departed outside to meet with Charles. Charles asked, "What is your sister doing in there?" Louis answered, "Wiping her chamber maiden of honor's feet with her hair and tears." Charles looked puzzled as Marie and added, "She is being the true angel that is her." Then Charles smiled and looked at peace now. Louis said to Charles, "I must surrender her to you before she wipes the feet of all in Europe." They all three laughed as Louis and Marie bid their farewells. Charles asked, "Are you not going to bid your farewell to your blood?" They both looked at him and said, "We shall never bid our farewells to her, for that which was lost is now found and we shall never lose her again." Charles shook his head as if he understood.

What he knew was his betrothed was loved by her family and would someday be once again loved by the French. Charles went to stand with the Pope in front of his carriage, with Faith's running second. When the Princess walked out with her escorts, she said to Charles, "Louis always rides behind me, why do you not? I can ride back to Paris if you so desire." Charles then in total shock, for never had one spoken to him like this replied with his wit saving him, "Your brother told me to ride in front of you for your safety. And I do so much want to take you to London." Faith looked at him saying, "You are saved this time my future husband. My brother worries too much over me." Charles replied, "My dear, you are worth the worry, for you are the love of Kings." Faith Maria then told him, "Be careful with your flattery, for I may run up to you and kiss you bringing the wrath of my brother upon you." Charles then replied, "It would be worth the price, however for now; hold on, here comes your brother running towards us." Louis said, "I need you over to the patio, bring all who are with you. We have one more task for you to perform." No one knew what was going on. Yet, for curiosity, we all ran to the patio. Marie motioned for them to enter the castle auditorium. Marie said, "Princess, go to the stage put on your crown and take the sword in your hand, I will be behind you telling you what to do, after I introduce you." Hurry my daughter, put on this wig and gown. Then listen to what I say and repeat it. Off went my dress, as my mother rushed to put on the new gown. That is when she first knew this was her mother; mothers have a protective instinct that will not let anything bad happen to their children. Faith Maria just stood there, for it was clear mother was in control here. She worked frantically as Heidi and Fejér came to her side. Marie said, "Girls, stand back, this holy divine duty is mine." They all looked at each other in shock, and once Faith Maria was dressed, they called daddy up to her. Marie then remarked, "Must all of you be here?" Faith Maria replied, "They are blood of my blood. Where my blood is, they shall be." Marie then motioned for the King to appear before them. Charles stood back in the corner and remarked to one of his commanders, "I almost had her didn't I?" They then did laugh. He further remarked, "At least I am not on my knees in front of her with that sword in her hand. She is innocent enough to make a big mistake. England would love that, my bride cuts off the head of the King of France. With all that has happened I would not be surprised." Marie stood behind Faith Maria and said, "King Louis XIII fall to your knees. As you now bow before your sister, blood of your father and blood of you, she shall bestow upon you, the title of Highest Knight in the Land, of which only she can do for only she if of you, and of your father." Marie then said, "Listen to me and say what I say," "With this sword my brother our fathers do give unto you the title Highest Knight in the Land." She then slowly tapped each shoulder and then together with Marie said, "Arise my brother for even our father and all with him honor you. For thou is the Highest Knight in the Land." When he arose, he grabbed his sister and started kissing her cheeks rapidly saying aloud, "I thank the Gods for my pure and saintly sister that he has returned to us. I love you . . ." Then Charles said to all, "My brother, please save some of her for me." Heidi, who had drifted back to the King, said to him, "Oh my royal highness, she still has enough for you, who shall receive the greatest love of all. For you shall be blessed among men to have your seed in her womb and behold the fruit thereof." Charles looked at her and said, "Did not I see you with the Princess today?" Heidi said, "Yes my master." Charles said, "You are not from England, so how can I be your master?" Heidi said, "I am the property of the Princess, for I am her chamber maiden of honor, which I may lay upon the ground for her feet to walk with comfort." Charles then replied, "Your never do that with that lady, oh now I remember, was it not you that she washed your feet with her hair and tears?" Heidi answered, "Yes, my King it was, and for that reason I will give my life and all my energy to save her from pain or injury." Charles then said, "With you in her bed, I can sleep knowing that love is beside her." Heidi then bowed to the King and replied, "More love than can fill the ocean my king." Faith now came in running to Charles yelling, "Why does my love bow to you my betrothed?" Charles answered, "Listening to her tell me about the oceans of love she has for you, I marvel at you Princess, and you have your King bowing before you and your servants offering their life to save yours. I am a very lucky man as your chamber maiden of honor did tell me. Now, let England bring you home." Faith Maria waved goodbye to her brother and mother and all the doctors and soldiers screaming out, "I shall always love all of you." Nonetheless, with that many tears of joy poured. The hour of departure was now almost at hand. As Faith Maria and her gang prepared to enter the carriage Charles yelled out, "Not all of you can ride in that carriage, chamber maiden, and ride with me." Faith Maria cried out, "Chamber maiden return to me, Charles, these are blood of my blood, and we all go as one or we do not go." Charles then said, "How my dear can all of you fit in there?" Faith Maria said, "It has a floor for me?" Charles then said, very well, my guards will ride outside." My daddy sat beside Faith Maria has Heidi and Fejér sat across from them. Faith Maria now at rest with those who loved the real her, rested her head on daddy's shoulder and began to cry. Daddy asked her, "My mighty queen, why do cry?" Faith Maria answered crying more, "I am not your mighty queen, I am your daughter." Daddy hugged her tightly and said to her, "Never forget that my child and if ever you need me, call for me since I am the rock for all my daughters. Do you understand?" Faith Maria then asked, "Daddy can I sleep on your lap one more time?" Daddy said, "My daughter, for as long as you want." Faith Maria jumped on his lap as she had many times at their family picnics and quickly went to sleep. Daddy told Heidi, when they all were little, all the other sisters would wrestle to get on mommy and little skin and bone Faith Maria would walk over to me and jump on my lap. Those days were not that long ago, and to think she now rides to marry a King after she just knighted another king. I think Ann has to be a little more careful whom she adopts from now on. They then all laughed. The convoy then started to roll. This time, it would be so different. The French soldiers had spread among all the people along the route to the port. The crowds were told that no one stands within two feet of the road. When the convoy is spotted, usually by advanced English Guards, all would go to their knees. When the convoy was approaching, all would bow with face in the ground. Any who failed to do so would be executed? No one was to stand under any circumstances or they would be shot. The resonance was, "A small boy almost killed the Princess. No one else will even be given a remote chance. No noise." The Princess had guards riding along each window. Immediately, upon departure a spirit of sadness still covered the Princess. Daddy started singing the old lullabies that always put them all to sleep. Faith Maria asked daddy, "Do you remember the first time we met?" Daddy said, "Yes, I never thought girls could carry so much mud. Even big girls like Fejér." Then all laughed except Heidi. Fejér told Heidi, "I will tell you all about it." Faith Maria now said, "I remember all the scrubbing, oils and salves from the doctors." Fejér added, "And the hard work little Ann did to fix all our boo boos." Faith Maria then looked at Heidi and said, "Your master was not always so famous, or hated, whatever I am now." Fejér continued with, "We were all hungry, clothed in rags with no hope until Ann, mommy, and daddy brought us into their home and shared everything, to include their love with us." Daddy then said, "We were not quite that bad, I mean some of you still had some teeth." Then Faith Maria reached up and kissed daddy's cheek. Heidi then said, "This is so remarkable." Faith Maria looked at Heidi and said, "If you would have seen us, you would have chased us away throwing stones at us." Heidi then said, "Only if you hid your eyes from me." Fejér then paused for a minute and spoke to Faith Maria in mind talk, "That which she says is true." Faith Maria then motioned her Heidi to come to her. She then kissed Heidi on the cheek and said, "I am so lucky to have you, promise never to leave me." Heidi smiled and started to kiss Faith Maria on her cheeks saying, "That promise shall I keep always from my heart and not the King's law." Fejér then complained, "Everyone gets kissed around her except for me." Heidi then jumped back and kissed Fejér on both cheeks. Everyone started laughing. In mind talk, Fejér told Faith Maria that Heidi was going to make an outstanding sister and once in the castle, we will have to introduce her to our sisters. Faith Maria agreed, and then started crying again. She then told her friends, "I want to live with my daddy and sisters." Daddy told her, "Faith, you are betrothed to the one man all the women in England want to marry. You got the one at the top. He stood by you all the weeks you were healing, each day praying for your recovery. I even saw him cry a few times." Faith Maria then replied, "He cried because he saw my face." Fejér then screamed at Faith, "How could you even think such a thing?" Then Heidi started crying. Fejér and Faith Maria looked at her and asked, "Heidi, why do you cry?" Heidi said, "My master cries because she has such an ugly chamber maiden." Faith Maria now squawked at Heidi, "How can you say such a thing?" Heidi then told Faith, "What I said was just a crazy as you thinking the King does not love your beauty." Then daddy said, "Girls, stop the crying and screaming or the King will have my head." Without hesitation, Charles knocked on the carriage door. The convoy had stopped. He asked, "Why is there so much screaming and why is the Princess crying." Heidi looked at the King and said, "She fears you think she is ugly." Charles then asked the Princess to depart from her carriage. As she did, he put her on his horse sitting in front of him. He then started riding to the back of the convoy yelling, "Look all and see my beautiful wife to be, the new Queen." The soldiers cheered as the people staying with their faces down. Later, the commanders told the King, "Be careful what commands you give, for if any in the crowds had stood up, they would have done so by your order. The King shared his bride to all, and then returned to her carriage asking, "Now my future wife, do I not love also your beauty?" The King was smart to toss in that "also" so he would not be accused "only" of loving her beauty. His mother had trained him well. As Faith Maria went to get back in her carriage, the King kissed her on the cheek. Faith Maria looked shocked and asked him, "How dare you, in front of your soldiers?" Charles replied, "Everyone was kissing you on your cheek, I just wanted to get one in before you no longer had a cheek." Faith Maria and her escort all then just laughed as Faith Maria gave the King a nice 'sexy' smile insuring that the king's soldiers could see it. Faith Maria knew from her days as a slut trying to keep her sisters alive that men fed off the victories over women for the other 'lucky' men. This indeed got flashier salutes while smiling as the King, now in his new glory, rode past them. Faith Maria now felt much better, the King had shown all his love for her to the soldiers in this caravan, and he finally gave her a kiss. She now thought about how this was the first time a real male lover had kissed her. It felt so wonderful. She now had a glow on her face as Fejér teased, "Goldie Locks got her first kiss." Faith laughed with the rest of them and then starry-eyed fell fast to sleep. When she woke, she spoke saying, "It is so sad that Charles and I did not have a chance to court, with flowers and gifts. When my brother asked me, I knew not who Charles was. The ironic thing is with him being the beggar at the ball, not knowing that I probably would have said yes there, just to see the misery in all those aristocrats." Then daddy said, "My dear child, I too am aristocrat." Faith Maria then said, "Not when you are holding me, as you share your home and lives with the poor plus give food to feed so many." Daddy then told her, "That is a daddy trick." Faith Maria looked outside, and saw all the people bow to the ground and then said, "It is so sad that they cannot have the freedom, I so wanted for them." The carriage now came to a stop. A soldier knocked on the door and said, "My fair queen, prepare to sail with your fleet." Faith Maria looked into the sea and could see no place without ships. She then asked a minister who was standing beside her, "Why do the ships have so many flags?" The minister said, "My fair Queen, the kings of the world have sent ships for your SAFE trip back to your England." Faith Maria looked at the minister and soldier and said, "I am not yet your Queen." The minister then said, "Oh my fair lady, when the King kissed your cheek you got your crown, my fair Queen. We have so longed for a queen since the death of Anne." Faith Maria then said, "I have a sister who was named after the former queen." The soldier then exclaimed, "That is so great, what is her name?" Faith and the Minister looked at the soldier and the Minister then said, "Son have mercy on our Queen and go rest somewhere to get your head out of the sun." Faith Maria and the Minister now both laughed. Faith Maria then said, "If were not that I grew up in England I do believe that a soldier would have scared me." Charles came riding back asking, "Why are my minister and queen laughing?" The minister then said, "My great and honorable King, our soldiers need to get out of this French sun." As he said Faith Maria began to laugh, and was soon followed by the minister. The King looked at both of them and said to the minister, "I forgave you for I know my betrothed has magic over the peoples' minds." The King then looked at Faith Maria and said, "Let us put you and your bloods on the largest ship we have, and I shall sail behind you, for if we sail in the same ship the pope will have my head. You shall give the command to take us home my fair Queen." Faith Maria told him, "In joy I depart France. My home is in England with my daddy and sisters. May I know how we shall go to London?" The King then answered, "Our fleet will dock in Bristol, then some ships will sail before we insure my Armies have control of the banks. My royal ministers and you shall sail in our ships to London based upon the wind. If it is poor, we shall arrive by royal carriage." Faith Maria nodded and replied, "Thank you my fair king." Faith Maria and her special friends walked towards the mighty ship that she would sail. The ship was so magnificent, truly befitting a queen. Daddy told her, "My daughter, I have never seen a ship so majestic." Fejér then commented, "I must be appropriate for a queen." They all laughed as Faith Maria locked her arms on my daddy's arm and allowed him to guide her onto the ship. The ship was remolded for total luxury. Each room had flowers. The queen had a large bed for her and Heidi, and two other large beds, one for Fejér and one for daddy. There was one large table for eating with rich assortments of food on it. Daddy's bed had some nice liquor beside it and the girls had a wide selection of wines. The ships were now leaving the dock. Faith Maria could see many people on the outside fence of the dock. They were waving and screaming they loved her. Faith Maria could not resist and had daddy, grudgingly obeyed as the opened her window and she reached out and waved. The cheers began to increase becoming so loud that many soldiers had to cover their ears. She then ran out on deck and yelled "Veni, vidi, vici." The King then yelled, "That you did my betrothed." Daddy was then once again surprised and asked, "When did you learn Latin, my daughter who came, and saw and conquered?" Faith Maria laughed and said, "Ann taught me." Daddy said, "Someday I need to rediscover that little tiger." Faith Maria laughed and said, "You will discover how blessed you truly are." She then led my daddy back into their chambers. A soldier commented to my daddy, "You are so lucky to be in the same chamber as the Queen." Faith Maria looked at him and said, "No my friend, it is I who is lucky to be in the same chamber as my daddy." When they got into the chambers, daddy said, "We must get some sleep girls, in England shall soon be upon us and our queen must now feed her subjects."

Chapter 06

A Royal Wedding

We give each our body that we all are not alone.
I give you my spirit until our life shall be done.
We are bound, each to the other, more
tightly than we ever could have said
Blood is red soul crimson shaded in our mystery
as we do now wed

We entered the docks in Bristol where the ministers told their King the wind were not favorable to cut down on the burning summer heat. The original plans to enter the Thames at Dover were cancelled when ministers received reports of low wind conditions throughout all of England. England could not afford to strange large warships in the low waters of the Thames, not being able to sail again until the seasonal rains. May of 1625 was brought on a hot summer. We then loaded into our carriages as the King said for Faith to lead the convoy, "We are in England, the home of your people. Have no fear." Faith Maria told the King that she had yet to be on this side of England before large crowds were England now forming. The shift from Dover to Bristol shifted many off the Thames. At least the first few days would go well. With so many in

- 207 -

the convoy, the King has fresh horses staged so the group could keep moving, just like a bullet into its target. Faith Maria wanted to avoid as many crowds as possible, and expressed her desire to the minister who then told the king. The King understood. Then in peace, Faith passed off to sleep only to awaken from a terrifying dream. She was dancing with daddy after her wedding when some ugly large beast came in and turned everyone into skeletons. It was so ugly, and I was so hot with no flesh to cover my bones. Fire was burning and people crying, as more came and were eating people. They were knocking down buildings and I heard one yell, "Where is the chosen one?" They all answered her saying, "We cannot find her." The large beast then yelled, "Find it, and search all of England, then Europe until I return. Warn them, when I return that if they do not give me the chosen one, I shall burn all of London. I shall give them only thirty-five years and shall return from my searches in 1660." The beast looked at me and laughed, saying "You foolish one, why do you sell yourself to a man? Do you not know how evil they are?" She gave me eyes. In addition, with my eyes I saw my wedding cake shrink, turn black, and two skulls drop upon it. Their eye sockets gaped at me. I then saw three red roses appear. This cake sat in a bowl of blood." Then my eyes began to melt with bitter pain, as if 1,000 needles were poked at them. It was the pain that woke me up." Faith Maria now was covered in sweat. Water was flowing from her body. Heidi was now worried as she had used up all the cloth she could find to wipe her dry. Faith Maria now went back into a sleep. The water in the carriage was gone. All knew the King had to be told. Heidi volunteered since she was French and only Faith Maria could ever punish her. She motioned for the driver to stop. She got out running to the King while crying aloud, "Help us." The King rushed to her jumping off his horse and asked, "How can I help?" He knew it was serious for the chamber maiden was crying. She told the king, "My master had a very bad dream and her body is sweating too much. We need more water and some blankets. The King pulled off his jacket and ordered that the carriage be given more water. He gave his jacket to the chamber maiden and said, "Put this on your master fast, now go." Heidi grabbed hold of the jacket and ran so fast to her carriage. The ministers were already in there covering her with fresh water to cool her and giving her water to drink. Some soldiers brought in some more clothe to help with the wiping. The King sent soldiers to get some blankets. He rushed into the carriage sitting beside Heidi and Fejér, since my daddy was looking for wood to make a small fire beside the carriage in the event she would need some heat. Heidi was so worried she forgot the King was beside her. Actually, she was extremely comfortable around the king, he respected her role, and she could tell he knew Faith needed me. The King always tried to make them feel well, and suffered so much for Faith Maria while in France hoping for her recovery. Heidi was removing layers of Faiths garments in order to be able to redress her in dry clothing. Finally, they were down to her last layer. She could go no further with the King among them. This was not a worry about the king, it was a worry that a soldier would tell the pope. The King remarked, "What strange garments does she wear next to her skin." Heidi said, "Oh, my king, have you not seen the garments a woman wears?" The King was now blushing and said, "Oh, why yes my maiden, it was just that hot sun temporarily made me mad. I do know one thing, not all women have such beauty there." It was now Heidi realized that Faith's nipples were showing. Faith Maria woke up feeling better this time, and said to the King, "Do my nipples bring peace to your heart my future husband?" The King replied, "I truly have ever to lay my eyes upon better?" Faith Maria then said, "Oh my husband, have you seen others?" The King then quickly remarked, "Not with the darn Pope breathing down upon me all the time, I do pray someday England makes its own church. I assure my betrothed that you shall be the first and last." Then Faith Maria told the King to come closer and whispered in his ear, "I do hope as a King you can discover a way to touch them while we kiss and not get caught. Can you do that for your deprived sick betrothed, so that if I die before we marry I will know your touch?" The King whispered back, "Your wish is my command." They kissed and the King proved why he was a King and touched his children's future milk bottles rather abundantly with only Heidi catching them. She protected the King. She protected them by providing extra concealment for the royal lovers. Upon completion, Charles looked at Heidi and smiled while he got out of the carriage. A soldier riding fast came towards him, saying, "My king, I have many blankets for our Queen." The King passed the blankets to Fejér. He then called his minister to him and looking at Heidi said, "I officially endorse our queen's selection as chamber maiden of honor of Heidi in all of England. Do this so when we return. Send soldiers in advance with your orders." The minister replied, "It shall be as the King has commanded." Heidi and Fejér had now undressed the princess, wiped her down making her clean and were redressing her with a combination of their clothing, joking by saying, "Faith, now we get some fun showing ourselves to men." Faith Maria then said, "Be careful my sisters, for you may not want to stop." They now took her outside to sit beside my daddy while he kept her warm. She told him, "I never thought after that burning in the temple that I would want heat again." Now a soldier came up and asked the Princess, saying, "Oh my Queen, a peasant family who gave you all their blankets would like to bow before you if you will let them." Faith Maria said, "Well I let so many French do it, I might as well let those who are keeping me warm join them." The soldier smiled and rushed back to get the family and bring them forward. The King yelled, "My soldier, where are you going?" He saw them heading towards the Queen. The soldier stopped and bowed saying, "My King, the Queen has given them audience so they may bow before her." The family now dropped to the ground as the soldier did. The King then asked the soldier, "Well you let me sneak in with the family?" The soldier said, "What if the Queen gets angry at me?" The King said as he walked before them taking the father of the family's hat, "Do not worry my soldier, she only gets mad at me. I will plead for your leniency, or we shall do our punishment together." They all laughed as they moved towards the queen. The mother began by saying to the Queen, "Oh great Queen, we all are so thankful that God has given us a Queen to control our King. (Hearing this, the King, with his head bowed and only his hat protecting him from the Queen scratched his throat.) At this time, the mother realized the King was beside her and the family all laughed. Faith Maria then commented, "My, what a joyous family we have here. I see you have a handsome husband, why does he not wear a hat. Is it to hide the face of your ugly son who stands beside you?" The family now laughed louder, as Charles lifted up his face and gave the hat to the father, saying, "Will you repeat that my betrothed?" Faith Maria said, "My dear Charles, will men never learn that they can never fool the one who shall marry them. I have studied you, and now know how you walked perfect. I knew you were walking with this family as you took your first step?" The mother of the family looked at her husband and said, "That also goes for you." Then the gang all laughed, to include my daddy who said, "Oh honorable king, that which my daughters says is true, even for me for my wife can even read my mind." Charles then said, "I guess my future will be more exciting than I thought." The mother then said to Faith, "I am so sorry our blankets were so poor for you our honorable Queen." Faith Maria then said, "Oh quite the contrary, I was going to ask you if I could buy them for ten pounds?" The mother said, "Oh no my Queen, if you want them you may have them for free." Faith Maria said, "Oh no, do not hate me so, Charles pays her?" The mother then said, "Oh I swear by all my ancestors that I have no hate for you." Then the King gave the woman the pounds. Daddy told him, "That too, is a part of marriage." The King said, "They never tell bachelors these things." Faith Maria said, "If you have been deceived, I shall release you from your oath." The King looked at his little juicy fourteen-year-old bride and said, "And be the only one in England who cannot love you, I think not my betrothed." The peasant family all cheered as the father said, "The King wiggled safely out of that one." My daddy then said, "That he did my friend, I do believe he will be a welcomed addition to our family and a fine husband for my daughter." Faith Maria then said, "I know daddy, I fell in love with him the first time I saw the poor dirty beggar." The King laughed as the peasant family looked puzzled, and then told them, "I shall tell our nation someday soon." They all returned to their carriages as some soldiers came riding towards the king. They told the King that all was clear before them. Even the secret spies are reporting the Queen is so safe that the people would carry her on their backs to get her to the wedding alter. Charles then said, "My people are wise for they know how to enjoy the good things in life." I will talk to my commanders and see what they want to do. The commanders told the king, "We have no need to show great force to our people. They want you chained to a Queen too much. We recommend that we take one hundred soldiers and go to Warwick castle and rejoice for a week to rest up. The Queen could use some fresh air and relaxation." The King then said, "Then to Warwick we do go." When they were within sight, Faith Maria was so shocked at how big it was. Even daddy said, "It is a great castle that in history did well for England. William the Conqueror was associated with it. I am sorry I do not know the details. I hated my history teacher." Faith Maria then asked, "Is this on the way to London? My father did not know, however Fejér did know saying, "I do not believe so. I believe Charles's father gave it to a Sir Fulke Greville." Faith Maria asked, "How did you get so smart?" Fejér then replied, "I was an aristocrat before my husband committed suicide." Heidi rushed to hug Fejér and kissing her cheeks told her, "I give my condolences if that is of any value. If for any reason you need someone to talk to or lean on, it must be my shoulder, okay Love?" Fejér nodded yes and smiled, then in mind talk said to Faith, "I do believe we have another sister here." Faith Maria nodded yes. As Faith Maria began to walk on the stones to enter Warwick, she had a flash and her body became cold with a severe pain in her back. In the flash, she saw a male servant holding a knife behind his back. Fejér, sensing something strange rushed into Faith's mind and looked for something not right. She was able to see the image. It was only an image and it was not from their time zone. She guessed that it would be a few years in their future. As she stared at the image, she saw the hand move into the man's master's back many times as the blood began to flow. She now saw the time as a calendar on the wall. It was in 1628, just a few years ahead." Faith Maria was once again placed comfortably on the ground as her ten-pound blankets once again covered her chilled flesh. The King then told my father that, "I have requested Sir Fulke to grant us a visit. The entire estate family graciously begged for the opportunity to serve their King and future queen. I do believe our fair lady is in dire need of some rest and relaxation." My father now thanked the King, as he returned to caring for his dramatic daughter. Fejér and Heidi also joined as the three of them and the Dutch Doctor worked to warm her. As her temperature was slowly restored, she started to regain her senses. Fejér now told Faith, in mind talk, "Fear not my sister, I saw your vision, and you are in no danger." She then spoke aloud, "Come now my sister, let us take you to our temporary chambers." As they entered the castle the Lady of the House quickly rushed up to her future queen and spoke, "Oh my beautiful Queen, allow my servants to escort you to our finest chambers." Faith nodded yes, and thanked her. The escort opened the bedroom door and Faith Maria looked in and gasped. Fejér and Heidi looked at, splitting up so that one was on each side of the Princess and gasped. The escort then asked, "Is this room suitable for our Queen." Faith Maria looked at her and said, "Absolutely my friend, I shall enjoy this room as if I were in the heavens." The escort said, "Oh please my Queen, hold off on heaven for a few years. We have been too long without a queen." Faith Maria looked at the escort, gave her a hug and said, "Trust me, my dear friend; I hope to torture your King for many years to come." The escort then said, "I am so lucky to have been touched by our queen and so proud to know that a woman will be keeping our King in line." They all laughed and the soldiers brought in the women's luggage, although it was quite light. The soldiers told the queen that any clothing that had been worn was being cleaned by the castle laundry staff and would be returned to them while they were dining at a meal. The girls now touched the beautiful curtains and soft gold trimming and to their amazement, all three fit in the elegant love seat. Faith Maria then joked, "So many chairs in this room, and I am so lucky to have those I love sacrificing them to be close to me." Fejér and Heidi started kissing their Queen each on a separate check and Fejér starting massaging her. As the Queen starting laughing, Fejér replied, "So you want to be a funny girl. It time to laugh now funny girl." Fejér then lightly massaged her new glorious Queen. Faith then gave a sensual moan, saying, "Bless you my lover." Heidi was now terrified and did not know what to do or say. Faith Maria looked at Heidi and asked, "Do you now not love me?" Heidi said, "As long as air is in my lungs, I shall love you." Faith Maria now gently took hold of her hand and placed it on her other breast and said, "I beg you then, serve me now." Heidi then started massaging her breast saying, "My Queen's was slowly becoming soft once more. At least this moment in time, she did not have the burdens of eastern Europe on her hands." Faith Maria asked Heidi, "I hope you are gaining as much hedonism as you are sharing now." Heidi then said, "Oh yes my love, I only pray that you let me serve all of you. Faith Maria then said, "That we shall enjoy, with Fejér as we all sleep tonight, OK my lover." Heidi asked, "Will the bed not be crowded." Faith Maria then told her, "My love, in our home with daddy all my four sisters and Fejér sleep in Ann's bed, leaving the other five cradles empty." Heidi then asked the Queen, "May I kiss you?" As she went to kiss Faith Maria on her cheek, the Queen detoured Heidi's head to her lips and gave Heidi a big 'French' kiss. Heidi came up starry eyed and simply sat back in the chair and softly moaned, "Wow that was so good. You know, I sometimes thought that I would die never enjoying the taste of another's lips." She now stumbled over to the white love seat in front of the white fireplace, sat down, and just smiled. Fejér then said to Faith, "I think you overloaded our new friend." Heidi then said, "Oh now my master, I am simply preparing for much more." Fejér said, "Do not worry Heidi, for you are the only who can sleep with her behind locked doors, except for the king." Faith then added, "Such great fortune for me. I have wanted to do this for a while, yet was scared." Heidi then said, "Why would you worry, what you command of me I shall always to, even if you command that I cut off my arm and give it to you, that would I do." Then Faith Maria replied, "Oh no, not that for my breasts would then hate me." They all laughed and started tickling and wrestling with each other on the nice soft King sized bed." Fejér then told Heidi, "Never forget, our love is only fourteen years

old, and in between ruling nations she must have some play time."
Moreover, tonight was a time to play. As the three lay down on the
nice sheet, it was time for Heidi to explore her queen. Faith Maria
laid down with the nice warm lanterns chasing the cold from her
flesh. Heidi looked upon the queen and remarked, "Such wonderful
beauty." Fejér then said, "Listen and do what I say and your master
will be pleased and relaxed." Fejér was so surprised at how Faith's
body responded to Heidi and said, "I think the master has found
the one with the key." Faith Maria did give unto her servant much
heavenly wine, more than when her sisters or Fejér. Heidi had
never enjoyed this wine before and told her Queen, "I do hope you
will share your cup with me again." Faith Maria told her, "We shall
both share our cups for now it is time I served you." Heidi fell onto
the sheet as Fejér and the Queen guided her in position. Then Heidi
just lay in total peace, as the Queen was able to pull her wine into
her cup. Heidi a martyr, which none of the sisters had ever seen or
known, although many had felt as such so many times in their
lives. Fejér said she had heard tales of them yet had yet to
understand one. This made the experience so much greater for the
Queen especially since Heidi would also explode with emotions at
the same time. Faith could feel the power of her emotions and it
brought her great joy. A few hours went by and then they fell fast
asleep. Faith Maria was so exhausted she did not hear
Máriakéménd calling for her. Fejér told her, "Let her rest, I will
join you." I wanted to see what the castle looked like so we opened
the window. The first place they wanted to see was our room. I
then asked, "Who is that freely exposed woman sleeping in Faith's
arms?" Fejér told her, "She is Heidi, Faith's honorable chamber
maiden. She must sleep with her Queen every night, except when
the Queen is with the King. She is a guard from her brother to
make sure she stays faithful to her husband." I then asked, "Does
she . . . ?" Fejér said, "Yes, and quite good for a beginner . . . ." I
now asked, "Do you think we should make her a sister?" Fejér said,
"She will, I shall introduce you guys to her soon." We now went
throughout the castle until I saw a big mean looking man who was
an important servant. I told Fejér, "That man shall kill his master

in a few years." Fejér told me, "Faith Maria had a vision about the same thing yesterday." I asked Fejér, "What does it mean?" Fejér said, "I think it has something to do with building your powers." I then told her, "We shall see." They all finished the tour and I, of course, and returned to the regular place in the night world." It was now time to get up. The minister had given us a schedule of upcoming events that the host requested the Queen attend. The first event was morning mass. He invited the bishop to this area. The bishop was early and appeared to be very nervous. Faith asked one of the servants why the bishop was so nervous. The servant told her it was because, "The pope is very fond of our Queen and believes that fewer Catholics will suffer in England because of her." Faith Maria told the servant, "Catholic as my French family and protestant as my English family, I want no people to die because of worshiping the God of Abraham. "When two brothers of the same house fight, the family also suffers." Little did Faith Maria know that her saying would soon spread through all of England, as many now said, "Our divided house shall have one Queen, our honorable mother." Fejér was feeding her many quotes as was Máriakéménd teaching her many old fables from her past, such as "It takes two men to make one brother . . ." and these short poems her father taught her:

All for one and one for all
My brother and my friend what fun we have.
The time we share brothers until the end.
One can be a brother only in something.
Where there is no tie that binds men,
Men are not united but merely lined up.

Since us, sisters had no brothers we always picture the two of our daddies. That would be a difficult road to walk, for only a King could try. For now, I thought I would tease the bishop so I ran up to him and put my arms around him, kissed him and told him, "I liked your message, and I want you to marry the King and I." The priest was so embarrassed he said, "He said, the

King must ask the pope" at which time he fainted. The King now yelled across the room, "My Queen, please do not torture the bishops as you did the pope." All in the room laughed while Faith and Heidi brought the King back to his conscience. The Lady of the house said to the King, "Our new Queen has control over the pope and bishops, which should work well for England . . . ." All agreed and talked about the events of the day. The Queen excused herself, took Heidi to her chambers, told the guards, "I shall rest for a while, do not disturb me." She got Heidi inside and told her, "Prepare yourself for my pleasures." Once Heidi and Faith Maria were 'disrobed', Faith Maria got a hair band to tie her hair back and some nice fluffy pillow for Heidi to lie. Faith Maria now enjoyed her damsel, as she desired. Heidi just lies there in astonishment, to have the most power woman in Western Europe working so hard to make her intimate pleasure was a reward beyond her prayers. The sensitivity and exotic drama that was unfolding put Heidi on top of the world, as she just lay there and cried in a soft voice, "I love my Queen, I was made to be a toy for my Queen. All that is mine is my Queens. Oh, how wonderful is my Queen."

Then Faith looked up at Heidi and asked, "Are you sure this is not going to damage your personality?" Heidi said, "When I begged you to be your chamber maid, I was begging to be yours and only yours. I can never be touched by another. You allowed Fejér to touch me. Now you give me the love that I could never have. I killed my personality when I gave my life to you and only you. I am so lucky to have a master who loves me so much. And I shall always love you forever and one day my master." Faith Maria then asked, "Can we ever be friends?" Heidi said, "I am more than your friend, because you are in me. If it were my will, I would even carry you so you would not have to walk." Then Faith Maria told her, "Oh myself, for I shall call you when we lay together myself, I must walk so my flesh stays firm to keep the King's eye, must I not." The Heidi said, "I will work hard with you to keep the King's eye on you." The Queen now said, "I do believe the Kinglike you also." Heidi said, "That is because he knows that if I beg you hard

enough that your love will force you to do what I beg you for."
Faith Maria said, "How could I ever say no to 'myself'?" Heidi
then answered, "I do know this, and that is why many times I have
told the King, "I cannot ask my only master that which you desire."
Then Faith Maria said, "In order to insure you a future least evil
take me, you need to pass some more things to me. I want him to
know that I do so much law and honor you. For why should you be
any different than others?" Heidi came back with, "Oh mighty
master, do you not know that when you die I must also die. It is a
law so that no other can touch the one the Queen slept with." Faith
Maria said, "Well, I had better live to be old. Still pass me his
requests. I want him to honor the one who I love so much. It will
give us more power; on things, he is afraid to ask me, he will not
be afraid to ask you. Let him think he was getting over on you. We
will get you many extra benefits while you blink your eyes and
'think' about it. Nevertheless, always say, I shall beg her. This way
it can never be counted as treason. Likewise, please always tell me
so I can defend you. For whatever she offers you, I shall offer
more." Heidi said, "Oh master please promise never to take your
love from me or me from your love." Faith Maria then told her,
"That you have earned, now let us rest for we have many more fun
things to do today." Now that I was asleep, it was time for me to
visit my sisters. Máriakéménd was teaching them about her
brothers, adding many exciting stories. These were the first stories
about boys that the sisters actually liked, for they were about them
saving Máriakéménd. The sisters naturally liked the three male
servants we had. India was quite, the other two had sisters that
chased and hit on them all day, which the sisters would always
laugh especially since the sisters did not hit them hard and the
brothers would pretend it was hard. The sisters were entertaining
the idea that some boys might be ok and that a King could maybe
be ok. We needed some more persuading. We all wondered if there
would be a King for all of us. Faith Maria suggested, maybe my
sons or the King's brothers. I told her, "I think your sons will have
too many girlfriends." Faith Maria gave me a kiss on the cheek. I
then asked her, "How long before you and daddy come back to our

house?" Faith Maria told me, "Ann, your daddy will be coming home soon; however I have to go to London and do a lot of work." I asked her, "What work do you have to do now? I thought you did all your work in France." Faith Maria then told me, "My work in France is done; now I have to prepare my new home and prepare for my wedding." I asked her, "Why do you have to do all the work?" Faith Maria told me, "I do not have to do the work, I have to tell other people to do the work the way I want it." I asked her, "Oh are you important now and can boss people?" Fejér told me, "Oh yes Ann, Faith Maria will be the number two bosses behind her husband who will be the number one boss." Ruth asked, "She will not be the boss of daddy will she?" Fejér said, "Yes, she is going to be our new Queen." Mary asked, "Is a husband a boy or girl?" Faith Maria told her, "A husband is a boy." Joy then screamed while crying, "Oh no, you are going to be prisoner of a man." Fejér told the sisters, "Oh no, she will be a Queen and if the King makes her mad, she can tell the priests to keep him away for it is against the law to hit a Queen." Máriakéménd said, while wiping away Joy's tears, "She will have many homes to live in. Being a Queen is a great thing because everyone will love her." Then Mary asked, "Will we be able to visit you or will the soldiers shoot us?" Faith Maria grabbed Mary and motioned for Ruth and me to join as she hugged us and said, "Daddy said you can visit me on holidays, a whole bunch of days in the summer and you all can come and help Heidi and me prepare for the wedding." Joy then asked, "Am I too big to help?" Faith Maria said, "You can come if you promise not to kiss the soldiers." Joy then started making sounds saying, "Yucky oh now I am sick, unlike you, I am never going to kiss boys. Never, never ever never)" Then all the sisters said, "Yucky yucky." At this time Máriakéménd, Fejér, and Faith Maria all started laughing. Faith Maria now heard Heidi calling, so she hurried back into her conscience. The Lord now wanted to show us the remainder of the house. As we toured a servant followed behind my dream and us who wore the black stripped clothes. Faith had to think of something fast. She told Heidi to walk slow and stand by a window. I shall walk back to join you. When he walks past you, trip him and scream, "Someone save me, and he touched my foot." Soldiers will be just behind me, and they always stare at my ass, so they will not know. Our plan worked like a charm. I turned to my soldiers and screamed crying, "Please save my chamber maiden before that beast attacks her." With us not being side by side, when the man regained his composure, he got up and tried to check to see if Heidi was ok. The soldiers seeing him moving towards Heidi rushed to him and constrained him then saying, "How dare you touch the Queen's chamber maid." He swore, "I did not know." The Queen then said, "And you know not who I am?" He bowed and said, "You are my Queen." Faith Maria asked, "Does not this Queen have a chamber maid?" The man said, "I know not about those things." Now the King and Sir Fulke arrived. Faith Maria asked Sir Fulke, "Why does this man not know of a Queen's Chambermaid?" The Lady of the house spoke out before her husband could answer, "My Queen, he knows of such things." The King demanded, "What is your name." The man, now bowing said, "Ralf Heywood." The King now asked, "My fair Queen, the love of my life, share with me what happened here?" The King was making the Lady of the house blush, knowing she would tell all about what a fine dignitary he was. Faith Maria now took a bold gamble, trusting the soldiers loved her and that they were watching her ass, as it was wrapped tightly in a dress she wore this afternoon to show her support for her room's decoration. The soldiers looked at the King and said, "Exactly as the Queen said. Exactly for us both saw it." Faith's gamble had paid off. The things she learned while keeping her and her sisters alive as a slut had now paid off for Sir Fulke. Sir Fulke said to the King, "Honorable King, and do as you will." The King then said, "I would ask our Queen however she would forgive him too fast. Yet to save her honor and love among our people, I shall defer the punishment to you." At this Faith Maria went over and hugged Heidi saying, "It shall be ok, my honorable Chamber Maiden." The Lady of the House joined them, wiping away Heidi's tears and trying to comfort her with words." Faith Maria now looked at the woman and said, "I warn you to keep him away from your husband for he will stab him in the back if not guarded." The Lady of the House now looked terrified and asked, "How do you know of such things?" Faith Maria then replied, "Is not a Queen also divinely appointed by our Lord to serve her people?" The Lady answered, "Yes, indeed." Sir Fulke then called Ralf before him and said, "You shall spend two years in my deepest dungeon and shall be removed from all my wills. My soldiers please take him to the dungeon." Faith Maria then thought to herself, "Two years will not be enough." Faith Maria said to Sir Fulke, "Is my chamber maiden worth only two years?" Sir Fulke said, "According to my judgment. You had the first judgment. Once I have judged, the judgment cannot be changed." Faith Maria looked at my father and Fejér and said, "Have my things brought to my carriage." She then looked at the soldiers and commanded, "Prepare my carriage for we shall leave immediately." She then looked at Sir Fulke and said, "I curse you for you shall die by Ralf's hand when you see it not." Within a few minutes, the entire convoy was prepared. The King came to Faith Maria who was sitting in her carriage and said to her, "We shall depart upon your command." Faith Maria looked at him and while starting to cry nodded her approval. The King departed from her and started yelling for everyone to go as fast as all could. Faith's escorts and maiden now brought their personal items to the carriage. Faith Maria then motioned for the carriage to depart and that it did. The King had one-half of the soldiers follow his queen. Faith Maria had the carriage depart high speed, yet when they were over the hill and out of sight, she had them slow down. The King caught up with her in a few hours, relieved that she had reduced her speed for him. He told his commanders, "This is the first real good sign that she and I shall be good together." He rode up beside Faith's carriage looked at her. Faith Maria stuck her hand out for the King to kiss, looking at him with sad eyes. Charles kissed her hand and said to her, "Be not worried my fair Queen, you shall receive your justice." The King then said to his minister, "Double all the taxes in this county." Faith Maria looked at him and said, "Thank you my dear honorable King for understanding the importance of the one who is my shadow." Charles answered promptly, "That I truly know, for I obey Heidi as I obey you." Faith Maria looked over at Heidi as their hands joined and both smiled at the king. This was the beginning of Faith's long time "daytime" depression. She now knew that as in France not all people could be trusted. She had worked to save the life of a man who did not deserve it. She looked over and saw daddy reading, '*Life of the Renowned Sir Philip Sidney*' and asked, "Where did you find that book?" trying to loosen the chilled mood in the carriage. My daddy then said, "I try to separate the writer from the words that he wrote." Faith Maria then asked, "If we are playing twenty questions, who is the writer?" Daddy said, "Your enemy." Faith Maria now looked at daddy with a shocked face, as he threw the book out the window. She started crying saying, "How can my daddy love my enemies? I thought I would always be your daughter." Daddy said, "I am sorry honey, I had started it last night and just was not paying attention. I hope you forgive your daddy who loves all his daughters and their mother so much. After discovering the author, I then felt it best to learn more about how our enemy thinks thus be able to better protect you, as is ultimately always my responsibility." Faith Maria appeared to release a small smile, and then closed her water-filled eyes and went to sleep. She had only one safe place and that was the night world. She would have to invite Heidi, for she hoped that Heidi would not tell, yet even if she did, she would be thought to be mad. Then she would be executed for violating her master's confidentially. It must be strange to be completely owned by a child. It was her position and not herself that owned her. Faith Maria now asked the King if they could stop by her home and bring back her parents and sisters to their castle. She also would like to have a couple of the girls and now since she had our daddy on the hook decided to ask him, "May I have a couple of the girls so that your daughters will have an easier time adjusting?" Daddy said, of course, your mother is really good at those types' tasks, I can ask her if you want me too?" Faith Maria perked up and said, "That is probably what I categorically need the most from our home. She knows how to get the servants to feel good and work hard. I know she goes to many weddings so she can help us plan. If I had my way we would stop at that little church in this small town and get married, however the "So called elites can have their day to outdo each other and I had better outdo them. This is such a waste of the people's money. By having a quick wedding here would turn the people against Parliament. I can see that Parliament and I shall go a few rounds before Charles send them home." Charles was under heat now from Parliament for the expense of the trip to bring the Queen back. Charles knew he had to stand his ground on this one. He sent back some soldiers to tell remind Parliament that the Queen is the sister of France and asked them if they were ready to finance a war with France. Charles said, "That will give them something to debate about for a few months. Now I can get some sleep." His ministers looked at Faith's carriage and then the King and then said, "You might have to wait to get some sleep, because we think you might something that will keep you awake." The King looked at the ministers and said, "Life is not fair for a man, he must work all day to feed the one that keeps him up all night." The ministers then told him, "You will soon discover that it is quite a wonderful bargain." The King then went to see if the convoy was ready to start. He asked Faith Maria saying, "My wonderful Queen, are you ready to begin?" Faith Maria looked at him and asked, "My fair King, let us go to that church and marry now, so I can ride with you in your carriage." Charles was somewhat surprised and sadly responded, "If it were my will, you would within this day be my wife, yet we must surrender to our crown as your brother surrenders to his." Faith Maria then, with tears starting to roll down her check said, "Like my parents surrendered me to the beasts to their crown." Charles then returned to his carriage to boast with his ministers who had heard the queen requesting a wedding today. They all laughed as Charles now said with more confidence than before, "I think the poor thing loves me. I must have finally grown on her." Parliament had sent recorders to report on the events of the trip. They did report to Parliament that the Queen wanted a small wedding in a Protestant church. Parliament reasoned that if Louis found out his sister had married in a protestant church, he would raid England, and thus this had to be kept a secret from the people who would have loved the news since many now hated her for being a Catholic. Parliament also decided to sweeten the ante for a royal wedding in London. They would have to sell the people on this and thus force the Queen into a wedding that they could not afford. Parliament would pull the monies from other projects and cover it up. They were the masters at covering things up or blaming them on the King and making themselves look good. Charles never worried about making himself look good because he was the law as ordained by God. The problem now is which God, the God of the Catholics, or the God of the Protestants. I hope that one of them would come forward in the event the crown needed some backing or his head could go tumbling. Faith Maria had planted the seed and now had parliament doing as she willed. They only way they could ever get over on her would be to impeach her, which she would sail back to France with a large fleet, keep them there, and be a Princess again. Being a Princess is much better than a Queen is because you have more freedom and protection. People always seem to love a Princess but grow tired of a Queen or the Queen is judged by what the King does. Since the convoy now had about fifty soldiers and five ministers, we would stop at night and camp to give the horses time to rest and feed. The Queen, her two girls and Daddy would sleep in the carriage. Faith Maria wanted everyone together, especially Daddy so that Ann would not be saddened. Faith Maria shared her ten-pound blankets from the peasants with the others in the carriage, the exception being Heidi who shared the same blanket with her master. The chill of the night soon gave way to roosters crowing and other birds chirping. Faith Maria and Heidi took a walk around the camp, staying in the camp since no soldiers would allow them out. That was the law and they had an obligation to protect the queen in these matters. Faith Maria did not care, for she knew the days of crazy games were over, at least in the daytime world, and that the security provided was for her benefit. She wanted to take better care of herself, because a stupid death on her part meant Heidi would also have to die. Faith Maria knew she had to accept responsibility because Heidi was more than her shadow now. She was a rock during this so fast changing daytime world. No more sitting around all day and hoping the family will play in some mud or who was it in the tag games they played. This day was different from other days, then why should not each day be different on the roller coaster ride to the top. The rain was pouring hard, in fact so hard that the horse's feet would sink into the road, creating danger for the horses behind them. The soldiers now took their horses off the road and traveled in the grass on each side of the road within about thirty feet of the road. The King and I moved along slower wish our carriage to the right, and the kids to the left side of the road to minimize the foot holes the horses would encounter. In the rocky boat, wavering of the carriage Faith Maria heard something hit their carriage. She looked out and something wiggling in the grass. She then heard musket fire; one of them hit her carriage. The drivers stopped the carriage and started firing back, and then tossed some bottles filled with black gold (oil) and rags that they were able to light with some matches. This lit up the area and Faith saw a small boy in a white robe with a long red scarf made of peasant cloth. She immediately ran out to the little boy and dropped on one side of him as her shadow (Heidi) dropped on the other side. The soldiers were now closing in on the attackers killed four of them and taking two hostages. The ministers demanded to know what they were doing, yet they refused to talk. One minister replied, "Let us now enjoy the benefits of two hostages. Soldiers, tie them up to that tree and start chopping off fingers on that one." He begged them to stop and his 'wife' agreed to talk if we would take them with us for safe haven. The ministers agreed and the woman told all. They had been paid by people in a nearby town to execute the queen, when a local crippled boy had crept through the woods to warn his queen. The ministers then sent to soldiers to destroy the small village and kill every person. Faith Maria asked, "Why kill everyone" as she stood in water soaked clothes in her sleeping shirt. The ministers answered being careful not to be caught by King enjoying their newfound fortune, "Because the women will avenge the deaths of their husbands and children of their fathers. It is the law of the old testament of the Bible." The King now came up and quickly wrapped his jacket over his betrothed noticing all the ministers were looking elsewhere, he said, "My dear wife to be, please save your blessings for me." Faith Maria whispered in his ear, "What do you speak about?" The King pointed to her breasts as Faith now added, "Oh you guys like this, if I take this shirt off I promise it gets better, here let me show our soldiers." The King now held her tight and said, "The soldiers are working hard keeping you safe, maybe some other day after I have some of our ladies share some of their wisdom with you." Then Faith Maria gave her special sad look and rested her head on his chest crying, "My King thinks my breasts are ugly." Charles now hastily remarked, "Oh no my love, the opposite is true, they are the most beautiful things in the world behind your face (tossed in to keep from getting into trouble) and I want such beauty just for me." Faith Maria then said, "I dream you are being honest with me." The King said, "I swear my love, all I shall ever want is you and that I will only share with Heidi." Faith Maria smiled and then asked the King about the crippled boy, "Can I take him back to London with me, since he did save my life?" The king, being glad it was not a crippled man eating beast quickly said, "Yes, my dear." He walked back to his carriage with the feeling of great victory. He was able to convince his innocent, naïve always wanting to share betrothed not to show all the soldiers her beautiful breasts. As he thought harder, that was a great victory for him. That was worth the trade to give her a crippled boy who had saved her life. Yet once again, Faith Maria was the one who actually won, she got a crippled boy to care for. Her and Heidi escorted him back to her carriage and once getting him inside along with Fejér told him it was time to change him into some dry clothes. He immediately started to beg my daddy, "Please do not make me take my clothes off in front of all these big girls." The desire to mother had clogged Faith's mind. They were big GIRLs to this little boy. Faith Maria fell head over heels for this child's innocence. Our daddy looked at the girls and said, "Will you big girls please wait outside and do not peak. I will make sure he gets his dry clothes on." Thus, all three big girls stood out in the rain with their backs to the carriage. The King came running up asking, "Are you women OK?" Faith Maria told him, "We have been labeled as big girls and kicked out of the carriage until our little boy finishes putting on his dry clothes." The King started laughing so hard that he almost fell down, as his ministers rushed to keep him on his feet asking, "Are you Ok our honorable King?" He answered, "The happiest I have been in so many years. See my women standing in the rain in front of their carriage. They have been defeated by a little crippled boy that they are making changes in his clothes. He does not change his clothes in front of big girls." They then all walked back to the King's carriage remembering the days when they were boys and big girls were dangerous. My daddy put the boy's clean clothing (actually his) on the boy and got the girls inside. The boy looked at Faith Maria as she sat down and asked him, "Are you going to have a big baby?" Faith Maria looked at him and said, "I do not think so, why do you ask?" He answered, "Because you have such big baby milk bottles." She teased him, "Do you like big baby milk bottles?" He quickly responded, "I am not a baby anymore, I am a big boy now." Faith Maria then quickly agreed with him. They all laughed in the carriage remembering how I used to call them big baby milk bottles. Fejér then asked him, "What is your name?" He answered, "They call me Isaac." The girls were now all huddled on the opposite row of seats from the 'boys.' They put a blanket over them and started working out of their wet clothes. Isaac saw the wet clothes being kicked to the floor and looked at my daddy and said, "Oh please Sir, make them promise to put their clothes back on." Heidi asked in a soft sweet voice, "Isaac is it ok if we put on dry clothes also so we do not get sick and maybe die." He answered, "As long as you are not tricking me." Faith, Heidi and Fejér were now falling deeply in love with this child as their maternal instincts were kicking in like rivers. It was so sad that he had one leg cut off. He must have infected it somehow and had to have it removed to keep his life. Faith Maria now said to him, "I forgot to thank you for saving my life." He looked at her and said, "I was trying to save the queen before you guys interfered." My daddy looked at him and asked, "Did you not see the King talking to her?" Isaac replied, "I saw her talking to a man that everyone was calling king." Daddy then said, "What is the woman who talks so close to the king, and he gives her his jacket to keep her from getting wet and listens to her, named?" He looked at daddy and said, "That is an easy question, that woman is called the Queen." Isaac looked at Faith Maria inquiring, "Are you the Queen?" Faith Maria told him, "As soon as we get married in London. Do you want to come to my wedding?" Isaac then qualified the request by saying, "Only if I do not have to sit beside any girls." Faith Maria told him, "Maybe my sisters, however do not worry, they hate little boys." Isaac then looked at Faith Maria as he was in a deep thought and replied, "I guess that would be okay." Fejér then asked him, "Isaac, why did you suffer so much to save the Queen?" Isaac told them, "I heard she loved her people." Faith Maria looked at him and said, "That is true Isaac, and now I love you the most." Isaac looked at her and said, "It is Ok for the Queen to love me since she is the mommies of mommies." Faith Maria then told him, "Then that makes me very special, right Isaac?" Do you think that once we get our clothes back in you will trade places with my friend and set between us and protect me?" Isaac then complained, "Why do I have to set in between you girls, I am a big boy and can protect you better by sitting next to the window." Faith Maria now said, "Oh yes, what was I thinking about, you are very much right." When he moved beside his queen Heidi said in her soft sweet voice, "Do you think you should tell your Queen about yourself?" Isaac then started talking, "My story is not a happy story, until tonight. When I go to where the other kids are playing, they either run away or call me names. They like to throw rocks at me. The rocks do not hurt as bad as the names. I then spend the rest of the day trying to find food. Sometimes it takes a long time to find some food. I hand around stores and inns. They give me the leftovers from the plates that their customers do not eat or the food that is spoiled. Once you get used to the taste it is not that bad and buy taking away the pains in the stomach that makes it taste so much better. When I was born, I had a mommy and daddy and two older brothers. Some bad men came by one day, killed all four of them, and then told me to give them all of our money. We had no money so they beat me so bad that no one in the village close to our farm could recognize me. Some of the town people decided I could not take care of our farm by myself so they sold our horses and farm and kept the money. They said my family died because I was evil. One night, some men took me out into the woods and chopped off my leg. Some poor old man found me and kept me alive. When I was better, he took me far away and told me never to go back to that town again or they would kill me. I accidently was lost and returned there yesterday after being gone for so many years. I recognized a few of the people so I stayed hid. I hid in an old barn. Then earlier last night, so many came into the barn to make their plans on how to kill the Queen. I thought if they kill the Queen then the King will have no children and be very sad. I do not want other people to be sad like me. When they left, I crawled out back into the forest, got my walking branch, and started to go to the road. When I got there, I hid in under some trees. I heard one of the man yell, "I found some tracks of a crippled person from the barn towards the road. It was then that your carriage came by, so I jumped up in the road to warn you when they started shooting. I do not care if shot me since a preacher once told me:

I will not be a crippled boy in Heaven
I realize my wings will float through the air
I can run and play with
All the other Children
There shall be no crippled boys up there

He told me that all the kids up there are nice and play with everyone." Fejér had sent this whole story to the night world. When we saw it, we all cried. We were now so puzzled because we could now see that not all boys are bad. If we had known Isaac, we would have hated many boys who were good. However, we did agree to make sure our big sisters inspect any boys we would want to talk with just to be safe. We now looked inside the carriage and I saw daddy crying, along with our sisters and Heidi. Isaac asked, "Oh I hope I did not make you sad, you are my friends, I promise to work hard and make you happy. Please for . . ." At that instant, an arrow came in through his head into Faith's shoulder. Isaac was immediately killed as parts of his brain splattered over a carriage of "big people" who loved him. Heidi jumped out of the carriage as Fejér jumped over beside Faith Maria to see how bad she had been hit. Heidi ran crying, "The Queen has been hit, please help." The Dutch doctor came rushing in, as did the king. When the King saw the damage, he yelled out, "Find those who shot my betrothed." The doctor carefully cuts the arrow into two parts, and then he had the soldiers take the body out and start cleaning the queen's escorts. He then laid her body on the ground on top of some extra clothing and started the long job of getting the arrow out. Fortunately, the arrow missed her arm bone and sunk deep into her muscle. He tried to rotate the sword. The sword would not rotate. He tried slowly to pull it back and it would not pull back. He decided to wait for the soldiers to return with the assassins and see what kind of arrowheads they had on them. In the meantime, the sisters watched this terrible murder and were very angry because they all had lost their new male friends (as soon as they would have been introduced). They all burst out crying as they saw this horrible event. Máriakémènd was also very shocked and called out for some help from her masters. Furthermore, at that instance large snakes surrounded the assassins trapping them. Now birds surrounded the soldiers so that they could not see and pushed them from behind to the assassins. The snakes now started herding them towards the birds. Then they all backed off and then surrounded them from a distance insuring the assassins did not escape. The soldiers then saw a white and gold figure from the sky, which told them, "Take these assassins back to your King so that he may punish them for injuring our queen. Tell your King to fear not for we shall heal the queen and she shall be made whole." A commander who was among the soldiers asked, "Who are you?" She replied, "In the days of old the Greeks called me Venus. I am now searching for the chosen one." She then vanished as the commander ran back to tell the King and the other soldiers. They would now testify that, "The old goddesses of Greece loved our Queen. She was blessed from the heavens." This would create other problems, especially with the churches that saw this as demon interaction. Máriakéménd also saw this and asked her masters about it. They told her, "Fear not Máriakéménd, for they are from the goddess Medica who also searches her loved one. She has brought the ones who tried to kill your sister to the king. We shall hide from her because she must not find the chosen one because the guards of this dimension are watching her and we cannot put the chosen one in danger." Máriakéménd now told the sisters that Faith would be okay. Ann asked about Isaac. She then looked over at the heavens and saw him flying and playing with other children. He looked so happy. Ann then asked, "He now plays with the children in heaven, we must let him go. Who is that beautiful woman that has hair of gold and such beautiful legs?" Máriakéménd said, "Fear her not for she searches for you." Ann asked, "Why does she not find me?" Máriakéménd told her, "The time is not at hand. She now works to help make Faith Maria new again. Let us prepare for your love tonight." Now Máriakéménd closed the window. The King was mystified by the tales the soldiers and his commander was telling him. The King decided to chop off the heads of the men, one at a time trying to get confessions and he killed his first prisoner whom he had promised sanctuary. He told his wife, "You knew of this attack and did not tell us. I shall tie you between the walls of this old building and the new woman upside down and you will watch your friends die one by one. Your only chance is to confess the truth. "The woman did not talk while they watched their men die one by one. Then the King had a local farmer beat the women with his horsewhip. After ten lashes, the new female started talking. She said, "We did not want the Queen to get hurt this time. Others will kill her later. We now wanted to kill the boy. He must die." The King now yelled, "When do you plan to kill the Queen." The woman said, "So many small cells are waiting for their chance. We are spread in many places." The King now had the woman lowered, wounds lightly wrapped. He said, "If they try to kill our Queen, you will die like the boy." He then told my daddy that all the Queens escorts sit on each one side while these two women will be tied tightly and be seated by the window on each side. Their heads will be also be tied to the window, thus any arrow would hit them first. If the Queen flinches, a release lever will pull the prisoners to extend the entire window. If these beasts must kill, let them kill their own." The King then ordered that thirteen women be captured from the town closest where they caught the prisoners. The people have to know that if they do not report these high crimes against the crown their loved ones will also suffer. When the young women were brought to him, he had their clothing removed and saved in case the Queen was to need them before the London and hung beside each other from the nearby trees that crossed a small local path. He made sure they were dead because he was still angry from the earlier conversation with the Queen's doctor. The arrows his soldiers had brought back would decide the next steps in her removal of the arrowhead. The soldiers brought in four traitors with one of them being female. When the doctor saw the arrows, he took one to the King to show him. The heads had broken shaving blades on them. If he pulled it back it would recut the flesh, leaving scars and possible long-term tissue damage. He knew that to push the blade forward would cut an additional two inches that would continue to extend the damage lengthwise of the injury, however if he pushed down and this straight up he could get the blade out with only about three-eighths inch additional damage. That would leave the Queen with at least two inches (width wide) of undamaged flesh and she would be able to use her arm partially or maybe someday completely. The King said, "Push the one where you push the least." The doctor had the King put rags into Faith's mouth to dull the scream and give her something safe to bite on. The doctor then pushed down and up cutting away the skin. As the cut started to break her skin, the doctor poured some scotch the soldiers had brought him into the damage area. He now gripped the head of the arrow and slowly started to pull. Now he rotated the arm and poured scotch into the other side of her arm where the arrow went in. The King asked, "Are you trying to make her drunk?" The doctor told the king, "I discovered in my lab that when alcohol was put on a bacterial culture the bacteria died. I do not know why, however I do know how. This should really help her recovery and reduce the chance of a killing infection or arm amputation." The doctor continued now to pull out the arrow from Faith's arm. Fejér, Heidi and my daddy fought hard to hold her down, as Faith's face was now solid red. Then slowly and carefully pulling, the doctor removed the arrowhead. In this instance, Faith Maria passed out. Her face was now a pale white as her body did not move. The doctor now started to put stitches in her wound. They told her escorts to, "Keep her head elevated and let her sleep for a while. She needs the extra rest for her healing." The King then had Faith Maria secured, his two hostages tied up for extra protection. The King told his guards to stay closer to the convoy and not to ride far ahead. "You are giving our enemies time to prepare an assault. Try to catch these assassins before they are able to get such close shots." Faith Maria now entered the wrong dark world. She saw a dark haired topless half woman sitting on a rock. The creature was a strong fish from the waist down. She was in a semi-closed cave with skulls floating around her. She had her back to a ship that was passing before them. Faith Maria asked her, "What is your name?" She said, "I am from Melinoë. She sent me to destroy you." Faith Maria then asked, "Why do you want to destroy me?" Melinoë then said, "For you are the chosen one." Faith Maria then said, "I am not the chosen one, inspect me again to see what I speak is the truth." Melinoë asked again, "If you are not the chosen one then how did you get here" Faith told her, "I know not how I got here, I was shot with an arrow the next thing was so great and next thing I knew is that I was here. Please scan me to see I speak the truth. Melinoë then scanned her and said, "You do speak the truth. We shall return you." Faith Maria knew she would find nothing since her nighttime world was protected in her mind and nothing could discover that. She could once again feel herself in her painful body. She cried for Máriakéménd who finally appeared and said, "Please help me from this pain." Máriakéménd then pulled her into the night world, while still her body alive by using time reversing. When Faith Maria returned,

James Hendershot

she would be with the pain as when she left. Faith Maria started to tell Máriakéménd about her vision and Melinoë. Máriakéménd told her that she was lucky for Melinoë was a prodigious evil goddesses, and to stay far away from her. Faith Maria assured Máriakéménd she would try very hard to stay away from this evil goddess. Then Faith Maria asked Máriakéménd to share some heavenly wine, as her soul was thirsty. She gave Faith Maria her heavenly wine, saying I shall refill my cup before the sister's return. It was now time for Faith Maria to return, since she needed to be an active part in the healing process. Days of pain now lay ahead. Faith Maria knew she was lucky, since it was only her arm and the arm could be put in a sling to reduce movement and pain. It had been awhile since she had this kind of pain, since the days of her beatings and rapes. The King assured her she would see the remainder of her revenge, after showing her the men's heads. The females were going to suffer a very painful death, for they had sinned the greatest by betraying their king. Charles decided to do the executions before London as not to tarnish Faith's entry. They would stop by a town called Aylesbury and execute the traitors there. The wife would be beaten and watch her co-prisoner burn. Then she too would be burned. It was now time to teach the peasants that attacks on the royalty would result in additional deaths. The King had some additional men thrown into the blazing fire so he would not waste such a good fire and show that all could be punished. They would investigate any leads about possible assassin cells by going to the towns and executing until the assassins stepped forward. Faith Maria was now satisfied with the executions however was now growing sad over all the heartaches that now being associated with being royalty. The only thing that was favorable was having Heidi and that was only because she now knew her. If she had met her, Faith Maria would have her sisters, which she was now growing apart. That was sad. The loss of Isaac also added to her misery and the treatment at the previous castle she had visited did not help. These stupid dreams were starting to bother her. The getting hit in the head by a boy in France and suffering a near death for that painful experience trapped her in

- 234 -

England. She would spend most of her future hidden in her castles and not doing what she originally wanted to do and that was to help people. Being at the top of the social ladder was not as fun as being pushed into a mud puddle by a sister. Now every time when she relaxed, death would come chasing her. Even a trip to the night world now could be intercepted into a near death experience. This Faith had great fear thinking about this, however for once she had a good dream. She saw a beautiful woman with warm eyes trying to push the clouds away with her head as she was trying to bring daylight in. She had a look of peace as she rested her head on relaxed fingers. Some light radiated from her right forehead. Her hair from the back of her head seemed to extend its light to a ship as if to protect it. Her eyes were locked on another ship as if she was preparing to save it. It was hard to tell whether she was the sea or if the sea was she. Faith Maria could not believe what was before her, a woman who appeared to be full of love and peace who was helping innocent helpless people. She wanted so much to talk with her and without warning; she fell into the cold spinning water and started begging to be saved. The woman lowered her finger into the water and Faith Maria swam over to it and crawled upon it from the water. The woman asked her, "Who are you?" Faith Maria answered, "My name is Henrietta Maria, however my friends call me Faith, and I do hope you call me Faith. What is your name?" She answered by saying, "My name is Medica, and I am here looking for the chosen one?" Faith Maria then asked, "Everywhere I go people are saying they look for the chosen one. Who is this chosen one and how did I get here?" Medica than asked, "Who else has asked about the chosen one?" Faith Maria said, "An evil ugly half fish woman named 'Melinoë' who returned by to the daytime world." Medica said Melinoë is an evil one who wishes to hurt the chosen one. You are here because I have watched you and have found favor in your deeds." Faith said, "My deeds of love and good are only rewarded by hate and evil, I now find it hard to love and do good." Medica then said, "My child, all who do good suffer from evil, yet remember that evil makes gods and goddess angry and it is a fearful thing to fall into the hands of an angry god, yet it is a joyous thing to spend eternity with goddesses of good." Faith Maria now asked, "Why do you say goddesses?" Medica said, "In my heavens are three goddesses that share the same being. Yet sadly, the chosen one has been taken from us by her lover, a god by the name of Bogovi. He takes her not for evil but safety while we fight the many evil gods in our dimension. We shall work hard to save and protect the chosen one." Faith Maria said, "This chosen one sounds special, and I would like to meet her." Medica, then said, "The chosen one took you and your sisters when you were hungry and with rags for clothing and shared and gave you her love. If you know not who the chosen one, ask Máriakéménd whom we sent to love and protect your small family. Henrietta Maria, we shall be with you. I tell you now a secret that will never come from your mouth. We shall take you from England when the people become a great danger to you. We shall move your sisters and parents to the American Colonies. You will be safe there. Your husband shall make many angry and fights with a parliament and a false parliament will behead him on 30 January 1649. This is for your safety since he was trying to locate you. We who protect the chosen one shall also protect you. Before telling anyone about the chosen one, please ask Máriakéménd if it is safe or you could place the chosen one in danger. You must help protect the chosen one, even though many times you will not be near her. You are to be Queen to protect the chosen one. When you are ready to return I shall send you back." Inside Faith Maria, she now felt a sense of purpose. She would naturally give her life to defend Ann. Now she had to give her life not in death but in life dedicated to protecting Ann. This mission she would enjoy so much. If any try to Hurt Ann, they would surely lose their heads. She now looked up at Medica and said, "Blessed is the chosen one to have friends such as you. I shall return now too soon we will be where Ann lives and I shall bring her to London with me soon." Medica said, "The chosen one is lucky to have a friend like you. The chosen one and her sisters now wait for you in your castle. If you need me, call out my name. Love and peace shall tarry with you." Then Faith Maria woke up beside Máriakéménd who had been resting on some pillows. As I walked over to her, she said, "So, you met Medica today?" Faith Maria said yes, as she knelt to pour her cup full of Máriakéménd's wine. Faith Maria asked, "Who is Medica?" Máriakéménd replied, "She is one of the masters. She is here to protect the chosen one and us. We must remember to treat Ann just like the other sisters so that when the evil ones watch us we will not give away our secret." Faith Maria said, "That will be hard for me, since I have always loved Ann so much." Máriakéménd, "You must keep on loving her, because any change could alert the evil ones." Faith Maria then asked, "Where are my sisters?" Máriakéménd told her, "They wait for you in your castle in London. Now that you have your fill of my wine, go now and find them." Faith awoke from her sleep, now in a room with Heidi. She asked Heidi, "Where are we?" Heidi said, "They have prepared a special room in this hospital for you as many people are working to mind your arm to perfection." Faith Maria asked Heidi if she would bring Charles to her." She asked Charles, "Will you please take me to our home in London? I wish to meet my sisters who wait for me." Charles slumbered as he stuttered saying, "Why do you say your sisters are in London?" Faith Maria told him, "In my pain I saw them in a vision." Charles then said, "The test of your vision shall be scored when we enter Buckingham." Faith Maria also added, "Our daddy would have gone to our home long ago if my sisters were in our home." Charles then replied, "I must wake up early if I am going to pull a fast one on you." Faith Maria told him, "My dear King, always remember this." They then kissed each other on their cheeks and Faith Maria asked one more question, "My king, when do we leave here." Charles told her, "You shall be able to travel in a few days. You shall enter London with power so those who wish to do you harm will see your strength. I shall return soon, if you need anything send our daughter, oh I mean Heidi, to me." Heidi then asked the King a question, "Your royal highness, is it true that Buckingham has a large entrance with two stairs to go to the upper floor and red carpet at the entrance, and trimmed in gold from below to the top?" Charles said, "That is true as you can also see the paintings by my mother and father and you shall someday see the paintings of my wife and me. Please take care of my betrothed." Heidi told the king, "That, my master I shall do." It made Charles feel good that she called him her master. This he would soon try to test. Heidi now prepared to clean and apply new healing salves. Faith was surprised when she saw her arm and all the swelling. Heidi told her that the doctor said that was the healing and that it was ok to try to move her fingers. Faith Maria closed her eyes at with her teeth crunched moved each finger one by one. They both became very excited as Heidi then told Faith Maria to lay back and relax and she would get some wine flowing. That relaxed Faith Maria that she slowly went back to sleep. She decided to go and look around Buckingham. Being able to shift time, she was able to see it during the daytime. She saw so many beautiful large paintings on the walls. To know someday future generations would look at her paintings created a sense of purpose for her existence. How would history treat her? She did not care because Fejér told her that the chosen one would take care of her. This palace was bigger than the home she grew up in, which was so much better than the streets she lay under men to keep her sisters alive. It would be nice to see them track some mud in as they ran across this big playroom. Well, maybe that would take some time, however there were many places for them to play without the prying eyes of a greedy public. What is more, her children, one who would be King or Queen would grow up here. She would fight hard to protect her children as she had her sisters. Somehow, she had to get to this palace and with her sisters prepare for a grand wedding. The people had given one for the queens before and they would for those who follow so why not also for her? She knew she had less than nine years before she would be transferred out by the orders of Medica. She could live with that because by then she would be tired of Charles anyway. To be protecting the chosen one was of greater than being a Queen of such irrational people. The next few weeks went fast as Heidi worked so hard to bring her queen back to perfect health. It was now time to practice her entry. She would have to wear a wig and paint just as mommy had to so many times. Now, she understood why mommy said it was not fun. She wanted to look powerful and yet compassionate, so she had a boy's guide her horse and many raging soldiers following her as she commanded them with her right arm, since the left one was still sore. The King also had musicians playing music for his betrothed. He loved paintings and just about all forms of art. Faith just wanted those with the ability to be given the chance as England could rise in the arts among Europe. Daddy and mommy also loved paintings so she would snoop around some storage rooms and pass some back to them as a thank you gift. The people now came out with great joy to see the famous Queen. A King without a Queen was not good, for now they would be balanced and have some new protection avenues for women and children. As the stories spread about the death of the cripple boy Isaac, which the Queen so much loved and the numerous attempts on her life, the people of London now believed that this year old had paid the price for her royalty. Being born of a King and Queen and end up being left in the streets to starve, and to have a little girl, named Ann to give her a new life, many wondered if the spirit of Queen Anne had returned to prepare the way for her son's wife. After all, do not all mothers seek out the best for their son so maybe, the new Queen was best of England? Thus, the celebrations began and joy came over London, for it was time to witness the royal wedding of their lifetime. That would be the test, although since she is also a Princess of France, everyone knew it would be good. England was lucky, because many Kings had to marry countesses for the availably of princess that would be compatible for an English Kingwas not that high. Her time had come, now finally her time was at hand. A palace that she was the lady of; no more hiding behind mommy as she would handle all the elite crap for her family, which was easier since she had four countesses living in her house. Now Faith's sisters did not have to worry about their status, for their King and Queen would officially recertify as soon as she was able to give the King his nighttime blessing. That would have been hard to act as if was the first time, however Fejér told her that she would get Medica to refresh her virginity and erase her special skills so that the King would be tumbling with a virgin, especially since the consummation would be observed. She secretly liked that and would make sure she moaned extra loud, so the kingdom would think their King to be sanctified and therefore would be able to raise an heir and a spare. A few loud squeals would also make him look mighty among his royal guards as the great pleasure of the Queen, and why not, he had won the respect of Daddy, and her French brother and mother, and they stood by her during so many tribulations in the journey to Buckingham. After giving her English mommy a ton of kisses, and hugs, and tell her at least 1,000 times, "I love you" she would feel at home again. Daddy watch Faiths entry and then the guards concealed him, Fejér and Heidi and got them into Buckingham to prepare the way for the Queen. The staffs would have to be given a heads up on some of Faith's likes and dislikes and some highlights on how to win her favor. The staff thought it would be good to buy some boys and put them in British uniforms to help with the Royal Couple's security. Faith Maria did really like that and broke the rules by kissing her guards when she passed them, with the King's blessings of course. This created the social rumors that the royal couple was family orientation, which distilled some fears. The King took her out for a quick ride to see the church they would marry. This was just a fast pass by, to help her get a fast idea for the preparations. She would have to come back with guards to make the final preparations for their ceremony. Faith Maria thought how lucky she was to have a night world where she could play and trade wine. Her daytime life would also be wonderful, for all she had to do was complain enough to keep Charles on his toes. She had some ideas on how to rebuild England back to its days of greatness and she wanted in England to explore and bring more people under the protection of the crown. The having one group be killed by other groups over such trivial things would have to be given a twist. If England pushed their ability to defend, they would get more acquisitions into the crown. She worried about the new world because trading with those Indians was not preventing bloodshed. She had time to debate with the ministers, parliament, and in bed where she had some extra ability to reward or not reward Charles for his agreement. Faith was so thankful that the weaker of the sexes had something that the stronger of the sexes wanted and that could at times even the score. She knew that was sometimes, for as in her home before Ann the mother of that house had no ability to gain any control, for refusal to submit was immediately punished by severe beating and marital rape. Their previous mother has been just happy that it was not a stranger raping her, as many of her friends experienced. Someone someday would have to stand up for these victims. Fejér told her that the chosen one would someday fix it; however, that someday would be in a place far away and long after the Earth was no more. They were now back at Buckingham as she was greeted by her shadow, Fejér, and mommy. Faith Maria ran up to her mommy and dropped to her knees hugging her tight and crying, "I love you" repeatedly. Faith Maria actually was crying so much that so many of the staff started crying. Charles looked around and said to the palace guards, "You have never seen one as this Her Royal Highness Princess of France." After about twenty minutes, Fejér and Heidi told the Princess, "Your highness it is time to prepare for the entry of Ann and your sisters." Charles told Faith, "We shall bring them in with many other girls, all with wigs of normal color to protect them from being seen by the public. Your parents have sold your old home and now live on a large farm nearby, with royal protection. No one shall ever see them except disguised on our wedding day. They shall play away from the windows, which more will be covered and in the private parts of your large estate." Fejér now realized the truth of what her masters had told her, "The chosen one shall be guarded by the highest in the land." They slowly pulled her up from her mommy who had pet her hair so much she now looked like a peasant who had been in a wind storm. Mommy looked like she was in another world, or was flooded with deep love. She now thought how lucky she was to have all these fine and wonderful daughters and bed bugs, for after Ann worked her way into mommy's bed in daddy's absence the remaining three of her daughters worked their way in, one at a time. It had been so nice having them with her at night and mingling everyone's unique bed posture into one smooth unit as remarkable. The daughters proved that all they wanted was to be able to love their mommy. Now they would march into Buckingham and be related to the royal crown. They marched with their padded petticoats, so everyone would look similar with a few different colored wigs to throw a twist to any royal terrorists. Neither Fejér nor Faith could pick them out until the four sisters removed their padded petticoats with only Joy not padded as much. Joy stood in front of all in the room with her developing breast exposed. One of the other marching girls picked up Joy's petticoat and wrapped in around her as the four girls were getting out of their size enhancing padded boots. Ruth claimed that walking in the soft padded boots was like, "Walking in the high air." The staff now surrounded them, and dressed them, then guided the other girls to some dressing rooms where they could change. An additional four girls had been brought in to substitute the four sisters on their departure. They would be dropped off in front of large churches throughout London; they would change clothes and leave with their parents after the service. Faith wondered if all this was necessary as Charles told her it would, "Last until after his inquisition when all who were here to kill her would give up their lives." The Queen was now tired with all the excitement so she asked Charles and her parents if she could, "Be excused and get her sisters settled in her chambers." Charles asked, "In your chambers?" The Princess replied, "If we are under the same roof we will sleep together unless you wish to have me that night. We have joined in some small areas so I think we can make it in my chambers." As the girls entered the chambers, they all rushed in to explore the chambers. The royal servants asked her if she needed anything, and she replied, "Some special sweets for the sisters and plenty of extra-large pillows." These were in their sleeping since no bed was large enough for all of them. After dessert was brought in for them to enjoy, and many large pillows and extra blankets made available, since even though it was early June, the palace would get cold at night. Faith Maria then instructed the staff, "No disturbances whatsoever." When they, all finished the deserts it was time to get on the pillows and visit after such a long separation. Heidi was a new addition and quickly won the favors of the sisters even though, with her there, only one side was free for the sisters to sit beside Faith and yet that position really belonged to Fejér. Faith Maria was now a big girl; actually, the biggest in England since being a Queen meant you were all grown up. Moreover, she would have to be in bed sometimes with a man. Joy argued that a King did not count as the younger sisters still had their reservations. The sisters soon found a solution by making a small circle in front of Faith Maria, Heidi, and Fejér. They included Heidi in the circle since it would not be polite to exclude her, as she would be with Faith Maria for the remainder of her days. Faith Maria would soon petition for her admittance with a short introduction period. However, now it was time for a trip to a nighttime beach so that Ruth and Mary could play big girl with Máriakéménd, Fejér, and Julie. The joy of walking on a sandy beach and warm sea winds, with multiple suns for a solid dose of Vitamin D on some planet in some faraway galaxy was a blessed experience by any means. Faith Maria and Joy stayed in the real world with Heidi and Ann. Ann would not leave Faith's side since she really missed her older sister and had grasped the concept that Faith Maria would be living in another homed. This was not the end because Ann now felt she lived in two homes. Faith Maria was dedicated to protecting this 'chosen one' and willing to remove any obstacle that would hinder their robust relationship. Heidi was helping them get comfortable with the palace, as each structure has its unique way of settling in at night. Fejér and Julie were now getting acquainted with each other in order to prepare for a compatible and consistent foundation for the sisters as they now were experiencing another style of life plus Fejér wanted to work her way back in with the younger sisters two at a time and put that extra fire back into their bonded unity. Truth be known, it was fun facing the new exciting challenges that were immediately ahead, such as preparing for Faith's wedding. This would give the girls their first taste of social extravaganza and a chance to out show the aristocrats. As the morning sun flooded the queen's chambers small bodies started sharing the joys of another day packed with adventure and so much energy to burn. Fejér gave a note to the door guards listing the food the chamber would need to break their fast and permission to knock when it was ready. The staff brought in the food and was so surprised to see the queen lying on the pillows that softened the hard floor. Then, snuggled up all around her were her sisters, the smaller ones taking small breaks from the new challenges that this chamber had hidden for them to discover. The staff strongly requested that Her Majesty and her Chamber Maiden sleep in the room's royal bed to no avail. The Princess had a rule, all, or nothing and did not care where her bones rested as long as a little tyke was bouncing off them. Some more stories were flying throughout the Islands now attesting to how 'Her Majesty' even though in a royal chamber slept on the floor with her sisters. The peasants of whom many did not have beds enjoyed this, as Faith's popularity would now return in the common people's circle. They considered it nobler to have great luxuries yet hold on to your values than becoming a greedy slave of those luxuries. Faith Maria simply attributed it to 'Blood of our blood' a power that unites allowing no option or desire for separation. Without the blood, the bond would die as one who also is without blood dies. Live or die together as one is "Blood of our blood." Máriakéménd and Fejér had done some time jumping the previous night after return Ruth and Mary. They watched other royal weddings to get some ideas for Faith's wedding. A few elements here and there would add a special touch to this ceremony. They decided to do little to Westminster Abby, maybe just a few things however Faith Maria liked the way it was and wanted to keep the people's touch that had been established for so many centuries in the Abby. That was a place of worship first and since God was creating the union, it should stay the way God liked or inspired its creation. Faith Maria and the King wanted to marry in a few weeks. Faith Maria had the ministers prepare the invitations and sent out a few days after landing in Bristol. They used the local government officials to distribute these invitations. Faith Maria wanted them sent out early since June was a month that many aristocrat families had preset plans. Daddy had told her that, "May through August is the most popular time of year to get married, considering summer weddings are full of sunshine and warmth." Máriakémend favored summer weddings since they, "are suitable for an outdoor setting such as a beach, a garden, or a beautiful yard. We can take advantage of the long days with an afternoon wedding, or highlight the glorious sunsets by saying your vows as the sun goes down behind you. What about using fresh fruits and vegetables to decorate — perhaps including clementine's and cumquats in our flower arrangements, or simply filling a large vases with dazzling yellow lemons. Add light to an evening wedding with torches and strings of lanterns in the trees. An extra-summery idea is to use gingham (lightweight plain-woven or checked cotton clothes, typically tablecloths with a few sunflowers in metal watering cans as centerpieces." Faith liked the flower decorations, since the royal garden had so many extra flowers including large fields of sunflowers. This would keep the costs down, or make more funds available for other areas. She had seen gingham used in weddings before and would give her more of a homier feeling. The outdoor activities would begin after the exchange of vowels; the royal couple would exchange them in a simpler version in the palace gardens. Faith Maria did not like the beach version since it would require the transportation from Westminster to the beach and then back to Buckingham. This would be too great of a challenge for the royal security. In addition, she had never worn clothes on a beach and to have a appearing as created by the Gods wedding on the beach would be way too taboo and could even result in getting burned at a stake for suggesting it. Why ruin a good thing? They would need the lanterns repositioned as many guests would still be celebrating into the nighttime hours, in which Charles could baste in his great conquer and Faith, with her shadow would ooze on away from the guests. Fejér added, "For all the non-aristocrat women in the bridal party, you must think about what heat, humidity, and moisture will do to your hair. Even some wigs of the aristocrat may have trouble and with the heat creating sweet under the wig, a few could fall or slide creating an opportunity for a good laugh. Most importantly, we must not try to fight our hair in the summer: straight hair will get straighter and limper, and wavy hair will get wavier and frizzier. Our royal staff with its professionals will design long-lasting styles. Thus, we can create unity with our hairstyle being not that diverse. A crown of flowers, or a single large flower tucked into your hair will look summery and beautiful. We shall deviate a little from the past so many diverse colors and hints of color in this wedding. Fejér will walk in with the sisters; holding Ruth's and Mary's hands with Ann and Joy following. Two of the palace boy guards will walk with the sisters. Faith would select which two. They would walk on the red carpet. Fejér would die her hair making it darker and harder for terrorists to target in on." Ann now asked for permission to talk and when granted questioned, "What about the food?" Fejér answered by saying, "Julie, Máriakéménd, and myself saw many weddings as we traveled through time last night in the night world. It would be wiser to follow Faith's desire to celebrate with the bounty of the season by filling our menus with fresh fruits such as strawberries, blackberries, raspberries, blueberries, grapes and apples. Between courses or as an additional dessert we will offer summer puddings. Tables with cheese, carrots, and strawberries, green peppers, celery plus a few items from our chefs including oven backed sliced potatoes dried out of course, with the table surrounded by our chef's favorite crackers will provide some finger foods for our guests. This should help reduce or prolong the effects of the liquors for the men and wines for our female guests. We do not want people getting crazy drunk. This will put some moisture back into their summer-baked bodies. We want to avoid any meats since that could encourage the guests to stay longer than we wish. " Faith decided only to allow limited guest tours inside the Palace due to security issues and would instead use some cottages not far from the palace. Special avenues would be roped that will allow carriages and pedestrians to a feeding area for the horses. We will have fresh English afternoon tea for all those who desire it. All shall need an escort card to attend; the only exceptions are the royal family and personal staff. These escort cards shall be displayed in Ivy topiaries, which will work perfectly as an escort card display and as a unique wedding reception decoration. Will can pin the escort cards to tea bags and then simply arrange them within each topiary in an ornamental shape. Those who complain about their card missing will meet with security who will match their name to the roster and then walk about to find the person with that escort name and determine who is being truthful. Escort card also allows for conversation that is more personal by keeping everything on a first name basis. We shall use rectangular tables. Cover them in gingham lightweight plain-woven or checked white cotton linens and surrounded each table with walnut folding chairs for a rustic touch with sunflowers to add color to the tables as centerpieces surrounded by an assortment of classic teacups and saucers. We will use some of the teacups to hold garden plants and vines that will creep across the table linens, mixed in cloche jars of various sizes, covering some of the teacups with plants. Our entertainment directly our wedding will skip alcohol and enjoy some competition games with rewards. We shall watch our knights' battle a couple rounds of Jousts; have supervised small bow children's archery, padded female fencing and some big horse racing. Rewards such a free tour with entry into a few nonpublic rooms, audience with the King and Faith Maria on their thrones and a few other low cost benefits would help enhance their public image. We will have a tea tour with the mothers through some special areas of the palace and children play time with the sisters, while the mothers relax drinking tea. We shall also have a late afternoon service in our chapels, one for Protestants, and the other for Catholics. The theme shall be about love and peace. The entrances will have a peaceful flower decoration. After the service, any who desire to leave may. The men will drink their liquors, women our wine and guards play more with the children. We want many of them to sleep on their way home." Now Julie gave more details about the summer wedding flowers. We cannot go wrong with an abundance of flowers at this summer wedding. There are so many varieties in season; we may have a tough time narrowing your choices down! We will fill the scenes with bright and cheerful flowers such as roses, sunflowers, red and yellow calla lilies, dahlias, Gerber daisies, cosmos, mums, and zinnias. Bright purple Dendrobium orchids are much less expensive during the summer months, so we can feel like a queen without the budget of one. Candles or small flower arrangements in the middle of fake snow made from small cotton balls or chipped wood painted white will add a special touch spotted among the tables. Another special touch is to use fake snow instead of an aisle runner. We shall send your guests home with a taste of the season: in June, a ripe peach and children will receive a treat box packed inside with sweets. Summer weddings are also perfect for seeds or small pots of flowers as favors. Since many warm or extra sunny days lie ahead of us, we shall also give out beautiful wooden fans. Our fruit will come from our royal orchards. Now we only have two more things to discuss, that being wedding dress and cake." Fejér now asked Faith if she "Had any changes to make or other requests?" Faith Maria said, "My sisters, you have read my mind. I was first thinking of a white wedding dress; however, since no one would ever want to wed in a cheap color as white. I saw a beautiful black dress and wanted to make one adjustment, and that is to have a nice long white drape in the back so that those who see me leaving shall see white and those who see me entering shall see the power of black. Those from behind will see a Princess, those ahead will see a Queen. Once in Westminster I will need some women also to cover my front with white as I stand before the priest, yet when I leave, I shall remove all the white, and all shall see me as a Queen. After discussing, the logistics of this switching the sisters all agreed that would not work and Faith Maria then went with the black for ceremonies and other dresses throughout the day. Her sisters wanted her to look like a powerful Queen to all who saw her on the streets and 'sexy' to all who attended the palace ceremonies. They drew some gown pictures and had the palaces dressmakers prepare them. They would all enjoy wide varieties of new gowns in the palace, so that the aristocrats would have their noses up slum kid's buts. The wonderful sweet taste of revenge could be at hand. Now they would enjoy the spotlight and play around the palace with children of the guests, for it was not the children's fault for the deeds of their parents; however, someday they would follow. At least they could see some freedom and happiness at the extreme top, as all in the palace had now grown attached to the special comfort this new clan emitted into the palace. Some claim to see the King playing marbles with Ann and Ruth, with Mary as their lookout, nevertheless Mary had fallen to sleep and allowed palace staff to discover it. This in no ways hurt Charles's reputation, quite the contrary it greatly enhanced it, seeing as a King who that enjoyed children would be an excellent father for the next King or queen. The initial discomfort for Charles was not knowing how this would react with his big strong King image, however as soon as the other large men who were or wanted to be fathers praised him for this play and so many even confessed to playing with their children or nieces and nephews. For they said to Charles, "They are blood of our blood, and nothing else can be stronger or greater." Thus, this had added to the power of his image, and having an exotic daring gorgeous wife would not hurt it by any means. He also remembered the first few years of his life, living without his older brother and parents when one of his father's friends in Scotland, and later to travel to England alone without his family. He then got close to his older brother, another Henry and just like his father in law, living on the other side of the road in the heavens somewhere. Henry died of Typhoid as Charles fought Rickets in his infant years. That is one reason he agreed with Louis to become Catholic in order to sweep away his sister. Charles crawled on the floor kissing dirt to get her, and all tried to dismiss him as a social defect, however he would now stand as King with the princess of France who had also made a sacrifice in her later adolescence after meeting him, gave up claim to the throne of France. Therefore, who was the real gold digger here, to cripple from Scotland or the young sex goddess from the top of the mountain in France. His point of no return was watching this little bundle as edge jumping energy fight for her life, as he has done in early life and not live life as Henry had done. When Faith had come back with all her powerful self-confidence, she looked into the eyes of a man who had become her slave. He did not care about how England would find out about his conversation, for he figured why not convert and get such a fine bundle of defiant reward, or struggle alone supporting those who would only strive to take his throne away. Wait until they went against his Henrietta Maria as Sir Fulke had tried in her prophesy had only a few years to be verified or rejected. That would lock her into a solid foundation in the Empire. Faith Maria had some issues to work out, yet her sisters would give her enough 'heavenly wine' to survive. They would have their day to show all how bonded they were. Faith was not going to be second place to no one nor was she going to play by his or her rules. She and her husband had fought off the snakes in their garden, and made their garden great. The power of her wonderful sisters was all they needed to dazzle the world. She would dance on the edge and watch them suffer until they also followed her on the edge, which would be the delight to so many noblemen. The girls had two more issues to work out before going final to the wedding, first was her private fifteenth birthday party, which they would keep private until they had children to announce her real age. Faith Maria was not very excited about the wedding since her brother had not let them leave France until they had exchanged vows, in front of Notre Dame in Paris. She thought that to be a better than Westminster, however each to his own taste. The sisters would be both bridesmaids with Ann doubling as a flower girl. The King's best man would be his brother Bobby or Robert to everyone else. He would stand in between King Charles 1 and King Louis XIII who would attend to show a hand of force supporting his younger sister and three young boys nominated by the royal staff, hopefully from their children at Faith's strong recommendation. Fejér nicked named the Kings, C1 and U13 (U for unlucky). She did not label Louis as unlucky but the country he ruled, which he even commented, "I still have fears about her near death and for her to give up her right to the throne due to violation of royal laws and customs made her worth so much more. These boys would escort Ruth, Ann, and Mary, acting official in the church, yet when back to the palace and as ordered by Faith, "I had better see dirty faces and clothes." Faith Maria had a good rationale for this in which both Kings. The three boys would stand surrounding the Kings and Charles's only remaining brother, since it was a king's brother that started all this, descending in size as Faith Maria would be escorted down England's lane by her English father who upon giving his daughter away would return to sit with Queen Marie and Prudence. Many aristocratic ladies of society could only envy the status that 'mommy' had today, even though Faith Maria begged that she walk with her and daddy down the lane, yet mommy said it would take away the role of daddy in giving away the first of many daughters. Faith Maria had worked a deal with the pope that when she arrived and standing in between the kings she would step back, walk to her mommies, and kiss them both while they wiped the happy tears from her eyes and return to stand with her husband and brother. That resulted in the whole lot standing and cheering. The pope began the first part by shocking the audience in having them reaffirm their oaths given at Notre Dame in Parris. After this, the pope and King Louis XIII descended across the stage and out the back. It was now a minister of Westminster that finished the vowels; clarifying them according to English and Protestant Laws and the laws of love (Faith Maria added this) which eased the Protestant Catholic conflict for at least the rest of this day of celebration. The previous royal traditions were all incorporated as Charles had them add one element from each royal wedding for the last six centuries, on display to add a touch of ancestral rights to the ceremony. An honorable touch to the wedding was the attendance of the King of Denmark who walked with King Louis in front of Faith and Charles. This added so much to the status image of the remaining sisters or countesses, as with the King of Denmark walking with them as all the members of the ceremony followed the King and Queen. The evidence was now fully established as this King was escorted by Ann's father for the remaining activities of the day, since Prudence entertained Marie and Fejér would entertain King Louis for the remainder of the day until the men and women separated. Henrietta Maria now could wear in public Charles grandmother's wedding ring. This allowed it to pass down from one Queen to a new one, yet Faith Maria would not pass it down, later growing bitter against her new Empire, being pulled out by Ann before her impeachment trials. Charles had so many groups of musicians playing music throughout the entire day. Faith Maria had the largest ring of all the women, and yet the ring presented no additional cost to the empire. Louis had funded most of Queen Henrietta Maria's expenses, insuring that the honor of his family was protected and projected with the esteem worthy of her name. As the differing factions melted their non-compromising positions and enjoyed a day in the middle with each having something at stake in this relationship. Throughout the ceremony they all developed, a sense of victory in that England had a Queen and she was in line for the throne of their largest so many times meshed together neighbor. A royal priced victory for their King he got them something good. The future kings and queens would have pure royal blood. Ann had one great concern, and that was the wedding cake. Faith told her, "Pick what you want in it and draw some pictures of what you want in it to look like, tell our chefs and it shall be, for I cannot eat it allowing me to still fit in these nice tight gowns and keep the eyes on me." Ann asked, "Why do you want to be in those tight dresses?" Fejér told Ann, "Someday you will discover why and you too will pass on the sweets." Ann remarked, "If it sweets or boys, I want the sweets." Fejér, Faith Maria, and Heidi all laughed. Ann looked at Heidi and asked, "Do you like boys?" Heidi told Ann, "No, like you I love Faith." Ann told her, "That is good." The wedding day was Faith's day, as she busted in her glory. Yet, in gardens sometime there is a snake and Faith Maria was about to be bitten. Faith Maria was now going to sign her first death warrant against the evils of her past. An au pair comes to her and whispered, "We have someone locked up you need to see." Faith Maria looked at the au pair and saw her sincerity thus joined her as they went to meet this 'stranger'. Faith Maria saw an older dirty vagabond and asked him, "Why do you disturb me on my day of marriage?" The toothless tramp then replied, "My, your breasts look just as soft as when I played with them." The Queen then said, "How dare you talk to the Queen like this?" The slug continued, "Do not you remember all the times I paid you to seduce me?" Faith Maria now could visualize the possibility of this, however the bum had received what he paid for and was now trying to take away from her the virtues such a grown man had bought from a young helpless starving child. Now the question really was being 'Does she pay again or does he receive again?' " Faith decided that greed and sloth were also on the table now and she would no longer give herself to this pedophile. She looked at him and said, "How dare you talk to your Virgin Queen like that?" She had passed all tests of chastity, thanks to Fejér and Máriakéménd so her defense was solid. Faith Maria continued, "My virginity was tested by all. You shall not entire my palace and tell my people such lies; guards, take him to the dungeon and bring back for my dogs his head." In addition as she commanded it was done, with the head being brought back after the celebrations. She looked at her au pair and laughed, "Why would a countess or princess even talk to such as him? I do love all people, yet when they lie to steal from me thus punishing me for my kindness, they must suffer." The house cleaners all gave her warm hugs and told her, "The innocent always suffer at the hands of evil." Queen Henrietta Maria just acted normal as this process unfolded, she wanted to draw much attention to it and let it unfold as a crazy bum wrongfully attacking the queen and the punishment to goes with such attacks. She could only think of the beauty of her mommy today. She was dressed in a pure white with dropping layers in her back and the front was not extended yet run flat down to show her support for Faith Maria and long dark brown hair flowing down her exposed back. Faith Maria ran up to her so many times and hugged her reaffirming their love. Mommy always loved Faith, especially the way she bonded with Ann, and mothered her younger sisters and worshipped her. Faith always followed her guidance without question and added the excitement and warmth to the family, especially on picnic nights. She would have walked the streets freely exposed to keep her sisters fed, yet in our home they were not only fed food but also love and the love they released had people who wanted it. We were a real family, even to the point of daddy making them countesses from Denmark and not France as for Faith. With Christian IV escorting the sisters and introducing them as royal countesses of Denmark and Norway, Ruth, Mary, and Joy were locked into a solid social status. Christian IV was popular in Denmark and thus that popularity spread into other countries, and today he got to visit with Charles I and Louis XIII, each having claim to this countess, princess and now Queen. Each with their claim or part would never hurt her. Nevertheless, Faith Maria wanted her sisters and chamber maiden and mommy glorified today. Fejér also wore a white gown, without the extenders and shoulder-less, with some light to share cleavage at top. She enjoyed bending over while talking to the noblemen, and promotes them choking on their drinks. These girls were devas in every sense of the word, Medica spared no curves or perfectly shaped muscles as many wondered, were they amazons or from a special part of the heavens that just made perfect women. How did such beauty mingle into one force, as they added glamour to the new fifteen year old, by a few days Queen? Even mommy impressed them, knowing that she cared for the children and raised such freedom loving children. They stood at attention when needed and wrestled in the mud when allowed. Many thought this to be a novel idea, train them hard, and let them play hard. Whatever it was did not really matter, as they were loved little children as the palace was their playground and the staff actually loved them because they also played with the staff's children, honestly, sharing and daring. The old castle had some life in it as Charles and Henrietta Maria cleaned some cobwebs out of their childhoods through the process. Many commented that with all the child guards in the palace it was now a kindergarten. Faith did not care, for it helped to build future leaders, most only until the sisters left for home. There was of course through the entire process one she served her master and true love with all her heart. Heidi never let Faith Maria out of her eyesight, even while talking with many gentlemen. Faith Maria dressed her somewhat like Fejér except putting a nice soft design in her white dress. The Queen personally dressed her chamber maiden and put on her makeup. Tonight would also be a special night for her as she would be in the group that watched the royal consummation. She and all the sisters would see Faith Maria being seduced along with other members of the church and ministry. Faith Maria told Charles they would give them a show and that she did bringing great glory to her husband with such remarks as, "My god, it is so big" as she reached for a nun's hand begging to be saved. Then Faith Maria would say as she moaned so loud, "You are so good, my husband, please do not stop." The sisters had been briefed about this in the nighttime world and told this was Faith's way to reward Charles for his loyalty and marriage. So many mystified verifiers left the room the next morning with all testifying the marriage was consummated and that there was every reason to believe would produce future royalty. Faith Maria also continued to moan great compliments as Charles fell fast to sleep. The nuns and priests wondered how long they would keep on bounding their bed. Most royal couples were finished in a few minutes, yet Faith Maria kept the cameras rolling for over three hours. The king, of course, received many compliments the next day as they all agreed, "Their King had given the young French princess a taste of British manhood." Word spread that the couple was made for each other and were now bonded by blood as Faith's rebuilt hymen broke as it was supposed to. England now had a rebuilt royalty stronger than before. Queen Henrietta Maria, Catholic, was going to shuffle some barrios and enjoy the life of a wife first and Queen second. King Charles had so many activities that cut back on the royals sleeping together, however Heidi was dedicated to serving her master and life in the Queen's chambers was robust. Faith Maria had never thought she would become bonded with Charles, yet as she became more intimate with him, he opened up more to her, sharing his deep feelings and thoughts. This bonding became so visible to the public for when they were on their judgment seats almost 99% of the time they ruled the same. Most judgments were made by checking guilty or not guilty without discussion, placed in a sealed envelope, and read by the court reporter. All day, agreement after agreement, this added to the validity of the judgment, and credibility of Henrietta Maria as a royal judge. The royal couple was bonded by mind and spirit. Once or twice a month when they did not judge the same way, they would go back into a closed room and debate it, yet the Queen always returned with extra winkles in her dress and facial makeup smeared. They would kiss and hug, then return and the King would say his verdict and she would agree. Many joked that Charles dazzled her with his manhood, and the poor love needed damsel would be smitten by it, yet even as a joke, it attested to her being a great spouse, for if she followed him, she believed in him. Everyone knew that if she disagreed, she had no fear in expressing it. Her summer of joy had ended, as her family would soon move back to their homes, now protected by the royal guards. Mommy no longer had to play by the aristocrats rules, for she was the English mother of the Queen and shared the role of mother with French Queen Marie in title only with each living on the other side of the shores. Faith would have her loved ones returned in royal carriages. She wanted all to know that she loved these people. Prior to their departure, Heidi was introduced to the night world and as part of the initiation had to supply the heavenly wine. She was so amazed, "How can this be?" Fejér told her that gods from another place and time were helping Ann and she demanded we all be with her. She said, "I never dreamed of supplying so much wine to so many. You all share so freely and make those who serve you want to serve harder." Faith told her. "In the nighttime world, no one served others because we were all Blood of our Blood, which means you must give up your blood and become one blood with Ann, who was the giver of the blood." Heidi then said to Ann, "Take all my blood, and let your blood make me one with you." Faith Maria told Heidi, "You must promise to serve and worship her all the days of your life." Heidi said, "She is so young, why do you worship her?" Fejér told her, "For she is the chosen one of Medica." Heidi looked at Faith Maria and said, "Do you wish I make this oath, my love?" Faith Maria and Fejér both told her, "Oh we want you to be with us forever as servants of Ann, for we have searched your heart and found you to be so worthy." Heidi then fell to her knees and licked Ann's feet saying, "I beg you to let me be your servant and to drown me in your blood." I looked down at her and could not help but love her, for she so much cared for Faith Maria whom would live in my heart the remainder of eternity. Therefore, I said to Heidi, "You shall be my chamber maiden in my kingdom that someday I will learn about. Give me your finger, I sliced a cut in it and sucked her blood until the small cut clotted then cut my finger and said to her, "Drink of my blood so that we may be one blood and you shall be blood of our blood for the remainder of eternity." I did not really know what this was about however Julie and Máriakéménd told me so many things that made me feel so much better about a day when I shall have my kingdom back, wherever it is in another place and other time. Furthermore, as Heidi did drink she turned pure white as a bright light. We had never seen this before, and then a voice spoke as Heidi's body returned, "The servant has been bonded with Ann and is the blood of her blood.

She shall be blessed by many worlds and known as the chamber maiden of the heavens." Heidi now stood up and ran over to Faith, her master, and asked, "Have I done good or evil to you in this night." Faith Maria told her, "You are the first to see your heavenly eternal body and the first to be given a title in the heavens." Heidi asked, "Is this good?" Máriakéménd asked her, after introducing herself and Julie, to go with them. Heidi looked at Faith Maria for permission as Faith Maria told her, "They are the servants of Medica and our teachers which we always obey." They took Heidi to a nice comfortable beach to set up on the sand rocks and asked her, "Do you know what is in those stars? The little one way over there (guiding her eyes to the point they were talking about), that is your daytime world. The heavens that you will be serving with the chosen one is greater than this entire sky by over 100 times. Medica told us that we must have your love in order to save the chosen one. We now beg for that love." Heidi stood up in anger and said, "You shall never beg me, but only ask and I shall do. Am I a part of the chosen one and am I blood of her blood?" Máriakéménd and Julie said with great excitement as they hugged her so tight, "You are the Blood of our Blood and we are Blood of your Blood, we are not one for eternity, now lets us return to the group and allow you to enjoy this great dot in the sky." When Heidi started to play she asked, "Do we not need to wear clothes, so no men find us and declare us to be?" Máriakéménd told her, "There are no men on this dot in the sky." Heidi smiled in amazement. She was part of something so much bigger and enjoyed it. Although she still so much wanted to serve Faith who would not let her hear, saying repeatedly, "You are blood of our blood, you are me and I am you, we are one so please take your part of me and fill it with joy and fun, so I may have twice the fun, please." Heidi could not argue with this and it brought her great joy. She was where she wanted to be and that was inside Faith. That is all that counted. She also liked the fact that she was part of a family and always so much enjoyed the bond these girls had with each other. She knew for a long time that it was special and powerful, yet never dreamed it was this special and powerful. Moreover, she would not have to mess Ann and the sisters, for she could see them every night now as grown women and consensual lovers. To be intimate with all of them was more than she could ever have dreamed. Her wine bottle was getting royal treatment and this was so much better than her oath of abstinence. Moreover, she would have something to do on the nights Queen Henrietta Maria was sleeping with King Charles I. Moreover, this was one of those nights, so they had to rush back. Heidi tucked herself into Faith's bed, all alone at night for the first since Faith Maria made her the Queen's Honorable Chamber Maiden and she was in for another surprise as all the sisters would be. Marchosias, a demon of evil, decided to visit her. It was this night that we all learned why Medica had worked so hard to pull her into the group. Marchosias said unto Heidi as she lifted her up, "I smell the blood of the promised one in you." Heidi said, "I have only the blood of my master whom I must serve till my death, for I am the Queen's Chamber Maiden." Marchosias then told Heidi, "You shall suffer tonight greater pains than ever before and you will tell me where the chosen one is?" Heidi than told her, "You do not take from me for I am owned by the queen." Marchosias told her, "The queen shall not save you. I shall drink all your blood and have the chosen one's blood." In addition, with this she did take her spiked razor fingernails and cut on Heidi's face. She then took hooks and lifted up Heidi's face as she kept singing, "My queen shall save me." Heidi was in so much pain that she became unconscious. In her, she saw a black woman sitting on a beach singing, "My queen shall save me." Heidi, with no face and soaked in blood called out begging, "Stranger, will you save me?" The stranger said, "I shall save, you. Will you tell who I am saving?" Heidi told her, "They call me Heidi; I am the Queen's chamber maiden." The stranger then told her, "I have heard great things about you Heidi, about your great love and service to the blood." Heidi then said, "I know not what you say." Heidi's face was gone and only blood covered her now. She could take no chances. Then the stranger said to her, "Do you know the chosen one?" Heidi then started singing, "My Queen shall save me." The stranger then restored Heidi to her former self-giving her back every drop of her lost blood and her great beauty. Heidi looked at herself then asked, "Which dot am I at in the sky?" The stranger said, "A dot not far from where Máriakéménd made love to you last night." Heidi said, "I know not this Máriakéménd you talk about." The stranger said, "If I bring her here to you, would you recognize her?" Heidi said, "If I recognize her I will tell you." Instantaneously, Máriakéménd appeared before her and bowing said, "Oh my great master, how may I serve you?" The stranger told her, "Take Heidi to the place you made love to her last night, show her the chosen one, and bring her back. Tell her not who I am." Máriakéménd took her to Ann where their spirits had drowned heavenly wine, and returned her. The stranger asked her, "Do you know the chosen one?" Heidi said, "I have in me and my body that lies below us dying the blood of the chosen one. I am loyal and worship the chosen one. I shall never tell anyone where my god is." The stranger then asked her, "Do you know that I too am a god and shall bring back your flesh as I have brought back your nighttime world, and shall destroy the evil demon Marchosias. She has brought pain to one who is loved by the master." Then Heidi saw pure energy and power slowly consume Marchosias as she cried in great pain, yet no one could hear her cry. The stranger had totally blockaded her since she could leave no trace of this demon. The stranger even fed back false information to the demon's cell sending them on a wild goose chase far away. Heidi was so amazed at the power of this god yet also felt relaxed since she never saw a female god before. Then Heidi watched every drop of blood return to her flesh and her face completely restored. Her body looked better than it was before. Heidi, now on her knees, asked the god, "Why do you want the chosen one?" The stranger said, "She is blood of my blood and blood of our blood. She is me and I am her." Heidi then said, "Why would you want to hurt the chosen one then?" The stranger said, "I have no thought of hurting my master, for my master is loyal to me, and gave me all that I am as I shall always give her all that I am, for I was inside her and am no more." Heidi asked, "Why, my god?" The stranger told her, "I am a goddess, a female such as you. To answer why, 'is still partially unknown, however Medica and I know that she charged the gods before being evil to the universal throne. The evil gods tried to destroy her, yet the god she is to marry brought her back here for her safety. If she is discovered, she will be punished badly by this evil throne, so we must confess to no one." Heidi said, "I wish I knew this chosen one so I could worship her also. May I ask the name of the goddess I now worship?" The stranger then told her, "My name is Sabina, the sister of your Ann." Now Sabina jumped into one of her flesh suits and appeared before them, as Máriakéménd was worshipping beside her. They were in a sandy part of this planet as even the sky was brown. Heidi then said, "I also am the sister of one called Ann, which must not be the same one you speak of." Máriakéménd looked at Heidi and said, "She is the same one." Sabina looked at Heidi and asked one more time, "Do you know the chosen one?" Heidi told her, "If I did, no amount of torture would ever make me betray her." Sabina then said, "Blessed is the one who is named Heidi, for she shall someday rule in the heavens." Heidi then said, "I do not wish to rule in the heavens, but only give my life serving my Queen." Sabina told her, "You shall rule for you are so loyal to the chosen one, and will never betray her. She will survive with you at her side. Your loyalty proven here today shall be told for all throughout the ages. You cared not for yourself, laying down with the truth inside you in great pain to die. Your life and pain could not force you to betray. Your Queen is blessed and so lucky to have your loyalty saving her sister. You are the blessed, and shall reign thrones greater than this Milky Way. Go and serve your Queen and her sisters." Now Máriakéménd escorted Heidi back to her body telling her, "You have proven to be stronger than any I yet to serve with. Do you not know pain?" Heidi said, "Pain I do feel and hate I do know, yet I also know love and loyalty. I will never betray those whom I serve for to do so would cause me greater pain." Máriakéménd replied, "Faith will be so proud of you." Heidi could feel herself melt into her body. She then became a little sad saying, "I so much more enjoyed being out of my body." Máriakéménd reminded her that she would be lying her body down in less than five decades. Sabina now reached out and hugged Heidi, "Someday, we will bring the chosen one and her disciples back to our throne. You shall be rewarded more than you can imagine." Heidi then replied, "Why would you want to reward me for such a small sacrifice for such a great love?" Máriakéménd and Sabina both now hugged Heidi. Máriakéménd took Heidi back to their nighttime land. Upon arrival, Máriakéménd asked the sisters to sit down and watch the following stream. She did not tell them what it concerned. They saw the evil Marchosias capture and attack Heidi without mercy scraping large deep cuts into her skin with her razor blade fingernails demanding to know where the chosen one was. Heidi had not answered. They watched Marchosias butcher Heidi's face and lift it off her. Heidi only sang, "My Queen shall save me" after which she slowly in pain laid down her life. The sisters were all in tears to include Julie and Fejér. Faith ran over to give Heidi a big tight hug shaking her while crying, "You are the greatest love I have ever seen." Ann also followed Faith Maria and wiggled in for a position. Ann told Heidi, "I feel so safe touching you. I hope no one else must ever suffer that much for me again. You are trying blood of my blood and you shall be with me for eternity and I will tell you where when the spirits tell me." We all touched and kissed her face crying at the thought of deep razor cuts throughout her entire body. We knew we had a special powerful bond that would get us to where we were going. I was now so angry that one, who was here to protect my sister by order of a king, would have to suffer so. I do not want others to have to suffer for me like that anymore. I told Máriakéménd to call the masters for me. She called them; and they appeared as white spirits telling me they "Could reveal no more for my security." I asked them, "Why was Heidi tortured so cruelly for my sake?" Sabina told Ann, "My precious and pure master, the demon called Marchosias who has sought for ages to kill you created a master plan to enter, with only a few minutes before I detected her. After restoring the Honorable Heidi, Marchosias was slowly erased from existence as was the memories of those she belonged. This is a bad thing, yet we shall continue to work hard protecting you until the day of your rebirth." I told them, "I do not know if I want any more rebirths, this last one was so exhausting." The spirits told her, "We must take a less active role in the next few years and defend you from afar. The nighttime world will also slow down to just one or two per month." I told them, "But Faith and Heidi will be gone from us. How can we visit them?" Medica told Ann, "As you have seen today, these visits can have a price, and we must strive to insure no more suffer like today as did the Honorable Heidi. In all the days of my flesh did not I ever suffer like that, nor in all my battles against evil did I make my enemies suffer like that. We must work very hard to insure this happens no more. In the days when we first developed our Empire, we did work hard to insure that all who were loyal to us should be saved. Let us not slow down now master." I asked them, "How can you protect us better by being farther away?" Sabina said, "By not leading your enemies to you. They cannot discover you if no one guides them to you, my master." I asked them, "Do you truly believe this?" Sabina and Medica both agreed, "Oh master, we only want one thing and that is for you to sit back on your new throne with your new disciples." I asked them, "What happened to my old throne?" They replied, "It is only served by one galaxy, whereas your new throne will have both a King and Queen and you will be served by six very large galaxies." I then told them, "Hay wait, Faith Maria is a Queen and her husband is a King, does that mean I will be married to a man because that would make me very sick?" Sabina told her, "Fear not Ann, He is a god and not of the flesh. He will give you peace as you give him peace." I told them, "Okay, as long as he is not a man, because I only like a very few men." Medica added, "Fear not Ann, for he is Blood of Our Blood." I told them, "He better be." They now had a light grin on their faces as they asked me, "Do you now understand, our master." I told them, "I understand much as you will have to teach me much in the future. I thank you for your service. You are free to do what you do." They then did slide out of sight and went somewhere that I did not know. I now had some bad news to tell my sisters. I began by telling them, "Our next few years will not be the same, for we will be learning to be cultured ladies without the help of Máriakéménd, for we shall only visit the nighttime world a few times each month. This is so that the chances of our sisters suffering today as the Honorable Heidi become slim. We shall now take fewer gambles, for the price that our Honorable Heidi paid was too high. We shall seldom see the ones we love so much, such as Julie, Heidi, Faith and our special lover, Máriakéménd. We shall all be strong so you can be my disciples around me as I sit on my new throne. Let us now wish each other luck as for the remainder of this night we all shall be given extra heavenly wine, so enjoy our love and drink enough to hold you till our next meeting." Everyone of course rushed to Heidi. She was so natural and humble, sitting at Faith's feet. Faith Maria was so honored to have such a wonderful chamber maiden. Heidi, of course could not give her wine to everyone at the same time, so the sisters stepped back and let Ann enjoy herself first. The remaining sisters hit Faith, Julie, Máriakéménd, and Fejér. The wine was flowing as slowly all worked their way to the Honorable Heidi to reward her for her great service. We all did not fully understand the road ahead of us as we all so much missed big sister. She was protecting over us at all times yet we were so glad that she had one such as Heidi protecting her. We were going to leave the palace officially tomorrow and go back home. Home life was going to change very much as those empty rooms would now have us in them practicing and learning from so many teachers. Our parents had so many teachers asking to teach the Queen's sisters. Their hardest job was verifying the teachers were not terrorists, even though no teacher was ever alone with any of them without two guards. The road to woman hood was boring, yet had its special private qualities. After our wonderful night together, we all did go the separate ways as soon we awoke to another day. King Charles I had his musicians play and guards on one side with royal staff on the other. He would have thirty carriages in the convoy with three royal gold and twenty-seven royal staff carriages. The three royal gold carriages would have none of the Queen's family in them. The Queen's family would be dressed in servants' uniforms and all carriages had one two guards, one of the horses and the other riding shotgun. One hundred soldiers would ride with the convoy, twenty-five on each side and twenty-five in front as well as the rear. Charles told the commanders, in front of Henrietta Maria, that if any of the family were hurt, heads would roll. The ministers told the Queen only to walk up to the golden carriages and not to acknowledge her family members for their security and King Charles looked at Heidi and told her, "That goes for you also, 'Sister." Heidi and Faith while smiling, bowed to the King and holding hands strolled down the convoy. They were afraid to let go of each other's hand for fear of running to the sisters and hug them. They stood strong and made it past the convoy without tipping their hand, for they knew the pain that could occur if they did not keep them secure. 'No more gambles' was Ann's new law and she made that law for them so that they could live and love for eternity. The convoy pulled out as Faith Maria, her shadow watched them leave, and then hugging each other cried in front of all. The servants bowed their heads as Charles came up and hugged them saying, "Whose sisters were these, my Queen or her chamber maiden?" Faith Maria told him, "All that I have I share equally with Heidi, for with her I am so safe, knowing her whole existence is dedicated to me." Charles looked at her and asked, "Do you have any sisters for me?" Faith

Maria immediately took off her hat and started chasing Charles around the courtyard, as Heidi stood there laughing. The servants immediately started blocking off escape routes for the King so the Queen could catch him easier. When she did, she wrapped her arms around him and started kissing him. She then said, "If you have a thirst for more love, you need to drink from this well, for it shall always have water for you." Charles told Faith, "I shall drink much since I know it is the best water in Europe." He then carried his queen into the Palace with Heidi behind them and all the servants cheering. No servant wants to serve royal couples that are prisoners to hate. Royal couples freed by love were so much better to live with, since most servants lived in the Buckingham for security reasons and on call availability for the crown. Faith now had a lot of time on her hands and was going to devote that to building a strong relationship as a foundation for the family she now wanted to have. She would dedicate her life to being a mother as well as mommy. That would take a lot of hard work, yet she knew the reward of young hearts raised in love. Charles very much agreed with her, wanting to insure that none of his children would suffer the pain of being raised without their parents. The royal couple continued their relationships with the children living in the palace as so many servants testified to the crowns 'family attitude' which was good news as all were eager for an heir and a spare, yet more importantly a well-developed family orientated King. Faith Maria and Heidi would spend many evenings looking out towards the home that had their sisters in it. Naturally they could not see the home, just feel the spirits in it. Faith Maria and Heidi could jump into each other's minds, which made Heidi feel so much better on the many nights that Faith Maria spent with her husband. When they both were in the Queen's private chambers, Faith Maria would completely serve the Honorable Heidi, including bathing her and comforting any sore muscles from her daily activities. Heidi so much begged Faith Maria not to do this, yet Faith Maria demanded that she "be given the privilege to serve one who had so much honor." When they slept together, Heidi would always wake up in the morning with her Queen sleeping at her feet. If the Empire only knew that great secret, many would walk away in total shock. Faith Maria just loved Heidi too much and had the greatest respect for her. Heidi was the other half inside her, whereas Charles was the other half outside her. The royal couple soon worked into their routines until one night Heidi and Faith received a visit from another unwanted guest. In the middle of the night, a dark night with no moon and dark gray clouds, a woman appeared in the window, touching the branches of a tree on each side turning them into pitch black. She wore a skirt made of what looked like thin woven hair and a solid black jacket with red wrist borders. She had a tight red vest with connected X running from her waist up to her upper exposed white chest, which revealed her black necklaces. The index fingers and thumbs were barely touching on each of her hands. Her red bright lips and long shaggy red hair highlighted her red face. Her greenish tinted eyes with big black pupils stared right through Faith Maria and Heidi as if they did not exist. As Heidi looked at this thing's lips she, thought that this beast may have just drank some blood. Something was not good here and they were freely exposed not only in flesh but felt exposed to danger with no protection. They trembled and were so afraid to talk in their minds. Then taking a change Faith Maria finally asked Heidi, "Do you know what this is?" Heidi replied, "No my master." The beast did not react thus the sisters now knew they could communicate with their minds freely. Heidi told Faith, "You must remain calm and display the strength of a Queen and ask her what she is called." Faith Maria said, "My love, I cannot, will you please save us?" This brought the fire out with Heidi as she boldly and politely asked, "Stranger, why you are here, and what your name is?" The beast shockingly replied, "I am called Azrael, the angel of death and I have come for you tonight." Heidi then replied, "Why have you made a wasted trip?" Azrael then answered, "I have not made a wasted trip. I must take the Queen first and leave you, for you will be executed when they discover the Queen dead." The beast went to touch Faith as Heidi slapped her hand and said, "I will give you a chance to escape and if not I will bring death upon you." Azrael then laughed saying, "Oh you foolish girl, did not you hear me say 'I am the Angel of Death'. No one can bring death into me. Now, the Queen is preparing to die and Azrael began to pull the air out of Faith. Heidi stood up and said aloud, "Oh mighty Sabina and Medica, your sisters beg that you save them." Then in a flash Azrael became freely exposed and started to burn. As she burned, Heidi breathed air back into Faith. They both watched as this beast burned and faded out of existence along with all memories of her among the other evil angels. Sabina and Medica would not show themselves in order to protect the sisters yet did completely make the room new once more. Faith Maria looked at Heidi in shock and then said to her, "My god girl, you just saved my life. How did you know the names to call upon and how could you be so strong and stand up to the angel of death? Are you human or a goddess?" Then an unknown voice spoke saying, "Faith, your chamber maiden in human and has the same fears as you. Her power is her love in serving you. You shall always be safe with you." Faith Maria asked, "Who are you?" She received no answer and looked at Heidi who told her, "I was promised protection by both the beautiful Sabina and Medica. They told me they would save me from any situation if my life were in danger. I have no life without you, so when your life is in danger, I will save you. Not for fear of my death but for fear of living life without you." Faith then said, "Do you know Honorable Heidi that you have now saved Ann and me from the claws of death? Will they ever learn not to challenge you?" Heidi then told Faith, "They will never learn and by the way, Medica showed me Ann in a flesh suit before she became a goddess and her beauty was so awesome." Faith Maria then said, "I wish I could meet them. You have done well Honorable Heidi, for the gods walk with you." Heidi became dizzy and fell to the floor. Faith Maria rushed putting water on Heidi. As Heidi woke up she told Faith Maria the news, "Medica and Sabina are going to take us and leave other spirits in our bodies here." Faith Maria hugged her tight and asked, "Will we die in pain?" Heidi kissed her and replied, "Of course not." Then they were flying through space like a lightning bolt. They saw so many colors and so many lights going everywhere. The power they felt was so massive. The felt heat and peace, as I filled them with so much warmth and love. Yet the faster they traveled, the lights grew no smaller. They could hear soft music and people singing. They then came to a frightening stop as four angels came to them and said, "We are from the trinity and shall take you through the dimensional walls. Fear not for we shall take you to the throne in peace. Let us go before we are discovered." Now they felt small as they would bounce off waves of light sometimes vertical and even sometimes in circles, always each time. The Angels were such great navigators that Faith later said, "It was a joy ride." Then after a few hours, the space became black and void. This was very strange yet the angels still looked calm. Then the waves started again, this time towards us. The angels were always prepared for theses waves predicting them when they were small. Heidi told them that their skills had improved so much, in which they told her, "We are now in our dimension." In addition, as they spoke this the space became filled with so many lights. Then they told the girls, "Before you in the smallest lights that are the deepest into our dimension lies the six galaxies of our Empire, each galaxy having over 1,000,000 planets to include Ereshkigal, which is now combined with ten other neighboring small galaxies since our goddess was hidden. Our heavens are very deep into our universe to protect against dimension jumpers, of which as of now we only possess that skill." Faith Maria asked, "How many dimensions are there?" One angel told her, "We have so far identified over 1,000,000. We have shifted many of them close to the dimension Ann now is hidden to reduce the chances of them jumping into ours." Heidi asked, "Why do you worry about them jumping?" The third angel answered, "For our goddess Lilith, or Ann to you, is at war with them." This great of an empire was mind boggling to the girls to say the least. Heidi asked another of her so many questions, "What has happened to our flesh?" An angel replied, "We have filled them with other spirits and reprogrammed them with your non secret memories. They will have your regular memories, with the exception of the wine drinking. We have notified Máriakémend and Fejér of this change, as you two shall replace Julie and Máriakémend since the roles are of very little use now." Faith looked out and saw a small yellow pyramid in open space. It grew larger and larger as white spaces and gray spaces were spread from within. It looked so beautiful and powerful. Heidi, the questioning spirit asked, "What is that?" The angels told her, which is our new throne, created by the god Bogovi. We shall go to the new throne for he wishes to speak with you. Heidi asked, "What were those lights we saw at the beginning of our trip?" The angel replied, "That was here for here can be there as there can be here. That is how we jump dimensions." Heidi replied, "Oh that is what I was thinking." Faith Maria started to tickle her saying, "Oh, so you want to be a funny girl." Then they entered the bright light and they could now feel their spirits being scanned by powerful forces. They experienced flashes of so many peaceful creatures studying them. Then a voice called out, "They are not from our enemies." They have now dropped into open space and were floating when a legion of angles caught them and guided them into the yellow light. As they approached, they discovered how massive it was in size. Heidi asked one of the commanders, "How large is this triangle?" He told them, "Larger than your Milky Way." They dreamed all the beauty of seeing. Once inside, they saw billions of angels going in all directions. "Where are we?" cried out Faith. One of the commanders told her, "You are inside the throne of Bogovi and Lilith." Heidi said, "We have heard of Bogovi, Medica, and Sabina, yet no Lilith." A voice spoke out, "She is the one you call Ann." Heidi then told Faith, "I never dreamed a place like this even existed, yet to say it is our little sister's throne is even more exhilarating. They now saw complete large cities with lights flashing on them. Their new guide told them, "These are some of the heavens. We have over 300 heavens inside here for all the saints from all of our history. They are guarded by billions of angels with the largest armies in our universe. We have another trillion angels who are fighting in the seventy-five galaxies we are currently at war with." Curious Heidi then asked, "What are all these wars over?" The guide told her, "They are fighting those who tried to kill your little Ann." Faith Maria then quizzed the guide, "Why do so many want to kill my little sister?" The guide told her, "She declared Rachmanism on them declaring them to be evil gods and hurting so many saints." Heidi jumped in, "Is that good or bad?" The guide told them, "The greatest good ever done in our history. Bogovi stands beside her dedicated to providing a safe universe for her to rule in." Faith Maria then replied, "Wow, this sounds like a great love." The guide told her, "Greater than any love in our universe. We all are waiting eagerly to Ann's return and marriage to Bogovi. This marriage has been approved by our dimensions throne." Heidi then asked in a puzzling tone, "Gods must get permission to marry?" The guide said, "Those who belong to the kingdom of the good and want the best for their servants." Then they dropped into one of the balls. It was a giant city of pure gold and coated with diamonds. Even a spirit could not look upon it for it was so bright. Glamour beyond what words could ever define. It was a volcano gushing out so much love and peace. Everyone was smiling and so happy. Joy was in their hearts. They could hear so much singing and music playing in such perfect harmony. Curious Heidi asked, "Where are we going?" The guide said, "I shall take you to Sabina and Medica; after which you all will go to Bogovi." Heidi said, "Oh that is good, for I really am so fond of Sabina." Faith had never met them even though they had pulled her from the angel of death and that was more than enough for an introduction for her. Somehow being a Queen of a small island on a small planet in a small galaxy did not mean much here and to think Ann, a small girl who pulled her off the streets and gave her unconditional love was the Queen of all this and Ann called her Honorable. That is a mystery for philosophers to debate for many centuries to come. Then they stopped and landed on a soft-sanded beach and looked over and saw a stranger standing before them. Heidi then got up and bowed to her knees, raised her hands and cried out, "We beg the great goddess Sabina to have mercy on us and reward us with an opportunity to fight evil and bring glory to you." Faith Maria was so shocked and the only thing she thought to do was that which Heidi was doing. Sabina came forward, and patted each of their heads and said, "You have been brought here for our great god Bogovi wishes to speak with you. She then took and rubbed Faith's head massaging it back and forth. Sabina said to Faith, "I have heard great things about you from my master. My master loves you so much. She told me you like heavenly wine. Do you want to drink from my cup?" Faith Maria said, "Oh yes my goddess. May Heidi join us?" Sabina then said, "Oh yes that will make my wine flow." She lay down on the sand and Faith Maria and Heidi buried their heads in her love and drank much wine from her cup. Sabina was so much at ease when she said, "My paramours, my master said you two were experts at getting wine. I do hope you will find much time to drink from me." Faith Maria then said, "My goddess Sabina, "Your wine is so fine I do pray that I may drink frequently from your beautiful dark bottle." Sabina then told the two that Medica would soon join them. She is more of a fighter than a spreader like me; however fear her not for we all have the same master, your Ann." Then did the sands to the back of them turn into a beautiful garden as a beautiful goddess did ascend up from below. Then this stranger asked, "Sabina, who are those two aficionados with you." Sabina answered, "They are the lovers of Ann. She has sent them to us. We are to go with them to the great Bogovi" Medica walked to Heidi and told her again, "This is the great Honorable Heidi, will you drink from our rivers of heavenly wines?" Heidi replied, "Yes, please of great goddess Medica, and may my master, Queen Henrietta Maria join us?" Medica told them, "Oh yes, and from what Ann told us, this shall be a great extravagance for me." Sabina told Medica, "My sister, you will enjoy the gifts our new sisters of brought for us." Heidi heard that statement and asked after she first worked Medica's flesh to extract the maximum wine as possible. Medica did moan and at times breathed so hard that Sabina had to hold her down and run cold water on her face. Then after two hours Sabina said, we must go to the Great Bogovi for he calls us now. As we prepared to go, Medica still lying down as Faith's head was still buried between her legs told them, "Bogovi has not shown himself to anyone since he smuggled Lilith into another time and body. He has declared his total devotion to fighting the war against those who tried to destroy his Lilith. We have put all that we have under his control as his strongest and most loyal allies. We have honored all requests he has made from us and we worship him with our true hearts, even though he tries to make us stop. We are the only ones allowed inside his light, which is always surrounded by his wise saints of the ages. He wants the four of us in his lights. We must now go, for I hear him calling." The four of them entered into the base of the throne inside the holy of holies. All guarding angels immediately bowed as they slowly drifted by. Sabina and Medica had Faith Maria and Heidi between them as they all held hands as they with great honor floated in. Then a loud trumpet sounded, and one spoke so loud that all around the throne could hear, "The goddess Sabina and goddess Medica are now here. May all give them great honor and worship." At this time, a calm force has started pulling them into the center light. This felt like millions of mosquitoes swarming around them as in the sound of compressed pure energy. As they entered inside the center, their spirits were enclosed by new flesh. He then made a small shallow lake for them to cool down inside a nice private bathing room. As the four freely exposed women stood before his light, Sabina began by saying, "Oh great god Bogovi, we who are your servants have brought before you Queen Henrietta Maria and her chamber maiden Heidi as you have commanded." Bogovi now began by saying, "I am honored to have such beauty before me. Why is the one beside you Sabina acting so shy?" Heidi answered, "Oh great god Bogovi, I have never been freely exposed in front of a male before." Bogovi then said, "Child, you have been freely exposed in front of thousands of male demons and angels, so fear not, for as you see the smile great smile on Medica's face, you are in no harm. I have brought Sister Faith, as Ann calls you, and the Honorable Heidi who saved the life of my little Ann to ask you if you will join the battle with me in bringing Ann back to her throne." Faith Maria leaped up and cried out, "Oh great god Bogovi, I wish to serve you anyway I can to bring Ann back to her home." Bogovi then told them, "Ann has requested that you also live here with her for eternity. Would you like that?" Faith Maria then asked, "Will each have her own man, or will all share yours?" Bogovi then said, "No my child, I will help you find a spouse if that is your will." Faith Maria looked at Heidi and then replied, "It is our wish to serve Ann for eternity." Bogovi then said, "Medica and Sabina and Ann have asked me to recognize you as their sisters and as such goddesses on Ann's throne. It shall be as your divinity has requested, yet not until Ann returns to sit upon our throne. First, I need your help in a mission not worthy of goddesses. If you do not want this mission, you can decline and I will make you both goddesses as you can today sit on Ann's throne between Sabina and Medica." Heidi looked at Faith and then replied, "Oh great god Bogovi, we must beg to be allowed to do any mission, no matter the status to help save our sister. We do not want the throne without Ann here with us." Bogovi then answered, "Lilith is blessed to have sisters such as you. We are slowly winning the war against evil, although many are sneaking past our blockades and hiding in the depths of our universe. Our universal throne is finding them and destroying them, yet it is a slow and time-consuming task. Unlike before, we no longer are in great danger of attacks and are winning in all our battles, as we are save the innocent saints as we fight, thus becoming slaves to time. I have no desire to hurt good innocent saints in the name of good. That cannot be. We shall win, especially with the great sacrifices that Sabina and Medica make for our joint cause. We must now give more attention to the security of Ann, as you know who has been a victim to unknown assaults. This cannot continue, as I cannot bear seeing such love as the Honorable Heidi suffering. I myself cannot see an ability to make as great sacrifice with such fortitude as the Honorable Heidi gave to the security of Ann. We cannot count on that strength of the entire enemy will study us and find a weak link. A small mistake could put Ann in an eternal lake of fire that could take me awhile to get her out. I do not want to chance that danger, as I believe neither do you. We shall immediately reduce our forces inside and around Earth to zero. That is why I need for Faith and Heidi to take over for Julie and Máriakémménd to return to our dimension. Somehow our enemy can detect a cellular deviation in one of their organs and that opens a highway to Ann." Heidi asked, "Oh great god Bogovi, can they not find it in my sister Ann." Bogovi then said to her, "Honorable Disciple Heidi, Ann in not from this dimension as I floated her spirit alongside the original spirit to join the flesh and sucked the original spirit back to me allowing Ann to be born 100% human. I believe that is why our enemies are so confused, for they can find no deviation. We shall add more dimensions between us and many powerful space forces to make programmed travel impossible except for secret travel rivers that we shall have flowing through it. We will be able to defend both the Honorable Disciple Heidi and Disciple Faith Maria in a flash. You shall never be in danger as our sensors will most times pick up the threat long before it deploys." Heidi then asked Bogovi, "Oh great god Bogovi, what will we do?" Bogovi answered, "My precious goddesses, you will go to them in the mind world and entertain and train them to fit in with their primitive societies. You and only you shall be in the nighttime world, which are on the other side of the universe, close to some sister dimensions that have offered you safe passage to our rivers. Ann and the sisters must never know who you are, for you shall be Komáromi and Siklósi and both have the beauty of Sabrina. Most times your duties will be performed at your subconscious level, sensing out deviations in normal patterns and sending the data back to us through a secret scrambled transformer at the end of the galaxy. My saints of wisdom have worked hard fine-tuning this network to perfection. I shall exhaust every ounce of my powers in protecting my Ann. I am still generating massive power that can remove the Milky Way from existence if Ann is placed in danger or spiritual prison." Heidi then asked, "Oh great god Bogovi, what did my sister do that created your love for her?" Sabina and Medica looked shocked, as Bogovi said, "goddesses Sabina and Medica that is a good question and something you all have the right to know as you will be building your own thrones as our universal throne continues to expand our boundaries. Honorable Disciple Heidi, I had been spying on Lilith as she built up her militaries and designed her courts. I did not know if she was going to expand into my galaxy since some of her empires had holdings in mine. As one of my spies ended up being involved with one of her queens, I was able perfectly to define all her goals and objectives. She was deep in a battle against evil in her galaxy determined to win. One of the empires had solar systems in both of our universes. I knew of her great power and strong personality along with being high strung. Yet when she came here, she was trembling and so humble. We have to visit for a while as she shared her heart with me. We formed an alliance that became stronger as even some of my servants married some of her servants. We knew we had a perfect match and it was our time to join as even our throne encouraged us. All my saints approved and all of Lilith's Lights of Ereshkigal approved. As we are the air, the air became a new us. Yet as we prepared for our big day of celebration evil attacked with such vengeance, even I barely wiggled out of it. My commanders were able to recreate the Ann for you, which is Blood of your Blood. You shall notice some differences in your new bodies. Lilith always wanted to represent all different kinds of people." Then Faith said, if Heidi tastes as good as Sabina, I am in for great treats." Bogovi said, "I do not know nor want to know that entire female rumble you girls are always talking about. If you destroy each other from consumption, remember I cannot save that which does not wish to be saved." At this all four girls began laughing and hugging each other. Bogovi then added, "You all will fit in well with that wife of mine, Sabina and Medica, please insure our new disciples know what they must for the safety of all, now go in peace and do what you do." They then all proceeded out of the holy of holies and then shot like missiles back to their resting throne and into their old holy of holies. Here they rested in the peaceful groves and ate fresh fruit and had some fish the Seonji had caught for them. Sabina and Medica showed the new disciples all the emergency procedures and briefings on suspected enemy threats. They also told them that many networks were established and to concentrate on Ann and their sisters. Heidi asked, "How many meetings should we have each month." Sabina told her, "Plan for two unless you have emergencies. Always respond to emergencies and then adjust the special as needed. Give Ann daily briefings concerning all things through the mind world. You will go straight to her unconscious, which makes the decisions on all matters. We feed highlights to Ann to her consciousness. We will tell her about you so she can help defend the change to your sisters. Even though you are safe, our enemies continue to improve." Medica now gave them a kiss and departed. Sabina then suggested that they test their new bodies while having some fun. They agreed as Sabina told them, "Let me teach you disciples something new. She took them to an outdoor comfort patio they had and put everyone in a special wine drinking position except Heidi who quenched the thirst of Faith. After a while, Heidi traded positions with Sabina and they continued to enjoy their flesh. After they had finished, Faith Maria asked Sabina, "What kind of people are you and Heidi, for your skin is much darker." Sabina told Faith, "We are Hyrum and you are an Ebonite." Faith Maria then asked, "Are there any differences in status or position between Hyrum and Ebonite?" Sabina then walked with them for a short distance telling the dynamic history of Lilith. "Lilith has worked hard so that sisters of all races can love in peace and equality. She sends me out to battle for Hyrum, their friends, Medica for Ebonite, and their friends. Medica and I share with the other races in freeing them from evil. Lilith receives a briefing from expert spirits, courts and the Lights of Ereshkigal She added, "Our Lights of Ereshkigal tell me that Lilith will be back on her new throne in five years at the longest. We have some emergency plans in position incase our concealment is discovered. We are in constant danger, because the God of this realm, as also Lilith and so many others are not bound by time so they can see what will happen in the future and could try to stop it now. We are fortunate that they cannot go back and capture the future offenders. You will soon be in rhythm with your focus area and will notice deviations immediately." Faith then looked over and saw a big beautiful white horse with large wings standing in the road. She gasped at such beauty and asked Sabina, "What is that and why is he standing up?" Sabina told her, "That is Lilith's personal horse and when she hears people walking she stands up to see if it is

Lilith. Lilith always cared for her personally and gave her a lot of kindness and love. That horse can fly like a missile through the air." Heidi asked, "You all keep mentioning 'missile'. We do not know what that is. Please tell us." Sabina then showed them a vision with missiles in them and a dated newspaper so they would know it was way in the future for them. Sabina then took them up to the horse and started to pet her. She could sense that Faith Maria and Heidi had been around her master and she appeared to get lively and perky. The courts sent their escorts here to take the disciples back to the little dot inside a very small galaxy that the Earthlings called the Milky Way. The journey back was as rocky as the one here yet the girls did not mind because they had been through it. Soon, they arrived in the nighttime world where Máriakémend and Julie were waiting and prepared for their journey home. They quickly reminded the girls where everything was and showed them where the secret things were. They had prepared a video stream to show them what they needed to do and how to do it. Within a few minutes, the escorts took them back to their home planets. The nighttime world felt strange for Faith now, as it hit her; she could no longer sleep or be with her husband. Heidi did not notice any big difference since most of her life was in Faith's chamber. Faith Maria would no longer be Queen Henrietta Maria. Heidi then told her, "We are now something so much greater, we are disciples to a throne so astronomically enormous. We have freedom to live in the holy of holies, where only the gods live, except for a few members of some special private and secluded races." She then went over to the viewer and watched what their sisters were doing. She could feel some big changes coming for the family. Would her sisters be able to adapt?

CHAPTER 07

SANCTUARY

Cultured for millennia like an exotic flower,
heavenly clotting light into red,
We are bound, each to the other, more tightly
than we ever could have said

Komáromi (Faith) and Siklósi (Heidi) looked down and listened to daddy talk. The Lights of Ereshkigal would implant ideas and suggestions in his mind or put environmental clues around him. The greatest concern now was to immerse the sisters into a program that would enable them to function as the Queen's sisters socially. They were now extreme upper class and as so had to know the graces and courtesies associated with this status. Komáromi had programed the new Queen Henrietta Maria with good memories of studying and playing with her sisters. She did not program information about the night world, the heavenly wine adventures nor did anything associate Ann being the chosen one. Siklósi did the same with her replacement and put the relationship as mostly professional with a few crazy adventures with the palaces children, such as throwing pies and cakes at each other. Siklósi programed in nightly bed wrestling activities with the Queen. There had to be a few activities that bonded them together. It was up to them to make their situations work. There are few worse situations than waking up into to the life of being the Queen with picture perfect memories to support it. Just to be safe Komáromi would scan Charles and the servants of the queen looking for any suspicions. When she found them, she updated the Queen's memory banks to make the required adjustments. Many times, to Komáromi's surprise this involved adding quirks in her style she never knew that she had. It was not anything too terribly bad, little things as the way she adjusted her dress as she entered a room or even the way she would fidget with her hair when asked questions she had to think about. Komáromi enjoyed learning about herself from those who knew her best while Siklósi enjoyed the humor about it until the roles were reversed. Thus, each had their fun. They were now however, more attune to watching the sisters. Joy was sprouting up fast as Mary, Ruth, and Ann still was about the same in height and weight and Fejér was still watching them; however, her role was dropping off fast. Mommy was spending so much time, almost 24/7 with the sisters. She also had the girls find leads for teachers who could come to the house and teach the sisters. Daddy was also searching for the more formal ones. The sisters were now wearing more academically attuned clothing. Very little play, just study and practice. They had to relearn everything new, although they had some fast tips while at Buckingham, those would not work here. In the palace, most guests were too busy bowing or worried about their perfection to pay any attention. Royal family had to be perfect. Ann did not really like that at all, yet knew to keep for sanctuary this was the only road to travel for not only her safety was at risk but also that of her family, since no evil spirit would ever accept the fact of their innocence even though her sisters had enough knowledge to raise a serious suspicion. At the end of this road lay their destiny. As for now, it was time to learn some manners. Guess no more contests to see which girl could fart the loudest a dinner. What would also add to some difficulty with this learning process was that they had limited access to Máriakémend and Julie, or as Ann now knew, Komáromi and Siklósi which now put Faith Maria and Heidi at their immediate disposal. Ann could not wait for the day that Máriakéménd and Julie would rejoin them. Ann's subconscious had already awarded Máriakéménd discipleship and Julie as her aid. She had not known Julie that long and wanted to save the discipleship positions for those who had contributed tremendously to her sanctuary. The betrayer demon in Henrietta would be judged special as the forward deployed spirits already had 'it' out of this dimension. Now they would set down and learn this from ground zero. Every action done in company ought to be with some sign of respect, to those that are present. No more sneezing on each other or tripping them so they fall in the mud. When in company, put not your hands to any part of the body, not usually revealed. Mary then asked, "What if my butt itches and Ruth will not scratch it?" Aethylswith, the first of so many of our teachers said, "Grab her hand, and go behind the trees and when she is scratching your butt you can pick her nose." We all said yucky nevertheless was never caught scratching our butts. Show nothing to your friends that may scare them. Thus, "Do not show them dead animals or snakes and spiders." Playing with those things is no longer permissible.

In the presence of others sing not to yourself with a humming noise, nor drum with your fingers or feet. We do not want sounds that attest to our foolishness conversely we want sounds that attest to our sophistication. Drumming your feet attest to nervousness and tapping your fingers attest to boredom. If you cough, sneeze, sigh, or yawn, do it not loud but privately; and speak not in your yawning, but put your handkerchief or hand before your face and turn aside. One yawn can have a whole group yawning while coughing on others can spread colds and other dangerous things that are airborne. Make sure you have a clean handkerchief each time you leave this home or I should say this mansion. The most exhausting thing about was that it did no good to use the mind world since it was real time and not time stopped and reversed as with the night world. It was so hard not yawning; nevertheless, it did help to keep all of us from falling to sleep. The one nice thing is that with the role playing that put some energized air back in our blood. Sleep not when others speak, sit not when others stand, speak not when you should hold your peace, and walk not on when others stop. Stopping when others stop shows your respect, as does the anger generated in response to perceived misunderstandings. Then one day then respond and at the same time, get rid of the anger before the sun goes down. Take not off your clothes in the presence of others, nor go out your bedroom half dressed. Then Joy said, "But the boys like watching me dress in front of them." Aethylswith then casually responded, "Well then I will ask your daddy to help you with this problem." Joy's face turned red as she gave up the temporary prestige she had received from the sisters for her daring humor and started begging for reconsideration from Aethylswith. She thought hard and then wanted to reconfirm that Joy could give up the undressing in front of boys. She confirmed this, however secretly within one year gave up on this battle. At play and at work it is good manners to give place to the last attending person, and affect not to speak louder than ordinary. If you must speak louder than the person or people you are, speaking until it is time to excuse yourself and join a less rambunctious group. This is because others around you will most likely hear you screaming and not the other members in that group, thus you will be thought the fool in the group. Spit not in the fire, nor stoop low before it neither put your hands into the flames to warm them, nor set your feet upon the fire especially if there be meat before it. Stirring the fire with your feet will flood the meat with ashes. Spitting should be done in private. We know that as young children you have had many spitting contests. That was as a child, you are now training to become women folk. The others actions quoted her could expose private body parts and put the smell of smoke in your hair or on your clothes. When you sit down, keep your feet firm, and even, without putting one on the other or crossing them. Young women folk never wear clothing, which requires their legs to be crossed. Firm feet provide evidence of confidence. Shift not yourself in the sight of others nor gnaw your nails. When you sit stay in your position. Moving your position imply insecurity and gnawing your nails are much like picking your nose. A woman would inspect her nail length while she is painting them. That is part of the pre-departure inspection. We were now starting to wonder if all this was worth the trouble. We could of course live all the time in our mansion, although we would have to attend church, special honorary functions and visits to Buckingham. Shake not the head, feet, or legs roll not the eyes lift not one eyebrow higher than the other twist not the mouth, and to wet with as if with dew no man's face with your spit, by approaching too adjoining him when you speak. No one likes someone who spits in their face when they are talking to you. Try to avoid getting into someone's personal space and avoid sending threatening vibes, most noticeably keep your spit in your mouth and keep your distance. Aethylswith had us stand face to face and spit on each other. We did not mind since we were all blood of our blood, yet we could understand how other people would not like it plus if other people did it to us. Kill no vermin as fleas, lice ticks in the sight of others, if you see any filth or thick spit put your foot gracefully upon it if it be upon the clothes of your companions, put it off privately, and if it be upon your own clothes return thanks to him who puts it off. No one likes to see mashed insects and their internal parts dripping from your hand. Turn not your back to others especially in speaking, shake not the table or desk on which another reads or writes, lean not upon any one. Aethylswith replied that the leaning not upon anyone was particularly hard for sisters with each other, thus we practiced this one every day. Keep your nails clean and well mannered, also your hands and teeth clean even without showing any great concern for them. Faith Maria and Fejér had drilled this into us, so we had no problems with this task and actually, Aethylswith commented on our excellent appearance of our bright white teeth. Do not puff up the cheeks, loll (move in a lazy manner) not out the tongue, rub the hands, or beard, thrust out the lips, or bite them or keep the lips too open or too tight. Be no flatterer, neither plays with any that delights to be a flatterer. We now understood way mommy hated this crap so much. Read no letters, books, or papers in company, but when there is a need for the reading you must ask leave: come not near the books or writings of another to read them unless desired or give your opinion of them asked also look not nigh when another is writing a Letter. Let your countenance be pleasant but in serious matters somewhat grave. The gestures of the body must be suited to your discourse. Have your body gestures, voice tone, and facial expressions match what you are saying. Reproach none of the infirmities of nature, nor delight to put them that have in mind thereof. Show not yourself glad at the misfortune of another though he was your enemy. When you see a crime punished, you may be inwardly pleased; however, always show pity to the suffering offender. We did this naturally and even to the extreme by crying too, as seeing suffering. Do not laugh too loud or equally important much at any public spectacle. This was the behavior of the poor as in competing too much to see who can laugh the loudest. Superfluous complements and all affectation of ceremony is to be avoided, yet where due to, they are not to be missed. Pulling off your hat to noblemen, justices, churchmen and make a reverence, bowing more or less according to the custom of the better bred, and quality of the person being higher if performed correctly. Among your equals, expect not always that they should begin with you first, but to pull off the hat when there is no need is affectation, in the manner of saluting and re-saluting in words keep to the most usual custom. It is ill manners to bid one more eminent than you are covered, as well as not to do it to whom it is doing. Likewise, he that makes haste to put on his hat does not well, yet he ought to put it on at the first, or at most the second time of being asked; now what is herein spoken, of qualification in behavior in saluting, ought also to be observed in taking of place, and sitting down for ceremonies without bounds is troublesome. If anyone comes to talk to you while you are sitting, stand up, though he is your inferior, and when you present seats let it be to every one according to his degree. When you meet with one of the greater quality than yourself, stop, and retire especially if it be at a door or any straight place to give way for her of him to pass. In walking, the highest station in most countries seems to be on the right hand. Therefore, place yourself on the left of him whom you desire to observe; however, if three walks conjointly the middle position is the most honorable the wall is usually given to the most worthy if two walks with each other. If anyone far surpasses others, either in age, estate, or merit yet would give place to a meaner than himself in his own lodging or elsewhere the one ought not to expect it, so he on the other part should not use much earnestness nor offer it above once or twice. To one that is your equal, or not much inferior you are to pay the primary seat in your lodging, and he to whom 'this offered ought at the first to refuse it but at the second to accept though not without acknowledging his own title. They that are in Dignity or in office have in all place's precedence but while they are Young, they ought to honor those that are their equals in girth or other characters, though they have no public charge. It is good manners to prefer them to whom we speak, before ourselves, especially if they be above us with whom in no sort of, we ought to begin. We were lucky in those above us because those were only the King and Queen. However, Aethylswith told us it was important to know these things so that others could not take us down, if not for you, but the position of the Queen's household. Let your discourse with men of business be short and comprehensive. Artificers & persons of low degree ought not to use many ceremonies to lords or others of high degree but respect and highly honor them, and those of high degree ought to treat them with affability and courtesy, without arrogance. In speaking to men of quality do not lean nor look them loaded in the face, or approach too near them at least keep a crowded pace from them. In visiting the sick, do not presently pretend to be the physician if you do not know therein. In writing or speaking, give to every person his due title according to his degree and the custom of the place. Strive not with your superiors in argument, but always submit your judgment to others with modesty. Undertake not to teach your equal in the art himself professes; it smacks of arrogance. Let their ceremonies in courtesy be proper to the dignity of his place with whom thou converses for it is absurd to act the same with a clown and a prince. Do not express joy before one sick or in pain for that, contrary passion will aggravate his misery. When a man does not all; he can though it succeeds not, will none blame him that did it. Being to advise or reprehend any one, consider whether it ought to be in public or in private presently, or at some other time in what terms to do it and in reproving, show no sign of anger, but do it with all sweetness and mildness. Take all admonitions thankfully in what time or place so ever given but afterwards not being culpable take a time and place convenient to let him know it that gave them. Mock not nor jest at anything of importance break no jests that are harp biting, and if you deliver anything, witty and pleasant abstain from laughing there at yourself. Wherein you reprove another be unblamable yourself; for example, it is more prevalent than precepts. Use no reprimand language against any one neither curse nor revile. We were now beginning to worry about Joy, for she appeared to be very tired every day. Joy told Aethylswith that she was missing Faith so much and was having bad dreams at night. Joy told us, "I can handle this, just, please give me some time." As soon as we were released from our studies, Joy would go straight to sleep. She now slept in the bed closest to the doorway. She never ate with us at home anymore. The girls told us that some leftovers from our kitchen were missing. She always seemed happy in the mornings, ate fast at lunch, and then drop off to sleep. Ethyl told us not to worry; she did not possess a temperature and still had a robust appetite. She attributed it to be the closest to the queen and never having to study formally before, and that time would cure this. Be not hasty to believe flying reports to the disparagement of any. Rumors destroy relationships. Wear not your clothes, foul, ripped or dusty but see they be brushed previously every day at least and take to heed that you avoid uncleanness. Mom would not let us wear our clothes more than once. They had to be cleaned before wearing again. Her mother also had that rule, and she drew it down. She always teased us, "You shall never know, for today you might meet your knight in shining armor, as he might want to kiss you." Now that Faith Maria was married and Joy was winking at the boys, we figured to be next so might as well be prepared for our King in shining armor. In your apparel be modest and endeavor to accommodate nature, rather than to procure admiration to keep to the fashion of your equals such as are civil and orderly with respect to times and places. Run not in the streets, neither walks too slowly nor with mouth open go not shaking your arms kick not the Earth with your feet, go not upon the toes, nor in a dancing fashion. Play not the peacock, looking everywhere about you, to see if you are skilfully decorated, if your shoes fit properly if your stockings sit neatly, and clothed handsomely. Eat not in the streets, nor in the house, out of the season. Associate yourself with men of good quality if you venerate your own reputation, for it is better to be alone than in the bad company. When walking up and down in a house, only with one in company if he were greater than you were, at the principal give him the right hand and stop not until he does and be not the first that turns. When you do turn let it be with your face towards him, if he be a man of great quality, walk not with him cheek by jour but somewhat behind him; but yet in such a manner that he may easily speak to you. Let your conversation be without malice or envy, for it is a sign of a tractable and commendable nature; and in all causes of passion admit a reason to govern. Never express anything unbecoming, nor act against the rules moral before your inferiors. Always be modest in urging your friends to find a secret. Utter not base and frivolous things among grave and learned men nor very difficult questions or subjects, among the ignorant or things hard to be believed, stuff not your discourse with sentences among your betters or equals. Speak not of doleful things in a time of mirth or at the table; speak not of melancholy things as death and wounds, and if others mention them change if you put up the discourse tell not your dreams, but to your intimate friend. A man ought not to value himself of his achievements, or rare qualities of wit; much less of his riches virtue or kindred. Break not a jest where none take pleasure in the mirth laugh not aloud, nor at all without occasion, deride no man's misfortune, though there seems to be some cause.

Speak not injurious words, in neither jest nor earnest, scoff at none although they give occasion. Be not forward but friendly and courteous; the first to salute hear, answer, and be not pensive when it is a time to converse. Detract not from others neither be excessive in commanding. Go not thither, where you know not, whether you shall be welcome or not. Give not advice without being asked and when desired do it briefly. If two contend together take not the part of both unconstrained; and be not obstinate in your own opinion, in things indifferent be of the major side. Reprehend not the imperfections of others for that belong to parents, masters, and superiors. Gaze not on the marks or blemishes of others and ask not how they came. What you may speak in secret to your friend deliver not before others. Do not speak in an unknown tongue in company but in your own language and that as those of quality do and not as the vulgar; sublime matters treat seriously. Think before you speak, pronounce not distinctly. When another speaks, be attentive yourself and disturb not the audience if any hesitate in his Words help him not nor prompt him without desired, interrupt him not, nor answer him until his speech is ended. In the midst of discourse ask not of what one argues but if you perceive any stop because of your coming you may well entreat him gently to proceed; If a person of quality comes in while you're conversing it is handsome to repeat what was said before. While you are talking, points not with your finger at him of whom you discourse nor approach too near him to whom you talk especially to his face. Treat with men at fit times about business and whisper not in the company of others. Make no comparisons and if any of the company be commended for any brave act of virtue, commend not another for the same. Be not apt to relate news if you know not the truth thereof. In discoursing of things you have heard name not your author always a secret discover not. Be not tedious in discourse or in reading unless you find the company pleased therewith. Be not curious to know the affairs of others neither approach those that speak in private. Undertake not what you cannot perform but be careful to keep your promise. When you deliver a matter do it without passion and with discretion, however mean the person be you do it too. When your superiors talk to anybody listens not, neither speaks nor laughs. In the company of those of higher quality than yourself, speak not until you are asked a question then stand upright put off your hat and answer in few words. In disputes, be not so desirous to overcome as not to give liberty to each one to deliver his opinion and submit to the judgment of the major part especially if they are judges of the dispute. Let thy carriage be such as becomes a man grave settled and attentive to that which is spoken. Contradict not at every turn what others say. Be not tedious in discourse, make not many digressions, nor repeat often the same manner of preaching. Speak no evil in the absent for it is unjust. Being set at meet scratch not neither spit cough nor blow your nose except there is a necessity for it. Make no show of taking great delight in your victuals, feed not with greediness; cut your bread with a knife, lean not on the table neither find fault with what you eat. Take no salt or cut dough with your knife greasy. Entertaining any one at table it, is decent to present him with meat, undertake not to help others undesired by the captain. If you soak bread in the sauce, let it be no more than what you put in your mouth at a time and blow not your broth at the table but stay until cools of itself. Put not your meat to your mouth with your Knife in your hand neither spit forth the seeds of any fruit, pie upon a dish nor cast anything under the table. It had been so easy for us to put food under the table because Charley would eat it quickly. It is unbecoming to stoop much to one's heart, keep your fingers clean, and when foul wipe them on a corner of your table napkin. Put not another bit into your mouth until the former be swallowed let not your morsels be too large for the mouth. Drink not nor talk with your mouth full neither gaze about you while you are a drinking. Drink not too leisurely nor yet too hastily. Before and after drinking wipe your lips breath not then or ever with too great a noise, for it is uncivil. Cleanse not your teeth with the Tablecloth, napkin, fork, or knife but if others do it let it be done with a toothpick. Rinse not your mouth in the presence of others. In Company of your betters be no longer in eating than they are, lay not your arm but only your hand upon the table. It belongs to the chief in company to unfold his napkin and fall to meat first, but he ought then to begin in time and to dispatch with dexterity that the slowest may have time allowed him. Be not angry at the table whatever happens and if you have reason to be so, show it not but on a cheerful countenance especially if there be strangers for good humor makes one dish of meat a feast. Set not yourself at the upper of the table but if it were your due or that the master of the house will have it so, contend not, least you should trouble the company. If others talk at the table, be attentive but talk not with meat in your mouth. Thus, our see food (seafood) jokes had to be put on the shelves. When you speak of God or his attributes, let it be serious and weigh reverence. Honor and obey your natural parents or foster even though they are poor. Let your recreations be brave, not sinful. Labor to keep alive in your breast that little spark of celestial fire called conscience. We all had survived an aristocratic lady-developing year, torment and all. We had practiced it so hard that we could feel ourselves changing. Not only were we complaining about these principles, yet also was James by telling us, "This crap is so boring." James reminds us that the father of the great eagle shall share these wise social skills in about one century yet to be, as he would continue to remind us. I just would say, "Oh James, type it for me." He did not have to heart to break a little girl's heart. I think that I will hate it when I become a big girl again. I will have no advantage. One of my sisters was developing much faster than the rest of us. She spent most of her time doing big girl things now with Fejér and sometimes mommy. Mommy was spending more time with her aristocratic friends and when she got home at night, she would explain to us how her situations mandated the use of some of the rules that Aethylswith had taught us. Many of mommy's friends were interested in these rules thus mommy had a printing company print them and gave them away freely. These pamphlets stayed in their family documents and in just a few years a gentleman by the name of Thomas Warner read one and saved it to be passed on the his children, with was read so many times it became memorized by most of his children, of special notice one named John. John like so many others decided to try his luck in the new world, and after a rocky landing married a girl by the name of Ann. They had a grandson in the 18th century that became a great warrior and political leader. The grandson published these courtesies before becoming the first president of the independent colonies. His given name was George, and from his father, a family name of Washington. The irony would be this our Queen Henrietta Maria would share these rules, which would sometime be used by those who would rebel against the throne she was part of building. This insured that many others suffered through these rules also and that the colonies would not behave as the savage barbarians they killed to get their lands. Father was not done with us by any means and learned of some growing discontent with Charles I, and his Queen and being so closely associated with them had to start looking for somewhere else to raise his daughters. His daughters were growing fast before him as Faith was popping out grandbabies in Buckingham. One little blossom was blooming before everyone's inattentive eyes. Joy would dress loose, casual around the house, yet by night right, and tight for the boys. She could make them howl to the moon. We did not know this, until one night I happened to awake as she was quietly leaving our room. She dawned some of our girls' hoods and outer coats and slid disguised out the door. I quickly went to my window and with our secret play rope dropped quickly to the ground to see Joy entering a carriage with a boy in it. How could she betray us just as Faith did? This was not a king's carriage and we agreed only to marry kings. Guess cupid was blasting poor Faith Maria with so many arrows. As she came back on this Saturday morning, I asked to talk with her privately. I started by asking her how things were going. She told me we should talk later after she got some rest. I then told her that I saw her getting into the carriage last night and that if she loved me she would tranquil my fears. Joy then guided me to a private room she had been using to spot Richard's carriage at night. She told me to sit and started massaging my back. It was so nice getting that special attention from a big sister once again. The anxiety of having another sister with a boy was very much depressing. Is this a decease, which all girls suffer? I might have to talk to mommy's Dutch doctor for some pills to fight this. Joy started by explaining the pain of losing Faith Maria for this was harder for her than the rest of us. As the years had been rolling by and having seen Faith's new babies had lighten up something inside. She was now longing to have a family. As she was walking one day, a clean well-mannered boy came up beside her. He did not know who she was. He noticed from her manners and courtesies that she would be presentable to his parents. He introduced them to her. They started to enjoy the walks in their large flower garden. Their house was comparable in size to our mansion. The parents continually praised her for being so well mannered. They continually asked where she lived and Joy told them she was visiting a friend, yet normally lives with her older sister. To add to her instability, the letters from Faith Maria had dropped off in both size and emotional tone. Big sister was pulling away and Joy now felt alone. Richard's soft hands and voice and romantic words were melting her defenses down. She now found herself longing all day to lie in Richard's arms through the night. They were forbidden to close the door and one of the servants always sat outside the room monitoring them. Richard's mother told the young lovers that this was to protect the noblewoman image of sweet Joy. Joy accepted this with little hesitation although Richard seemed to be suffering from this policy. They would talk about so many things and started to plan their future. Joy was now thirteen, thus she was of age to marry, if daddy and mommy approved it. She would have to sell them on the idea, and that would take some time. She would do this by looking depressed and spend a lot of time alone, which she usually slept. I would now help her any way I could, because little sisters can never deny an older sister in need. I had always loved Joy, as she was our link to Faith Maria who was our link to Fejér who was our link to mommy who finalized our link to daddy. Ruth, Mary become masters at working this network, actually so good that Faith Maria and now Joy would recruit our services. She was totally hooked on Richard until one day he told her they could no longer see each other. Joy pleaded with Richard to tell her why. He told her that his parents now forbid it. Joy was now extremely hurt that people who said they loved her and would let her lay beside their son throughout the night could betray her. She charged into the family room demanding an answer after first declaring her love for Richard. His mother told them they had discovered Joy's identity. Richard then told his parents, "I care not what bad things she may have done in the past, I want to spend my life with her." Joy now feared that they might have discovered her prostitute past. Notwithstanding, at hand this turned out not to be the case. Richard's mother then qualified the conversation by attesting that Joy did not have a dishonorable past, yet to the contrary had one of great honor and distinction. Richard then rebutted with, "Then why can we not be together?" Richard's father jumped in and said, "Son, we are not even worthy to clean her feet." Richard quizzed again, "Are we talking about my soul mate here? How can she be so high, you act as if she is the Queen or something?" Then Richard's mother told him, "Not the Queen my son however the queen's beloved sister, whom she has sworn to protect with her armies." Richard looked at Joy in shock and asked her, "Why did you deceive me and place our lives in great danger?" Joy had already talked to Faith Maria about this and the new Faith Maria was not that much worried about it and was only concerned if she would bring him to Buckingham this summer concern only been to prepare romantic sleeping quarters and the proper chaperones. Joy then said, "I did not deceive you Richard, you never asked me." Richard then told her, "Who would ask a woman if she was the queen's sister, for even I know her great love for you." Then Joy, who like Faith, could always think on her feet, responded, "Do you think that I would lie beside you at night without Her Majesty's permission?" The room then became silent as they all began to shake nervously. Then Joy said, "She is going to be mad when she learns that you had me lie beside you so many nights and then dumped me." Richard's mother then said, "I assure your royal highness that Richard is not going to dump you." Richard then bowed before as did his parents and begged for mercy. Then Joy looked him square in the eye and said, "How can you give me your unconditional love now?" Richard told Joy, "My love was before knowing who you are, and if you still want it, I shall love you as you want me to?" Then Joy looked at his parents and asked, "Will you guys be interfering anymore." They then said, "Oh no." Then Joy told them, "My sister wants Richard to spend the summer with us at Buckingham. She is preparing a very nice romantic chamber for us. Does this have your approval?" The parents said, "Oh yes, whatever the queen wishes that shall we concur with." Joy then decided to up the stakes and then commented, "If the Queen will allow us to sleep together unsupervised, then it does not seem fair to me that we have a guard and open door." Richard jumped in, for he sensed a great gain for him in the pleasure department, "Yes mom that does not seem fair." Then Richard's father said, "Richard, if you joined Joy in the family way, you must marry her and only her. You cannot steal her god given gift of virginity and be unfaithful to her afterwards. That is not my law, but the law of God and can be punished by execution. Do you understand?" Then Joy helped take him off the hook by also asking, "Do you understand? Before I give myself to you, you must ask me to marry you." Richard then said, "That has been my plan for our second meeting." Joy then asked the parents, "May we be excused?" The parents then bowed and said, "Do what you want our future family addition." Joy and Richard then slept together their first free night. Joy told me that his touch did something so strange inside, it took away all her fears, and this good feeling just made her want to surrender. However, she was able to fight it off for a while as the detailed discussions, yet with each word, her defenses slowly weakened. She was the Queen's sister and followed the chosen one, so why was she here surrendering all to Richard's soft words and magic filled hands. She now thought about how this romance completely changed Richard's life. Upon cementing the foundation of their relationship, he had written so many poems about their love, he did not want to attend his private schools or continue to be active in any of his clubs. He did as Joy did, stay up all night beside Joy as they both struggled to make it through their long and now lonely days. Joy only wished that she could say the things to Richard's face what she felt about him throughout the day. Richard would read to her a not too old poem his felt capture our now joint fate

> How appealing is the winning
> Of a kiss at love's beginning,
> When two mutual hearts are sighing
> For the knot, there is no untying!
> Yet remember, among your wooing
> Love has delight, but Love has ruing,
> Other smiles may make you fickle,
> Tears for other allures may trickle.
> Love he comes and Love he tarries
> Just as fate or daydream carries,
> Longest stays, when sorest shedding,
> Laughs and flies, when pressed and bedding.
> Bind the sea to slumber stilly,
> Bind its odor to the lily,
> Bind the aspen never to quiver,
> Then bind Love to last forever.
> Love is a fire that needs renewal
> Of fresh beauty for its fuel;
> Love's wing molts when caged and captured,
> Only free, he soars enraptured.
> Can you keep the bees from ranging?
> Alternatively, the ringdove's neck from changing?
> No! Nor fettered Love from dying
> In the knot, there is no untying.

He copied this poem on paper for her and every time she could get alone throughout her long days, she would read it and promise to herself she would not release this knot and remain caped and captured by Richard for him to enjoy how he saw fit. She had no fuel, since she quickly consumed it trying to get back to Richard. She wanted to be helpless with no energy to escape his powerful touches. Every flower now yelled out at her, "Give thyself to your love." Joy was able to hide her drop in attention from Aethylswith and wiggle slowly past her younger sisters, who now feared it was a middle girl changing into a big girl thing. They helped their new sister leader as much as they could, shielding her from additional detection, especially from their parents. The girls who served in the house also cared for her and not only concealed her detached condition but helped her sneak out to meet Richard and upon return escorted her safely back to her cold and empty bed. Richard's teachers noticed the difference in their student. In the meantime, a most unlucky thing happened. One of his teachers had caught the lovers by night, and was enraged beyond reason. Thinking that Richard was engaging with women of the lower class, that his teacher spread this scandal all over London. Joy feared revealing her identity until she had received her parents' permission. She did not know how to stop this before Richard's parents were hurt by it. It was sadly too late to prevent that. His parents sat down with them and confirmed that they would protect Joy's identity and would now have their servant's aid in smuggling them in and out. The scandal was now starting to spread like wildfire thus Joy prepared a letter to be given to Faith. Richard's parents provided the servants to deliver the letter to Buckingham. Joy's letter to her Queen detailed the scandal at hand and the reasons she wanted the scandal stopped. Thus, Faith Maria sent an Army to capture the teacher and hang him in the central park of Joy's hometown. A sign was erected which said, "This teacher's scandal hurt innocent people." The guards also visited the local newspapers telling them not to spread stories about Richard or his family. One newspaper reported demanded to know the source of these punishments. The reported soon replaced Richard with a sign, "Do not threaten your Crown." The guards also visited Richard's teacher's family and friends to weed out any sympathizers. The Army then visited Richard and his family. They were so astonished to have the top commanders of this Army visit them and render honorary courtesies. The Army then headed back to London. Richard and his family could now conceptualize the power that young Joy truly had. Richard now believed very much in true love and decided to pass the final point of no return with his now to be lifetime love.

He only part he cared about Joy's power was the part that would protect the life of their special love. Neither had to search, having found the special love in their lives. Joy knew her soul mate had been discovered for in her dreams she often would weep secretly whenever she saw Richard with another girl and how she was too proud to admit it. Joy finally told Richard about these dreams and made him promise he had no other lovers. Richard in shame held down his head and confessed to having another female in his life. Joy broke down in tears wrapping her arms around his legs and crying, "I promise to give myself to you. Why must you break my heart?" Richard then told her, "I shall bring my female friend here so we both may enjoy her." Even though Joy thought she might enjoy Richard's female friend, she could not bear the thought of him with another female. She would pretend to accept it and when this female touched Richard, she would fight her with all her might. She knew now that if she could not have Richard, then she would fight any other who would try to take him. She never pictured Richard as being interested in, group sex. He had told her that she was the first and would be the only. Is it so important in love to tell lies? Is it when you are on your back while your lover with great personal pleasure painfully penetrates your flesh seeking only to deposit his seed deep inside you? Now all of a sudden, love seemed to be nothing but hurt. Throw your heart and body out of a beast to consume. Why did not anyone warn young lovers about this? When you only parents and all other couples acting so much in love, you assume that it is the road to happiness. Richard now told Joy it was time to meet his other lover. He called out, "Suzy come to my bed. In addition, in came Suzy, walking with all fours across the floor and then, without hesitation jumping up on the bed beside Richard. Joy found herself helplessly pulled to Suzy and petting her hair and saying the words she never thought would come out of her mouth, "Good Girl." Suzy reached down, put a flower in her mouth, and gave it to Joy. Joy started kissing and petting, what just a few minutes ago was her declared enemy, however now her new friend. Richard's other female started licking Joy's face. Suzy was such a gorgeous little puppy. Joy finally decided that she could not play this game any longer. Therefore, she confronted Richard and professed that she loved him too much, and then he was the only man that she had ever or would ever love. Although Richard knew of her feelings for him, he was still taken aback and never expected her to react this way. Joy was trembling from her new anxiety. She told Richard that their love was now to be of a part of her and the fear of losing it was unbearable. Although he was touched by her undying love for him and wanted, so much to return it the bond was now choking him also. Joy had said something that awoke this fact in him. A relationship is something that both parties must work on. Joy appeared to be ready to work; however, he now questioned if he would be able faithfully to work on it. Realizing that he had someone so important in his life and also that he in no way wanted to let her get away, he decided to confess is helpless attempts to escape her. His whole mind was flooded with these new fears. Richard was afraid that Joy could easily select someone new and he would be left lonely and helpless. For once in his life, he felt the fear of losing someone also. Joy was always waiting for him and professed never to give up their love. All they could do is treasure what they had. Time was too slow for those who wait; too swift for those who fear; too long for those who grieve; too short for those who rejoice; but for those who love, time is eternity. All they had to do is hold each other tight. They had passed the first four obstacles in their relationship. Queen, Richard's Parents, Public scandal, and Self-Doubt yet still had Joy's parents to join their lifetime journey. Self-doubt was especially troublesome for the young couple, since they had such little time or opportunities to develop a solid foundation to base their conclusions. Little signs that were so easy to misinterpret were destroying them. They only now knew of one sure positive way to get with of these doubts and that was in bed. When Richard was in Joy, he felt her bonding love. When Richard was in Joy, she could feel an eternity of security and love. Although their stamina was quite developed, all good things must end and each time they started it had to end. Joy could now feel Richard's loyalty as he so much enjoyed sharing himself with her. They had a nice magical flare that seemed to penetrate each other's heart. She now completely had no defense nor wanted any defense against Richard, only to surrender all she was and had to him. Richard would ride with in the carriage to and from Joy's home. At home, the seams were starting to rattle as daddy was having more family meetings. He wanted to prepare the family for a new lifestyle as he was becoming more and more of a Puritan and wanted us to join him. At first, this was yucky and daddy would get mad at Joy for sleeping through much of it. How was soon to have a solution to that problem, yet not the solution he wanted. The servants were making one security mistake each night and that was going the exact same route, any waving from it when within one mile of Joy's home. Joy paid no attention to their routes since she and Richard would be kissing every minute on these short trips trying to store up enough love to survive their separation throughout their miserable days. Then one night after a complete night of extreme passion Joy decided, it was time to ask her parents if she could marry Richard. The passion in her could no longer stand the length of the days apart. This was the day they had both dreaded and longed to manifest itself. The carriage moved along very peacefully as not to arouse any suspicions when Joy heard two big thumps on the top of the carriage. The driver tapped their door and standing on the side as to allow them to protect their intimacy told them, "Fear not, for we had a large tree branch fall on us. We have it cleared and will be moving again." Two new killers had landed on the top after killing the driver and shotgun with their crossbows. They landed in the carriage throwing the dead driver and his partner off the road and into the ditch. They now changed the direction of the carriage heading out of town rather than to Joy's house. Joy asked Richard if he noticed we were going a different way. Richard told her that his father might have changed the route for security purposes. Then the carriage drove up to a small house and a woman came out and invited them inside. She told them that some evil gangs had been reported in the area, thus the drivers brought them here until the sheriff would tell them it was safe to travel again. Joy and Richard went inside the house and once inside discovered the house was packed with people as they entered from the other rooms. They then surrounded the couple who were too occupied with kissing. Then several knives were forced in Richard's back as blood now came from his mouth. At this point, several men tied a now hysterical Joy with ropes and gagged her mouth. They now spun Richard around and with an ax cut off his head. They now brought his head to her, with his blood dripping on her clothes and told her, "We shall remove the gag from your mouth. If you scream we have agents in your house now and them if we do not pick them up they will kill all in your house, do you understand?" Joy shook her head yes. They then told her to kiss her lover goodbye. Joy kissed the head of Richard, asking him to wait for him in eternity. She then looked at the mob and asked them, "Why do you do this terrible thing to us?" A woman and four teenage children came up to and asked her, "Do you know who we are?" Joy looked at the woman and said, "You are the devil." The woman then told her that her dead husband had been one of Richard's teachers and that Joy's sister, the Queen had him executed. They now stripped the clothing from Joy, tied her and began to beat her. The mother would rotate with her children as the mob cheered in a normal tone as not to disturb or alert any passers-by. At this moment, I woke up and started screaming, "Joy is missing." Fejér, Ruth, and Mary did not understand why I would betray Joy. I ran to my parent's room and cried, "I just had a bad dream and Joy is in trouble. I had to think of something quick so I told them I saw her standing by the road and some men pulled her into their carriage and headed for out of town. Daddy sent India to get the sheriff. Daddy then took me, with the two brother servants and we began our search. The girls and sisters in my house were very angry with me now. I had no time to explain to them. They had to have Faith Maria in me. In the meantime, the entire mob started beating on Joy. She was about ready to pass over when something told her to hang on. About an hour of living hell later, we showed up with the sheriff and his gang. They were on horseback, which went so much faster than our buggy at night. As we, all surrounded the old house people came running out. The deputies started firing their crossbows killing them or injuring the ones who made it back inside. The deputies rushed in and got Joy. The rapists were too afraid to challenge real men and instead only bolstered their power on young women folk. What the deputies brought out for us to see was terrifying. Joy was nothing but bruises and whip marks. Her eyes were swollen shut and she could move no part of her body. I fell beside her and wrapped my arms around her crying, "Joy please stay with us." Joy wiggled my hand for me to put my ear by her mouth and she said to me as she gave up her last breath, "Please let me have Richard in your kingdom." I told her, "That shall be." She now died in my arms and this created inside me a whirlpool of hate and anger. My mind called for my spirits as I told them, "Join Joy and our Richard and take them to my throne and destroy to demons that did this to her." Then in a flash did the house ignite, as my spirits pulled the deputies out the windows. The sheriff believed that the terrorists set the house ablaze to avoid execution. He could not explain his deputies flying out the window, then how those who fell out the second story windows were not hurt as they went crashing onto the ground. My father told him, "It only proves that there is a God for the just." The Sheriff shock his head yes and answered, "I know I will join your family in church this week." My heavenly escorts were able to find Richard and Joy's souls and took them to my throne where Medica and Sabina welcomed them. Sabina warned Joy, that since Richard was the only male here she might have to share. This was great news for Richard as Joy remarked, "There is enough of my soul mate to share with all of the females here and still have plenty for me." Medica then said, "My child, you first shall be able to enjoy him and be married as we have prepared bodies for you both as you shall live and love on a nice very peaceful planet in a mansion. You shall only concentrate on your love, yet shall bear no children. When Ann and the disciples join us, you shall return to our throne to spend eternity with us. We have a very special friend who will be living beside you with her husband. Then Joy looked over, saw Máriakéménd, and ran to her falling at her feet and begging that she not leave them. The Joy looked over at Medica and cried out, "How can I steel Máriakéménd from my sisters for we all love her so much?" Sabina answered, "My child, this is the wish of The Chosen One, for she now has Faith and Heidi in your night world with other spirits in their flesh at Buckingham. The Chosen One; has declared that each person who was their hurting you shall have their spirit brought here for a punishment 1,000 harsher than any in the hells of your dimension. She will also have the Queen order the execution of all their families to include parents and siblings. They will be beaten then paraded freely exposed down the middle of London and nailed to crosses and painted in the blood of cattle so the ravens can eat them alive." The Richard asked, "Oh beautiful and gorgeous goddesses, may I beg that you have some angels help my parents in their grief at my loss." Then Medica answered, "Oh such handsome and strong man, your parents grieve over you and Joy for they did so much truly love Joy. We shall help them and give them blessings so that their road shall have peace and comfort." Then did both Richard and Joy bow down and thank Medica and Sabina as in a flash they were inside a giant wonderful palace. They had many wonderful servants and personal secretaries who briefed them completely on their engagements so they would look real for them. Shortly thereafter, Máriakéménd appeared at their door all alone. Joy asked her, "Where is your husband?" She told Joy that she rejected the husband they gave her and asked instead if she could live with us. Joy immediately responded yes and said that she would sleep in one of the rooms in their master chamber. Joy looked at Richard and said, "Máriakéménd is blood of my blood thus you may do with her what you desire. To touch her is to touch me. Máriakéménd then bowed to Richard and added, "I shall serve you with the same heart I serve Joy." Richard then asked Joy, "Why did you not tell me about this Máriakéménd?" Joy then said, "Because she was given to us by the Chosen One and we were bound never to tell about the Chosen One." Richard asked, "Who is the Chosen One?" Joy and Máriakéménd answered, "She is the goddess of the largest empire in this region." Richard then asked, "How did you find her?" Joy said, "Her blood found us and she filled us with her blood that we all would have her blood in us. I now wonder why she let us die." Máriakéménd answered, "For she knew your father would reject Richard and you would lose your love thus she brought you here so that you could live your love without barriers or fears." Joy and Richard then both said, "Wow, she did all that for us? Why?" Máriakéménd answered, Because Joy has the blood of The Chosen One."

The situation back on Earth was not as joyous as the throne of The Chosen One. Even the heavens were rumbling. Lilith's spirits were swapping reprogramed spirits from her Hells with the evil spirits associated with Joy's death. They swapped them one by one, insuring that each were carbon copies of the other. They were then escorted to Medica and Sabina as no one displayed a side of them none ever want to see. Lilith had made them strong. Ann was not having so much luck, as she and her daddy held each other crying as they watched the deputies gently wrap Joy's and Richard's parts into the best body bags they had, and then took them to the best funeral parlor to prepare them for their trip to Buckingham. When the royal couple discovered this news, both went into a rage. Charles had actually grown fond of Joy, as she was the closest sister next to Faith in age. They had developed a solid sibling relationship that earned the respect of so many in the royal circles. Charles then called for three Armies to bring back Joy's and Richard's bodies and families to Buckingham. He also ordered the execution of all who were part of that terrorist group and their complete families. The sheriff was able to find enough evidence to identify all who were in there from the horses and documents they left on the horses, such as membership rosters. I ensured that every person there appeared on these rosters plus their addresses. Faith Maria had suffered so much as now did Joy. The line was going to be drawn here. Our recent Intel reports revealed that the investigators of the spirits so long followed Faith Maria or Heidi and considered her family to be of no strategic importance. They were that close to us and now we had a few more months to revamp our procedures and exit plans. This was not important now, for my daddy and I had to tell our family about this. We rode our friend back to our house with the deputies escorting us. Mommy had something that went off inside her, which proved to me we had our mommy of my heavens, as she came running out and one look in our eyes fell to the ground crying. Daddy and I comforted her as I told her, "Mommy, the bad men burned up in their house." A sense of panic hit our mansion as never before experienced, especially as all three of our male servants returned, and were standing in the yard with their heads bowed. All of our girl servants came out surrounding India and their brothers. They looked at these men as tears were rolling down their faces. The girls then ripped their dresses and felt the ground crying and screaming as they beat the ground saying, "Oh God, please no." Fejér now brought out Ruth and Mary who were horrified. Even Fejér was trembling trying to negate what she believed had happened, yet could find no evidence to the contrary. She tried to avoid mommy; however, she no longer had the strength to do so as her eyes, against her will, were pulled over and locked onto mommy's eyes. One look and that was it. Fejér dropped to the ground, ripped her shirt and began crying and begging no as she also fell to the ground hitting it crying, "Please come back." Mary and Ruth were frozen and scared completely out of their wits. They then asked me, "Ann, where is Joy and Richard?" I looked at them and motioned for them to come to me. When they got to me, "I whispered to them, "They are now in heaven." Then tears fell down their eyes as I hugged them as tight as I could. They were brave little girls and were only worried about where they were now. It is so strange that the youngest among us could see the entire picture. Then my daddy asked softly, "Ann, who is Richard?" I then said, "Daddy, she went to get him and bring him back here today to ask if you would give her hand in marriage." Daddy then said, "Ann, did she love him and he loves her?" I answered, "Daddy, they truly were deep in love and were meant to be together." All the servants, Fejér, Ruth, and Mary agreed with me. Then daddy said, "I thank God she found love before she died." Daddy then asked, "Ann, where can I find this young gentleman?" I told him, with more tears flowing down my cheek, "Daddy, he died trying to save Joy." Then mommy cried out, "Oh God, why?" Then she, Mary, Fejér daddy and I hugged Ruth. Our female (The Girls) servants all made a circle around the three boy servants as they all hugged as one large family. We all loved Joy with all our hearts. Our circle was now broken as we have now learned that there was something else that could take one of our circle instead of marriage. This just hit us so fast an unexpected. We all agreed with daddy that at least she found love before she died. Daddy then asked, "Who should we send to tell Faith?" I told him, "I asked the sheriff to do that. She will very soon know." Daddy looked at me rather surprised in my administrative ability to inform my separated sister. That was so easy for me, since I always considered them one. I also told my spirits to make sure that Komáromi and Siklósi were notified. Komáromi (Faith) would be shocked, yet by now being in the spirit world would have a better understanding of the transfer process. The sheriff came to our house the next day and told us that three Armies were on their way to take Richard's family, the bodies, and us back to Buckingham. The Armies were sent massive amount of soldiers. Charles had many wagons with the Armies, as he wanted everything packed out of both homes and delivered to another Palace where the families would live in a highly secured and protected place. Mommy and daddy were too grieved to contest this. I just made sure that our servants who wanted to live with us join us. Fejér wrote very impressive letters of recommendations for those who stayed back. She still had her aristocrat stamp and as such signed on behalf of the Queen with the stamp that Faith Maria had given her. That was an open ticket to work in the best of the best mansions. The girls helped the soldiers take the most important items and sort out the items that would be taken the next trips. Very few owners of mansions move to a new place due to the logistics involved and usually mansions are sold with the furniture in them. We all had our favorites as Komáromi and Siklósi searched our minds to determine what was of value and wanted. Daddy knew we had to move to a new place. Luckily, we moved to a town on the oceanfront into Oxford Castle. Oxford Castle allowed daddy to keep his shipping business and added to the jobs in the local villages although many of his workers moved into the local area and started building new homes. This was a boom for the locals as Daddy quickly established himself and his expanding business. He found that the overhead was much lower here than in our previous home and with no competition he was able easily to increase his business. He had the Kings protection, which helped him so much. Other businesses did not have this protection available thus were forced to stay around the King's forts. Daddy did not really care about this. He wanted the security of his family. Richard's relatives included his parents, two older sisters, one of which was married and had two girls our age. They were Amity and Siusan. At first they were very reserved around us, however Ruth broke that barrier down and then when in private they became our good friends as we always walked Ruth, Amity, me, Siusan, Mary. We kept them inside us and around me. That way their parents and grandparents could see that, we went by the kid's rules and not big people's rules. Naturally, we all cried when we saw Joy and Richard's bodies. Another thing that bonded us, knowing we would go without dread, someday to their graves and serve our Ann. None of us wanted to let them go. My only consolation was when my spirits kept telling me they were ok. I do not remember much about their funerals as we all were in so much grief. Faith had difficulty and sharing her feelings with us and acted more like Queen Henrietta Maria than Faith. Mommy said it was because she felt guilty for her death. The standard procedure was to kill the family with the violator; however, her tender heart would not permit it. Her heart was now building up its walls as she watched all the relatives of this terrorist group be beaten and displayed freely exposed to all of London and then be nailed to crosses with the words "Servants of Satin" written above them. They did not touch their heads so as not to let it resemble Christ being crucified. In addition, as they neared death, they were given water and then burned alive so their souls would have the fire to lead them into hell. Queen Henrietta demanded that as many people as possible see this punishment and she warned that next time it would be 100 times fold. She also now declared official that

Catholic was her religion and she wanted nothing to do with the Protestants that supported this murder. "They may kill fewer, however I can kill many," was her cry. This was when Daddy started to separate us as much as possible from the throne, for he was Protestant and wanted us to be. We went to church dressed as peasants and were smuggled back into the palace by some of our trusted guards. Daddy knew that there would religious troubles for a long time coming so he was now looking at starting new in the colonies. He did not like the feeling of being caged inside this wonderful castle yet knew as long as he lived in England he would have to live secured or attend each of our funerals. Mommy and daddy grew close to Richard's parents, explaining to them how the adoption of the Queen, was only as his daughter bringing home stray animals. They joked that after forbidding Ann to bring animals home, she brought children home. Daddy was big about no royal treatment by Richard's family to us. He said we all paid a terrible price to get in here and the time for paying was over. Richard's parents were also interested in the Protestant teachings, and wanted Amity (who eventually had a well-known town named after her in the colonies) and Siusan who like Ruth and Mary faded into history. My claim to fame was a granddaughter who was an accuser at some witch trial and many grandsons down my line who became famous generals. That however, was in the future, and after the day that they buried my mother and me. My father joined us with a group called the Puritans, who were discontent with the Church of England and wanted religious moral and societal reforms. Daddy did not get involved with the societal reforms since that could bring him to class with his son-in-law and daughter. They, at times went over the line, which made going to the colonies essential for survival. Life for our family gradually changed yet I had to stay here because the change added to my security. The first thing they taught us was how they punished. It was almost as Faith Maria wrote it, however she could not since she was now a devoted Christian. Bad people would be hung and burnt for witchcraft, put in the stockades, or pinned while people threw rotten fruit at you. For lying, they might burn a hole in your tongue. For stealing, they might chop off your fingers. We complained to daddy about these rules nevertheless he declared that we must save our souls. I wish I could have told him that his soul was already saved nonetheless I could not take away his need to protect his girls. Daddy told us to study the bible all the time since the convicted may plead the benefit of clergy, in which case, if they can read a passage from the Bible without one mistake, their sentence will be reduced. Our gang of five girls practiced this every day, because we were now growing into one. Another punishment was stocks where the convicted would have his head and hands placed in a locked stockade for the remainder of the day, and the community would be invited to pelt him with food. The convicted must clean up anything he was pelted. We never threw anything at the big people because we knew they would get out soon so we avoided them. One-day a mean old man saw Amity eating without first saying a prayer. She had to wear a sign, which is a milder punishment than branding. She had to make her own sign to hang around her neck, which told that she did not pray before eating. Many old people yelled at her. We all surrounded her as much as possible, however the big nosey people would stand over us and look down. Another method they used which I hated to hear the people crying was branding where the convicted was marked with letters that stand for their crime—HT for hog thief, A for adulterer. The branding can be on the cheek, forehead, or even a few mildly of the hand or finger. The next one was the one mommy hated, it was the ducking stool and was for women only, usually used in the case of gossip. The woman shall be confined in a chair and dunked in water. Mommy said the men just did that because they always made the woman wear tight shirts and they could see the outlines of our breasts easier. Daddy told mommy not to spread that or they would be dunking her also and that the perfect outlines of her breasts would give the old buzzards a heart attack. Either way the women still spread gossip, and would qualify their statements by talking to their husbands first, thus they would say, "My husband said . . ." The boys were not so lucky to be dunked in water; they most times got a whipping. A number of "lashes" was administered to the back of the convicted. Lashes usually ranged from five to twenty. I got in trouble once for falling to sleep in church and some fools signed their death warrant when they punished me by public shaming. Even though a milder form of punishment, they made me pull on a rope through the town, while the community was invited to point fingers at me, tell me I was naughty, and pelt me with small objects. I yelled back them and told them if the preacher was not so boring, I would have not fallen to sleep. The ones the through grapes and cherries at me, I yelled their names. My four sisters walked two to a side with me writing down the people's names who threw things. That night we visit many of them, letting out their horses and throwing sticks into their windows. We were able to get back in the palace before being caught and our favorite soldiers gave evidence that we had not left. We only knew one way to keep them on our side, thus we called them into my room and let them watch us change our clothes. They were ours now. They were just like cattle going into the butcher's shop. As our dresses went down so did they. I sometimes question if a vagina can bring a man down faster than a god. I am glad that my kingdom does not have flesh, except for the living. We may wear our suits when we want to play with flesh, even just to feel the cold or take a deep breathe. I now begged my daddy not to make me go to church, that we wanted to be a Catholic like Faith. He told us the Catholics would no longer take us and that we our attendance at church on Sunday was mandatory and anyone not in attendance risked a fine or, for repeat offenses, time in the stocks, a public whipping or for me a dunking. We were not permitted to express negative opinions or to question anything relating to the Bible. Because Puritan society, law, economy, and industry are based on perceived biblical attributes, a member is not sanctioned to speak against any of these elements, because he or she was then deemed to be indirectly condemning the Bible. The punishment for these crimes varied and included fines, whippings, and executions. Why had daddy been so far off in this one? His mind was clouded by the death of Joy and now he was giving us a life of misery. The only defense we had was to stay hidden in our chambers because some of the servants who were already here would spy on us. They drew great power from this and shifting their firewood from a neighbor's house and watch, as they tried to deny stealing it. We enjoyed putting dead rodents in their water pails and snakes in their houses. They were so far off on the definitions of sexual transgressions, for if Joy and Richard were here they would be put in prison for the remainder of their living days. These beasts believed the human body and condition to be unclean, unholy, and depraved. If they took baths often then their minds would not be so unclean. Sex with their animals did appear unclean. I would love to tell them to look at my throne body and then tell me it was not clean. No pleasure was to be taken from sexual relations. One thing I learned when creating all my daughters was that there is a lot of pleasure in this act. Sex was merely a means of reproducing. I guess if you did not succeed the first time, you could try repeatedly. Spouses displaying affection toward one another was considered lewd and unseemly. We were told about a soldier, that after returning home from a three-year military tour, kissed his wife on the doorstep of their home and was promptly placed in the stocks for two hours as punishment. "Fornication," which meant intimate relations between unmarried people was heavily condemned, with a range of punishments from a large fine to a public whipping for both parties, and even execution for repeat offenders. That insured many young people had no chances to explore their feelings and emotions. Adultery was also punishable by death in many communities, although in more moderate areas, the punishment for adultery involved public humiliation via a public whipping and being forced to wear a large, scarlet letter "A," so that everyone was aware of the offense. We did not have much to look forward to with our roles very much defined. Women's roles within our communities were comprised of two features. The first being that women were considered the weaker vessel in both body and mind" and "her husband ought not to expect too much from her." The second feature was the way that women manipulated their born roles in order to fulfill their own aspirations and goals. The community leaders were male, and they readily accepted the supposed inferiority of women. This belief made men react harshly or ashamedly to women who openly objected to this gender role. However, many women were safe from public exposure because they usually exercised an indirect authority within the community. However, the women that were not easily influenced to remain silent, with consequences could be life altering. Our marriages may have seemed harmonious because the male was the undisputed head of household and the wife a subordinate; it was not the case in many marriages. To begin, there is indication of female shaping. Female shaping was used to enforce the female role, which was that women should not challenge men, women should never show temper, should be subordinate to their husbands, and allow their husband to handle all financial matters. There was a great deal of emphasis on that cosmology that women were frivolous, greedy, fickle, nagging, gossiping, and vain. The purpose of stressing women's weaknesses was to warn men not to be influenced by their wives. However, women had a great deal of influence in society, and that not all women were willing to accept or respect their traditional role in society and in the home. The woman who did not accept their role acted in a diversity of manners. The most injurious to a husband was if the wife had sexual relations outside the marriage. The husband would be humiliated and he then was subjected to the questioning the legitimacy of his own children. If a man caught his wife having an affair, he could bring her to court, and if found guilty, there was the possibility that she faced a penalty of death. This was not the same punishment the husband would face if found cheating on his wife. He would be punished with either a fine or a whipping. However, most women did not press charges against their husbands for extramarital affairs because that was one more aspect of marriage that women were expected to tolerate. Even though women were not usually expected to press charges against their husbands for extramarital affairs, they could bring their husbands to court for battery. Women's battering their husband has occurred in our society as indicated by our court records. Few men made the step to bring their wives to court because of the humiliation that it would cause the man. This would mean that he was not able to control his wife, which was one of his male roles. The women who did go to court due to extramarital affairs, battery, or the need to have the court order the couple to live together, despite their wish for a divorce, were a minority of the population in England. The majority of women accepted their inferior status because of their religious devotion. The evidence that this social system was faulty is clarified by the existence of widows. When a woman became widowed, she usually inherited her husband's property and money, and she was permitted to become active in public in order to finish his business. After years of dependency, many widows had to turn to either adult sons or male relations because they did not have the knowledge of how to conduct their finances. Children are automatically expected to be subservient to their parents. "Submissiveness represented in the image of the saints' love and obedient receptivity to God's righteousness." Women were countenanced to have direct authority over their children because they held an image of God with a nursing breast, but it was not as common of the image of God as a father was. Because she had direct authority over children, the mother taught her children religious piousness, manners, discipline, and affection. Oddly, mothers had to be cautious with the amount of affection they gave their children because they were expected to be the parent that breaks the child's will in order to teach discipline. For instance, the mother would have to wean the child from breast-feeding once the child was around two years old. This time in a child's life was considered strenuous; however, it was the mother's duty. As a result, the mother would gain status in a society for their nurturing methods. Most women lost half of their children in infancy, and one out of five women died in childbirth. When a woman gets near the end of her term, she would assemble a group of women to be present and help her while she is in labor. Due to the high mortality rate, midwives adopted the motto a "Living mother of a Living child." I always said it was God having mercy on the children by letting half be born into real human homes. Childbearing and mothering were just two of women's duties. Food and clothing fabrication became principle duties. In England, there were fairs, markets, and peddlers that sold goods. Women had to create a trading network within their communities for food. In these networks, women learned to bargain and judge goods. Women played numerous major roles concerning work and religion and were quite knowledgeable in a wide assortment of topics, especially those related to child-rearing, household duties and serving the Church. Yet, despite being subordinate to their husbands at both home and church, goodwives played an important part in the economies of their households and husbands entrusting them with a wide range of down-to-earth responsibilities. These included maintaining the needs of the household and actively performing at church functions while leading a lifestyle based on religious purity, chastity, and devotion to one's family, husband, children and fellow men and women within their communities. Women, without regard to age or social status, were supposed to be dutiful daughters, acquiescent and faithful wives, wise mothers, prudent household managers, and kind neighbors. They were not advised by their husbands, clerical leaders to take an active role in the political, or the religious life due to the patriarchal system in which they worked and lived. Although women were not permitted to speak their minds at home nor in the church, they were not denied the basic privileges of religious observance and worship and were generally encouraged to meet with their fellow sisters in Christ to pray and meditate on an immense range of subjects, especially those related to personal virtue and growth. The church officials became nervous about these meetings because they believed that women, even though they were supposed to be weak, were able to bring men down and that they influenced the success of a minister. Women were the largest attendants in congregations and their responsiveness to the sermons affected the popularity of the minister. Women were not allowed to pray publicly with a congregation and could not lead prayer, and they were not supposed to interpret the Scriptures because they were not considered educated enough. They also believed that Eve's role in original sin exemplified woman's inherent moral weakness. They did not know of Adam's evils nor me. They feared that women were much more susceptible to temptations, and that they possessed qualities that could be exploited and become sinful. A woman was to love, obey, and further the interests and will of her husband. If she was a good mate, she had fulfilled her God-given duty. The role of sin played a huge role since they believed in original sin, meaning that all people are fundamentally sinners, except the elect. Puritans wanted to abolish sin in order to form an ideal society, but this was an impossible task. The integral role of sin was that it was around every corner, and that Puritans needed to be aware of sin when it surfaced and manifested, since all are born sinners and the devil was behind every evil or unfortunate deed. They did not know how humankind is the basis of evil, and not those of the spiritual word. They have a big surprise waiting them. These views are reflected in sermons that were filled with such fire and brimstone that children began to stay home from church because they had nightmares from the sermons. The role of sin, and therefore the devil, proved costly for the Puritans, with an example being the witch trials, which my (as in Ann) granddaughter was an accuser. What was scary is that they felt no remorse about administering punishment. In Puritan society, the average age for marriage was higher than in any other group of immigrants—the average for men was twenty-six, and for women age twenty-three. There was a strong imperative to marry; those who did not were ostracized. The Puritans married for love, there were no arranged marriages, which was nice indeed. Courtship practices were strict, and weddings were simple affairs. First cousin marriages were forbidden and second cousin marriages were discouraged. Daddy told me it was stricter in his days, and always made us laugh by telling us how mommy laughed at him the first night they slept together. Banners had to be published before a marriage could take place. A publication of the Banners was the public announcement by the minister during a normal church service that two people wish to marry, and an invitation to the congregation to declare any unlawful reason why they should not marry. Women were, of course, subordinate to men. Married women were not allowed to possess property, sign contracts, or conduct business. Their husbands owned everything, including the couple's children. Divorce was rare, and a separation would mean no access to the children. Only widows who did not remarry could own property and run their own businesses. Puritan women were expected to bow to their husbands and fathers, and to obey their orders; nevertheless, they supported each other. During childbirth, they excluded the men, and comforted the mother-to-be with beer as well as prayers. Women had to dress modestly, covering their hair and arms while in public. Women found guilty of immodest dress could be stripped to the waist, preventing revealing their breasts and whipped until their backs were bloody, which would expose their bodies thus giving the old perverts a cheap thrill. Public humiliation could include confessing one's sins in front of the church congregation. Schools were small with all students in the same room. Students sat by row according to grade level. Youngest kids sat in the front and the older the students sat the furthest back in the room. The dropout rate was quite high so the room looked like a triangle with the most students on the front couple of rows and the number of kids tapering off as the rows progressed towards the back of the room. The subjects were quite simple, reading, writing, and arithmetic. Little critical thinking, and no free thought or free expressions were entertained. You learned things by memorizing everything and quoting it back. The teacher may have you stand up and recite your times tables from 1x1 up to 12x12. Grammatical sayings were also memorized to help students learn how to write correctly. "I before E except after C and sometimes Y"; when two vowels go a walking, the first one always does the talking." Religion was a big part of education. The Bible was the source for virtually all of their in-class readings. Bible stories, along with their morals, were drilled into the students' heads. The majority of the teachers were men—very few women went into teaching and they were often widows. Often the teachers knew little more than the students knew, and were often only a page ahead of the student in the textbook. The books themselves were very scarce, but virtually all families had a copy of the Bible in the home.

A thump on the back of the wrist or a slap with a ruler on the palm of the hand was common. Teachers would rotate their eating schedule among their student's parents and would even stay (lodge) with the families of their pupils for a week or longer at a time. They always came to our palace first, and if staying with one of our servants attempted to stay in our palace. Mommy would not permit this and even received criticism from our church of which she told them, we shall do and only do our share. Daddy of course received criticism for this in which he simply replied, "Our matters at home are governed by her." She did not want them in our house extra since we ran our home the way we always did and that was all three of us almost living in mommy's lap listening to her tell us stories. Mommy slowly weeded out the troublemakers on our staffs. The girls were bringing in girls they met in the area that were not so zealous. The church of course, received complaints about this as my mother told them, "Stay out of our palace or I shall notify my catholic daughter and we shall have some new heads rolling down our streets." They stayed out of our business. Mommy complained to daddy, "How dare they interfere with this home. I shall hire private tutors for my children." Daddy agreed we could have private tutors for extra teaching; however, the girls would have to go to the churches' school. Their classes were held year-round with no summer break and very few days off except for holidays. This made it hard to go to Buckingham. Our church did not want us to go to Buckingham. My mommy went to the elders and asked them to sign a letter she was going to send to her daughter about the sisters of the Queen's annual visit to Buckingham informing her that the church refused to allow it. No one would sign it. My mommy called them "spineless hypocrites" and laughed at them as she departed. There were no school districts as it was just one school after another with no real organization, which gave way to abuse by the local church. Children were expected to behave under the same strict code as the adults, doing chores, attending church services, and repressing individual differences. Any display of emotion, such as excitement, anger, fear, was discouraged, and disobedience was severely punished. Children rarely played, as toys and games were scarce. Puritans saw these activities as sinful distractions. My parents never punished us as neither did Amity's and Siusan's parents and we were allowed to play together in our chambers. However, unlike young girls, boys had a few outlets for their imagination. They often worked as apprentices outside the home, practicing such skills as crafts or carpentry. Boys were also allowed to explore the outdoors, hunting, and fishing. On the other hand, girls were expected to tend to the house, helping their mother's cook, wash, clean, and sew. The church allowed few books to be written for children, and those written often warning against bad behavior and described the punishment that children would suffer from sinful acts. All they could think about was punishment. The whipping post and the pillory, which was a wooden frame in which the boy or girl had to put in their hands and head, were the more severe forms of punishment. If you were caught talking in class, your knuckles might be thwacked with a ruler. If you fell asleep in class, you might be picked up from your seat by your left ear or even have your ankles burned in the sun with a magnifying glass. Tardy students had to clean the blackboards or pick up trash around the school. If the teacher happened to be a clergyman, he could also scare students with threats of eternal damnation if they would not behave. Great pains were taken to warn their members and specifically their children of the dangers of the world. Religiously motivated, they were exceptional in their time for their interest in the education of their children. Reading of the Bible was necessary to living a reverent life. The education of the next generation was important to further "purify" the church and flawless social living. Three English divisions were banned, religious music, drama, and erotic poetry. Drama and erotic poetry led to immorality. Music in worship created a "dream" state, which was not beneficial in listening to God. Since the people were not spending their time frivolously indulged in trivialities, they were left with two godly diversions. The Bible stimulated their communal intellect by promoting discussions of literature. Greek classics of Cicero, Virgil, Terence, and Ovid were taught, as well as poetry and Latin verse. They were encouraged to create their own poetry, always religious in content. They punished all children by offering free schooling. The next few years saw us grow further apart from our daddy. We just could not understand why he allowed himself to be bound by such stupidity. My spirits tell me that I never had this kind of trouble with my planets. Then the bomb hit, which shattered the unity of our family. Ruth was caught freely exposed with a boy. It has been a set up since the boy's father and neighbors were there to trap her. They took the boy back to his house and paraded Ruth freely exposed down the streets of the palace. Mommy ran out to stop them, yet they hit her and tied her up accusing her of obstructing justice. At this time, the guards came rushing in and started shooting their crossbows. Down went the father and his friends. Mommy, once untied, put her jacket over Ruth and after giving her a kiss told her to go inside and stand by a guard. Mommy then demanded to see the boy and once he came out, she called him a devil and ordered the guards to kill him. Mommy knew that it always took some hard promises to get a little girl to take off her clothes and that this was a setup. She then told the guards to blind his mother; wanting the filth that thought they could humiliate them have a burden and a reminder every day to the rest of their lives. She figured a blind woman would not be a serious threat. She knew that if an activity involved one of the children, the mother was usually involved. She then looked at the remaining of the servants and warned them that she would conduct an inquisition if she ever heard about this again. Mommy had reached her limit. When she went in she found little Ruth crying, more from shame than any pain. Mommy, being the best there ever was, had a way of knowing the truth that we could never figure out. It was as if our souls were connected, in which I knew they were not. Mommy asked Ruth to give her a kiss and while hugging her told her, "I am your mommy and I shall always, no matter what love you." Then mommy asked, "My daughter tell me what happened." Ruth told her that he was different down there and that girls used to be boys, but they were bad so their parents cut off their pee bug. I did not believe him, so he showed me his and it was different, then he told me if I take off my pants he would prove to me that I had been a bad, and that my parents had cut off my pee bug. When my pants hit the ground, he grabbed them, and yelled for his dad who came with his friends raiding from everywhere. They told him to go home and they tied me up calling me a witch. Then they hit me with a belt and told me to start walking. Do you believe me mommy?" Mommy told Ruth, "A boy had told her the same thing and she ran to the church to ask the minister if it was true. The minister took her to the boy's house where his daddy whipped him good. Ruth, I do very much believe you, and I am sorry that I have not warned you girls about the evil of the boys. Please, my little princes remember this, when your pants go down with a boy you will always get into trouble unless you are married like mommy and daddy." By then all four of was there beside Ruth and we held her one by one telling her that we were so proud of her. She remained hurt by this for some time, a big consolation being that the boy was not alive to torment her about it in school. Luckily, we never had to go to that terrible school again or associate with them filthy dogs. Mommy could take this no longer and now was the time for action. Her little girls would never be stripped and marched freely exposed down a street while a toothless peasant was beating her. Daddy argued that the boy did not take off Ruth's pants. Mommy argued that only a stupid male would want to see an area where there was nothing. She then threatened to take us and leave. As she packed our clothes, put us in our carriage, and started for the palace's gates daddy ran out to stop her. He ran up to the carriage and asked mommy if they could discuss a compromise. He had tears rolling down his cheek as he looked in and saw Ruth, Mary and me. We also had tears and cried to mommy, "Mommy, please talk to daddy." Mommy agreed and told us to wait. This was her bargaining chip. Daddy asked mommy what she wanted to change the most, and mommy told him to get free from the pack of demons that he was letting rule our family. I never want to see an English Puritan church again. Then daddy confessed to her, "They did go too far by marching my baby freely exposed down the street and beating her. I think we should take some of my ships and go to America." Mommy looked at him in shock, as she never expected this degree of support for his family. She asked him, "When shall we go?" He said, "I shall have my company start packing what you girls want to take. Remember; pack what you think you will need and that we must go light." Then daddy called the guards in and in front of mommy told them, "Any who come from our church to admonish us, execute them." When mommy heard that, she kissed daddy on his cheek and while running out screaming, "I love you Edward." Daddy asked the guard, "Do you think she is staying?" The guard said, "Sir Edward, you have the same powerful force over the ladies as does King Charles." Daddy asked, "The King and LADIES." The guard quickly qualified it by saying, "Oh Sir Edward, I meant the King and your daughter only of course." Daddy smiled and winked at him and started to pack. Mommy rushed back to the carriage to get her girls. She told us, "We must start packing girls; we are going to the new world." I asked mommy "Is that far away?" Mommy told us it was, and then Ruth said, "Yeah." While we were walking with Mommy and daddy was watching his four women come back in the house, I asked mommy, "Can Amity and Siusan come with us?" Mommy, then said, "We shall go to their grandparents chambers and invite all of them face to face." I then whispered in mind talk to my spirits, 'please let them join us.' Richard's family rejected our offer except for Amity's, and Siusan's parents, who accepted. Their parents were good friends with mommy although they did not really like daddy. We celebrated with great joy for we five were ready to come alive again. Sure enough, the small church could not let go of the power it once had and came to the gate to demand execution of mommy and Ruth. That was the final blow for daddy as he ordered the guards to execute all of them, along with all the servants that came to the palace, and burn their church. Mommy and I told the girls to pack; we were going to the colonies. They only wanted to be with us, which was what we wanted. Daddy wanted this to be of their free will so he destroyed their indenture contracts in front of them and told them their debt has been settled. Nevertheless, they beseeched with their true hearts to go with us. Daddy shook his head as we all ran up and let them pick us up and swing around in joy. They are the most wonderful servants any could have and they would be spending time with me for eternity. Daddy put three ships in our fleet. Two were for protection and we would all be on the third one with a few guards. Our group was made up to five adults, which were our parents including Amity's, Fejér, three family servants from their family and nine of our female servants that we always called our girls. Mommy told daddy he was lucky to have so many pretty women on this journey in which he agreed saying, "Finally, I might get some work out of my crews." Mommy never thought of that, yet with a shy smile, had to agree. All three ships were loaded with our clothing and personal items and a few pieces of furniture. Mommy sent a note to Faith explaining why they had to leave England and the persecutions the Puritans had put on our family. Faith Maria understood as so did Charles who was under pressure for Faith's Catholicism. He told Faith Maria he would stand by her, as he too was getting angry over all the problems with the churches. Daddy gave his top executive orders on how to run the company and how to deliver the earnings and requests for major purchases to him. He had set up some trading lanes with the colonies many years earlier and was able to make good profit from it, especially since he had some new cannons on board that could shoot further and thus defend against the pirates of the seas. Soon, we were on the seas, and our parents worked hard to rebuild our families into one. That was better for us girls as Amity and Siusan were now with us every minute every day. We were now teenagers so our parents only had to worry about the boys and us. Daddy warned the crew, "Touch not our children." They were more interested in our 'girls' then us. Deep down we were happy for that since the girls were getting older and needed to think about starting families. Three of them were in the family way before we reached Massachusetts Bay. For each daddy asked for, the father to meet with him. He married the couple and gave the father a job in his new company headquarters in the colonies. With news of this the other two fathers stepped up, were married, and received positions. The three soon to be mothers greatly thanked my daddy by chasing him around the ship trying to kiss him. Mommy caught daddy for the first kiss, Fejér caught him four our second girl, and we five girls caught daddy for the third girl as the crew, with the happy daddies, cheered. We were so thankful that daddy loved us so much. Fejér had been secluded much during the Puritan disasters actually preparing to leave. Mommy and we five beggars kept her chained to us. We could have not have had a life without Fejér. Then one day our journeys changed. As we looked out at the peaceful sea as we had done so many times before, the sea changed. It grew fierce as the winds pushed us back into them. Our ship started spinning around and from side to side, as some of the crew fell overboard. Then one wave came in and crushed Fejér's head open in front of us. As the blood poured over us, I knew something was not good. Then another wave spun two large broken poles at us, as one went into Amity and the other into Siusan. Then two more hit Ruth and Mary. I had the five bodies my best friends shooting blood all over me. Could this be the end? I told James it was too early to end this book as he agreed to listen to the rest of this story, and then boom a pole bashed beside my head, causing me to go blank. Once again, I was spinning like inside a modern washing machine. What was happening to us?

Chapter 08

Adventures in Time Jumping

S pinning and spinning to where, once again I do not know and am alone. Why is this happening? This time I am not rising or dropping, nor do I have any escorts. I am now lachrymose being separated from my spirits, "Where are you?" Then the light came on again as I spun to the Earth's surface in a canyon that I remember flying over after I was booted from the Garden of Eden. The Earthlings called a place that looked like this the Grand Canyon. Considering that I had never seen it, except a few times while cruising above it, I did not really know. What I did know is that so many planets in so many galaxies had places like this. It was as if there were ancients, which traveled throughout the dimensions drilling big holes, disfiguring the worlds they visited. I did not know where I was or even what dimension I was in, since a big fragment of my entry was unconscious. As I climbed down the tree I woke up in, to my joy I was once again a big girl. Guess the little girl times are over for a while, I hope. As I walked in this loneliness, I heard a noise as a few branches crunching on the ground caused by something walking over it. I quickly climbed a nearby tree. I could hear the noise going up a tree beside me. I truly do not know what to expect, since being in an unknown place is not where I woke up today, being halfway from England to Massachusetts Bay. The air felt wonderfully clean as it entered into my lungs, compared to the dirty air in England and salty air of the ocean. Thenceforth as I heard the noise in the other tree, I looked over. I was frozen in my tree behind some branches. Then I looked over and saw the most beautiful sight I have ever seen. I saw the beauty that was greater than anything I can remember seeing in any dreams. I saw a big part of me in the other tree a reservoir of my feelings, hopes, and love. I now yelled in a warm loving voice to the other tree, "Fejér, meet me on the ground". We both rushed down the tree to the soft sandy ground. Fejér did the same and we slowly walked towards each other, making sure, it was not a trick of our illusions, as some get from wanting water in a desert. We immediately touched each other as to say if this is a trick take me your prisoner for I care not. This resulted in intense hugging, crying, and kissing. It was as if we had been apart for a long time. I guess a long distance can qualify also. Fejér then asked me, "Who are you?" It now hit me that I was now in a grown female body so I told her, "I am Ann." Fejér then told me, "Yes, I can see the resemblance." I then asked Fejér, "Do you know where we are and why we subsist here? Also, are we alone or do others exist?" Fejér shared with me that she only knew something went wrong in our security and that the spirits will tell us soon since they cannot talk now. If others are here, I do not know. We must search each day just in case." I asked her, "What shall we eat, and how shall we survive?" Fejér said, "There are plenty of fruits and wild vegetables that are edible. We must avoid hunting since the smell of blood could invite unknown dangers. Until we know we must be very careful." We continued walking and eating some fruit until we finished our first day. Fejér recommended that we sleep in the nearby trees. The first night was scary as we heard some strange noises. We did not know what creatures roamed at night, so the tree was working well for us. On the second morning, I was wakened by some noises of something walking beneath me. At first, I thought it was Fejér; however, I looked up above me and saw her still sleeping. As I froze myself on the branch that supported me, I looked down and saw two grown women walking below us. I yelled down, "Fear not, I am your friend." They stopped and looked around to see who was talking. I rushed down and walked towards them. They were shocked and shaking, too frightened to run and petrified to stay. I knew I had to get to them fast before they passed out. About halfway there, I yelled, "I am Ann and now I am a big girl." They started to relax some as I approached. They now did not want to leave for fear that if I really was Ann they would not be with their best sister. Upon reaching them, I petted their hair and gave each a kiss on the check. I then asked, "What are the names of these two grown gorgeous women?" One responded, "I am Amity." I then looked at the other and said, "Could you then be Siusan?" She reached over to hug me saying, "That I am." I was somewhat taken back when she reached for me and as she spoke I regained myself. One would think that seeing something so obvious would not elicit fear, however the not knowing what to expect when in an unknown place creates crippling anxiety. Amity asked me, "Are you alone?" I told her that Fejér was in the tree above us. I told them it would be better if we stayed up the tree until we knew if this area was free of danger, thus the three of us went up our tree. As Fejér seen them come up she painted her face with a big smile and asked, "Who are you two fine young ladies?" They then introduced themselves and asked, "Has anyone seen Mary or Ruth?" Fejér then said, "We have not nor do we know if they are even here?" Amity asked, "Where could they be?" Fejér said, "Your guess is as good as mine. However, we will never find them here so let's start looking." I lost tract of the number of hills we went up and down in the last afternoon. Then the peaceful sky turned into an active breeding place for a storm. The soft rolling land now lost its trees. Fejér suggested that we look for a cave and not walk in the open. The quiet gave way to the roaring sounds of unknown beasts as one was squealing at such a high pitch we had to put our hands over our ears. Then Fejér painted her face with absolute fear. We looked at her as our hearts stopped beating, sweat soaked us, and a couple of us had puddles of urine under them. When Fejér got scared, we knew trouble was upon us once again. I casually looked over and was very much shocked as my eyes grew the size of oranges. Fejér said, "Ok women, we need to walk away while staying low. I do not think they will hear our sound." We were so terrified, I think we all walked one inch above the ground if such a thing were possible. I started to talk to my spirits with mind talk telling them, "We need a cave." We heard a loud thump as our ground started to shake. The wind was blowing towards us now in a light breeze, which was good for us so our scent would not be blown towards those terrifying flesh eating beasts. We could smell blood and the foul odor of internal organs. The beasts would occasionally start fighting with each other over choice body parts. These beasts were as fast as lightning. As we were, walking Amity fell down grabbing Siusan's leg and loudly whispering, "Help." As we looked back, she lost her grip on her sister's leg and vanished into the hole. Oh not now, I mean we are trying to save ourselves from beasts and now this planet is eating us. Fejér started smiling. I asked her, "You really think this is a time to smile?" She then said, "Follow me." She got down on the round, and lowered her face into this people-eating hole and called for Amity. Amity answered. Fejér asked her if she was ok. She affirmed that she was ok. Fejér next asked her, "What do you see down there?" She told Fejér, "I see a lot of darkness and two small lights in front of me. Fejér then asked her to move away any rocks that could hurt us as we jump in and to use her voice as a target for us. Fejér added, "After whom identify where you want us to land, move back fast." Fejér then sent me in, followed by Siusan, and herself last. Prior to going in, she placed additional vegetation around the hole to help conceal it, optimistically buying enough time to find a safe outlet. After everyone got himself or herself together, she led us to one of the lights. As we started to get close to the light, we heard a noise on one of our sides. The darkness prevented us from seeing whom what it was. We now walked slower and softer. Then Siusan stepped on a branch and the branch started screaming. We immediately surrounded this thing and asked, "Who are you?" We had not seen any humans yet, so we were somewhat excited to discover if there was human life here. The trembling voice, was now crying saying, "My name is Ruth, please do not kill me. I will be your slave if you want." Then Amity said, "Ruth, my name is Amity and I sure would like to have a new slave." Then in an instant, something came out from behind Amity, grabbed her, and then started osculating her. Fejér then said, Amity turn around so we can save you. She turned around and Fejér and I pulled it off her. I got on top of her and asked, "Who are you?" The stranger said, "I am Mary, we are lost here." Then Fejér told her, "I am Fejér and you both are no longer lost." I was now so happy that I had my four sisters and big sister together again. We all started hugging and spinning each other so excited to be united once more. Then Mary asked Fejér, "Fejér why do we all have big girl bodies?" Fejér only answer was, "Outside of not knowing, I can only guess that it might be to help us survive until help arrives. Do you know your way around this cave?" Mary said, "We walked around a few of the side tunnels to find water, outside of that we have been keeping still and staying alive." Fejér asked, "Do you know of any exits or have you seen any lights? Ruth told her, "If we go up around that tunnel there and walk for a while you will see a small light." We then did as Ruth said and soon we saw the light. In addition, we walked and walked for so long, taking three big naps along the way. Fejér told us that after each long nap we were starting a new day. Then finally, after what seemed forever the little light started to get bigger. As we walked up to the entrance, Fejér went ahead and scouted it for us. She vanished and as we were approaching the entrance, she reappeared with great news. She told us that there was a nice beach and a couple of orchards alongside the sea. It was a sea because the water was fresh. We are protected by a large cliff that closes off the beach a few miles down the shore on each way. There are also many grape and berry vines on the lower parts of the cliff. We are safe here. We need to drink some water and clean our black bodies and soak our feet. We all still stayed very close to each other, using the excuse of helping clean each other to hide the fear of not being as safe as a sister could be. Even though we had, big bodies we still were small girls inside. Fejér then told us to watch her now as she vanished into the sea then within a few seconds came up with two fish. She laughed saying, "Tonight we

shall eat, and someone makes a fire and start cleaning these fish."
We had no idea how to make a fire until Amity told us to watch
her. She had a nice big diamond on her finger that I had given her
as a present. She gathered some twigs and then reflected the
sunlight off the ring onto the twigs. They began to burn thus; we
put a few large pieces of driftwood on them. Fejér kept coming up
with fish, she actually caught twenty-four of them as we each had
four to put into our famished bodies. Ruth had picked some berries
and we all had a nice meal. After this we all lie down beside each
other, because there is no way any of us are going to sit alone. As I
lay beside Fejér, she whispered into my ear, "You want to see how
the heavenly wine flows from your new wine glass." I then told her,
"Oh, please discover for me my precious love." She lay me down
and buried her face between my legs and started to get my wine
flowing as I lay there moaning in ecstasy. Amity and Siusan asked,
"What are they doing?" Ruth told them to come over here and
watch. Fejér was completely putting me in another realm of
physical relief. Mary and Ruth were petting my hair and kissing me
while playing with my bosom. Amity and Siusan were stunned, for
they had never seen this before, or even knew not it was possible.
Now I rolled Fejér over and told her, "See how this gets you." As
Fejér lie there she told Amity and Siusan, Do not fear, for we have
done this often for many years. Do you want Mary and Ruth to
play with you? You will never regret it." Then Mary gave Amity a
big hug and said to her, "Let me serve you now." Amity did not
know why she went along with this except that I looked like they
were enjoying it and they had all been her close friends for so long,
and her parents were not here for her to ask. She felt her legs give
way as they now lay on her back. Then Mary calmly opened up
and she could feel herself releasing to Mary and Mary into her. She
sighed, "Wow, this is so great, Siusan do not be afraid." With that,
Ruth wrapped her now big arms around Siusan and started kissing
her as Siusan did as her sister and let their flesh go to the ground
now lying together. Her heart gracefully opened wide as a new
sensation she never thought possible crippled her flesh. She
wondered, "How can Ruth, Mary, and Ann know such a great

thing? Wonder what other great things they know." After some time Ruth and Mary told them, it was time for them to learn. Ruth then told the newbies "Do not be shy or afraid of us. We are your devotees and have no desire ever to hurt you. You will get joy in feeling our joy." Likewise, they did learn fast as we were all pretty much paired off now. Amity and Siusan were no longer walking around. It was now Mary and Amity, with Siusan and Ruth following. Fejér and I always lead the way and all three groups held hands all day long and at night. I believe this was not a coupling act as much as it was a way to not feel alone and have some sense of security. As her first hopefully safe night approached, Fejér put us all in a circle and asked Ruth, Mary and myself in mind talk if it was time to add Amity and Siusan to our sisterhood. I readily agreed saying, "I so much want to add them to fill in for what Faith lost to marriage, and Joy lost to murder. I will give all my blood if that is what it will take." Mary and Ruth readily agreed, thus Fejér began the ceremony. She looked at Siusan and Amity and told them, "We have another very special club that we belong to and that is to be followers of Ann, the chosen one." Amity answered, "We will follow Ann even if she is not a chosen one. By the way, what is a chosen one?" Fejér then told her, "It is time you all knew, "Ann, before you became a baby in the flesh, you were the goddess of a great empire. Your empire had to hide you from great evils that were and still are trying to kill you. Your kingdom fights with many other kingdoms killing the evil. Soon they will be ready for you to return. Your kingdom has more worlds than the stars you can ever see in our skies and you have great power that cannot be tapped now for it will give away your security." Ruth and Amity looked at me and said, "Wow." Fejér further added that, "Any who were blood of Ann's blood would become one of her disciples and have great mansions and lead Armies." I then looked at Amity and Siusan and said, "Fejér, Mary, and Ruth have my blood in them. Do you want to be one with me and share the same blood?" Siusan answered, "I care not about your empire, and I just want to love you forever, take all my blood, and give to me what will not hurt you." Amity then added, "You have been the greatest love in my life and without you I would only want death, so take all my blood that when I die I shall be in your arms." Then I said to them, "I ask not that you die, but that you live with me forever and ever." They then asked Fejér, "What do we do?" Fejér told them, "She is a goddess, give her what a goddess should have." They both fell on the ground each holding on to one of Ann's legs crying, "Oh please great one, and do not forget those who love you so much." Then I told them, "Prepare to drink my blood so that my blood shall be in you forever. For once my blood is in you; your blood shall be the same as mine." I then took my diamond ring, cut my finger, and poured my blood into their mouths. They cried out, "I can feel it cleaning my body. All power and glory be unto the goddess I worship." Then something different happened this time, the turned pure white one at a time then changed back. I ask Fejér what was that and she said, maybe we should all drink your blood again, as she kneeled and opened her mouth with Mary and Ruth instantaneously beside her. I had a big cut so I could give them all a nice drink and they also transformed. I thus put my finger in my mouth attempting to clot my blood, as I also transformed and when I returned the cut on my finger had vanished. Fejér then said, "I think your transformation may be coming soon, my lord. Let us now rest so when it does we shall be ready." I then asked Fejér, "Will you let me sleep in your arms please?" Fejér replied, "Of course my precious love." The other two couples paired off and slept in each other's arms to keep warm and feel safe. We were to get our first sisterhood night together. Fejér also told Amity and Siusan, "Someday we will take you to our nighttime world and tomorrow we will show how to mind talk." Amity said with great excitement, "Wow, I think my life is going to be more interesting than I ever dreamed." Moreover, with that, Mary started a little song and we all sang slowly together. We did not know what lay ahead of us tomorrow however we knew what lay beside us tonight and that was the Blood of Our Blood. Then we all peacefully, with feet that had been soaked in water and flesh had no longer was covered in dirt, bellies filled with meat and grapes and redeeming blood and our carnal thirst quenched. That had us snoring. Then around the witching hour in the night, we all awoke to rocks flying across the top of our cave. Then they started to hit close to us, as we all stood freely exposed against the cave's walls, looking for any cover we could find. Then the large opening to our cave started to fill with rocks. We now saw the cave wall vanish as trees without leaves now stood where the wall once stood. Yet this was only the introduction. We now could see fire rising from the cave floor and with that we saw a black owl, a spooking grave marker or something and so many skulls lying on the cave's floor. Then we saw a beautiful woman kneeling with her head down and her hair touching the fire. I went to save her as Fejér grabbed hold of me saying, "Don't Ann, it is a trap." Now appeared a thing that had a skull face; with hands of flesh and a long dark robe with a hood. He had a heavy iron pole in his left hand with a razor sharp sickle on top. He looked at us somewhat stunned that we would not save the helpless woman, as she now started to beg for mercy. He lifted up the sickle and cut off her head. We all quenched, then I got angry and I stood up and walked towards him as he reached for me I told him, "Touch me not, or you shall burn." He grabbed my shoulder to pull me into the fire. The fire stopped. He flinched, then I said, "Burn you beast." Then he made his blue eyes light up as he went to speak yet could not call for help. He cried, "Who are you." I told him, "I am the woman you just killed." Then the fire completely consumed him as he vanished. As I turned around all five of my girls were on their knees bowing to me saying, "The goddess Ann is our master whom we serve. Have mercy on us." I looked at them and said, "The only thing I will have for you is your heavenly wine" as I dropped on Fejér and Amity forcing them to the cave floor on their backs and asking, "Can I lay in my sisters arms. All five of them reached out their arms and hugged me flooding me with kisses. I then told them, "If this is the reward for being a good goddess then I think I shall always be good." It felt so good to have finally been able to save my sisters. I asked Fejér, "How did I do that?" Fejér told me, "Your love for us was so great that you reached into your subconscious and pulled out a nibble of your power." I then told them, "My love shall always be that great."

Then as we were just about at peace with the results, the cave floor behind us turned into water with red and black and something started to ascend out of the water. Her hair had a style I could not identify and her eyes were fierce and so powerful. I asked her in a nice voice, "Who are you?" She then told me, "I am one who you said you would love me forever." I then told her, "I see no reason not to love you now, my love who are you?" She answered, I am blood of your blood, I am you, and you are me." It was Ruth's turn to say, "Wow." I told her, "I know not what you are saying, yet I know you would never lie to me, I can feel that." She then said, "My goddess is still so warm and wise, I am Medica and I live inside of you as does Sabina." We have lived too long without you my god. Please hurry back all your kingdoms may worship you." I then asked her, "Medica, why can we not go back now?" She told me, "My god, it is still too dangerous, however the time shall be soon as your millions of Armies are fighting harder each day." Now it was Mary's turn to say, "Wow, this is bigger than I ever dreamed my god" as she was kneeling with her hands clasped together. I walked over, kissed her head, and said, "Yet I would give all those Armies up if that was the price to spend eternity with my sisters." Medica told her, "You will not have to give up anything." Then she departed and the water now turned bright blue and a peaceful light did glow as a goddess of great beauty came up out of the water on a gray boat filled with air, a wonderful site for six hungry hearts. I called over in yearning, "Who are you?" She looked at me with eyes of warmth and said, "I am your love and you are my love." We all rushed into the water to get close to her by surrounding her. She looked at us and replied, "My, I have a lot of friends here don't I." We all said, "You do." Then Amity asked, "Where did you get flesh like that." This stranger looked at me and said, "Your Ann made them for me a long time ago." This time we all said, "Wow." Then I asked again, "I can feel that you are my love and that in all things you would always tell me the truth. What is the name of my heavenly love?" She then said, "I am in you and you are in me." I then said, "Medica already used that one." She now added, "I am Sabina and we three are one in all things." I then said, "I think I will need to visit the other side of me someday." Then Amity said, "I bet your heavenly wine tastes the best." Sabina then said, "My sister, Amity, when you come to our throne I shall walk in the flesh before our whole kingdom and let you drink the wine from my cup in thanks for the pure love you have given my god while in your flesh. It is easy to love a goddess when you see her on a throne, yet to drink her blood from only the declaration of her love to you is a great love. I cannot wait the share my wine in the vineyard of eternal love with all of you, however so sad, I must leave for Ann's safety." Then she did vanish as all the rocks were placed back where they belonged and the cave entrance was open to let the morning sunlight enter. We all agreed to catch up on our sleep and to dream about Sabina. Fejér told me, "Ann I knew not how great your kingdom really was. Our eternities shall be blessed and full of love." I then asked, "Do you think the six of us can keep Sabina's cup empty?" Then Siusan said, "Who cares, the joy will be in trying." We had really converted her fast and she was on this wagon to ride for a long time. Sabina had released a hidden energy in all of us, a reward for finishing our journey. We woke up late in the day, and all around us were fish, all cleaned an in cloth back packs. We asked Fejér if she did this and she said she had not, and asked, "Where would I get the cloth?" We then went outside and at the entrance was a nice fire with fish already cooked for us with large wooden bowls filled with grapes and berries. We all looked at each other and then Amity said, "I think we may, finally, have an admirer." We all agreed that it would be nice to have an admirer who would also double as a provider. We ate all the food that was before us, trying to put back into our bodies what all this anxiety had taken out. We then all bathed in the sea and lay on the grass beside the shore to get some sun. As nighttime approached we wondered if once again we would have special company. Just to be safe we all crowded beside each other as we used to do in my bed at mommy's house. The night slowly conquered all of us as our bodies were meshed tight against each other. If one moved, we all would be alerted and we wanted it that way. Then about maybe one hour before dawn, a bright white light appeared before us. It gave off warm heat that helped chase the damp cold out of our cave. As we tried to look at it, our eyes would hurt so we tried to peek just a little through our fingers. What we could feel was the kindness that radiated from it. I then asked, "Who are you?" He then said, "I am an angel sent by Bogovi to update you on your situation. We had to take you out of the ship in the ocean since some angels and some of your angry daughters were about to identify you and turn you into the local throne. We thus had to destroy all the bodies except for yours in which we placed a lost soul in it. We destroyed your sisters' bodies to keep the enemy from thinking others had joined you. We would love to see the surprise on the demons that walk into this trap by bringing a false soul to the throne that will imprison them in doing so. We hope that will take away some of the aggressiveness in these threats. You are now almost seventy million years into your past, long before humankind of any kind walked the Earth. Yet even here, you have met danger. We now are going to deliver you to a vacant ancient city deep in the Earth. We have been able to sabotage their sonar systems, which will keep you, secure until we can find another place for you to live. Bogovi has declared that your time on Earth shall soon be finished. He has also discovered that this throne does not know that you had attempted to attack them with their word, so still stay low so you can avoid the other you from clashing. We shall have a small light ahead of you to guide you to this ancient city called Angkor. It will be a long journey and we will have food positioned for you throughout your long journey. I must now go; you will see us no more, unless an emergency shall present itself. We will pull you to your next time jump when it is secured. Go with the love of your Bogovi." Ruth now asked, "How many are yours Ann?" I said I did not know. The spirit said, "You shall soon know." Then the light did vanish. I asked Ann, "Who is this Bogovi?" Fejér told me, "I know that you were preparing to marry him when an army of evil gods attacked. That is all I know. They erased so much from my memory to protect you in case of danger." I then said, "I think maybe too many lost too much because of me." Fejér said, "That is so far from the truth, because of you millions of planets are now ruled by goodness and justice and love instead of hating, evil and deceivers. A dawn filled with peace and joy. No other in history has done as much as you. That I do know. More girls are given your name that any one person in all of history in all the dimensions as declared by our dimension's throne. So never think that too may have lost for you but know that so many will give everything for you." It was now Ruth and Amity's turn to say, "Wow." Amity said, "I do not think my name will ever be famous." Then Ruth said, jokingly in innocence, "Now Amity, that is a terrifying thought." Then we all laughed as Fejér said, "Ladies, we need to pack up and head down to Angkor. The lights seemed to lead us up and down. That was because there were not that many tunnels that ran extremely deep, so they tried to get us as deep as possible for as long as possible, since we were the only humans on the planet. I now marvel that we survived on the surface as long as we did. The lights always told us that fresh and sometimes cool air was ahead. Usually our food supplies would be just a little ahead. We usually slept not too far from the lights if they were overhead. If they are easily entering and exiting, we must keep moving. No one wanted to leave the cave for fear that we might not make it back in. Something was working very hard for our salvation and we wanted to keep within the safety zone they had provided. The days came and went as we continued to see so many marvels. I had never messed around much underground yet the things I was seeing now were amazing. I would start having our planets build underground some in order to have additional protection from invasions and provide more surface space for producing food. What is more amazing is that enough raw materials will flood these beautiful underground caverns that will produce oil for the abusive fossil fuel civilizations that find time to destroy each other while destroying this planet. That shall never happen to any planet I rule, for if they do, I destroy it, and make a new one and brings worthy saints to spend the remainder of their living days in peace and beauty. The smell of a new planet busting for the bearing of life is much like this place we are walking through now, except the lack of light and dangerous life, I hope. We had to walk around this underground sea to make it to the light. We took our time walking around the sea, as we found plenty of fresh prepared meat for us. Our spirits were trying to make us all fat I guess, however the continual walking, climbing up and down seamed to keep our waists in favorable form. I cannot imagine what it was like not to be trapped inside these shells. I did not notice this in my England body because I only knew of it except in the nighttime world and even there we felt bound in our bodies, as proven by the heavenly wine we gorged ourselves on. I will conceptualize on that later, for now enjoy the beauty of this journey, and surprisingly the warm heat that now floods this hidden paradise. The seafood we were eating now looked much different from that on the surface, yet had a fresher, more robust taste and felt energy packed. Guess we are lucky for not having to see them before they were cleaned, as I am now feeling that traditionally I never favored flesh, except when it was offered to me as a sacrifice and that was absorbed through the smoke. Some poor priests had to consume the overdone flesh. No wonder so many of them were skinny. I can feel some memories starting to come back in pieces, which makes each day exciting. Moreover, to be honest, my main concern for returning is to get my sisters, the ones who suffer for me each day to their rightful reward. My mind is trying to figure out how I can enjoy them if I am really three spirits in one. Guess I will have to have a door in me that one side says 'do not disturb' and the other side saying 'Sabina is here.' The latter sign will pull my sisters in like an arrow flying from a crossbow. Back to our present paradise, the beauty appears to be ongoing. When we first started this voyage to our sanctuary I thought we would be crawling into small holes, not enjoying what appears to be underground worlds. We are now traveling underneath golden ice cycles reflecting the light we are following. We do not look to either side for fear of falling into dark emptiness; however, I am not foolish enough to think it does not lack a bottom as I nor any of us want to verify. It feels like we have walked forever now, up and down, as we are now, according to Fejér starting our deep twisting descent. The twisting always leads into another tunnel. Thus, just before the twist we walk a small ledge with our backs tightly against the cave wall as it leads into another twisting descent. Fejér told us this is necessary to prevent raiders from above someday to invade. She had always pushed some rocks in a certain order that made the ledge appear and then once safe in the next part of our cave, she would rearrange the rocks again and close the ledge. I told her, "A ledge does not prevent spirits from following us." She told me, "Yet spirits rarely search for humans in places humans cannot go." I guess she is right. As we now started to ascend once more, the tunnel led into a large open space in which we saw some candles light up. Then we saw four faces appear before us, the front one had her right side cover with a black broken mirror, and behind her were two large fierce looking faces without bodies and one broken face above a big bright green color ring on her right hand. We could only see one eye and it was focused on something above and behind us. We all froze and I have asked since now when we are in danger my sisters all look at me, "Who are you?" All four of them replied, "We are the Daughters of Usha, now you need to ask what we are?" I then replied, "And you need to ask what am I?" They all started laughing as the first looked and said, "You are a scared thing." I told them, I have no fear." As I said that rocks began to fall upon us, and I looked up and said, "Stop" and the rocks stopped in midair and I then looked at these daughters and said, "I can have them hit you if that is your desire?" Three of the four heads vanished as the remaining one said, Rock does not hurt me, for I will simply reappear. I then released the rocks on her, and she did disappear and reappeared to a spot to the left of her. As she disappeared, we quickly went to where they were, which simply a few feet from us was. When she reappeared, it was in front of me. As she scanned where we were, she said, "Never returned you invaders for I shall stop you." I touched her and she was only a light. I told her, "No light shall stop us." She then yelled out, "Where are you?" She could hear us but not see us. I then said, "Why do you try to hurt us?" She replied, "I am a protector of Angkor." I asked her, "How long have you been a protector?" It replied, "Let me check my clocks and calendars . . . Then she continued seven million of your years." Fejér then asked me, "How is that possible?" I told her that time was like space in that it has no boundaries and it went both ways. As a new year is manifesting itself, on the + side, another year in the past manifested itself on the − side so that time like space can balance itself. In addition, time simply keeps repeating itself. Someday Angkor will once again thrive as it cleans the surface as it has for so many times." Fejér asked, "How long have you been my goddess, and I told her only a few million years, so I am a relative newcomer and a reproducer, for have made around seventy million daughters and watched twenty-five million of them die at the hand of the god of this world. I still hate that to this day. Yet the flesh did not meet with a spirit which offers some consolation, as I have been replacing them in my throne, now with power and net flesh." I then looked at this holocaust before me and said, "Your lights are no more" at such time, the lights did go out. We all then did some investigating yet found no threat. It was simply a forward security plant. Within a few hundred feet, we started discovering caves that were hard to justify being created by natural means. The walkway now looked like it was used for movement of large items. Our guiding light was now brighter and bigger. We were trying to figure out how large items got into her to be taken, I suppose, to Angkor. It did not make any sense, why have large transport tunnels that go nowhere. We still received our prepared food at the regular times, and you can only guess how we felt, being women, and enjoyed prepared food. That is nice. During nighttime, we still sleep tight as two coats of paint. I always wiggle up to Fejér and my sisters' wiggle up on both sides of us and a couple on top of us. I inspirationally enjoy this great bond, and the way they believe in me faithfully. I shall always strive to keep their trust and belief in me. The nights have now been so quiet and still. We could feel the absence of the surface. We only knew one thing now, something was trying to keep us safe, and that something had a stake in us. Mary acted strange today complaining about missing Faith Maria and Heidi. As I thought about it, I asked Fejér, "Does the night time world exist in this time era?" Fejér did not know, thus I decided to ask the spirits calling upon them claiming this to be an emergency in which in reality it was because my sister was suffering. My spirits then appeared before me saying, "Oh greatest goddess of all the dimensions, how may we serve you?" Strangely, I still felt like a little girl in this big body and still was not comfortable with the supposed greatness. The only thing I knew was I was in a deep hole in the Earth way before human life was in existence. I now asked them, "Where are my sisters, Faith Maria and Heidi?" They answered, "They are now called, Komáromi and Siklósi and they are safe in the night world." I continued my investigation by asking, "Then where is Máriakémend?" They then told me, "She is in your throne enjoying her eternity." I then told them, "My love for them is so great I wish for them to be with me for I need them so much. My love for them prevents me from ordering it. Will you ask them if they wish to return to us?" These spirits now turned into many lights and I could see three people, one vaguely on the left, just beginning to walk towards us. Then the spirit asked me, "Do wish for Joy and Richard to serve with you now?" I said to the spirit, "They suffered greatly because my spirits did not protect them. They shall see my revenge on those who failed to protect one that I love so much. Her suffering must end, as I can no longer take a chance on her suffering again. With this in mind, I wish for them to remain in my holy of holies until I return." The spirit said, "I shall report to Bogovi your decision and have him provide you the support you need. I now have your sisters in new fully functional bodies." As I saw their faces, I fell to my knees and cried, "Come hold me my sisters." They rushed to me and held me while lifting me up saying, "It is not good for a great goddess of all good to be on her knees." I answered, "My love for my sisters fills me with so much happiness that my legs cannot support it. Never in my long history have I been so blessed." Then Máriakémend answered, "Nor ourselves for being so blessed to serve such a wonderful goddess." We all joined in a great celebration as I then had to request I be given an opportunity to speak. I then said the my lost sisters, " I wish to introduce Amity and Siusan, who are our new blood sisters having declared themselves also my servants and have drank freely of our wine." Máriakémménd, Faith Maria, and Heidi rushed over and introduced themselves to their newest sisters, for any sister of mine was automatically a sister of theirs. The spirits then told us, "You are close to the giant city of Angkor and shall arrive early tomorrow afternoon. Is there anything else that we can humbly serve our master?" I told them, "Your service today has been so great, I shall always be so thankful for what you have brought back to me today, for that which was lost is now found." What the spirits did leave, leaving behind a large feast of food for us to celebrate. I told my sisters, "It is so nice to have spirits which brings so many good things, yet these things would have no joy unless shared with my sisters, for as I watch you eat I can remember how so many times we ate together, to put energy in our body's to return to vigorously jest with great joy. United again, then I wondered if we should also have Julia with us. Máriakémménd pleaded on her behalf and as I was getting ready to ask, a bright light with a white dress came walking through the wall.

Máriakémménd then commented, "If that is Julie, then that dress is coming for the sisters to enjoy her wine." As Julia materialized she immediately fell on her knees and cried out, "How may if serve the master of my blood that we may still be Blood of our Blood?" I told her, "I wish that you once again are our sister." She, still kneeling, replied, "With great honor she who rules my heart and that I shall follow the remaining days of our eternity together." It was Siusan's turn now, still being amazed by the new spirits who are part of their sisterhood, "Wow." We all laughed as I walked over and hugged her giving her a kiss on each cheek and reaffirming my love for her. Fejér then recommended that we all take a wine break so the new sisters could be welcomed properly. We all got ourselves bonded again and in the next morning, after a well-prepared seafood breakfast we started on our journey. I liked that instant response until Julia busted my bubble by telling us that they already had her here and was simply waiting for a good time for her to enter. I should not be too disappointed since they are starting to figure out what I need, so that part is good. As we all walked, we were now a big gang, consisting of Máriakémend (I had first picked on as we walked with arms tightly wrapped around each other, especially since she was more aware of what dangers could lie ahead in the spiritual realm. I loved all my sisters yet Máriakémend was always the one I was most drawn to, since she had struggled so hard in her life), Fejér, Julia, Faith, Heidi, Mary, Amity, Ruth and Siusan. We were now almost the size of a small Army of ten, with every one of us now having bodies that could break any men's hearts, yet that did us no good since we lived on a planet with no men. Guess that is how Bogovi planned it. I cannot blame him if he did. Our new temporary sanctuary was now visibly before us, the ancient city of Angkor. We now saw something greater than anything I have seen since my rebirth. Fejér tells me, "Your daughter rules a great empire on so many planets to include many in your empire that builds great cities under the ocean." I told her that someday I would like to meet her. She told me, "You shall meet Atlantis again someday." Now, Faith is going my mystified followers with her first, "Wow." I naturally ran over and hugged my big sister. We all had Joy in our hearts yet knew since she had Richard in her life she needed to be with him. This city had so many layers and light. I wondered how the light could still be working after so long. Julia told us that the Angkor had built special sunray collectors in the mountains that were able to convert into energy for their cities. She justified her knowledge by telling us, "I ate a long of knowledge pills about the Angkors. The strangest thing is how they just stopped. Nevertheless, many were washed away from existence." I had a sneaky hypothesis that I would keep private for the time being. Looking upon the enormous empty city I jokingly replied, "There are so many mansions we each could have one." I thought it was funny so I started laughing, and then suddenly noticed no one else was laughing. They were all on the ground crying as if their hearts had been broken. I asked my sisters, "Sisters of my love, why do you all cry?" Then Fejér, acting as the spokesperson for their group, said in tears, "We do not want our own mansions, master, we want to be with you at your feet, loving you with all of our souls." I then looked at them and said, "I too need this from my sisters, nevertheless I cannot, nor will I force my will upon any of you since we are Blood of Our Blood and my blood flows through you thus my heart must unite with your hearts. Your will must also be my will. Now let us find a small place where sleep." They all came back to life. In a way, I hope this time is long, since to have disciples with hearts that are united, as one is something that not all gods are rewarded. I can see so many steps going everywhere. I wonder how the people moved around in this great city. Then Julia showed us special rooms that were located on all corners and midway between the corners. These rooms could fit twenty people comfortably. She told us the ones on the corners were for local trips and the ones in between for big jumps to the further points in the city. They also had central stations in the middle of the city for jumps to the surface and to other cities. Their military had their own jump stations. We tested it, all at once of course, and jumped around the city, catching as many sites as possible. We eventually made it to the big highlighted one in the middle of the city. Julia told us this was a command and research center. Research was very important for them, so they kept it close to their military. We wondered why they had to have a military and Julia told us she did not know, moreover we could get some answers from their command archives. Julia started looking strange like disks and studying the different categories and put in our first disk. A complete video stream appeared before us. She told us that this looks like an alien invasion on another city. We were glad that the people who lived in this city did not look like that at Julia verified these cities on Earth were inhabited by humans. It looks like these aliens recut a temporary large entrance so their ships could invade at will. What is strange on this stream is that the aliens were capturing the humans and taking them back to a large ship that floated by very fast. So many ships were entering as their Armies

were gathering up the people and then when they got their quota buried the entrance with a material that kept multiplying until the city and the entrance were completely sealed. It then over time turned into rocks and soil. We could not figure out why they did not take all the people before they departed. The area above the city for about four hundred feet turned into hard solid rocks that eventually smashed the city. In smashing the city, it also converted all material in the city into stone, thus completely erased from existence. This almost appears to be an act of war, yet strangely, this city had no military. This explains why the Angkor was big on having a strong military. The military was for protection from aliens. We watched a few more cities to be erased until they attacked a city that had a military. The military destroyed the aliens before they had a chance to enlarge the city's entrance. The military also attached the mother ship in space. The aliens had transferred the humans to the central part of their ship for added security. That proved to be what saved some of the civilians in that the attacks were destroying the outside of the mastership. This cuts off their power and communications. The humans were able to enter the ship and attack from within while searching for any prisoners, which would have been captured from other destroyed cities. They battled their way to the central area where the large prison was located. The humans had been stripped and hands chained to the short ceiling and left hanging. A few had whip marks on their backs. Unfortunately, not all were still alive. Some had their feet cut off with large drains below them. There were a few empty chains. They also found a room with human bodies hanging with skin missing, head removed, and insides cleaned as one would clean an animal. They were catching the humans as they went hunting. The humans freed as many of the fellow Earthlings that were alive and then took a couple hundred prisoners exited the master ship and then destroyed it. Upon returning, they released to fellow humans who returned shortly thereafter. They had nowhere to go so they were placed in a holding cell and then auctioned off as slaves. They were able to keep the money for receiving their sale and given a freedom date. This system worked well for them as many acquired marketable skills that allowed them to be productive members of this new society. The fate for invaders was not as welcoming. They were starved only giving the minimum to keep them alive. Then each day, one hung upside down in front of the military center beaten with twenty-three lashes and left to die. Most died within a few hours. These painful executions were recorded, and broadcast deep into space. After this great victory, all cities began building large militaries and joined in their space transportation development. They were actually more advanced than any future fossil fuel nation or empire. This was an astonishing revelation for my small group, yet it did not explain the current existence of Angkor. We all decided to find a small room somewhere so we could all bundle up for the night. Máriakéménd told us she knew the place where our spirits had selected for us to rest and dine for the evening. The dine part had us on Máriakéménd's soles as we went to discover our home for his night. It was just one stop from the city's center and soon we were going up the stairs to the fourth floor. Máriakéménd told us that four was a lucky number for her people because it was an unlucky number for their enemies. We entered our small cozy apartment and for my first time since returning to Earth we had running water and heat from something else than wood. This was wonderfully nice as we all set down at a nice large table and ate our seafood and fresh variety of vegetation. We all enjoyed the fresh spring in the water. After eating, we started telling some of our stories to Amity and Siusana. I could see the peace that flowed through their bodies as these stories brought them closer to us. They now believed more in my divinity, although luckily for me their faith had kept them at my side. I was rather sad about not having our nighttime world, however for security reasons we could no longer go there as our enemies had focused on it. In fact, the roles of Komáromi and Siklósi (pending receiving their original names from my throne) were reprogrammed with a complete different past and no information about me. All memory of me was erased from Buckingham and I no longer had any spiritual connections with any human in that time era. Their actions now would be as recorded in history. They developed such different personalities, I no longer recognized them, nor did I feel any type of bond. Our nighttime world was still active as the spirits programmed many fake leads, which kept our enemies very busy. We got one more surprise this night. Just when we were thinking, that our tribulations would recede, our enemy again attacked. A beast that looked like Usha appeared again. This time he had three fierce dogs with him. They had razor sharp teeth as they crushed the empty skulls into a fine powder. The dogs had a fire behind them. Then one dog leaped at us, thus breaking the chain that held them back. The dog pushed Fejér to the ground and started biting her and clawing her with his needle sharp claws. At first, I thought this was an illusion however the screams and blood shooting everywhere from Fejér proved otherwise. Seconds now meant death for Fejér so I commanded it to stop, yet their master just laughed at us. My sister is dying and I have no power to save her. Why have powers if not with you when needed? Then Julia ran to our counter space in the kitchen and moved a couple of rocks and the dogs and their evil master vanished. Julia had saved our lives. I asked Julia, "What happened to my power?" She told me, "For security reasons you will have no power while we are here." I told her, "What security, my sister is in big trouble and fighting for her life?" Julia told me that this was an internal Angkor protection attack. I asked her, "Which idiot did not check this room before leading us to it and not ensuring that it was secure?" Julia answered, "I know not, however we shall no longer take chances?" We then found some cloth in the apartment, and soaked it in water trying to clean Fejér's deep wounds. I could see that we were losing Fejér and that she would soon die if we could not save her. Julia now got up and started moving some more rocks at which time a light shined on. The light went up and down her blood soaked body. Then the light vanished. We now all worked as hard as we could stop all the bleeding. Fejér continued to cry in great anguish. I hated this, being a burden I could not bear. The sight of her great suffering made me realize how helpless I really was. To watch a loved one painfully die in front of me was crushing. This misery was soaking all of our souls as we were losing the battle. This paradise was flooded with serpents. Fejér was dying in front of us. She was now coughing up blood as she was burning up. She no longer cried from the agony, as if she was giving up. We all now could just cry as we looked upon her. All cried except for Julia. I thought this to be strange, however many express grief in their own ways. Fejér had now lost too much blood for any hope of surviving. The only thing we could do now is hold her hands and be with her as she crosses over. I am now very much angry and I want to find who keeps screwing up our security. As I was getting ready to demand the spirits return, the bright light in our ceiling came back on. It now focused completely on Fejér for about one minute and then went back out. We all now jumped for joy. The light had completely remade Fejér who was now standing up receiving vigorous hugs from her sisters. I now started to suspect the Julia knew this all along. I went over and asked Julia if she knew this was going to happen. She told me, "I did not know for sure. I had seen in their medical journals how they had perfected the light of healing. I saw a few examples, and this one started like those examples. I did not want to give my sisters any false hope thus allowing them to prepare and brace for the worst situation. Sadly, we must now protect ourselves. We need to get some weapons from the military headquarters tonight." I then told her, "I understand the wisdom of your words, Sisters . . . Let us now go and get some weapons." We were a relieved when we discovered our steps had lights on so we could see where our little huddle was wobbling. Then we looked out the door and saw pitch black. We were all sitting back on this, however Julia walked out, and as she moved the lights came on. Julia to me now is evidence where thinking ahead and being prepared for alternate situations is a lifesaving absolute. A goddess without power is worse than a human with no power, because the loss of hope and faith. I am so lucky that my disciples still have their everlasting faith. I need no power to be in this group because I am in each of them. That is a good feeling as we now walk down the street to the military headquarters. Julia warns us to be very careful how we enter for there could be alarms or traps. She went in first, and caused all the lights to come on, and tested the room for our security and then motioned for us to enter one at a time following the path she had entered. When we all got in, I went over and hugged Julia, telling her as I was kissing her, "Please, never put yourself in danger because you are truly one of my sisters and I do not want to lose you. Do not take chances until we all discuss it. You are with us and my blood as in the Blood of Our Blood." She then, while falling to her knees and hugging tightly my legs, "I shall obey my master; however, I shall let me die for her if needed." I then with one hand on each side of her face lifted her head to where she could see me and said, "I will not permit that, however I will let you live for with me, now arise, and continue the great works you have so far done for us." I just am not prepared to lose any of them, especially since I do not know if my spirits can take them to my 'throne'. Each has been a part of my life during this sanctuary period. United we seem to overcome past disasters. Julia picked out our weapons. Each received a rifle style laser and a pistol style laser. Additionally, we each got a small portable medical light and a knife. We had a belt to hold it on our waist. Julia was a special contribution to our future. They always seem to enjoy when I baby them, pet them, touch them and of course share our heavenly wine. They are the best. We all agreed that it would be better to find a new place to sleep tonight. Julia led us to a community building that had some small rooms for homeless people. We found a little room and crowded in and on top of each other with rifles resting against the noses of the sisters on the bottom and started snoring. If any alien had seen us they would have thought, we were on with ten heads, twenty arms, and legs and always as we all always-clasped hands now. We just were not at ease in this deep hole in the ground. I also wanted to be somewhere with more contact with my spirits. This is wrong to put me here, helpless to watch my loved ones suffer. Yes, we made it through our tribulations so far. How long our luck would last was anyone's guess. The next morning we found our morning seafood, which even that is getting old. Putting me in a body that needs more food to function and then give it seafood three times, a day is not hitting the mark with me anymore. I do not think I should be happy for getting something when everything has been taken from me. It is time for me to start raising some anger with this whole situation. After eating, we decided to return to the police and research center where we were the previous day. Julia and now Fejér had a crippling curiosity about the fate of the Angkor, especially after seeing the lifesaving performance of their medical lights. As we scanned through their history, we could see rather harmonious civilization, with few public executions. They were also making many trips to planets in other deep parts of the Milky Way establishing new colonies on these other planets. We now were moving closer to their end and it was not pleasant as a river of fire flooded the city and thousands of warriors came out of it fighting and killing many. The fire was a strange fire in that it did not burn what it touched. It disabled any form of communication, and all public power sources. The people were trapped where they were with no defense as the police center was also locked tight. However, within about ten minutes, the research center activated the emergency power and their public laser weapons were set on auto and automatically started destroying the invaders. They discovered the four sources for the 'fire wave' zapped it is trapping the forward warriors in the open where they were picked off quickly. In this short battle, they lost one out of four of their population. Even though they had survived this massacre, the public was demanding revenge. Thus, the military launched campaigns to find these invaders with little success. They rigorously searched and searched, going into places they normally would not go. This turned out to create the small hole in their dam that flooded them triggering destruction. One ship returned later than it was supposed to and just minutes before the next scheduled ship. Thus, considering that no dangers had been detected on the detoxification phases on all other ships returning from the current sector that was being searched, they let the late ship pass on through so they could inspect the ship behind it. They did not consider that each ship was searching different solar systems and this ship searched a planet that had bacteria that was not compatible with their human life forms. Like most deadly and destructive biological agents, they mass-produced with the availability of oxygen in the air. They would enter the humans when breathed in and consume all the oxygen that entered the host body until the host body died from suffocation. The entire population was killed the first night, as alarms went off not allowing any ships deployed to return. After these agents consumed all the oxygen in the underground capsule, they rushed to the surface to indulge in the vast quantity of oxygen. Nevertheless, their rush to the surface was the last place they rushed because when they met the sunlight they immediately died. The deployed ships were now long gone as they went to live with the new deep settlements on the other side of the Galaxy. History provided enough storms and Earthquakes to seal the entranceway to the surface and the city became a sealed treasure deep inside the Earth, staying intact until I would destroy the Earth much later. That was a strange thought that just passed through my mind; I was actually a part of the end of this extremely evil planet, having more evil in one planet than in many of my evil solar systems. This planet turned out to be the black hole of evil, hate, pain, greed, lust to name just a few things. I knew one thing; I had to get my sisters out of here as soon as I could. For the first time, I was starting to get homesick, although at times I am still hazy about the Bogovi that Sabina and Medica are always deliberating. There had to be some form of deity in place for the Angkor, yet they were left as lambs to the slaughter. I now remember that every planet in my Empire had a strong network of my forces protecting them. Having so many daughters was a great asset, and the millions of armies I was able to create. I had the desire and I did it. Over seventy-five percent of my temples had a visible angel to help them. Love had to have a weapon to fight hate, as good must be stronger than evil. Evil feeds itself with the active spiritual interaction and the ability to create mystery about Good. Good must also feed itself with active spiritual interaction. What still amazed me is how evil unites to meet any challenge before it, yet good tends to stay self-contained geared towards defending itself. Evil pinpoints its attack on a specific targeted threat. That is why I am here. With millions of armies, fighting throughout an entire universe my enemy stays concentrated on me, yet they with any luck will not get me. Billions of weapons pointed at me, and every one of them must be taken out since each one can tap into their central power source and unleash their total punch on me. This is why I do not like it here because I have nowhere to run. I have no way to voice my concern so I might as well put my helmet on and hope for the best. We all rolled back the disks and watched some family streams. I could see in each of my sisters, especially Faith, since she was married and actively trying, a longing to reproduce. This maternal instinct is so real I could see small tears going down their faces. They had not the right situations such as Fejér's husband trying to secure enough income to provide for a family they both wanted, only to see her husband commit suicide after his business crumbled. Máriakémènd was the only one, besides Julia, that lived a life and died, yet her life had not been fair, learning that she had to sell her body to survive. Heidi had surrendered her opportunity for a normal life to be Faith's chamber maiden. Faith Maria no longer needed a chamber maiden, however since Heidi was Blood of Our Blood, thus she belonged here, and here is where I want her. Mary and Ruth, Amity & Siusan were actually still little girls as I was until my memory started to return. I still do not know the history of Julia, nor do I really need to know, she has my blood in her and I want her with me. I sometimes even wish that Joy could be with us, as she so many times guided me and helped me given that she was closer in age and still not a 'big' girl. I understand that she must stay with Richard. I can now see myself as being greedy, because I want to keep my sisters, yet the thought of me leaving them is misery and breaks their hearts. They want me and I want them, thus I shall keep them however, in order to keep them, I owe them the chance to go through the seasons of life. With this in mind, as I return to my throne, they will all be given new bodies and a chance to marry, even if I have to nudge their candidates, and to have babies and to grow old and then join me in my throne, if they so desire. They will not go through the pain of death since it is my decision to breathe life into them, thus I will take them when they can no longer live in the flesh. I will wait until we get back on my throne before telling them this. I will motivate them by letting them hold their first baby. That will put them on one of my planets, in a royal family of course with my priests knowing they are chosen ones. For now, I just want to get them there safely. We now ate our evening seafood and decided to find a safe place to sleep. Julia did not like this center since it had too many alarms, which would manifest deadly holograms. We found a hospital about two stops down from the center. We went inside and found a resting area with beds. Julia double-checked it to make sure it was not associated with any lights. She jokingly told us, "The last thing we need is a sex change operation and wake up as boys." Ruth now complained, "Now that I have a big girl's body, I have no experience with boys as also lacking is Mary, Amity, and Siusan. Julia then told all of us to follow her. They went to a special 'entertainment center' as she pushed a few buttons and told them to, "Hurry in and get laid." They looked at me and asked for permission, and I told them, "Sisters, you do not want to miss this electrifying exotic experience, now hurry." They all jumped for joy as, they were rushing in, I could hear them saying, "We have the greatest sisters." Then about three hours later, to our amazement, they came out soaking wet, hair looking like someone had stuck their tongues in an electrical socket, and limping with humongous large smiles. Fejér now said, "Dang, all of us should have gone in. I asked them if everything was ok, and Ruth answered by saying, "It was soooo wooondeeeeeerfull. Thanks for making me a woman." Then Faith Maria said, "Darn, I had to marry a King and never got laid like that." We hugged our younger sisters as they now had a taste of life. I can still remember how Ruth and Mary would tell everyone all day long, how she hated boys. She would never say that again, at least for a while. As we know, relationships with boys can be Topsy-turvy at times on the roller coaster of love. It is so amazing how the simple free times, at least for most women, in life can overload the senses with visions and the aroma of the heavens. In addition, the experiences must be duplicated for each vessel of being. We are now so excited from the excitement of the newest members of the heterosexual club. Their fortune will be my ability to control when they become with child, thus ensuring they can raise their families in an environment that can provide for them, however if they ever click their slippers three times, I will be there. We now found some water and rags to clean our sister's love struck bodies. They had actually tangled with some loaded males, as it took us a lot of water to unload them, however we did, and they were able to join us for a nice night's sleep. Moreover, they fell to sleep like a rock falling from a cliff. They slept so hard they forgot to snore. The rest of us were also very excited as we felt the right thing had been done and they had the love and support that they needed to develop into fine young women. Our tired bodies gave way to the night as we all fell to sleep even more bonded than, and I thought after almost losing Fejér we would never feel more bonded than we were then. Yet each day was becoming better than the day before although to many more days in this underground disaster area would drive me crazy. I wanted some sunshine and wide open space. I just felt we were too much an open target here. Then in the middle of the night, we all awoke finding ourselves spinning in the stupid tunnel again. This time we hung onto each other as hard as we could connecting ourselves into a tight circle and even interlocked our legs. We all had that "Oh no, what now" look on our faces. Then the night turned into day, the dark into light. The silence started giving way to small chirping sounds of birds and we all gently landed falling off our feet and now laying in the middle of a grass prairie. Oh wow, my rocket scientists really hit me good this time. At least we were in high grass, about three feet high. There is nothing like a gang of ten freely exposed females dropping into a wide-open prairie. I guess my so call fiancé is taking very good care of me. He must want all to witness what he is getting. I never could understand men. I complain about being an open target deep in time and way below the surface is an open easy target, so we are blasted into the wide-open where if anyone would have had trouble killing me can do so now at complete ease. I was now going to test my connections, and demanded my spirits appear before me. I then fell into a sleep and my spirits appeared before me. They asked, "How can we serve our master?" I yelled back, "First thing is not to leave me without my power again. Second, clean up my security spirits and burn a few of them. I am tired of being helpless as my sisters bleed in great pain and we are barely able to save them. I want no more surprises. And what idiot put me here?" Then all got silent as the spirits vanished and my sisters now appeared beside me and a large voice said, "It was me who put here, my love." I then screamed out, "Who are you?" The voice answered, "I am your protector and servant in love who is named Bogovi." At this time, Máriakémónd surprised me as she was kneeling and said, "Wow." With her down my sisters, all dropped immediately, however I continued to stand. Bogovi replied, "You are wise in your selection of disciples as we shall serve their needs for eternity." I then cried back, "As our protector why have you not protected me? Why do I live in fear as I wipe the blood and hear my sisters scream as they crossover? This is not fair. Why can I not have my powers and my throne back?" Bogovi then told me, "You are the one who I love the most; however, the throne of our dimension will not let you return yet. My throne and your throne plus all the galaxies we have freed from evil fight hard daily to get the required safety for you to return. If it were in my power you would be here beside me." Now Julia joined the wow club with a big, "Wow, I had no idea the greatness of your throne." Bogovi told my sisters, "There shall never been a throne greater than ours. Each day galaxies begs to become a part of the empire and join the battle to "Bring Lilith home." I then asked, "Who is Lilith?" Bogovi said, "That is your real name. Your name is the name of power, love, good, and peace." I then started moaning as my body was twitching and floating a few feet off our ground. Faith then questioned, "It not Lilith the one who kills babies?" Bogovi then answered, "That one only lives on the world you are in, by all means avoid her." I felt so much better than I can ever remember. I told my sisters, "Fear not, I am getting a gift such as our sisters received late last night." Then they all started mollycoddling my hair and guarding me from any physical dangers. Then Bogovi let me down easy and now told me, "We have brought you here because the Oakley are so spiritual and are in tune with the Earth. They can better battle off attacks from evil. You are now safer than ever before. You will learn many new things and have some more great experiences. I have returned to you more power than before. You must use it wisely. We shall Bring Lilith Home." We now fell into a deep sleep as our freely exposed bodies soaked up some sunshine we had been deprived of lately. I am now getting excited to get back to my throne, and get a whole bunch more of that twitching and exotic spiritual stimulation. I now feel so much more at ease understanding the cards I am being dealt. It is a good hand. I will be spending the rest of eternity thanking those who gave so much for me. I am so glad that I took the high road and fight for the right of the good to live without being raped, beaten and stripped of everything by evil. This is a small detour along that high road, I can easily believe the high road shall be mine again, and it will be so much better than before as the good and the just shall have the life they so much deserve, as they shall watch the witched suffer with the full punch of my wrath. Evil will never roam freely again nor will good be deprived of that which I have promised them. I know my throne has great wells of love that are fed each day and given to my servants as we all work so hard to make sure the freely exposed (except for me) are clothed and the hungry are fed. All the starving I have seen in my very few years on Earth is horrifying. I have in my chosen ten disciples (sorry, husbands must support their wives), five who came to me dirty, beaten, raped and starving surviving only by selling their greatest gift. Fejér, Faith, Joy, Mary, and Ruth, are my reward for the principles that I have built my empire. Máriakéménd was only saved from further suffering by crossing over into the land of the dead. Amity and Siusan follow me by total faith. They had everything, yet gladly gave it up to follow me believing before seeing, as is also my case now. I enjoy when those who have food, love and happiness gives it to become a part of my love, and be fed by my empire drowning in peaceful rivers of happiness. Julia did without a doubt save our lives in Angkor. Her desire to serve with all her energy pushed her to enter my service well prepared. They shall have new body suits after their time in the flesh is finished, and live in my holy of holies being served and loved by my Seonji warriors. As we slowly started to get up, we saw about one hundred Indians surround us. I had learned about Indians in our nighttime world and from some scary storybooks daddy bought me plus the Oakley on my New Venus. At this time, an old man with many feathers on his head come up to us and started yelling at us. As our universal translators started to kick in, we now understood what he was yelling about as he told us, "Women, you must put on clothes so my warriors do not forget how to be braves. Then a young woman came up to us with small leather robes and some strings made from dried and tied vegetation. The woman passed them out to us, as we quickly got dressed. The freedom we had enjoyed from our nudity was over now, also by our choice, since the testosterone flowing through 100 plus warriors seeing a variation in some fresh meat motivated us to get those robes on as fast as we could. We now walked back to the village, yet strangely, the girl had tied our hands behind our backs. I asked her why and she told us, "To keep the warriors away. They will think you are prisoners and not desire you." We walked for many miles as we now started going up a big hill and at the top, we could see many hills with flowing hills. As we were standing there, their chief saw off into the open plains a small herd of buffalo and yelled at his warriors telling them to go get us some meat. They immediately raced their horses to kill some meat that could keep them alive. The oldest game on this planet, kill to live and live to kill. Consequently, sick yet the pains of an empty stomach give us no choice. I have heard people tell me that the animals do not feel it. Even though I am the ruler of a great empire, I also have some basic reasoning skills. The animals run away from the force that is trying to kill them. They bleed. They cry out in pain. Sometimes other members of the group will return to fight with them. The coldness of theses killings and it is killing, because something that was living, breathing, seeing, smelling, tasting, making noises, and moving ceases all these activities, is that they many times target the old and the newborn. Now, that is cold. They must kill these buffalo in order to live. If they do not kill them, they will reproduce beyond what the Earth can produce to keep them alive, or other predators will start to feed off them. Either way, they must die. This is so sad and why my throne funnels a vast supply of "divinely created" meat. Meat that is created without all the other organs needed to sustain it. My people can eat without killing. I have always had a problem with "I am a saint, even though I kill other living things for my personal satisfaction. I must have this or I will die." We must survive as a team, and team has no I. I knew a prophet who was very wise named Daniel. His greatest discovery that has been ignored by the generations that followed him was the fact humans can live from beans and not meat. The killing is for the need to kill and say, "I am good." I still feel guilty about eating the fish that Fejér prepared for us. I have no excuse for eating that. I did not make the rules for the bodies we must now live. I prefer the flesh suits I have at my throne, they do not take in and release out. This waste is still a mystery for me, except that when you live in the open, the smell of it alerts predators, so they can find and kill you swifter and easier. That is not a creation based on goodness and love. Somebody has fed a lot of hogwash to this planet. That is why the rest of the meat we ate, after that first killing was created by my spirits. I do not like the feature that as you continue to do something, the part of your body that is doing it becomes sore and painful, like my feet are now. The girl who is guiding us with some warriors tells us we shall be there soon. When we arrived, I saw a string of maybe twenty crosses zig-zaged on the outer side of their camp. She told us it was for young men who did not want to be warriors. She showed us our tents, yet still did not free us. I asked her why and she told us, "We fear you will accidently wander off and be killed by wild beasts who hunt here at night. You have nothing to fear. She then collected our robes, saying the warriors are leaving now, so you have nothing to fear. She brought us no food, as my spirits have drifted away once again, saying the warriors will bring our food from their hunt. Then we could feel rumbling in the ground as the warriors rode in on their horses. The chief got off his horse, and started yelling at the warriors as they rushed into our tent and drag us out feet first and tied us to the bottom of the crosses. Then their medicine idiot came past us and threw some dust on us. It burned as it hit our skin. Then he ran to the chief and brought him back. Now he poured the remainder of the dust onto Mary and as it burned her, she yelled out crying, "Save me Ann." As I tried, I once again realized I have lost my powers. Julia told me in mind talk that the Indians spirits were blocking it. The chief then told us, "We have proven that you are from evil spirits. Today four of my warriors died while hunting the buffalo. Our great spiritual leader had verified you are from evil. Each shall receive five lashes and be tied to the cross you now are before and in the morning; you shall be beaten until your evil spirit leaves your body. Do you have anything to say?" I said, "Before the next moon I shall destroy all of you, and you shall be judged by my daughters." That made him angrier and he gave me five more lashes. This brought joy to my heart in that I am able to suffer much more than the innocent ones who foolishly follow me, yet pain because that darn whip hurts. I had one more thing to enjoy, and that was that they also went to bed tonight hungry. They had us tied up on the prairie side of the village and to add to my misery we had a full moon tonight. I could see each of my sisters suffering, yet the stupid aficionados kept singing. "Bring Lilith Home." I told them to declare me as the evil one and to save themselves. Mary looked at her other sisters and then cried out, "We wish to die being true to you and as your faithful servants. This is such a small price to pay for the great love you have given us." I then cried out, "Spirits, why have you abandoned me?" At that time, the sky grew dark and the wind started blowing down the Oakley tents. Lightning flashed at them, killing some, as they cried in terminating pain. The chief yelled, "We must kill those demons before they kill us." They then started throwing spears at us; however, the wind shifted them past us. Some tried to shoot their bows at us yet the bows broke. We were escaping each event by the hair of our noses, in which as fine young women, we had no hair in our noses. Then the warriors started screaming and running away from us. We looked around and could see nothing. Subsequently, a few minutes later, we heard a large pack of wolves heading towards us. We could hear more screaming as they were biting and killing anyone they saw. The lightning was not hitting more frequently and spread out as the warriors were escaping in a wide variety of places. The lightning exposed the skies for us. I could see the head wolf issuing his commands. As we were helplessly watching all this drama, the woman who led us back here and ran out with some boys, the little runts zipped up our poles, and with the knives, they had in their mouths freed us as fast as the lightning was striking. They were happy in that they got some praise from some big girls. We all were helped down our poles by the small boys who took good care of us. As we gathered in a circle, the woman reached out and petted one of the wolves, then called for him to stand in the circle we had made. That wolf had our undivided attention as she had him and a few of his friends walk by us. She told us to pet them. After a few short minutes, we were comfortable with them as they would sit for us and shake a paw. This was so amazing. She now told us, "These wolves will take you to my master who will care for you. Go forth my goddess." I asked her, standing before her cold and freely exposed with bloodstains over my body, "Why do you call me goddess?"

She told me, "My master has had a vision about you and knows your greatness, your kindness, your love, your war against all evil and wants you to come to her camp so she may be among the lucky who may also worship you." I told her, "I trust you speak the truth. What happens to you now and the boys?" She told me, "We will be okay; the boys got scared and ran into the forests, did you not see them go?" I gave her a kiss and told her, "I do hope someday I can have you among those who fight evil with me." She answered with a big smile saying, "I too will beg the spirits each day for that honor." Afterwards, we walked until we approached a small stream where before us were ten horses. We got on them and the wolves guided us up the stream for about four miles and then over some rocks that led us into a thick forest. Here we turned to our left and soon came to a wide opening where we were able to journey with some speed as we rushed around a large hilltop and up then up a hilltop until the morning light did shine. The wolves now stopped the horses and tugged at our feet as if to tell us to get off. We got off and they stood up and kissed our face then they chased the horses away. Then we started to walk along the side of this rocky hill when we looked over and saw a topless Oakley female. As we approached, I said to her, "Fear not, we do not come to hurt you, what is your name?" She said, "My name is Filkeháza, and I fear not." I then asked her, "We have many wounds and have not eaten in a few days and have no clothes, will you care for us?" She said, "I shall care for you. Oh my, some of your wounds are deep. Why do you have more than the others?" I told her, "Because I am guilty and they are innocent. Why is one as blessed in the gifts of a woman and beautiful as you live out here all alone?" She told me, "I shall surrender all my blessings to you. I had to leave the evil village below for their evil smells up to our spirits in the sky. They told me to leave or I would die with them." She then brought out a leather bag of some smashed roots in it and poured some water on me and passed the bottle to Fejér telling her, "If you need more water there is a spring behind that rock right there" as she passed her some more fabrics from an old English dress. She rubbed the roots on my wounds and then took them over to my disciples explaining to Fejér how to do it. As she worked so gently on my skin tirelessly also massaging me I told her, "That which I have now is feeling so much better because of you Filkeháza." She then said, "We need to hide in the forest in case some lost warriors find us." Then as she stood up, she froze and started twitching and sweat rolled off her skin as her eyes were rolling up and down and back and forth. I asked her, "What is wrong?" She said, "A friend of mine is in danger. I need for two of your friends to help me." I told her, "I shall help you and my friend Julia." I motioned for Julia to join us, and we started to run across the field. Half way their four horses joined us and we rode back to the stream and up it. As we were getting close to the village, we saw some wolves dragging a woman through the stream. Filkeháza rode to her and picked her up putting her on the spare horse. She kissed two of the wolves, gave the other two a pat on their heads', and quickly got back on her horse as we all raced away. We rode fast through the stream until finally it met with a small creek. Here we rode up the hill for a while, then got off by some rocks and started walking. The horses rushed back down the creek and back up the stream to exit on the opposite side and once again put the search party on a wild goose chase, while we three carried our wounded friend to the cover of the forest where we laid her down. As we did this, we rolled her over and for the first time, I saw her face. Shoot, what a shock. This beaten totally bruised from head to toe with broken bones and one eye hanging out was my friend who saved us from the village. I asked Filkeháza, "Do you know her name?" She answered, "She is the servant of good named Bács-Kiskun." I then touched her face lightly as she cried out in pain and I said, "Bács-Kiskun, who did this to you?" She said to me, "After we departed from you some warriors were hiding in the brush and they captured us and tied us to the whipping pole. When the evil chief returned, he demanded to know where you were so he could beat you and kill you. I refused to tell him. He then brought each boy in front of me and chopped off his head demanding that I tell him. I told him, you must kill me since I will never betray my goddess." He laughed at me, "Is your goddess the one I beat and tied to this cross? You need to be more meticulous about who you worship you fool. Beat her till she lives no more." The warriors were beating me when the wolves came back to raid the village. They freed me and drug meeeeeeee too (girgling) sorryyyyy (girgling) my journey is over." I grabbed her and yelled to my spirits, "My spirits, in the name of my throne I demand that you return her to me. She shall serve on my side here." Then did a peaceful blue light descend upon the hill and as it lifted up Bács-Kiskun was complete again. My wounds were also gone, as I could hear my sisters running towards me and when they found me they said, "Look master we are whole." Then as we looked around, we could not find Filkeháza. I asked Bács-Kiskun, "Do you know where she could be?" She told me, "I fear she may go back to the village for revenge, for two of those boys were her sons." I just closed my eyes and began to cry. Why must so much suffering happen each day of my journey? I now yelled out, "Spirits give Filkeháza back her sons and send the spirits of the other boys to torture all in the village until no more live." I then called all my sisters to meet in a circle. I showed them the vision of Bács-Kiskun's suffering to protect us. When the vision had finished, they all were crying. Mary then asked, "Can we please make her also our sister?" I then looked at Filkeháza and asked, "Will you surrender your body and name to me?" She answered rapidly, "My body, my soul, my name, and my life." I will decide her name when we arrive at my throne. I then positioned her in our spiritual river and drank her wine. As she lay there in ecstasy, she cried out, "My, you are a goddess that knows all things about her servants." I then asked, "Will you drink from our cups" and she did one by one work so hard many times choking on her wonderful devotion. When she finished we all rather wobbly stood up again and I asked her, as we all now touched her, "Filkeháza, will you follow me and worship no other but me?" She answered, "With all that I have and will have, I lay at your feet." I then took a knife that Filkeháza had lying there and cut my finger and said to her, "You must drink of my blood so that your blood will be mine." She answered, "I truly wish that I could drink of this blood forever and ever." As she sucked on my finger so hard that no more blood flowed out, we could all see the devotion in her pure heart. Then did her and I turn pure white and back to our flesh again. I said, "My sisters, today we have another sister in our family. She is now Blood of Our Blood. My blood runs now through the flesh she serves me. We all did hug, kiss, and jump together, all the foolish things women do when they get excited. Later that evening Filkeháza returned to her tree houses. She found me and dropped to her knees thanking me. She said, "The spirits have told me that you gave back the lives of my sons. They will say tomorrow that I may receive them, as all in the village shall die this night. I wanted to rush back to thank you for your great mercy and ask you to stay and meet my sons, who do remember you." I asked her if she wanted me to ride with her. She told me that the spirits told her to leave me in the camp so that the demons would not be given extra opportunities to discover you. That works for me. As she departed, Bács-Kiskun showed us the little secret kingdom that Filkeháza had carved out for her as she lay in tears each night missing her boys. The thing that kept her going was that someday when the boys got older they would all ride off beyond the mountains together. Each day the mountains were getting farther away from her until she felt you in the air. She then sent me a note with one of the wolves to spare your life. As we were walking and all talking, Siusan and Mary must have rubbed themselves against some vegetation that they were allergic. Within one hour, they both began swelling terribly. Bács-Kiskun found some roots in Filkeháza's collection and started rubbing them on the girls. We wrapped them up and laid them in a comfortable place to rest as Bács-Kiskun gave them some tea made from Filkeháza's special roots. We then prepared them for their nighttime rest. The rest of us followed Bács-Kiskun just a few feet away as she went to lie down. Faith told her, "My new sister, you are one of us now, please join us so we can welcome you and fill you with our love." It would take a little time to build up some experiences and get to know our newest member. I really want to get her story and Julia's story soon, if not for at least a few more pages for that grouchy James. It was now time to fall asleep and even though early in the evening with the sun still up, we were now all on our way to sleep. Then in a flash, I saw a pillar of fire drop straight down to the Earth, only a few miles on the prairie side of us. At this time, Julia asked Bács-Kiskun, "Isn't that where your old village is?" Bács-Kiskun looked around and replied, "I think so, wonder if Filkeháza and her sons are ok?" Then I got a chill in my back, and could not take the suspense anymore and started to get up and call my spirits. As I got ready to call, I heard some horses come rushing in. Filkeháza jumped off and cried out, "We no longer must hide our paths as we come to and fro. The evil village is no more. Our wolves prevented any from escaping and luckily for them the fire was exact." She came over and fell to her knees thanking me for a future with her sons. She then asked me, "Our spirits wish to meet you. Would you like that?" I told her, "If it is your will, I will for the one that also holds my heart." Filkeháza answered back, "If I were a man that would be the answer to my prayers." Bács-Kiskun then replied, "You cannot be a man for she is the champion for women and their freedom." Filkeháza then smiled looking somewhat puzzled and collected her sons to for the first time in so many years to sleep with her. Mommy's wings were over them tonight. As I fell to sleep I was awakened by an old, weather torn faced Oakley man who had his eyes closed. In his hand was a small spirit box that had birds traveling in and out. The robe he wore also had a bird embroidered on it. I looked at him and began to walk around him. I felt so sorry for him. I finally worked my way around him and stood in front of him. He then said to me, "My child, do you not have clothes?" I told him, "I enjoy the freedom of not hiding my beauty." He then started to chuckle and said, "I have passed the years when I could enjoy such beauty. I now worry about you getting cold, here take my outer robe." I told him, "Your kindness is so sweet, yet I am not cold, for the love inside me burns hot." He told me now that his name is Gluscabi and asked me if he could tell me why he is here. I asked him, "Oh please my friend tell me why you are here." He now told me that his story began so many ages ago in my encounter with the Eagle of the Wind. He asked me, "Can I tell about my foolishness in my days of youth when my eyes could have enjoyed your beauty?" I replied once again, considering that his years made it hard to remember parts of a conversation, "Of course my new friend, please add joy to a young girl's heart. He then began with a new energy, "Long ago, I lived with my grandmother, Tolna, in a small lodge beside the big water. One day I was walking around when I looked out and saw some ducks in the bay. "I think it is time to go hunt some ducks," I said. Therefore, I took my bow and arrows and got into my canoe. I began to paddle out into the bay and as I paddled, I sang:

> Ki yo wah ji neh
> Yo ho hey ho
> Ki yo wah ji neh
> Ki yo wah ji neh

However, a wind came up, and it turned my canoe and blew me back to shore. Once again, I began to paddle out and this time I have been singing my song a little louder . . .

> Ki Yo Wah Ji Neh
> Yo Ho Hey Ho
> Ki Yo Wah Ji Neh
> Ki Yo Wah Ji Neh

Even so, again, the wind came and blew me back to shore. Five times, I tried to paddle out into the bay and five times, I failed. I was not happy. I went back to the lodge of my grandmother and walked right in, even though there was a stick propped across the door, which meant that the person inside was doing some work and did not want to be disturbed. "Grandmother," I said, "What makes the wind blow?" Grandmother Tolna looked up from her work. You," she said, "Why do you want to know?" Then I answered her just as every child in the world does when asked such a question. "Because," I said. Grandmother Tolna looked at him. "Ah, Gluscabi," she said. "Whenever you ask such questions I feel there is going to be trouble. Besides, perhaps I should not tell you.

However, I know that you are so stubborn you will never cease asking until I answer you. For that reason, I shall tell you. Far from here, on top of the highest mountain, a great bird stands. This bird is named Füzérradvány, and when he flaps his wings he makes the wind blow." "Eh-hey, Grandmother," said I, "I see. Now how would one find that place where the Eagle on the Wind stands?" Again, Grandmother Tolna looked at me. "Ah, Gluscabi," she said, "Once again I feel that maybe I should not tell you. Nevertheless, I know that you are very stubborn and will never die down asking. So, I will tell you the place where Füzérradvány stands." "Thank you, Grandmother," I said. I stepped out of the lodge, and faced into the wind and began to walk. I walked across the fields and through the woods and the wind blew strong. I walked through the valleys and into the hills and the wind blew harder still. I came to the foothills and began to climb and the wind still blew harder. Now the foothills were becoming mountains and the wind was very strong. Soon there were no longer any trees and the wind was very, very hard. The wind was so strong that it blew off my moccasins. Nonetheless, I was stubborn and I kept walking, leaning into the wind. Today the wind was so strong that it blew off my shirt, but I kept on walking. Today the wind was so strong that it blew off all my clothes and like you I was without clothing, nonetheless I kept walking. Today the wind was so strong that it blew off all my hair, but I still kept walking, facing the wind. The wind was so strong that it blew off my eyebrows, but even so, I continued to walk. Now the wind was so strong that I could hardly stand. I had to pull myself along by grabbing hold of boulders. Nevertheless, there, on the peak ahead of me, I could see a great bird slowly flapping its wings. It was Füzérradvány, the Eagle on the Wind. I took a deep, cool breath. "Grandfather," I shouted out. The Eagle on the Wind stopped flapping his wings and looked around. "Who calls me Grandfather?" he said. I stood up. "It's me, Grandfather. I just came up here to tell you that you do a very good job forcing the wind to blow." The Eagle on the Wind puffed out his chest with pride. "You mean like this?" he said and flapped his wings even harder. The wind, which he made, was so strong that it lifted me right off my feet, and I would have been blown right off the mountain had I not reached out and grabbed a boulder again. "Grandfather," I shouted again. The Eagle of the Wind stopped flapping his wings." Yesss?" he said. I stood up and came closer to Füzérradvány. "You do a very good job of requiring the wind blow, Grandfather. This is so. But it seems to me that you could do an even better job if you were on that peak over there." The Eagle on the Wind looked toward the other peak. "That may be so," he said, "but how would I get from here to there?" I smiled. "Grandfather," I said, "I will carry you. Wait here." Then I ran back down the mountain until I came to a big linden tree. I stripped off the outer bark and from the inner bark; I braided a strong carrying strap, which I took back up the mountain to the Eagle on the Wind. "Here, Grandfather," I said. "Let me wrap this around you so I can lift you more easily." Then I wrapped the carrying strap so tightly around Füzérradvány that his wings were pulled into his sides and he could hardly breathe. "Now Grandfather," I said, picking the Eagle on the Wind up, "I will take you to a better place." I began to walk toward the other peak, but as I walked, I came to a place where there was a large crevice, and as I stepped over it, I let go of the carrying strap, and then the Eagle on the Wind skid down into the crevice, upside down, and wedged therein. "Now," I said, "It is time to hunt some ducks." I walked back down the mountain and there was no wind at all. I walked until I came to the tree line and still no wind blew. I walked down to the foothills and down to the hills and valleys and still there was no wind. I walked through the forest and through the fields, and the wind did not blow at all. I walked and walked until I came back to the lodge by the water, and by now, my hair had grown back. I put on the fine clothing that I now wear, a new pair of moccasins, took my bow, and arrows, went down to the bay, and climbed into my boat to hunt ducks. I paddled out into the water and sang my canoeing song:

Ki yo wah ji neh
Yo ho hey ho
Ki yo wah ji neh
Ki yo wah ji neh

To the contrary, the atmosphere was very hot and still and I began to sweat, as it was difficult to breathe. Soon the water began to grow dirty and smell bad and there was too much foam on the water, I could barely paddle. I was not pleased at all, returned to the shore, went straight to my grandmother's lodge, and walked in. "Grandma," I said, "What is wrong the air is hot and still and it's making me sweat and it is difficult to breathe. The water is filthy and covered with foam. I cannot hunt ducks at all like this." "Gluscabi," she said, "What have you done now?" I answered just as every child in the world answers when asked that question, "Oh, nothing," I said. "Gluscabi," said Grandmother Tolna again, "Tell me what you have done." Then I told her about going to visit the Eagle on the Wind, and that I had managed to stop the wind. "Oh Gluscabi," said Grandmother Tolna, "Will you never learn? Tabaldak, The Owner, set the Eagle on the Wind on that mountain to make the wind because we need wind. The wind keeps the atmosphere cool and fresh. The wind brings the clouds, which give up rain to wash the Earth. The wind moves the waters and keeps them fresh and perfumed. Without the wind, life will not be safe for us, for our children or our children's children." I nodded my head slowly. "Kaamoji, Grandmother," I stated, "I understand." Then I went outside again. I looked in the direction from which the wind had once came and began to walk. I walked through the fields, forest, valleys, and up the hills, there was no wind, and it was difficult for me to take a breather. He bore on the foothills and began to climb and I was really hot and sweaty indeed. At last, I came to the mountain where the Eagle on the Wind once stood and I went and looked down into the crevice. There was Füzérradvány, The Eagle on the Wind, wedged upside down. "Uncle," I cried. The Eagle on the Wind looked up as best he could. "Who calls me uncle? He said. "It is Gluscabi, Uncle. I am up here. What are you doing down there?" "Oh, Gluscabi," said the Eagle on the Wind, "A very ugly naked man with no hair told me that he would take me to the other peak so that I could do a better job of making the wind blow. He tied my wings and picked me up, but as he stepped over this crevice he dropped me and I am stuck. And I am not

comfortable here at all." "Ah, Grandfath . . . er, Uncle, I will get
you out." Then I climbed down into the crevice. I pulled the Eagle
on the Wind free, placed him back on his mountain, and untied his
wings. "Uncle," I said, "It is good that the wind should blow
sometimes and other times it is good that it should be still." The
Eagle on the Wind looked at me and then nodded his head.
"Grandson," he said, "I hear what you say." Consequently, it is that
sometimes there is wind and sometimes it is still to this very day.
Tabaldak, The Owner, called me out and brought me to his heavens
telling me that my job for eternity is to protect the Eagle on the
Wind and other small birds of the sky. Therefore, my story goes.
As I stood up, I went over and looked at the peace in content in his
old rugged face. I have experienced in my short time back on Earth
how so many threatens the old with hate and evil, only wanting to
take from them for their own personal greed. I now feel the need to
look for those who are evil in the old and turn them in older than
the one they tortured. This visit helped me, as I was now being
eagerly waiting to see what would appear before me next.
Appearing before me now a beautiful powerful woman with hands
rose as a sign of power with her focused eyes. She had lightning
behind her with sunshine bouncing from her face. She was
between the heavens and the Earth that was below her. A powerful
Eagle glided in front of her. She looked at me and said, "My name
is Wakantanka. I am the protector of the Eagles because they like
me talk to Wakinyan who speaks mysteries. The tale I have
selected for you today so you can understand our servants is a story
about "A warrior and one of my eagles. Long ago the Delaware
believed that if a brave could pluck a feather from the stern of a
live eagle and wear that feather, he would not only always be brave
and of great courage, but good fortune would always watch over
him. Consequently, young hunters used to try to catch eagles by
putting pieces of wolf meat on high cliffs, eagles being very fond
of wolf meat. Once a young brave lived that was very reckless,
ambitious, and daring. He wanted to obtain eagle feathers for a
headdress and preferred to pluck the feathers himself from live
eagles, so he found a high place where eagles often came and

baited the place for a few days with wolf meat. Then he defeated a large wolf, took it to this spot, and hung a large piece of the flesh near the edge of the cliff. He then hid behind a big tree, with a forked stick, ready to capture an eagle. Before long, an eagle came to take the tempting morsel, but the young brave considered this eagle too small and drove it away. Soon another came, but this one also did not seem to suit the brave. He drove away several others, not being satisfied with the plumage of any of them. All at once, he heard the flapping of heavy wings and there alighted before him an eagle much larger than himself. This eagle instead of looking like the others had red feathers, as if dyed in blood. This eagle did not take the wolf meat, but came straight to the brave, seized him in his talons and carried him away to a high cliff, from which it was impossible to escape, except by jumping down, which would have been certain destruction. On this cliff was a large nest containing four young eagles. The large eagle left the brave in the nest and said to him, "You shall stay here and care for my young until they are large enough to carry you back to where I got you. I am the principal honcho of the eagles. Your greed and ambition have brought you to this. You were not satisfied with the plumage of the birds I sent you. Now you shall stay here and suffer for your greed, and perhaps when you return you will be glad to take such feathers as we give you." There was nothing else for the young brave to do but rest and guard the young eagles, and this he so well made, as to win the friendship and love of the young eagles as well as the old eagle, who occasionally came to the nest, bringing in his talons a deer, rabbit or other game. Finally, after the brave had been there many days and the young eagles had learned to fly, they would sometimes be away nearly all day and leave him alone. He would become very lonely and wonder if they were going to leave him to die of starvation or eat him up, or whether they truly meant to take him back where the old eagle found him. He was not kept long in suspense, however, for one day; the great eagle came again and said, "Now, my young friend, my grandchildren here shall carry you back to where I found you. I will continue to ensure that they do not drop you until you reach the place in safety." Accordingly two of the young eagles seized the brave in their talons and flew toward the cliff where he had been tempting the eagles with wolf meat. It was not far from the nest and they soon arrived at the place in safety. There the brave found some eagle feathers, which he was glad enough to take without plucking them from a live eagle, and he returned with them to his people. The lesson he learned from his adventure is that opportunities will eventually cease to occur if you continue to ignore them, hoping for a better one." I looked at Tétiand told her, "I have found this trait sadly not to be among the humans, and since I am not a goddess on this small pebble with the evil of a giant mountain, I am helpless." Tétithen told me, "I ask not for your help but show you how our servants continue to fulfill our dreams. We have looked into the future yet may not tell our servants the terrible things the white men will do to us. How they will destroy our food, kill our great braves, rape and sell as sex slaves our women, and butcher our babies. Nevertheless after they destroy my servant's homes they will then fight a big war killing brother against brother, and then destroy their clean rivers, fill the clean air with death and then destroy the land." I looked at Tétiand said, "That is true my new acquaintance. However, evil lives in all men, although not as much as in the white man. For in the very few days I have been with Filkeháza and Bács-Kiskun I have seen evil and faced death, my clothing taken away and beaten. I had to destroy that nest bed of Gomorrah." Tétithen said, "That is true, if not for the liveliness of the wolves, we might not have come across today. I have discovered the great deeds of your empire and ask in someday I may join your empire." I told her, "I shall send escorts back to you, for I have many servants who need to be reminded about the important lesson you shared with me today. Another beautiful Oakley woman appeared before me and told me her name what Chibiabos the sister in the wolves. She further added that she has many looks only in her appearance, since she spends her days with her brothers, the wolves. She wanted to tell me a story about Wenebojo and her cronies. I smiled and told her, "Please tell me." Györköny then began, "One day Hahót saw some people and went up to find out who they were. He was surprised to discover that they were a pack of wolves. He called them nephews and asked what they were doing. They were hunting, said the Old Wolf, and looking for a spot to camp. Hence, they all camped together on the edge of a lake. Hahót was very cold in there were only two logs for the fire, so one of the wolves jumped over the flame and immediately it burned higher. Hahót was hungry, so one of the wolves pulled off his moccasin and tossed it to Hahótand told him to pull up the sock. Hahót threw it back, saying that he did not eat any stinking socks. The wolf said: "You must be very particular if you don't like this food." He reached into the sock and pulled out a deer tenderloin then reached in again and brought out some bear fat. Wenebojo's eyes popped. He asked for some of the meat and started to roast it over the fire. Then, imitating the wolf, Hahót pulled off his moccasin and threw it at the wolf, saying, "Here, nephew, you must be hungry. Pull my sock out." There was no sock, only old dry hay, which he used to warm his feet. The wolf said he did not eat hay and Hahót was ashamed. The next day the wolves left to go hunting, but the father of the young wolves came along with Wenebojo. As they traveled along, they found an old deer carcass. Old Wolf told Hahót to pick it up, but Hahót said he did not want it and kicked it aside. The Wolf picked it up and shook it: it was a nice, tanned deerskin, which Hahót wanted, so Old Wolf gave it to him. They went on, following the wolves. Hahót saw blood and soon they came on the pack, all lying asleep with their bellies full; only the bones were left. Hahót was mad because the young wolves were so greedy and had eaten up all the deer. The Old Wolf then woke up the others and told them to pack the deer home. Hahót picked up the best bones so he could boil them. When they reached camp, the fire was still burning and Old Wolf told the others to give Hahót some meat to cook. One of the wolves came toward Hahót belching and looking like he was going to throw up. Another acted the same way and suddenly, out of the mouth of one came a ham and some ribs out of the mouth of another. My wolves have a double stomach, and in this way, they can carry the meat home, unspoiled, to their pups. After that, Hahót did not have to leave the camp because the wolves hunted for him and kept him supplied with deer, elk, and moose. Hahót would prepare the meat and was well off indeed. Toward spring, the Old Wolf said they would be leaving and that Hahót had enough meat to last until summer. One younger wolf said he thought Hahót would be lonesome, so he, the best hunter, would stay with him. All went well until suddenly the evil manidog [spirits] became jealous of Hahótand decided they would take his younger brother away. That night Hahót dreamed his brother, while hunting a moose, would meet with misfortune. In the morning, he warned the brother not to cross a lake or stream, even a dry streambed, without laying a stick across it. When Wolf did not return, Hahót feared the worst and set out to search for him. At last, he came to a stream, which was rapidly becoming a large river and he saw racks of a moose and a wolf. Hahót realized that Wolf had been careless and neglected to place a stick across the stream. Desolate, Hahót returned to his wigwam. He wanted to find out how his brother had died, so he started out to find him. When he came to a big tree leaning over a stream that emptied into a lake, a bird was sitting in the tree looking down into the water. Hahót asked him what he was looking at. The bird said the evil manido was going to kill Wenebojo's brother and he was waiting for some of the guts to come floating down the stream so he could eat them. This angered Wenebojo, but he slyly told the bird he would paint it if it told him what it knew. The bird said the manido, who was the chief of the water monsters lived on a big island up the stream, but that he and all the others came out to sun themselves on a warm day. Therefore, Hahót pretended he would paint the bird, but he really wanted to wring its neck. However, the bird ducked and Hahót only hit him on the back of the head, ruffling his feathers. This was the Kingfisher and that was how he got his ruffled crest. From now on, Hahót told him, the only way he would get his food would be to sit in a tree all day and wait for it. Then Hahót heard a voice speaking to him. It told him to use the claw of the Kingfisher for his arrow and, when he was ready to shoot the water monster, not to shoot at the body, but to look for the place where the shadow was and shoot him there because the shadow and the soul were the same thing. Hahót then traveled up the stream until he came to the island where the chief of the water monsters was lying in the sun. He shot into the side of the shadow. The manido rose up and began to pursue Hahót who ran with all his might, looking for a mountain. He was also pursued by the water, which kept coming higher and higher. At last, he found a tall pine, high up on a mountain, and climbed it. The water continued to rise halfway up the tree. Wenebojo, having outwitted the evil manidog by trickery, at last found himself stranded in the pine tree. He crept higher, begging the tree to stretch as tall as it could. Finally, the waters stopped just below Wenebojo's nose. He saw many animals swimming around and asked them all, in turn, to dive down and bring up a little Earth, so that he and they might live. The loon tried, and then the otter and the beaver, but all of them were drowned before they could bring back any Earth. Finally, the muskrat went down, but he too passed out as he came to the surface. "Poor little fellow," said Wenebojo, "You tried hard." Nevertheless, he saw the muskrat clutching something in his paw, a few grains of sand and a bit of mud. Hahót breathed on the muskrat and restored his life, and then he took the mud and rolled it in his hands. Soon he had enough for a small island and he called the other animals to climb out of the water. He sent a huge bird to fly around the island and enlarge it. The bird was gone four days, but Hahót said that was not enough and he sent out the eagle to make the land larger. Having created the world, Hahót said, "Here is where my aunts and uncles and all my relatives can make their home." Then Hahót cut up the body of one of the evil manidog and fed part of it to the Tolna, who had once saved his life. Into a hollow, he put the rest of the food and when some of it turned into oil or fat, Hahót told the animals to help themselves. The Tolna was told to work only in the summertime; in the winter, he could rest in a snug den and sleep, and each spring he would have a new coat. Before that, most of the animals had lived on grass and other plants, but now they could eat meat if they wished. The rabbit came and took a little stick with which he touched himself high on the back. The deer and other animals that eat grass all touched themselves on their flanks. Hahót told the deer he could eat moss.

The bear drank some of the fat, as did the smaller animals that eat meat. All those who sipped the fat were turned into manido and are now the guardian spirits of every Indian who fasts. Hahót then named the plants, herbs, and roots and instructed the Indians in the use of these plants. Wenebojo's grandmother, Nokomis, also has a lodge somewhere in that land. Did you like my story, oh great one?" I replied, "So very much Györköny and I really want to thank your brothers for saving me and my sisters. I shall forever love them." Györköny bowed and said, "It was and always will be our honor to serve you. We know you have a long rich history with your Oakley and have courts to protect the animals and birds. Your kingdom is so great." I then told her, "As the wolves are your brothers, you are my sisters, and as I find more Oakley tribes that have lost their spirits I shall call upon your spirits when your red man no longer lives freely. Györköny then stood up with her brothers and said, "Thank you for your kindness oh great one" and they all vanished. Then another beautiful Indian spirit appeared. She told me her name was Pawnee. She started by saying, "I have seen the beauty of your white horse that you will ride when returning to your throne. I can feel his spirit with my brothers and sisters my horses. She then told me her story how she is now the horse spirit after I became a horse and then ascended to be the horse spirits. I was the lucky one as others have tried and died instead." She began, "A chief had many horses, and among them a stallion which his wife myself often rode. The stallion and I became enamored of each other and cohabited. I grew careless of my household duties and always wanted to look after the horses. When the people moved camp, and the horses were brought in, it was noticed that the stallion made right for me and sniffed about me as stallions do with mares. After this, I was watching. When my husband learned the truth, he shot the stallion. I cried and went not go to bed. At daybreak I was gone, no one knew where. About a year after this, it was discovered that I had gone off with some wild horses. One day when the people were traveling over a large open place, they saw a band of horses, and I among them. I had partly changed into a horse. My private hair had grown so long that it resembled a tail. I also had much hair on my body, and the hair of my head had grown to resemble a horse's mane. My arms and legs had also changed considerably; but my face was still human, and bore some resemblance to my original self. The chief sent some young men to chase me. All the wild horses ran away, but I could not run so fast as they, and was run down and lassoed. I was brought into my husband's lodge; and the people watched me for some time, trying to tame me, but I continued to act and whinny as a horse. At last, they let me free. The following year they saw me again. I had become almost entirely horse, and had a colt by my side. I had many children afterwards. There was a village, and the men decided to go on a warpath. Therefore, these men started, and they journeyed for several days to the south. They came to a thickly wooded country. They found wild horses, and among them was one of my spotted ponies. One man caught the spotted pony and took care of it. He took it home, and instructed his wife Skide to look after it, as if it were their chiefs. This Skide did, and, further, she liked the horse very much. She took it where there was good grass. In the winter time she cut young cottonwood shoots for it, so that the horse was always fat. In the night, if it was stormy, she pulled a lot of dry grass, and when she put the blanket over the horse and tied it up, she stuffed the grass under the blanket, so the horse never got cold. It was always fine and sleek. One summer evening she went to where she had tied the horse, and she met a fine-looking man, who had on a buffalo robe with a spotted horse pictured on it. She liked him; he smelt finely. She followed him until they came to where the horse had been, and the man said, "You went with me. It is I who was a horse." She was glad, for she liked the horse. For several years, they were together, and the woman gave birth, and it was a spotted pony. When the pony was born, the Skide found she had a tail like that of a horse. She also had long hair. When the colt sucked, the woman stood up. For several years they roamed about, and had more ponies, all spotted. At home, the man mourned for his lost wife. He could not figure out why she should go off. People went on a hunt many years afterward, and they came across these spotted ponies. People did not care to attack them, for among them was a strange looking animal. Nevertheless, as they came across them now and then, they decided to catch them. They were difficult to catch, but at last, they caught them, all but the woman, because she could run fast; however, when they caught her children she gives in, and was apprehended. People said, "This is the woman who was lost." In addition, some said, "No, it is not." Her husband was sent for, and he recognized her. He took his bow and arrows out and shot her dead, for he did not like to see her with the horse's tail. The other spotted ponies were kept, and as they increased, they were spotted. So the people had many spotted ponies." I told her, "Oh, I love these stories, as I sit here my giant winged white horse is racing through my mind as is my beautiful white ground horse who loves to play in the sea. Thanks for bringing those memories back to me." Pawnee then, as she said now on her knees to me, "My lord, I shall tell you my best horse story. The Sun God, HaJohano, starts each morning from his home in the east and rides across the skies to his home in the west." I then remembered one of my revealers who had a similar task. She continued, "He carries with him his shining gold disk, the sun. He has five horses, a horse of turquoise, one of white shell like yours, one of pearly shell, one of red shell, and one of coal. The skies are blue and the weather is fair, the Sun God rides his horse of turquoise, or the one of white shell, or the one of pearl shells. However, when the heavens are dark with storm, he mounts the red horse or the horse of coal. Beneath the hoofs of the horses are spread precious hides of all kinds and beautiful blankets, carefully woven and richly decorated. In the days gone by, the Dine (Navajo) wove rich blankets, first alleged discovered in the home of the Sun God. He lets his horses graze on flower blossoms, and drink from mingled waters. These are holy waters of all kinds; spring water, snow water, hail water, water from the four corners of the world. The Dine (Navajo) uses such waters in their ceremonies. When any horse of the Sun God trots or runs, he raises not dust. It is glittering grains of minerals, such as are used in religious ceremonies. When a horse rolls and shakes himself, shining grains of sand fly from him. When he runs, not dust, but the sacred pollen offered to the Sun God is all about him. Then he looks like a mist. The Dine (Navajo) says that the mist on the horizon is the pollen that has been offered to the gods. A Navaho man sings about the horses of the Sun God in order that he, too, may have beautiful horses. Standing among his herd, he scatters holy pollen and sings this song for the blessing and the protection of his animals:

How joyous his neigh!
Lo, the Turquoise Horse of HaJohano,
How jubilant his neigh,
There on precious furs outspread, stands he,
How exultant his neigh,
There for blended waters holy, he drinks,
How festive his neigh,
There in the mist of sanctified pollen
hidden, all hidden him,
How jolly his neigh,
These his offspring may grow and flourish evermore,
How merry his neigh!"

I told Pawnee, "That tale is also so wonderful. Someday when I return to my throne and your Indians no longer need you, I shall invite you to care for my horses. My spirits tell me that my horse looks for me every day. The winged one stands ready to protect me if I need to be protected as I enter. He is so protective of me. He forces all to bow except my trinity. They also tell me my other might land White horse races around the beaches every day to see if I have returned. I hope you will be able to enjoy them and any horses you wish to bring in my throne." Pawnee, still on her knees now put her face to the ground and with tears and hair washed my dry feet. She said to me, "I pray to be your servant for eternity." I told her, "My humble child, I shall answer that prayer for you. Now go in peace." Then there came another beautiful Indian female spirit. She told me her name, "I am the one called Fulókércs and I shall now tell you my story oh mighty one. In the beginning of time, people lived in harmony with the land. They lived in harmony with their brothers and sisters, the plants, trees, animals, insects, snakes, the fish and the birds. The people realized that the plants and animals were of spirit, and were placed here on Mother Earth to help them. The people were grateful for the help of the animals, the plants the trees and for they wanted to honor them. One day they heard a beautiful song from a bird, and they became aware how this tiny creature made them feel. They wanted to sing in return, to make the spirit of the animals feel as they did when they heard the songs of the birds. Therefore, they asked for songs from the spirits to sing to their brothers and sisters, the animals, plants, fish. Songs came to the people, songs to be sung in the spirit of the eagle, the spirit of the tree, the spirit of the water—songs for all of their relations. One day Ching Woo was in the forest and he heard one of these songs being sung by the people. The song was being sung in his honor, and their voices were carried by the wind into the forest. When Ching Woo heard this beautiful song, he felt honored and respected. He went to the edge of a clearing in the forest, and saw that the people were in ceremony. As he watched and listened, he saw the people making offerings to his spirit, and he heard the kind words that the people spoke of him. They referred to him as a Brother. Then he heard the people ask him for medicines help them. At that moment, Ching Woo realized that he must make a journey for the people and bring back medicines for them. All summer long, he ate and ate, preparing for his task. Finally, when autumn came, he knew it was time. He sought out a lodge where his physical form would be safe while his spirit travelled. As he approached his lodge, he looked back on the world, as he knew he would be gone for several moons. Finally, with the words "All My Relations," he entered his lodge. Therefore, the spirit of Ching Woo began its pursuit into the spirit world. As he journeyed, he collected the medicines, which the people had asked for. He sat in council with the spirits of the Plant people and requested from them the medicines for the people. The plants agreed to give their medicines, as long as Ching Woo would cultivate and fertilize the land for them, so that they would continue to come back year after year. Ching Woo agreed to do this. Finally, after many moons, Ching Woo's journey was ending. He wanted to let the people know that he would soon be returning, so his spirit found me in our Bear Clan, as I was praying in the sweat lodge. Ching Woo came to me and spoke to me, "From this day forward, you will be known as Ching Wooiskw, the Bear Woman. I have a request for you. I am soon returning to my physical form, as I have completed my spiritual journey. Would you be as kind as to prepare a Feast for me, as I am weak?" I knew that when a spirit requested something from a human it was to be done. I listened to Ching Woo's request as to how the Feast would be prepared and what ceremonies would be involved, then I took the request of the people. I told them of my vision in the lodge, and shared with the people the details of Ching Woo's request. The people were happy and instantaneously began arrangements for the Feast. I spoke about the berries, which Ching Woo asked for. I said that Ching Woo wanted the berries that he feasted on throughout the year, and he wanted to honor the spirit of the plants, which provided him this food, as they also provided the food for the people. Therefore, it was. People brought berries, which were dried and stored over the winter. Strawberries, which were the first berry in the spring, blueberries, fruit of summer, blackberries from the fall, and cranberries, gathered in early winter. Then, the men went out to their barrages 'and gathered fish to be included in the Feast. Four days after the Bear Spirit spoke to me the appointed day for the Feast of the Bear arrived. The berries, the fish, and more food were all made by myself. As the people sit in a Sacred Circle, the ceremony began with the lighting of the Sacred Pipe, and as the pipe was shared with the people, a story was told. The story told of why we must always honor the Bear Spirit. In the fall of the year we honor him for his long fast, and the journey he is about to make in the spirit world for medicines for the people. In the spring, we honor the Bear for the medicines he brings back from his long journey. In both ceremonies, a woman of the Bear Clan prepares the Feast of the Bear, and in both ceremonies, a song is sung to honor mine. Therefore, it continues to this day. Ching Woo tills and fertilizes the ground to help plants grow, and during the long cold winter, he journeys to the spirit realm to seek medicines for the people. And each year, in the fall and the spring, native people gather together for a feast in his honor." As she prepared to sally forth, I had to give her a hug, as I remembered the great warmth that a bear can give in the cold parts of the year when they travel with you. I have some planets, which have enter continents forbear to room with plenty of fish, ground insects, and berries. I now walked towards Fulókércs, pet the hair on her head and the bear beside, and said, "I so much enjoyed your story. I do hope that you will come and help me with my bears when the red man no longer needs your medicine." She told me, "I will serve you and you may call upon me if you need anything that I can do for you. My sister shall now come to tell you her story, as we are so much related. She is called Kelphit and she is now arriving. I shall depart as I wait to serve your throne." Now Kelphit arrived and on her knees saying, "Oh mighty one, I am called Kelphit the spirit of autumn and I wish to tell my story of how my sister, Fulókércs brought me into being." I told her, "Kelphit, I eagerly await your story." Kelphit began by saying, "There were four hunters who were brothers. No hunters were as good as they were at following a trail. They never gave up once they began tracking their quarry. One day, in the moon when the cold nights return, an urgent message came to the village of the four hunters. A great bear, one so large and powerful that many thought it must be some manner of monster, had appeared. The people of the village whose hunting grounds the monster had invaded were afraid. The children no longer went out to play in the woods. The long houses of the village were guarded each night by men with weapons that stood by the entrances. Each morning, when the people went outside, they found the huge tracks of the bear in the midst of their village. They knew that soon it would become even bolder. Picking up their spears and calling to their small dog, the four hunters set forth for that village, which was not far away. As they came closer, they noticed how quiet the woods were. There were no signs of rabbits or deer and even the birds were silent. On a great pine tree, they found the scars where the great bear had reared up on hind legs and made deep scratches to mark its territory. The tallest of the brothers tried to touch the highest of the scratch marks with the tip of his spear. "It is as the people feared," the first brother said. "This one we are to hunt is Püspökladányi, a monster bear." "But what about the magic that the Püspökladányi has?" said the second brother. The first brother shook his head. "That magic will do it no good if we find its track." "That's so," said the third brother. "I have always heard that from the old people. Those creatures can only chase a hunter who has not yet found its trail. When you find the track of the Püspökladányi and begin to chase it, then it must run from you." "Brothers," said the fourth hunter who was the fattest and laziest, "did we bring along enough food to eat? It may take a long time to catch this big bear. I'm feeling hungry." Before long, the four hunters and their small dog reached the village. It was a sad sight to see. There was no fire burning in the center of the village and the doors of all the long houses were closed. Grim men stood on guard with clubs and spears and there was no game hung from the racks or skins stretched for tanning. The people looked hungry. The elder sachem of the village came out and the tallest of the four hunters spoke to him. "Uncle," the hunter said, "we have come to help you get rid of the monster." Then the fattest and laziest of the four brothers spoke. "Uncle," he said, "is there some food we can eat? Can we find a place to rest before we start chasing this big bear? I'm tired." The first hunter shook his head and smiled. "My brother is only joking, Uncle." he said. "We are going now to pick up the monster bear's trail." "I am not sure you can do that, Nephews," the elder sachem said. "Though we find tracks closer and closer to the doors of our lodges each morning, whenever we try to follow those tracks they disappear." The second hunter knelt down and patted the head of their small dog. "Uncle," he said, that is because they do not have a dog such as ours." He pointed to the two black circles above the eyes of the small dog. "Four-Eyes can see any tracks, even those many days old." "May Creator's protection is being with you," said the elder sachem. "Do not worry. Uncle," said the third hunter. "Once we are on a trail we never stop following until we've finished our hunt." "That's why I think we should have something to eat first," said the fourth hunter, but his brothers did not listen. They nodded to the elder sachem and began to leave. Heaving his sigh, the fattest, and laziest of the brothers, lifted up his long spear and trudged after them. They walked, following their little dog. It kept lifting up its head, as if to look around with its four eyes. The trail was not easy to find. "Brothers," the fattest and laziest hunter complained, "Don't you think we should rest. We've been walking a long time." However, his brothers paid no attention to him. Though they could see no tracks, they could feel the presence of the Püspökladányi. They knew that if they did not soon find its trail, it would make its way behind them. Then they would be the hunted ones. The fattest and laziest brother took out his pemmican pouch. At least he could eat while they walked along. He opened the pouch and shook out the food he had prepared so carefully by pounding together strips of meat and berries with maple sugar and then drying them in the sun. Instead of pemmican, pale squirming things fell out into his hands. The magic of the Püspökladányi had changed the food into worms. "Brothers," the fattest and laziest of the hunters shouted, "Let's hurry up and catch that big bear! Look what it did to my pemmican. Now I'm getting angry." Meanwhile, like a pale giant shadow, the Püspökladányi was moving through the trees close to the hunters. Its mouth was open as it watched them and its huge teeth shone, its eyes flashed red. Soon it would be behind them and on their trail. Just then, though, the little dog lifted its head and yelped. "Eh-heh!" the first brother called. "Four-Eyes has found the trail," shouted the second brother. "We have the track of the Püspökladányi," said the third brother. "Big Bear," the fattest and laziest one yelled, "we are after you, now!" Fear filled the heart of the great bear for the first time and it began to run. As it broke from the cover of the pines, the four hunters saw it, a gigantic white shape, as pale as to look as if almost freely exposed. With loud hunting cries, they began to run after it. The great bear's strides were long and it ran more swiftly than a deer. The four hunters and their little dog were swift also though and they did not fall behind. The trail led through the swamps and the thickets. It was easy to read, for the bear pushed everything aside as it ran, even knocking down big trees. On and on they ran, over hills and through valleys. They came to the slope of a mountain and followed the trail higher and higher, every now and then catching a glimpse of their quarry over the next rise. Now though the lazy hunter was getting tired of running. He pretended to fall and twist his ankle. "Brothers," he called, "I have sprained my ankle. You must carry me." Therefore, his three brothers did as he asked, two of them carrying him by turns while the third hunter carried his spear. They ran more slowly now because of their heavy load, but they were not falling any further behind. The day had turned now into night, yet they could still see the white shape of the great bear ahead of them. They were at the top of the mountain now and the ground beneath them was very dark as they ran across it. The bear was tiring, but so were they. It was not easy to carry their fat and lazy brother. The little dog, Four-Eyes, was close behind the great bear, nipping at its tail as it ran. "Brothers," said the fattest and laziest one. "Put me down now. I think my leg has gotten better." The brothers did as he asked. Fresh and rested, the fattest and laziest one grabbed his spear and dashed ahead of the others. Just as the great bear turned to bite at the little dog, the fattest and laziest hunter leveled his spear and thrust it into the heart of the Püspökladányi. The monster bear fell dead. By the time the other brothers caught up, the fattest and laziest hunter had already built a fire and was cutting up the big bear. "Come on, brothers," he said. "Let's eat. All this running has made me hungry!" Hence, they cooked the meat of the great bear and its fat sizzled as it dripped from their fire. They ate until even the fattest and laziest one was satisfied and leaned back in contentment. Just then, though, the first hunter looked down at his feet. "Brothers," he exclaimed, "look below us!" The four hunters looked down. Below them were thousands of small sparkling lights in the darkness, which they realized, was all around them. "We aren't on a mountain top at all," said the third brother. "We are up in the sky." Likewise, it was so. The great bear had indeed been magical. Its feet had taken it high above the Earth as it tried to escape the four hunters. However, their determination not to give up the chase had carried them up that strange trail. Just then their little dog yipped twice. "The great bear!" said the second hunter. "Look!" The hunters looked. There, where they had piled the bones of their feast the Great Bear was coming back to life and rising to its feet. As they watched, it began to run again, the small dog close on its heels. "Follow me," shouted the first brother. Grabbing up their spears, the four hunters again began to chase the great bear across the skies. Therefore, it was, the old people say, and so it still is. Each autumn the hunters chase the great bear across the skies and kill it. Then, as they cut it up for their meal, the blood falls down from the heavens and colors the leaves of the maple trees scarlet. They cook the bear and the fat dripping from their fires turns the grass white. If you look carefully into the skies as the seasons change, you can read that story. The great bear is the square shaped that some call the bowl of the Big Dipper. The hunters and their small dog (which you can just barely see) are close behind, the dipper's handle. When autumn comes and that constellation turns upside down, the old people say. "Ah, the lazy hunter has killed the bear." However, as the moons pass and the sky moves once more towards spring, the bear slowly rises back on its feet and the chase begins again. That is how I came to be. Now all things living must pass through me. Before they had only summer and winter, now they have me to prepare their harvests and the things they need for she that follows me, the winter spirit." I thanked the autumn spirit and of course gave the same invitations as I did for the others. The next spirit told me she was the winter spirit and that many did not like her, however she began her story as a punishment for complaining people, and is as follows, "At one time there was only warm weather, and there was never any snow or ice. In spite of this, the people complained about their condition. Sometimes they grumbled about the heat, other times they blamed the Creator for sending rain. After listening to their dissatisfied comments for many generations, the Creator let the sun travel further and further away from the villages. The days grew shorter and colder. Even though they wore extra clothing and added, heavy bark and thick animal, skins to the covering of their homes for protection many people died from the extreme cold. In fear, the people called upon the Great Spirit to send the sun back to warm them again. In mercy and forgiveness, Csongrádi-oo directed the sun to return, but each year there would be a season of short days and cold weather to remind the people of their ungrateful complaining. From that time, we have been taught to offer thanks for every beautiful day regardless of the weather. Poisonous plants grew from the graves of the rebellious people who had died during the extreme cold as a further reminder of our dependence upon Csongrádi-oo to provide for us according to His wisdom rather than to pacify selfish demands." I thanked her for her story and asked if I could now return to my disciples, as the sun spirit was getting ready to be dragged across the Earth. I felt bad in that now I was somewhat overwhelmed as when you get too much of a good thing the tastes turns from delicious to bitter. I did not even ask for winter spirit's name. Later, I would have one of my spirits render her the appropriate divine protocols. She now told me that the elders wanted to say goodbye. I have always respected my elders although few now can claim to be older than me. So I with a false expression of joy agreed to the request. Next appearing before me were four giant chiefs who were almost one with the wind as they floated over a small Indian village. I could see a brave on his horse worshipping them. I could also see highlighted by the moon a wolf rendering his respects. They now turned to look at me and said, "We hope you have enjoyed our limited introduction, for we have thousands of spirits who control all things who wished to speak with you. We have seen how you favorably treat our Oakley brothers who live in your throne. We know you still have your journey before you and if you need our help call upon the wind and the spirit of the wind will tell us. We wish you go in peace as do we." They all vanished as I had now fallen deep to sleep to be awaken by a terrified Julia. Is not this the way all things happen. So many nights I have wakened early to be bored or lonely while, my sisters snored, yet today I am tired and sleepy and wakened up. Oh well, they are my loves so I must care for their needs.

I awoke and said to Julia, "What is wrong my lovely sister?" She said, "Please come, save Siusan, for some disease took away her beauty." As I approached one of my favorite sisters, she was standing in the darkness of some trees that were hiding the morning sun. As I looked upon her I said, "So, you have decided not to hide your great beauty?" Siusan fell to her knees and said, "Oh master, please forgive me for I feared if you saw the real me and not the beauty you loved you would hate me." I said, "Oh Siusan, did you not know that my love is with your spirit and that the flesh is only a toy to play with or to hide our soul. Did you not wonder that when you died as a child and returned as a big girl that your true beauty was once again hidden?" Siusan, now crying and holding my feet as her warm tears flowed down my legs said, "Oh master, I thought that it was to hide your shame in me, and that you needed to find a reason to cast me aside." I now fell down to my knees and hugged her with both of my arms as Julia and the other sisters now stood in shock and told my lovely sister, "I chose you because of your great Harvey beauty. I once had a Harvey people, yet her sister tribes destroyed all of them. I have so long searched for another Harvey. I shall never cast you aside as I am white and you are blue, we have the same blood for you are Blood of Our Blood. From now on you shall sleep on my left and Ruth to your left and Bács-Kiskun to my right and Fejér to her right. As I walk, you too always walk beside me. If I must chain you to me, I shall." I now turned to my sisters and said, "Today you all shall know my secret. My spirits remembered a commandment I gave them long ago to find me a Harvey. The Harvey lived on my New Venus, yet I was so busy fighting off evil demons as my planet was raging with evil. The sister tribes of the Harvey killed all of them, sparing none. I have searched for so long and then one night I had a vision that told me a concealed Harvey lived in England. They found us and then discovered that a love could manifest itself with Joy and Richard, so we prepared their introductions. You know the rest of our story. That which I lost is found and I shall not lose it again. I hope that you will love her as I do." At this time, my sisters regained their peace and ran to hug their first Harvey. Bács-Kiskun now came up to me and asked, "Oh great master, why do you wish for me to sleep to your right an honor I have yet to earn." I answered her, "Bács-Kiskun, you shall do great things for our throne and in that you have earned it. I must find you a personal sister so that all in my group has personal sisters." She had now fallen to her knees and thanked me. I bent over, kissed her head, and said once again, "My love for you is so great and I hope you help me with Siusan." Bács-Kiskun answered, "Oh yes, my goddess, with all my heart and soul." I now walked over to Filkeháza who was with her two sons. I asked her if she knew Bács-Kiskun was going to go with us and if she wanted to join us. Filkeháza declined the offer saying, "I have too long been parted from my sons. I wish now to make them a nice home and be their mother till my death." I told her, "Filkeháza, you shall have a fine strong warrior for a husband and you will have a nice teepee filled with much food and animal skins. Your two sons, plus I shall give unto you another six and they shall grow strong and healthy, and give fine squaws to bear them forth many children. In this realm when you pass over to death, all your memories vanish. You shall then be given the memory of how you saved us. And I shall take you to my throne where you will be loved for eternity and live in a mighty mansion." Filkeháza said to me, "You are truly a goddess of love and when I cross over after receiving all the gifts you have given me, I shall serve you for eternity." As I kissed her forehead I told her, I shall also serve with you my child." Her sons were beside a nearby tree playing, and when they saw their mother kneeling before me as they said, "Mother, who is that in which you bow before." She told them, "She is the mother of all things." They then bowed beside her. I then said to her sons, "You are blessed because you believed without seeing, thus now you shall see." As I moved, my hands a nice white horse appeared and I jumped on the back of it and told Filkeháza, "I shall soon return." I then looked up and said, "Thank you Pawnee." We could feel a nice wind blow by us as my horse looked back as to also say, "Thanks." I then said, "Do you wish to ride with me?" She then appeared on a spotted horse and slowly manifested herself into flesh riding her horse towards me giving me a kiss and said, "Let me show you some wonderful beautiful lands. We now rode off holding hands as I felt such a peace. This was the closest I have felt to be back on my throne. It has been one of my happiest times since being back on Earth. I did this activity so much in my holy of holies, as my spirit would work on all my divine duties, my flesh suit would enjoy the peace and warmth of being one with my friend in my horses. They were always so loyal, gentle, and willing to do, as I wanted. If I wanted to go to a place, they too would go to that place. No threats or punishments needed just some sugar, a little corn, and some high grass to graze. No big houses or fancy clothing, just a nice warm petting and they were so satisfied. As we rode, she told me more about herself and the joys she had as being one with her horses. I thought it is strange now that I knew more about Pawnee than I did about Julia and Bács-Kiskun; however, we had time on our side. Back at the camp Filkeháza's son were now very excited, for today they finally meet Pawnee. All Indian children were taught about Pawnee, and how if they were cruel to the horses, she will come after them. Filkeháza knew now that their lives have been changed for the better, for they would believe in the other spirits and grow up serving them and their mother Earth in the process. As we were returning to the village Pawnee stopped me and told me, "The spirits had given her a vision last night. In my vision, they told me that you had one more mission before returning to your throne. Your throne wants you to pass one challenge before bringing a stronger and richer you back to your throne. One more servant so much needs your love. You can deny the mission and that servant will suffer greatly or accept the mission in the name of love and willingness to shed your blood." I looked at Pawnee and asked, "If I go, who will care for my sisters?" Pawnee said, "The elders will protect and provide for them and also teach them many legends. You will return instantaneous back to us, however your mission will require much time." I said to Pawnee, "How can I set on a throne while one suffers because of me, is it not the one on the throne to suffer so others may not suffer? I shall go and give my blood." Pawnee got off her horse as we were now in our small opening for our camp. She lifted up her arms to guide me down safely, and then fell to her knees and cried out, "You are truly the goddess of love and mercy." Then she and her horse vanished. I then slowly walked away as my horse vanished. Filkeháza's sons loved this, as their amazement level would now reach new levels. I then called for my sisters to join me. When they all surrounded me, I started talking to them, "I must now leave you before we can all ascend to my throne. The elder gods of my universe need me to suffer one more mission before I go home." Fejér then asked, "Will you be safe my master and if not may I come to suffer for you?" Then all my disciples begged to go and suffer in my place. I could only hug them and let my tears soak into their warm bodies as a kissed them and told each how much I loved them. After a few minutes, I got up and told them, "I can survive great sufferings, however your spirits are still so young. I do promise you that I shall return. Now they gave me some more hugs and kisses. Oh, their kisses and hugs felt like sleeping in my holy of holies. They were I and I was they. I knew I would have to have the Indian spirits to hold them back or they would find a way to find me. They had great powers they did not yet know about. We finished our goodbyes as even Filkeháza and her sons were in our circle. I so much understand why she wants to give her life to them. Then my journey began and ouch, this one is not going to be fun. Immediately I was in a place where the spirits were occupying deformed bodies mingled into one deranged horizontal rainbow. My spirit was now being stretched by a mighty force and thousands of needled being driven into me like bullets. I can see this is going to be one of those warped suffering experiences to satisfy some divine thing with a deranged mind. I marvel how loyalty is tested by the degree of suffering. The last thing I want is for my sisters suffer for me. That is too much pain for me. That is one part of the divine bull crap, which I do approve. The peace I have now is that someone will get to cheat some divinity of the thrills of making someone suffer. Darn, those needles continue to sting as they go out after being driven in. I now wonder if any part of me had not been hit, ouch that piece of crap just got my eyes. Ha, ha, now they are not getting to see me trying to avoid their stings of death. I will just lie still like a floor that they are on stomping the daylights out of me. At least it so far is not as bad as the lake of fire I lived in for 1,000 years.

I could now feel myself being pulled into a painful female body that was in chains. The sun was now coming up to usher in a hot summer day in Rome as a simple cart, pulled by horses, freely exposed its way along the streets, which were slowly coming to life. I could tell this was Rome, the head of an Empire, which at its top was the antichrist. This city would take the Christian Faith Maria and fill it with pagan rituals that would destroy so many lives throughout history. They did more to keep the demons as helpless victims than even Samuel could have hoped to do. Our cart had chained along both sides slaves that are on their way to the market to be sold. I looked over and saw a woman the guards all called Drusilla who looked accordingly miserable as we were pulled along the road. She wondered how her life had come to this point. Her father and mother had both died, murdered by their more aristocratic owner who had ordered both of them to be killed when he had found that his adulterous mistress had become pregnant with the bastard children of her slave lover rather than his. The owner, a member of the Senate, had ordered both of them to be crucified and of the twin girls to be sold as soon as they could walk. Since then Drusilla and I had known only the life of a slave. I was her twin sister named Auriel. Our minds and memories had been molded together. I was hit with sixteen years of pain and misery in one shot. So many memories of our struggles, challenges, heartbreaks, lost friends, mountains, valleys, beatings, a collection of misery that my mind was constantly fighting to keep in my unconsciousness. I believe all this transmitted misery in me, as these memories would trickle out, as a leak in a large dam. It was so hard for me to know my past, as I knew my age, and remembered bits and pieces of my life. The one thing I do know is that there is one foundation, which I have stood beside my entire life. A force that has soaked my soul with her spilt blood and that piece of me is called Drusilla. As I continue my life under Drusilla's, umbrella, stabbed so many times that it barely slows the flooding rains of pain, as we both live on the edge of life. Now when she hurt so did I, thus lucky me got a double dose. We were both Hyrum and lucky us, as we had some of 'blessed' flesh suits, though scared and marred, the Romans always insured they did not harm the front portion of their female's bodies, much the same, as they would not mar the visible parts of their horses, for to do so reduced the value of their livestock. Such actions were the same destroying their wealth, as their accumulated value determined their social rank. As concerning female stock, they used smaller whips and beat closer to them thus ripping their backs striking with more accuracy and a concentrated area. When we were sixteen we had been sold and become the concubine of another senator and when we had failed to please him sexually, he had had us sold. As property, when we were owned we were expected to outperform all previous seductions, and if we were mediocre, they would allow the male slaves to rape us. Thus, we performed as hard as we could; however, there are those times when a greater performer had performed before us. Since our performances were totally submission and we appeared trustworthy, our reward was to be sold. Our master would go into extremes promoting our talents in order to receive higher financial rewards. We had no choice but to struggle hard to get a higher price, since if a new master paid more, we would be treated better. Drusilla remembered the time she had lost her virginity, not slowly and tenderly with a man she loved but in a swift, violent coupling, without meaning or love which had been little more than a rape. I was not so lucky, for me a group of about twenty soldiers returning from the long ship voyage from Egypt back to Rome saw me and having lusted after the Hyrum in Egypt that they could not touch decided to make up for lost time. They raped and beat me for three days. The only reason they left was the danger is that all my blood might make their uniforms dirty, for it was bad to have slave blood on a uniform in Rome. I could feel all that now. My memories of my earliest life on Earth were now so distant memories, as I only remember trees and big deep holes. I cannot see how those memories could be true, since everyone I talk to enlighten me that such things are impossible and may be a sign of my insanity departing me. Thus, I attribute them to having been beaten or starved one too many times. I had only one love, and I have only loved one my complete life, every second that I can ever remember Drusilla was with me. I know I had suffered, yet she had suffered more, many times behaving as a wild animal to protect me, and of course being duly punished as our master would avoid me, not wanting to deal with Drusilla again. Inside me, I could feel the love of Drusilla. She had cared for me so much in my life, so often offering up herself so these Roman monsters would ignore me. I knew that Drusilla longed for a more meaningful life for us where she could stop the dull drudgery of slavery and fear of being nothing more than the sexual plaything of her master and mistress whoever desired the sexual love of a man or women. She often fed me off to the mistress and she suffered with the master since the master was so much more painful and sadistic. We had now reached the age of twenty. Our bodies would have been the envy of Sabina and when she finds this in my memories, I will see her blessings bouncing through our holy of holies. We also had nice developed and muscular bodies after years of toiling and carrying heavy goods. The Romans considered their female slaves to be working alongside the males when not seducing their masters. These seductions were considered special breaks for the female slaves. All that work was now cast in my spirit. Our breasts were well formed with large nipples, which may sadly be the only reason we have not been fed to the dogs as of yet. Drusilla had large brown eyes and long dark hair smooth, which flowed down her back when it was not tied in place. Her hair was the thing that brought her pride, as she demanded mine resembled hers. We were so surprised that her past owners had not cut off our hair, so that their wives could have wigs made out from it. She always kept my hair in piggy tales so the masters could not pull on it and would make it loose and free when I was with the mistress since she liked it when my heart was buried in the service of their pleasures. For now, we were to be sold again, so we had look well because spiritual slavery was so much better than working in slave camps where death knocked on all doors. With spiritual slavery, if you pleased the master and mistress you would get lighter duties that the other slaves and some rewards if you pleased their guests. Our cart came to a halt and the smell of fruit and manure, synonymous with the market, rose in Drusilla's nostrils. She had been here before and knew that she would again in time. Our time as slaves had made Drusilla rebellious, wild, and untamed yet for me I knew the game. Look pretty and kiss Drusilla and that always activated the animal lust in them, a lust that had to be satisfied if we were to live another day. In the past, we had turned this to our advantage. Drusilla once escaped, but recaptured after a few days. When she had been returned to her master, he had extracted from her a pitiless revenge. In front of all the other slaves, he tore her clothing from her body and left Drusilla freely exposed, leaving no mysteries for one to see. The master had then bound her arms and legs, and left her tied up at the front gate, inviting any passing soldiers of the legions to do whatever they wanted with her. They quickly learned that if they punished me with her she turn to a wild animal. If that failed or she sensed it would not prevail, she would get on her knees begging them to spare me because I was innocent. The smell of both of us tied freely exposed at the gate made many soldiers leave with their sexual perversions satisfied. Lucky for us they carried some animal fat in one of their pouches. This would help them get a big shot of calories and helped them when they had anal sex with slaves and animals. That kept us from having our rectum scared with pain for a long time, or actually damaged worse, since so many Romans enjoyed fearing and terror they created in the flesh they were destroying. I knew one thing, that if there were a God he would destroy these people and never let their name associated with him. That thing we knew, for so many souls were up their somewhere demanding revenge. We wonder how such if great God could ignore these, yet we had to face reality. The gods, who had to be mighty as was their statues, only favored the real people, that being the Romans. Back to our punishment, for some strange reason the soldiers believed in the buddy system with slave girls. One would place their evil male privates in our private while the other greased his male privates with animal fat and cam in the back door, as they would say. For some reason they treated us as a special treat since few slaves came from Africa and actually resembled Cleopatra. This worked to our disadvantage as Cleopatra was viewed by many as the whore of the Caesars. Thus, they expected better and more from our frail torn bodies. Most of the soldiers came from the barbarians in Europe and their conquered lands. Nevertheless, this was one of the longest nights of our lives on the other hand when the morning had come; we were released and had not been beaten. The slaves had found some fresh clothes for us and after that day, we had kept her thoughts about escaping to ourselves for my sake. Drusilla looked about her at the bustles of the market place. Carts of fruit, vegetables, and other goods were being unloaded. There were also several more cartloads of slaves, all looking as unhappy and miserable as we do. The wagon master tied his horse and walked to the back of the cart. "We are here, now move!" Slowly the three other slaves, one man, and two women stood, their chains chiming and began to walk to the back of the cart. Drusilla was the last and she could feel the chains round her wrists and feet chaffing against her skin. The others began to walk but the wagon master, an unpleasant, sweaty man whom she did not know by name but had always feared pulled Drusilla closest to his sweaty body. Drusilla shivered, feeling his rough hands against the bear arm skin of the arms. He then pushed her against a pillar. "Your ex-master has something special planned for you, Drusilla." The wagon master slipped his hand down inside her tunica and grabbed her bosom, pinching her nipples callous. Drusilla gasped in surprise and anger as she felt his rough hands groping and fumbling for her privates. Although she was a slave, she did take kindly to having her breasts groped by this sweaty ox. Drusilla tried to back away from the man but she was trapped by the pillar. "The fun I could have with you!" grunted the sweating man as his hand explored further inside Drusilla's tunica. She tried to back away further, trying to avoid the feeling of his palms against her breast but the pillar was immovable, and she just whimpered as the man pawed away at her. Drusilla could not believe this grunting imbecile, was raping her there and then. She felt her nipple grow hard as his hand squeezed further and she gasped, half in a mixture of fear and surprise and the other half in anger at both herself for getting aroused by the pain, the only thing her life had ever shared with her, and at this unknown man who was invading her most private area. The man pushed aside the thin material, exposing her nipple. Drusilla looked around wildly, expecting someone at least to notice what the man was doing but everyone was either too engrossed in his or her work or ignoring what was going on. Something like this was not regular occurrence in the market where slaves were concerned. They were the lowest form of citizen and could be used and abused by anyone who saw fit. The man bent his head down and clamped his teeth around her exposed dug. Drusilla felt unexpected moistness that she had not felt before. Just as Drusilla thought he was going to rape her in full public view, the man was pulled away from her breast. Drusilla gasped in pain as the man's teeth grazed her breast. She saw her chance and brought her knee up swiftly, connecting with his hard groin. The man crumpled to the ground, roaring in pain and anger. He slammed Drusilla against the pillar, his hands looking for the edge of her tunic to rip away and leave her freely exposed for all to see. At that moment, a sword entered Drusilla's vision and her that it was handled by a young Roman legionnaire. "If you wish to go raping young slaves, whoremonger, I suggest you do it somewhere else," said the soldier. "I did not mean anything by it," whimpered the wagon master. "From what I saw you were going to rip off this slave's tunica and rape her against the pillar. Now get out of here before I turn you into a eunuch!" The wagon master jumped onto the back of his cart and rode away at great speed, the mocking laughter of slaves, citizens, and soldiers ringing in his ears. It would be a long time before he would dare show his face in Rome again. After checking that Drusilla's clothes were not damaged and that she appeared to be shaken but nothing more, the soldier ushered Drusilla inside the market. Drusilla had experienced worse in the past but she was grateful that she had escaped the encounter with nothing more than damaged pride and her breast groped, although she could soon be put on display in the slave market, and when at the market, all privates were examined, to insure the new master's satisfaction. Drusilla always wondered why the Romans have such strict laws with sex between the aristocrats yet wives either ignored or participated in the sex with slaves. Sex with slaves was their right as the master race, the race created by their gods, to kill beasts for food or even sport and to enjoy their slaves, who were created with the same body parts. However, even animals have the same parts, yet they cannot talk.

Drusilla reflected later, what a pleasure it had been to drive her knee into the wagon master's groin. Drusilla walked into a short tunnel and emerged to find herself with the other slaves, with me at her side in a small area partitioned off from the rest of the market. The one male and a female slave that had been with us a few minutes before had already been sold. The other female slave was sitting on the floor and looked up as Drusilla came in. "I hear you had some trouble from the wagon master?" whispered the woman. Drusilla looked the woman up and down and realized that this woman had not been in the cart with her. She must have come in from another entrance. She was dressed in the standard clothing of a slave, a simple rough tunica, tied at the waist with a belt and her hair cropped short as opposed to Drusilla who had her hair tied back. Drusilla realized for the first time how attractive this woman was and she was little older than she was. She could not be a slave as her body had no marks of being beaten, nor did she have the 'poor life look' and struggle and strife. Her breasts were a little smaller than Drusilla but she was still attractive although a little plain when compared to Drusilla. "What is your name?" asked Drusilla. "You don't need to know that," replied the woman, "What happened to you?" "The wagon master groped me . . . he . . . I don't know." said Drusilla, flustered that she did not know what to feel or say. "Let me guess, he pinched your breast and then tried to suck it and then tried to rape you in broad daylight," said the woman. "Yes." "He does that all the slaves. I think it's because his manhood is so small, he has to try it on with other women." The woman paused as the curtain parted and the auctioneer looked in and then closed it. "I've been taken before," said Drusilla, wanting to pour her whole heart out to this unknown woman. "I bet it could hardly have been called love making. It was probably at the hands of a previous master who stripped you and did whatever he felt like with you. Are you a mother?" "No!" said Drusilla, shocked at the forcefulness in her voice. Drusilla added, "However, I am bonded to my twin sister, as we are the only family we each have. She is the reason I live, her safety is my primary duty. "The woman stood and walked over to Drusilla and kissed her. It was the first time that Drusilla had been kissed by another woman and she found herself. At this time, she realized that this woman is not a slave, but a buyer and she appeared to be nice, thus she pretended to be deeply aroused by the passion that the woman was putting into it. She had always passed me off to the mistress, which the only thing I enjoyed was that the mistresses most times were more caring and gentle. I had, a couple of times been with mistresses who were evil, empty of love and only wanted to be superior. I usually gave these mistresses a good dose of, "Oh, how lovely is your hair and how did you find that vase on your counter, you must be a very wise, as well as extremely beautiful. Are you a secret goddess?" I would then pretend to worship her. That most times put them on the pedestal they were so craving to be. These trick had its rewards, as I would continue to be humble, they would have me beside them being also served great foods by their servants. The need to be superior and have power is a mountain that is difficult to rise above. This was the curse of the Romans. If Julius has 100 slaves then I must have 102, and the upward spiral leaves them on a beanstalk far above the clouds, and nowhere to go, but down. Our greatest joy in life was when we one of these Roman monsters come tumbling down.

This woman then came over and kissed me asking who I was. I told her, "I am Drusilla's twin sister." Drusilla was a little scared at the thought that at any moment the guard could come through the curtain and separate us forever. Drusilla would give anything to stop this happening. The woman's tongue explored deep inside Drusilla's mouth with more 'false Roman' loving passion than she could remember. Yet in this passion, Drusilla found it difficult to determine if it was false or true. Drusilla yearned to be freely exposed with this woman, exploring her freely exposed body and letting her body explode with a full and unstoppable sincere pleasure, as pleasure she had yet to experience. Just as Drusilla was wondering if this heaven would end, the woman broke the kiss and walked over to the curtain. It parted and the guard came in. "We agreed a price of 8000 denarii, guard." said the woman. "Yes." said the guard. "And how much for the dirty looking African beside her?" asked the woman. The guard said, "I will throw her in for 3000 denarii since she is so quiet." The woman bent down in front of Drusilla and picked up a small leather purse, giving Drusilla an opportunity to look down her cleavage. She was stunned by this view, as it was nothing new, for she was also woman. This was more, for she had shared this purposely, and had not forced her. The mystery of discovery was now driving her wild. The coins rattled in the purse. A few moments Drusilla blinked in the sunshine as the woman led us to another cart and we all climbed on the back. For a few moments, we were silent as they remembered the stolen moment they had shared. As the horse and tumbril left the city and headed into the countryside, jolting along the dirt tracks, the woman turned to Drusilla. "My name is Sallyarin. My lover who you are yet to meet is Juliuus. I know that you are called Drusilla and you and your sister are my new slaves. Do not worry you will be well treated. My lover wants a new mistress. And your new mistress wanted a new lover." "What does that mean?" asked Drusilla. "It means that you will do what we ask. It will not be onerous. In fact, later today, we will go a little further." Drusilla stared out of the cart, trying to make sense of how quickly her world had changed. Could this be as wonderful as it appeared? Not long ago she was being groped and half raped. Now she had been kissed by a beautiful woman and then . . . what? She did not know but she had a feeling that she would enjoy finding out. After all, they were not chained in this wagon, and only our new master was taking us to her home. She trusted us, thus we would trust her. Whatever happened with her new master, Drusilla realized that despite her new master and mistress would enjoy the experience, she herself would take some pleasure from it. Drusilla realized that she was about to embark on a journey of sensual exploration that was entirely new to her and previously reserved for me. This was different from her love for me, for she felt I belonged to her, and thus give me the upmost respect. Notwithstanding, this woman was our master, she was from the master race, yet appeared to get joy from appearing as a slave. As we continued our journey, a small band of Roman soldiers stopped us and demanded we tell them where we had escaped. They inspected us and prepared to bind us when her neighbor comes to our group to inspect what was happening. The neighbor demanded that our master be set free. The soldiers were shocked, yet this man stood tall and strong and had authority in his voice as would any aristocrat. Soon, we were on our way, as our mistress invited this neighbor and his family to have dinner with them within a few weeks. He accepted and we all went our separate ways. Drusilla's mind was preoccupied with thoughts of our new master. Instead of a rough, sexual groping and humping from dishonorable men, we would be treated as human beings for the first time in our lives. She asked me why I did not tell her the joy of being with another woman and I told her, "Being forced it is not joy but anguish." Drusilla looked across at her new mistress and looked more closely at her, allowing her gaze to travel down from her blonde hair, over Sallyarin's breasts to her long legs. Drusilla ached for the time her new mistress would be freely exposed before her. Moreover, she wanted to see her new master's husband and find out what kind of lover he would be for me. I had to be safe before she could surrender to the great explosions insider her. I told Drusilla, "My sister, we must first do as they wish in or we shall suffer worse. I do not wish to see the old wagon masters. Drusilla looked out over the fields of grapes and olive groves as the cart bounded along and then it turned off the track and travelled a short distance farther before it came to a halt outside a large white villa, several miles from the city. "We are here, girls." We climbed off the cart and entered the cool house. "You must be tired and hungry after the day so far. We have a room for you. It is small but comfortable with clean clothes. You will sleep this afternoon and meet my husband later on this evening. You may bathe in our pool and remove your old world from your skin. I will provide oils and lotions to add a shine to your dark shin, to bring to your surface your already hidden beauty. He is currently busy with other affairs at the moment but you will meet him after dinner." Drusilla and I were led through the main hallway and into a small room. Sallyarin was right. It was small but was the first room we had ever had that we could call our own. Actually, it was for Drusilla; however, she had to have me under her wing in order to maintain sanity. The one thing I had of great value was my sister, for without her I would have been gone long ago. My shyness and quietness often come across as rude however if I said something wrong, I got into worse trouble therefore, I kept safe by saying nothing. Drusilla slipped off her tunica and was soon pulling off mine saying, "Let us cool in their pool and remove our old and prepare for our new then we shall rest my sister, stay very close to me for we yet know what shall become of us. As we held our hands, we could feel a hope flowing through our souls. Tonight we lay down without being raped and blood oozing out of our wounds. We then fell asleep on the floor, dreaming of what the night would bring. During her dream, Fejér appeared before her saying, "Drusilla, who shall be blessed more than any ever to be born among the Romans. You shall rule beside the greatest goddess over the greatest empire ever to be. Your empire will have more stars that all who were ever born or died in Roman Hands. We have found favor in you in your care of The Chosen One. Rest in peace and care for your twin sister. Fear not for your reward is at hand." Drusilla awoke so confused. Why would she have a dream about caring for her sister, whom in an instant she would surrender her life to protect. She did not care for a reward, yet feared not being beside her only love. Her reward was the love of one who has been with her all the days of her life. Drusilla now reclined on our bed, savoring in the warmth of the sun's rays at the end of the day. Our room viewed their fields planted with grapes and olives. She had no idea how far the city was but Drusilla realized that it could not have been that far away. The sun was warm and relaxing and Drusilla realized that she had been both fortunate and lucky this day. If she had been alone with the wagon master, he would have been a lot less indiscreet than he had already. She shivered at the thought of what could have happened. Drusilla knew that if they had been alone it would have involved the man tearing off her clothes and raping her on the floor or against a pillar there and then for all to look upon with pity. As she lay on the bed, the sun began to disappear slowly over the hill and Drusilla realized that for the second time that day she was thinking about sex. She had reached an age when just thinking about it was not enough. After what had happened this morning, she wanted to be loved in every possible way with her master. She wanted her master to kiss her. She wanted to pleasure and witness her sister pleasured by a kind man at the same time. She wanted long, slow lovemaking, as she had searched her entire life for this experience. Had the wagon master awakened something more in her? The thought of being simultaneously loved and molested appealed to her. Drusilla closed her eyes and thought about the journey with her new mistress who intrigued her. The moment that she had pressed her lips so powerfully against Drusilla had been one of much needed tenderness after the terror of being fondled and exposed in public. It was known that women to have affairs with other women. Common prostitutes and rich women were often known to have passionate affairs behind closed doors but for her mistress to kiss in what was a public setting was daring in the extreme. Drusilla knew that she would now become a slave to the mystery of their possible love. The woman, she knew, Drusilla could love but the man. She would just have to wait and see. She now asked me and I could only tell her, "Relax and feel each move without the fear of making a man angry. Compliment her superior traits, which when compare to us was a task, which would surrender many traits. When you feel something, show the emotion for women lovers depend much on the emotion. The sun had disappeared beyond the hill when Drusilla awoke, feeling the warm night air coming in. Beside her on the bed lay two fresh, clean tunics made of woven cotton. It felt fine in her hand and was certainly of a better material than we had ever known. Drusilla stood up from the bed and looked at the last light in the sky, warm reds coalescing into yellows, purples, and blues. Drusilla lifted off her old tunica and looked at her freely exposed body in the slowly decaying light. Her nipple and breast was slightly sore and tender from where the wagon master had pinched and molested her so freely. There was a slight bruise where his teeth had been so roughly pulled away from her body. Yet apart from that, she was healing slowly. The new tunica was a different design to the one she had known all these years. It was woven in white cotton and tied at with three small buttons. Although it was similar to her previous one, this would not allow any man with wandering hands to invade the holes in the arms as the wagon master had done. Rather than put it on over her head, she had to step into it and then lift it up before buttoning it at the shoulders. When she was ready, she looked down at her now clothed body. The tunica was cut in such a way that her cleavage was slightly more exposed than she had in the previous tunica, which now lay on the floor. She now turned and dressed me. She looked at me and said, "I am blessed to have your love. Do-nothing foolish tonight and we shall see what hand has been dealt into us. Drusilla tossed our old ones on to the bed. She might keep them another day but this new tunica was much nicer. There was a knock at the door. Drusilla opened it to find our mistress standing before her. She motioned her to follow, and led her to the lounge. In the middle of it was our new master. As the mistress led us out of our room, she turned around to Drusilla and gave her another long, passionate kiss. Drusilla had not been expecting this, but then again when she felt her mistress's tongue explore her mouth; she received more readily than she had at the slave market. Drusilla found herself becoming deeply aroused by this woman and felt her nipples go hard. Sallyarin pushed her against a pillar and kissed her some more, her hands falling down Drusilla's body, inspiring her even more. Just as Drusilla thought that Sallyarin was going to remove her clothes, she broke the kiss and smiled. "Alas, my lover wants to see you first before we make love." Drusilla stared at Sallyarin, dazed and confused. She longed to be exposed in front of this woman and to see her mistress freely exposed. Drusilla decided to break all protocols, pulled the other woman back to her, and forcibly kissed her mistress with as much passion as she had ever felt for any other man or woman. Sallyarin tried to break the kiss but Drusilla would not let her get away again so easily. The more her mistress resisted, the more Drusilla explored her mouth. Finally, Sallyarin broke the kiss and forced Drusilla against the pillar, smiling. "I've never known a slave be so passionate. You've been longing for me all day haven't you?" Drusilla stood, shocked at how daring she had just become. "Yes, mistress," was all she could say. "My name also is Sallyarin. I will be your mistress. Your sister will be the lover of my lover. You have been badly treated in the past but now your treatment will be according to your works as those bad days are gone." Sallyarin walked off and beckoned Drusilla to follow her. They rapidly came to a room. On the floor were several cushions and rugs. It was well furnished and well lit. In the center was Juliuus, a big man and the lover of Sallyarin, dressed in a toga. He was tall, about six feet tall with dark hair. His hazel eyes explored our bodies and I thrust my breasts out purposely to allow his admiring gaze to travel from my head, down my exposed cleavage to the floor. "I see Sallyarin made a good choice." He walked over and kissed Sabain on her cheek. Then he beckoned her to come and sit in the middle of the room and sat down. I stood in front of him. Juliuus motioned for me to sit but I shook my head, preferring to stand. I was unsure what my new keepers wanted of us. Did they want a servant girl or a lover? "She is unsure," said Sallyarin. "I don't blame her. Let me guess, Drusilla. This morning you were taken to a market, half raped, kissed by Sallyarin, and then brought here. Confusion is an emotion that I would probably be feeling if I was in your shoes." There was a silence for a moment and Drusilla realized that the world outside had grown dark. The bird song of the day had gone to be replaced by crickets chirping outside. Drusilla realized that she was both hungry and thirsty and realized that we had not had anything since breakfast, ten hours, and a lifetime ago but she was happy when, as her gaze searched the room, there were simple meals laid out and ready. "Are you going to say anything?" asked Sallyarin. "We are tired, hungry, and parched. You have shown me such kindness as no master or mistress has shown before. Nevertheless, we would like to know our duties. What is expected of us?" "I thought Sallyarin had explained that." Juliuus rose and stood close to us "Your duties will be like this." He pulled me close, wrapping his muscular arms around me and kissed me. I was surprised at how much I enjoyed this kiss from a man I barely knew. He was warm and passionate, like his other lover and she moaned with pleasure as one of his hands cupped her breast through the thin material of the tunica. I held him close until they had both got as much from the kiss as each other had and then he broke it. Drusilla realized that Sallyarin had been watching them the whole time but she was not jealous. "You will love us both," said the second Sallyarin "You will pleasure and be pleasured. You sisters shall eat soon but before then there is something you must do for us." The master and mistress walked off to the other side of the room and talked. After this, Sallyarin returned and told us that her lover needed to run an errand and would return early in the morning. She could sit down at the table and eat and when finished return to our room and leave the tunics we had on outside the room to be cleaned. Drusilla then asked her, "Mistress, did not you have anything you sought us to do before eating?" She replied, "We need some more things before we enjoy that opportunity. My lover will have them by early morning." As we sat down to eat I told Drusilla, "We must eat good today for tomorrow we will eat less." Drusilla then looked at me and said, "Oh my foolish sister, have we not been as one for twenty long years and have I not lead in such a way that we survive. I tell you now that we shall have some nice days serving these new masters." I looked at her and told her, "Do you not know how great your love has been and the pain I felt each time you took pain from me. Yet I tell you that tonight is our last night in this lovely mansion." Drusilla had a puzzled look and asked, "If you know this do you know if we shall still be together?" I then told her, "Tonight as we sleep I will tell you how we can stay together for eternity. We must bring these small knives to bed with us." She took her knife, I took mine, and we retreated to our small comfortable room. Drusilla asked me about my strange behavior. I told her, "My lifetime sister, my memories are flooded with me at your side. However, I tell you that, "We still have to carry some more burdens, and I ask you do you love me?" Drusilla then answered me, "You know I have loved you since the beginning of our days and that I would do all things for you, you are the reason I love my sister?" Then I asked her, "My sister, I have been with you all of our days and yet also have existed since before the days of this little Earth. Do you believe me?" Drusilla then answered, "It is not that I believe or not for what comes from your heart and mind also comes from mine, so if you say the sun is black, then I shall see the sun is black." I continued with, "Soon I must go back to my throne, will you come with me and serve in my kingdom?" Drusilla then replied in a strong voice, "My sister, I care not about any Empire, I care only for you and life without you would be death for me, I cannot live without my purpose and I will follow you through anything or anyplace just to be at your side. I hope you will have mercy on me and let me love and be with you for our eternity together. Since the days of my birth I served only you." I then looked at her and asked, "Will you drink of my blood to be one with me?" Drusilla then said, "I shall drink anything you want and all the blood you can give me as long as you are have no harm." Then I cut my finger as Drusilla pulled the knife from me and said, "Oh please Auriel, do not make me see pain upon you and us both suffer." I told her, "My sister, there is no pain, now drink of my blood so I may be in you." In addition, as she started to drink I asked, "Drusilla, will be serve me as your goddess?" As she was performing her duty my finger working hard to make sure the wound would not hurt me she cried out, "You have been and always will be my goddess, for I have loved and worshipped you all the days of my life." I then said to her, "With this act you are Blood of Our Blood as my blood now flows through you we are united, now look and see what awaits us in the near future." With my words, we both turned into light and we could see my throne and my eleven sisters standing around it.

Then we returned to our Hyrum bodies, and my sister washed my feet with her tears and wiped them with her hair as she had so many times in our wonderfully pain and miserably filled short life, so far. She now said to me, "Oh great master, I deserve none of the gifts you shall give me and beg to have all your mercy and to be your slave for eternity, and that you not punish me for my love and service to you by separating us. I beg to serve my sister for eternity." I then told her, "You will always be one of my sisters and live with us in our holy of holies as pain, shame, hunger and misery shall never enter us again. Now let us prepare for the misery of today. For today, you are commanded to let me suffer for you." Drusilla in her angry way said, "I cannot let you suffer for me for if you suffer so shall I. You know this has always been my way with you." I then told her, "I command you not to, yet ask that you have faith that we shall pass through this last tribulation together." She then kissed me and said, "My love for you will kill me if I see you suffer too much my life long sister." I understood this completely understood this completely. Then as the morning, some field slaves came in and pulled us out of our small room before we had a chance to dress. They drug us outside, and then tied us to the whipping posts. Then the mistress came out and said, "The master has decided that he wants barbarian women from the north, thus you shall work in our fields. I shall first beat you with a whip, as that also gives me pleasures. Now make sure you cry loud and beg for mercy." I then yelled, "You are a stupid slut yammer, after today all your organisms shall be of blood." Sallyarin's anger now became very evident as she screamed. "You will beg me for mercy, or you will die today powerless quiet one. Your mouth has given you much pain." I then said to her, "You slut, you have not the power to make me cry and beg for mercy." I looked at Drusilla and said, "Beg her not for being silent will give her misery." Sallyarin then commanded her servants to bring her the black monster of death. This was a whip with many minuscule endings. It had woven into them many minute razor-sharp stones. She then began to beat me. I could feel the blood rushing out of my back. She next had her slaves retry me with my front facing her. She now beat my face, my arms and legs and afterwards, my breasts. The pain rushed through me and flooded me so much that I no longer knew where I was. Millions of small cuts on top of smaller cuts flooded the ground with my blood. However, I have not moved since I now only reasoned that the perverts that sent me here had to get their joy from seeing my great pain, as did Sallyarin, and they would have to find somewhere else to fulfill their fantasies. Sallyarin subsequently said these words to me, "If you do not beg to save yourself, you will beg to save your sister." She thereafter started beating Drusilla; nevertheless, she showed neither pain nor begged for any mercy. She was being strong for me. She saw the price I paid and did not want to let the purchase go without its reward. She knew this to be the only way we could be together. She then looked at Sallyarin and said, "Your kisses feel like you have been kissing dogs, do you favor them as you are a sick skank?" Sallyarin beat Drusilla as hard as she had me. Soon the servants said to her, "If you continue they will die and be free from your pain, yet if you stop now they shall suffer for a few more hours." She thus sat in her chair and masturbated in front of the servants as she watched our blood slowly pour from our bodies. Later in a flash, her orgasms turned into flowing blood as the servants rushed with rags to stop it. They then rushed to get the doctor who examined her as she now lay in great pain. The doctor told her she could never have orgasms again nor have any children, proceeded to remove those organs, and sealed her intimate area used for receiving penetration. She would never again enjoy sex from male or female. The doctor slowly burned as many nerve endings in her intimate female sexual organ. They gave her strong drink, yet it did not dull the pain. The doctor asked her, "Which god did you anger today?" She then looked out at Drusilla and me as we hung there in total sleep. She cursed at us, "May you Africans burn in hell." As we could hear her crying in pain and seen her blood flow everywhere Drusilla then said to me, "My sister, you are truly a goddess, please remember me today." I looked over and saw the pain she suffered being loyal to me, I told her you will have my wish and continued declaring to her, "We shall live in the same home and sleep in my holy beds." With this, our spirits started to flow out of our bodies, and we appeared in a strange room in the clouds. There were men, women, and other things appearing before us. We stood before them completely exposed only covered with our blood. The old man who sat in the center of the back now spoke, "We wish to serve you before you leave oh greatest goddess." I asked them, "Who are you?" Additionally, they said, "We are the Highest of the Roman gods and goddesses." I then revealed to them, "Why do you love wickedness so much? Can you see what your wickedness has done to us?" The old man then said, "It was your foolishness that did this to you." Let us introduce our titles and ourselves. I am both Zeus and Jupiter—King of the Gods and my wife Juno—Queen of the Gods. All shall now stand and bow to you giving you their names and title. Neptune—God of the Sea, Pluto—God of Death, Apollo—God of the Sun, Diana— Goddess of the Moon, Mars—God of War, Venus—Goddess of Love, Cupid—God of Love, Mercury—Messenger of the Gods, Minerva—Goddess of Wisdom, Ceres—The Earth Goddess, Proserpine—Goddess of the Underworld, Vulcan—The Smith God Bacchus—God of Wine, Saturn—God of Time, Vesta—Goddess of the Home Janus—God of Doors, Uranus and Gaia—Parents of Saturn, Maia—Goddess of Growth, Flora – Goddess of Flowers, Plutus—God of Wealth." Drusilla now looked at them and me and said, "My master is your throne larger than this?" I told her, "My sister, this small group is but a piece of sand in the oceans to our empire." I then looked at Jupiter and said, "I have felt the evil and wickedness among your servants. I now know that you receive joy from this suffering and that without humans to play with you will soon vanish into the dirty air. Thus, I tell you that soon, the Romans will turn away from you and worship a new god, a peasant that was beaten and crucified, worse than I was. This way you shall remember my curse upon you. They will no longer need or want you and you will have no joy. They shall only remember you on a few pages in their millions of pages and see your statues crumble like those who made them. Their children shall play with small images of you and as they grow, shall burn and destroy those toys of no fun. Now, go and search the galaxy to find your parts." With this, I did turn them into stone and blast them into many atomic parts throughout your small Milky Way. I then said to my sister, let us now be made new you as you were created and me as I desire and meet your other sisters as we prepare to go to our home. The Roman Gods now only lived in the evil Romans distorted imaginations. Many, who have eyes, cannot see this. We now slowly floated with our hands held as Drusilla would not let go of my hands, not to enter my throne but to hold on to the only love she ever had. My thoughts shifted back to the Romans, as I now had an issue with their new religion in about 300 years. I thus decided that the Romans would absorb that religion and corrupt it. The curse I put on them shall cause great suffering on both themselves and those who foolishly follow their doctrine.

As we floated, the lights got warmer and flooded us with joy. Then we slowly reappeared a few short feet from our little camp. As we walked into the camp, my sisters asked me, "Did you forget something master?" I asked them, "Why do ask?" Then Julia said, "Master for you just told us you were to going on a mission. Did you change your mind?" I looked at them and said, "Since I went back into history for twenty years I can return when I left." Ruth then said, "Oh master were you really gone for twenty years?" I then told them, "I shall put my memories and the memories of my twin, Drusilla into our mind so you can all see all the things that we suffered together." Then Máriakémènd asked, "Is she your twin sister, and are you identical twins?" I then answered saying, "Our bodies were exact, down to the lowest identical cell. My sister Drusilla loved, cared, and suffered with me through each step of our journey. Then Mary started screaming, "Oh master, why would you suffer a death like that and not cry for your spirits to save you?" I then said, "The same is that I would suffer from any of my sisters. I knew not of you nor any part of a life except that of Drusilla and myself. Please form our circle with my twin and me in the middle. I then introduced her to each one" and when she came to Bács-Kiskun, "Behold Drusilla, your special soul mate." Drusilla then said to me, "I have a fear of not pronouncing her name, for we have yet to learn how to speak such word. Will you teach me how, so that I can be perfect like you since I gave all them to you?" I then asked her, "Drusilla, will you promise to love us unless at least one agrees you can play with another? Fear not her name for I shall change it when we arrive at my throne." Drusilla now guided my hands to hold her blessings and said, "You may take from me whatever you want as long as you not take me from you, my sister, and goddess." I then said to Filkeháza, "Now would be a good time to take your sons for a walk." She called for her sons to follow her and quickly departed our camp. We all promptly introduced Drusilla to the river of our love, she became absorbed in the river, and we all did enjoy this new heavenly wine, as her cup was being filled and emptied as never before. She begged for more as even all the sisters could give no more and she gave a wonderful greeting in which all the sisters, especially Siusan, came to me thanking me for this new wonderful addition to our family and all your other life memories being protected and shared by our river. After many hours of being welcomed and getting to know each other we all, in great exhaustion, went over to the tree in which our seafood was delivered each night. Tonight, we had no food. My sisters asked me why, and I told them, "I do not know since I have been gone for twenty years. Let me ask." Then as I went to speak, the Earth turned dark, and a big light in the heavens shined down on us, as we all stood hold one hand of two sisters so our circle would not be broken. A very loud voice said to me, "Lilith, we have found in you, the Greatest Love that a goddess may have and your blood shall free over one million galaxies from evil, as your Empire shall be as a cancer, forever and ever growing and freeing those who suffer. Consequently, evil no longer can touch you as all dimensions now give you access and the sword of justice that you now own. This sword cannot never be defeated or taken from you. Your name shall include this additional title 'holder of the Sword of Justice' or words to that effect as your courts may recommend changes. You are now without question the greatest known goddess. Your price has been paid in full by the laws of the highest divine of all known realities. Prepare yourself now and your 'Blood of Our Blood' sisters to return to your throne. Your work is now finished and it is time for you to receive your reward." Then the light finished and I looked at my sisters and told them, "Our work is done and we shall return to my throne before the sun gives light to another day. Then Mary asked with tears in her eyes, "Master, will it hurt?" I then told my disciples, "We go to a place where you shall have no pain, hunger, thirst, and never be cold and filled with more love and heavenly wine than you can ever remember. Your spirit will flow in mine, and my spirit in you. You must trust me this last time." I then walked over to Mary and wiped the tears from her eyes with my hair and then I told my sisters, "The saddest sight for my eyes to see is tears from your eyes. Let me take those tears away. Stand back as I take us back to your new home." I then pointed my new Sword of Justice to the sky and commanded, "Take us to my throne." Instantly, the sky turned dark and the Earth juddered and at first was moving slowly away from us, and then the Earth Vanished as did the Milky Way and like rockets we spun into the dimensional wall which quickly opened its doors as we shot through it, closing it immediately afterwards. We now headed for another wall and its doors opened for us. Now, we were weaving between walls to position for entry into my dimension. We were now going in a straight shot as planet and the stars moved aside as we passed by. I held on to my new sword, as I knew now it would keep me from all evil and protect my throne. I would eat it when we arrived home. That would make it one with me. This trip is so different from the others in that I am conscious and can see and feel all things. It is so nice finally to be going home, for the last thirty some years have been a challenge, yet I do have my rewards hanging on to me. I can now recognize some galaxies in my dimension, yet we are not going to Ereshkigal. We are going high above it. I can now see some mighty lights start that are slowly getting larger, oh so large. It is easily over 100,000 times the Milky Way. We are being pulled into this light. As I point my Sword of Justice, I now feel disappointed. I had so much wished to return to my throne and lie in the souls of Medica and Sabina. Medica will enjoy our new sister Heidi as Sabina will feast upon Faith and Drusilla. I can see Sabina wearing some more "blessed' body suits. Yet now it looks like our reunion will not be now. We are now passing through layers of different colored lights. Red, green, yellow, blue, purple and then white. We are now stopping in the white layer that has no surface. Our flesh falls off as our spirits now shine. Now we are landing on a large, maybe 100 miles bright white marble surface with thousands of large white beautiful columns. I can see many large statues of myself, Sabina and Medica. Where are we? I have never been in a place such as this. Our journey is now ended. I can feel none of my sisters, nor can I feel myself. What happened? Yet I can see no danger. Could this be a trap, or even evil intercepting our path? I must look strong for those who a traveling with me. I scan everything yet nothing matches my memory. Mystery once again floods now secretly through my mind. I know not where we are.

TIME FOR SALVATION, SHOWERS OF BLOOD

OTHER ADVENTURES IN THIS SERIES

Prikhodko, Dream of Nagykanizsai
Mempire, Born in Blood
Penance on Earth
Lord of New Venus
Rachmanism in Ereshkigal
Salvation, Showers of Blood
Tianshire, Life in the Light

AUTHOR BIO

James Hendershot, D.D. was born on July 12, 1957, living in old wooden houses with no running water until his father obtained work with a construction company that built Interstate 77 from Cleveland, Ohio to Marietta Ohio. He made friends in each of the new towns that his family moved to during this time. The family finally settled in Caldwell, Ohio where he eventually attended a school for auto mechanics. Being of a lover of parties more than study, he graduated at the bottom of his high school class. After barely graduating, he served four years in the Air Force and graduated, Magna Cum Laude, with three majors from the prestigious Marietta College. He then served until retirement in the US Army during which time he obtained his Masters of Science degree from Central Michigan University and his third degree in Computer Programing from Central Texas College. His final degree was the honorary degree of Doctors of Divinity from Kingsway Bible College, which provided him with keen insight into the divine nature of man.

After retiring from the US Army, he accepted a visiting professor position with Korea University in Seoul, South Korea.

Upon returning to a small hometown close to his mother's childhood home, he served as a personnel director for Kollar Enterprises. Eleven years later, he moved to a suburb of Seattle to finish his life-long search for Mempire and the goddess Lilith, only to find them in his fingers and not with his eyes. It is now time for Earth to learn about the great mysteries not only deep in our universe but also in the universes or dimensions beyond. Listen to his fingers as they are sharing these mysteries with you.

INDEX

V

Váci 37, 38
Veszprém 37, 38, 39
Victoria 20
Viscount/Viscountess 109
Vlad the Implaler 23

W

Wakinyan 368
Westminster Abby 244
William 46, 49, 55, 66, 77, 78, 88, 90,
    136
William the Conqueror 212
Wind Eagle 363, 365, 366
Wind EagleI 367
Wuchowsen 365, 367

Y

Yanaba 360, 363, 370, 386, 410

Z

Zeus 409